Doppelgänger

CHUCK DRISKELL

DOPPELGÄNGER

Copyright © 2012 by Chuck Driskell
Published by Autobahn Books
Cover art by Nat Shane

First Edition: May 2012

autobahn

BOOKS

In memory of my father, Charles Sloan Driskell.
Marine, Friend, Husband, Dad. He was the best.

PART ONE

Effortless Commencements

ONE

DECEMBER, 1940

THE STATUESQUE man in the Wehrmacht gray officer's uniform closed the dossier and removed his pince-nez. He tilted his head back, rubbing the bridge of his nose. The other man, also in uniform, sat on the opposite side of the desk, waiting patiently. After gathering himself, the first man, Colonel (*Oberst* in German) Emil von Marburg, tossed the dossier to his desk and locked eyes with his associate. He pressed his lips together, whitening them, slowly shaking his head.

"He'll never do it."

"Yes, he will," countered Lieutenant Colonel (*Oberstleutnant* in German) Frederick Heydte, the commandant of the academy, as it was known colloquially amongst the few who were familiar with its existence. Heydte was a shorter-than-average block of a man. He had shoulders like cantaloupes, a barrel chest, and a blond-topped head shaped like an artillery round. Rather than just extend normally, his massive hands seemed to explode from the sleeves of his wool winter uniform—a lumberjack's hands. Heydte's full lips poked out thoughtfully as he seemed to ponder his explanation. "He's our eighth product in four years, and thus far, no one has shown a higher degree of intelligence or..." he paused, searching for the phrase, smiling when he found it, "...cold-hearted willingness."

"It just seems too much like a stunt."

"Sir, all due respect, it isn't. It's..." he searched again for the proper expression, "a display of loyalty."

The colonel leaned forward, hardening his prominent face, his rigid, bony finger poking the mahogany desk. "*Murder* is what it is, Heydte. Murder of a German citizen."

1

The lieutenant colonel shrugged, his voice even. "I prefer to look at it as the strategic disposal of an insignificant asset to confirm the validity of a major one." He, too, leaned forward. "And, after the non-performance of several of our operatives, are you truly willing to send another man into the United States without first knowing his steadfast loyalty belongs to the Reich?"

"*You* trained those men, Heydte. *You* brought them to me and *you* said they were sound." Von Marburg sat back in the chair, pointing at Heydte with the pince-nez. "And I'm not quite sure I would call their disappearance something as casual as non-performance." He turned his attention to the winter gray sky out the window. "Abject failure seems a more fitting term."

A flash of pink appeared on Heydte's thick neck. "Indeed, sir, I did train them. And that's why I'm recommending such extreme measures with this man, and any subsequent operatives."

A chilly quiet fell between them. They were in a private second-floor office in Potsdam, on the outskirts of Berlin. Each wall of the office was three-and-a-half meters tall, covered in row after row of leather-bound books, most of them dealing with psychology or history. Beside the desk was a vintage globe of the earth, and on the far end of the office, an antique clock announced the seconds with its slow, steady ticking. It was minutes past nine in the morning. Von Marburg, a handsome man of fifty-two, who, before his conscription during the Great War, had begun his career as an investment banker, broke the silence.

"Are we still in contact with the three men who haven't failed us yet?"

"Yes, sir. Weekly, at a minimum. And we don't know the status of the other four. There could be a good reason for their silence."

Von Marburg's head whipped around. "Good reason? A good reason?" He took a loud calming breath, again massaging the bridge of his nose as was his habit. "Perhaps, if this Faber is so good, we should use him to locate our missing four?"

Heydte shook his head emphatically. "I wouldn't advise that, sir, for two reasons. First, each operative has been compartmentalized. There is nothing to be gained by their knowing any details of the other operatives. I'm quite sure each of them suspects others have come through the academy, but why give them such confirmation? All it would do is potentially jeopardize additional operations, and by compartmentalizing the agents we make each one's mission completely independent, as well as all associated risk." He glanced at the door before looking at the clock. "And second, as you're about to see, using him to find the others would be a tremendous waste of a truly gifted man."

Colonel von Marburg adjusted himself in his chair, reaching inside his uniform jacket to retrieve a leather cigar pouch. Using a cutter from his top drawer, he prepared the cigar, lighting it with a gilded desk lighter. He puffed away, making sure the cigar was well lit before turning his slate-gray eyes back to Heydte. "And what about him is so special?"

Heydte assumed a thoughtful expression. "I just think you're going to be surprised...pleasantly. I know I was. Nine months ago we started with eighty candidates. Six months ago it was down to ten. In every elimination phase, Faber stood head and shoulders above the rest."

"In what way?"

"In every single metric we track, he finished first. Every one. Never before have we had a candidate so far ahead of his peers."

"Perhaps his peers were duds," Marburg quipped.

"Negative, sir. This was as good a group as we've run through. Their average testing, as a group, was higher than the previous classes to come through the academy. The Führer's education system is truly beginning to turn out a new breed of warrior. This one is the best I've seen."

Von Marburg feigned adulation as he patted his heart. "A Nordic God? Perhaps Nietzsche, if he were still alive, would have fainted when he discovered this exemplary *übermann*."

"I think you should just see for yourself. And please, ask him anything you like."

The colonel nodded, drained, motioning with his hand. "Then just bring him in."

Heydte stood, walked to the heavy wooden door. He opened it and issued a command in a normal tone of voice. Colonel von Marburg could hear the footsteps coming at standard quick-time—two steps per second—laid out for the militaries of the world by the Prussian master of drill, Baron von Steuben. The soldier entered, marching through the door and across the Oriental rug, clicking the heels of his polished boots as he stopped before the desk. Under his left arm, situated perfectly, was his hat. His right arm extended outward, giving the Nazi salute.

"Heil Hitler! Sir, Oberleutnant Gerhard Faber reporting as ordered, sir!"

Colonel von Marburg frowned at the overdone formalities. He allowed merciful silence to descend on the room as he studied Heydte's prize student. The uniform and boots were perfect. His hair was short and well within regulation, his twenty-something face unlined and indistinct. He was neither handsome nor ugly, falling somewhere in between. Marburg guessed many women would describe his looks as average or, perhaps—on his best night, and in the correct light—pleasant. He was of average height and slightly stocky build and, thus far, there seemed to be nothing remarkable about the man. He appeared to be the archetypal German line soldier, of the type you might find in any barracks throughout the burgeoning Thousand Year Reich. After looking him up and down, the colonel halfheartedly returned the salute and motioned for him to sit.

Von Marburg turned, joining his bleary eyes with Heydte. He gave him a look that said, "*This* is the man you've been bragging about?" Heydte, wearing a smirk, motioned for him to proceed.

The colonel turned his attention to the lieutenant and fingered the cigar, twirling it over the ashtray. "Where are you from, Faber?"

"Sir, I'm from Hannover, sir."

"Lose the boot-camp double-sir formalities."

"Yes, sir."

"Brothers and sisters?"

"Three brothers, sir."

"And where are they?"

"Each are dead, sir."

Von Marburg raised his eyebrows. "Dead how?"

Gerhard showed no trace of emotion, like a seasoned poker player. "The oldest one murdered the second oldest one ten years ago. He, in turn, was killed while fleeing from the polizei. My remaining brother was killed last year in Libya, sir."

The colonel placed the cigar in the ashtray and flattened his palms on his desk. "Why did your brother kill your other brother?"

"Because he stole food from him, sir."

Von Marburg cut his eyes to Heydte before coming back to Gerhard. "A murder over *food?*"

"Yes, sir."

The colonel shifted in his seat. "Did you see it happen?"

"I did. We were eating what little food we had at the time, and when my oldest brother left the room, the second oldest one took his potatoes, sir."

"And did he shoot him?"

"No, sir."

"Well, how did he kill him?"

"Broke his neck, sir."

"As in, threw him down some stairs, or off of a balcony?"

"No, sir. Michael came back into the room, stared at his plate, asked who took his food. I told him. He walked behind Bernard and grasped his neck. They struggled for a moment before he snapped Bernard's neck, and then he left the house."

Von Marburg struggled to swallow. He turned his eyes to Heydte, still sitting by the door with his hands folded over his lap. The colonel returned his attention to Gerhard. "Did this...scar you?"

"Sir?"

"Are you haunted by the memory?"

"Not at all, sir. Bernard had it coming to him."

The colonel's mouth was dry. Very dry. He stood and retrieved a glass of water, filling it from the pitcher, drinking half the glass, staring out the window as he spoke. "Faber, don't you find it queer that you don't seem to be bothered by your brother killing your other brother?"

"Perhaps queer to some, sir. But not in our household."

Von Marburg finished the water and sat. After clearing his throat several times, he addressed Gerhard again. "Speak some English."

"What dialect, sir?"

"American dialect." At that moment something occurred to Von Marburg. He held up his hand, stopping Gerhard. "Wait. You can do British, too?"

"Among others, sir."

A thoughtful nod. "Very good. For now, just American."

"Which American dialect would you like to hear?"

Von Marburg's eyes again cut back to Heydte. "I thought our language people only taught a generic American dialect? That persnickety schoolmaster told me it was what a person might hear in middle America, like Nebraska or Missouri."

Heydte nodded. "Yes, sir, that's correct. Lieutenant Faber has mastered many of the American regional dialects on his own."

"How?" Von Marburg asked.

"They have a Magnetophon, sir, at the language institute," Gerhard answered. "After classes, in the evenings, I would practice by listening to the recorded accents."

The colonel narrowed his eyes. "Then recite the American first general order in a southern dialect."

Gerhard nodded. "I will guard everything within the limits of my post, and quit my post only when properly relieved, sir."

Marburg didn't look at Heydte, because he knew he was wearing his shit-eating grin. Fully fluent in English, Colonel von Marburg often enjoyed American movies without the hideous German studio overdubbing. He'd recently watched *Gone With the Wind*, noticing the distinct difference between the black actors with authentic southern accents and the white ones, forcing the drawling accent so thickly that they sounded comical. Gerhard's, however, was spot-on.

He asked to hear a New York accent. Gerhard repeated the general order, using a more clipped dialect, making the soft vowels machine-gun quick. He added in a nasal inflection, lifting his sentences at their ends. His elocution was masterful.

The colonel questioned Gerhard for a full hour, amazed at the machinelike precision with which he responded to the queries. Gerhard had jade-green eyes and rarely blinked. He focused on the colonel, answering each of the questions with refreshing frankness. Finally, Colonel von Marburg placed one of his hands on top of the other and looked to Heydte. "I have no more questions."

Lieutenant Colonel Heydte stepped forward, removing an envelope from his uniform pocket. He placed it on the front of the colonel's desk, directly in front of Lieutenant Faber, tapping it once. "In that envelope, Lieutenant Faber, is the key to your final hurdle before we pronounce you ready for deep immersion work."

"May I ask what the hurdle is, sir?"

"Certainly." Heydte paused, licking his lips. "You are required to kill a German citizen in order to complete your block of training."

Lieutenant Faber's green eyes moved from Heydte's to Von Marburg's, to the envelope and back to Heydte's. "I understand, sir."

Heydte nodded. "I will personally release you at twenty-one hundred hours tonight. You will have twenty-four hours to return to me. In that amount of time, you must kill the person named in that envelope, by a headshot from a pistol. It goes without saying that you cannot get caught. In fact, the killing should baffle the authorities. And the only way to do that is by leaving no trace." Using a handkerchief, he reached into the jacket again, producing a compact Sauer 7.65 millimeter pistol, one of the most common firearms in Germany. He laid it on the desk with the envelope. "If you do get caught, we will profess no knowledge of this and you will certainly be executed, especially given your family history. Additionally, we'll offer forth manufactured iron-clad evidence that will not only pronounce you as the killer, but also an enemy of the state." Heydte smiled as if he were a rich uncle sending a nephew on a ritzy Danube cruise. "Finally, if you do not kill the person in question, as prescribed, and arrive back here in time, you will be considered a failure and will be dealt with appropriately."

Gerhard was expressionless. "I understand, sir."

Lieutenant Colonel Heydte handed the envelope to Gerhard. "Open it."

Gerhard inserted a finger under the flap, tearing it across the top. He pinched the heavy, cream-colored paper between his fingers, sliding it out and opening it. The two officers watched carefully, neither of them breathing, as Gerhard stared at the paper with the single name and address printed in its center. After half a minute, the lieutenant refolded the paper, placing it back in the envelope. He handed the envelope back to Heydte before taking the pistol from the desk, gripping it with his right hand, his trigger finger outside of the guard. He made eye contact with Heydte first, then Colonel von Marburg.

7

"I understand my orders. It will be done."

Heydte twisted his head to Von Marburg. He mouthed the words, "Told you."

AT ABOUT that same moment, across the Atlantic and several hours before sunup, seven men filed into the modified top floor of what was once a turn-of-the-century grand Pennsylvania hotel. The top floor, sixty feet above ground, had once been a rustic restaurant, offering rare game and commanding views of the Poconos to the west. The walls were still adorned with antlers, ancient muskets, and across the back wall three prized bucks, a fourteen-point white tail in the middle. Three years before, when the embryonic department of the government known only to a few as the Signals and Gathering Sector (SGS) came into existence, its director, realizing a private training area was needed, purchased the defunct hotel and nineteen hundred surrounding acres. The property was immediately surrounded by a high-voltage electric fence, topped with concertina wire. Inside of that an even taller fence was constructed, and the entire perimeter, all twelve miles, was placed under the patrol of an Army battalion stationed in nearby Stroudsburg. Even the highest levels of the battalion's leadership were unsure of what existed inside the inner fence. However, if any unwanted guests were to gain entry, they would most likely be disappointed at their find. Other than the old hotel, the property contained a twenty-five meter firing range and a MOUT (Military Operations in Urban Terrain) site, but beyond that, nothing permanent existed that would seem out of the ordinary or catch a person's eye.

Unless training was in session.

And on this particular night, a thirteen-month training block would end. One man would be declared the top of his class—the winner—eligible for a very special mission. The other would finish in position number two—the loser—moving on to join the regular day-to-day functions of the SGS. Both men were fluent in German. Both were skilled tacticians. They both were familiar with nearly every weapon in existence, and both felt they were clearly superior to the other.

The first man, Barrett Hancock, had been born and raised in the mountains of Northern California. A graduate of Stanford, he spent the next six years of his life in the San Francisco Police Department, leading the force's marksmanship team. After joining the Army in '38, Hancock was quickly recruited by Special Duties, the precursor to special operations, and several months later drew the attention of the budding SGS. A sycamore of a man, Hancock was six feet six inches tall and weighed in at 240 pounds. He had smooth, tan skin and a helmet of white-blond hair. A football and basketball player at Stanford, Hancock had the ability to run the 100-yard dash, even at his size, in only ten and a half seconds. Most of the brass favored him as the choice to infiltrate Germany, not only due to his Nordic appearance, but mainly for his physicality and weapons prowess.

The second man to take part in the competition was Roland Buhl. Raised on a struggling Virginia pig farm, he was the opposite of Hancock in nearly every way. Schooled at home by his now deceased parents, Roland tested extremely high in raw aptitude scores. His parents were first-generation German immigrants. Therefore, he spoke fluent, working-class Ripuarian German and displayed a sinewy toughness that only a person who has always worked with their hands can demonstrate. He was of average size, and nothing about him, to the naked eye, seemed different from any man one might meet on the street. However, contrary to the leanings of the chain of command, two of the Ivy League behavioral psychologists on the SGS's payroll insisted that Roland was the better of the two candidates. With his high aptitude for learning and lack of formal schooling or training, they felt he was the more moldable piece of clay. Add to that his unremarkable countenance as well as his language skills, and they felt he could blend into most any Germanic situation without causing anyone to look at him twice.

The fact of the matter was that their preference, or that of the brass, was of no importance. Tonight's competition—man versus man—in true American fashion, would decide the winner. The rules were simple: disable the other man, to either unconsciousness or verbal submission, for victory. No weapons were to be used, only hands and feet. The competition was largely dependent upon stealth, but at some point, brawn would have to factor into the equation. This clearly made Hancock the heavy favorite to move on.

The two men would be inserted from opposite sides into what had come to be known as the maze. Surrounded by twelve-foot hedges, the maze was an enclosure, square, a hundred and fifty yards in each direction. It had once been the gilded rear courtyard of the hotel, and, with a few subtle changes, had been transformed into a gladiator arena of sorts. The marble neoclassical statues were still there. The fountain was still in the center but turned off due to the noise, the surrounding reflection pool's blue water shimmering under the hard winter moon. Several grassy berms had been added, as well as the occasional three-foot granite wall. Other than that, the entire area was wide open.

Both men wore identical indigo suits, specially treated with a dusting of phosphorescent material. The material would not aid the other man in seeing his quarry, especially with such a powerful moon, but it did make both combatants stand out to the men on the top floor of the facility. The wide picture windows had been treated with an amber chemical, and when the phosphorous material was seen through the window, it glowed like a firefly's ass.

The seven men took their seats, four in the front, three behind them. The seats were elevated theater-style. An attendant served strong coffee. A flask was discreetly passed, and four of the men—not unlike spectators at a highly-anticipated prize fight—added a touch of good cheer to their drink. Once the attendant left them, the man seated at the front left broke the relative quiet.

"I'd lay good odds that big Hancock sends our German immigrant straight to the medics. And if anyone twists my arm, I'd also give decent odds he hospitalizes him in the process."

Another voice, this one gravelly, joined in. "Hell, Lucian, he may kill him. Outweighs him by fifty pounds, doesn't he? All that time playing sports and serving on the SFPD. Johnston down in intelligence said they used to send Hancock in special just to rough up the hard cases. Said he used to get a hard-on by beating the shit outta people."

"This Buhl kid," said a third man. "I spent three days peppering him with questions. He's a hard bird to figure out. Seems like he's from another planet. Like some of his wires are crossed."

"Grew up on a farm," the first man said. "Insular, isolated. Hell...bein' from Virginia hill country...he may be inbred." Chuckles all around. "And a German on top of that. Only interaction he had was with his family and a pig's teats." All of the men laughed aloud but one.

Sitting on the back row, his eyes narrowed as he awaited the combatants' entry, was Colonel Matthew Silver. Silver had recruited Roland and spent more time with him than all the other men combined. He was heavily vested in the young man, and while he had to agree that, on paper, Hancock was the heavy favorite, he wasn't quite ready to cast his lot with the California kid who had likely never faced much in the way of a worthy adversary. Silver kept quiet, massaging his sweaty hands, waiting.

"There they are!" one of the men on the front row yelled.

At precisely the same moment, the trainees entered through heavy steel doors on opposite sides of the maze. True as advertised, through the treated window, both men appeared to be wearing lighted jumpsuits. The seven officers leaned forward as the one on the front left reminded them of the rules. "Neither one can stay still for more than a full minute. There's two refs next door, and if either man does, he gets one warning from the horn, and on his second offense, he's immediately disqualified."

"Does Buhl know Hancock?" the man next to Silver asked.

"Yes," Silver answered.

"Shit," the man breathed. "If that's the case Buhl will probably try to get disqualified on purpose."

Colonel Silver shook his head. And on his mouth was the wisp of a smile. He'd seen what Roland could do. These assholes had no idea.

ROLAND BUHL stood in front of the door he'd just been pushed through. There was only a whisper of a breeze and nothing else. There were no crickets this time of year, only deafening silence. His chest was rising and falling as if he'd already winded himself. Adrenaline.

Easy, boy. Easy.

He glanced at his arms and the top of his feet, seeing the ghostly blue set off by the round disc of the moon floating off to the right. Marking the moon's position, Roland knew that he needed to stay to the left of all available cover to avoid its light.

In front of him, twenty feet away, was a Zeus-like statue. Roland padded forward, moving to the statue's left, staring straight ahead. He controlled his breathing, finally holding his breath and listening. After several seconds, he heard an owl screech far in the distance. Nothing else. His internal clock counted the seconds. Roland didn't want to have to take a warning for sitting still. He needed to keep moving. He'd been still for thirty seconds as he narrowed his eyes, scrutinizing the maze bathed in moonlight, looking for Hancock.

Where are you, big boy?

He knew Barrett Hancock. He didn't care for him. Arrogant and brash, Hancock strutted the halls of the facility all day like the self-appointed cock of the walk. Bragging about this and that, never pausing to give Roland a dime's worth of credit for getting as far as he had. Once, Roland had tried a different tack after a difficult shooting exercise. Both men had attained perfect scores. Roland, trying to be the bigger man, complimented Hancock by telling him he was a fine shot. "I know," Hancock replied, turning his back and strutting away. And the brass ate it up. Roland could just hear them up in the penthouse, betting that he was going to throw the competition just to prevent a beating at the hands of the gargantuan California kid.

Weak thoughts, Roland. Focus. Don't think about it—prove it. Time to move.

Dropping down to his stomach, Roland slithered like a snake to the grassy berm off to his left. The frosty grass crunched under his weight, feeling icy cold to his stomach. He was now near the head of the maze, at the point closest to the facility. He could imagine the brass upstairs, staring nearly straight down at him, ruminating over the level of fear that the poor Virginian pig farmer must be feeling. He shook his head to clear it.

Focus, damn it! Lose the insecurities.

Roland crawled to the top of the berm, scanning the maze.

It was an old trick, perhaps the oldest, but old tricks became tried and true for one reason—they worked. Clawing into the earth with his fingers, he located a pebble. Scooting back so as not to display his motion in the moonlight, he threw the rock at the Zeus statue, satisfied at the plink it made. He peered through the darkness, seeing the flash to his left.

The big Californian was moving in his direction.

BARRETT HANCOCK heard the sound. He wasn't overly concerned about revealing his position to a man who, without a weapon, couldn't do a damned thing about it. Even still, he knew the cadre was watching from up above, and he wanted to at least try to demonstrate his furtive capabilities. Moving in a crouch, he used one of the granite walls as cover as he waddled toward the front of the maze. Upon reaching the wall, he chewed on his tongue the way he always had in football when lined up at end, awaiting the snap, anticipating his chance to maul the quarterback.

C'mon, show yourself, you little prick.

What would be the most impressive way to demonstrate his prowess?

Punches were always exciting—like home runs in baseball. Who doesn't like seeing someone belt the long ball, or get knocked out cold? Of course he could use a body lock, or a neck crank, or maybe even a full-Nelson. He shook his head no, his mind made up. Unless the situation didn't allow it, he'd disable the little Virginian peckerhead by punches. He wanted to bloody the little bastard enough to send a message that he was not to be trifled with. Ever. It was no different than the methods he'd used in his own locker room in sports, at the police academy, and at officer candidate school. One good ass-beating usually did it, too. Once the others saw what kind of man he was, they'd trip over themselves to avoid any sort of conflict.

Roland would have to be the SGS object-lesson.

He stopped breathing, listening for movement. Clink! There it was again. It sounded like rocks hitting the statue just up ahead. Stupid redneck wants to play tricks. Hancock lifted his head, glancing to the left and the right. The only two hiding places were the grassy hill or the granite wall and—

There!

Roland flashed by, running to the statue. Hancock leapt to his feet, his fingernails clawing at the wall as he moved around it, sprinting to the statue to finish this stress-free finale that to him was nothing more than exercise. Knowing Roland would probably try to kick him like a girl, Hancock took a wide angle around the statue, stopping on the darkened far side. Searching...looking...whirling...

Roland wasn't there. *Sneaky little sonofabitch!*

"HE DOESN'T see him," the man on the front row said. "Big galoot ran right to that statue and never saw him slink around to the other side."

The men were all standing. Realizing the confrontation was near, like spectators at a horse race they had moved to the window, each of them standing so close their breath fogged the specially-treated window.

"Slick maneuver by the little guy," said one man. "I'll give him this: he moves well."

"Doesn't matter," answered the man with the gravelly voice. "Once Hancock gets a hold of him, it'll only take a second."

"Where's Buhl anyway?" asked a third voice.

Six sets of eyes were looking to the right, in the direction Roland had run before disappearing behind the statue. Hancock was searching in that direction also.

Colonel Silver's eyes, however, were looking left, and that's when he saw Roland's glowing form emerge from behind one of the berms and close the distance like an angered hornet.

ROLAND RAN with hardly a sound, slowing at the last moment to unleash a right kick. Hancock was in an athletic stance on the shadowy side of the statue, facing away, his feet shoulder width apart, his hands at the ready. He must have heard Roland coming because he'd just begun to turn.

It was too late.

Roland's foot connected with his groin area, making Hancock roar in pain. Instinctively, Hancock spun, his meaty left fist swinging like a Colombian bolo. Roland saw it coming, ducking underneath the massive hand, unleashing an uppercut into the big Californian's gut.

Just as Roland's punch connected with Hancock's rigid abdomen, the former athlete's haymaker crashed into the statue, shattering his hand and making him shriek in pain. Roland watched as he pulled his mangled hand back like it had been burnt. Still in close quarters from his uppercut, Roland seized the big man's balls, clawing at them with both hands. Just as he knew he would, Hancock bent double, his testicles surely tender from the kick. Roland then unleashed a furious upward knee, colliding with the giant's nose and face, sending him down in a heap. He leapt to the man's back, sliding his arm underneath Hancock's throat, ready to choke him to submission and end the exercise.

But Barrett Hancock, no surprise to Roland, was a game opponent. He grasped Roland's arm as he sprung up and forward, somersaulting him off in a textbook judo throw. Hancock staggered to his feet, his breathing ragged due to the thick blood pouring from his now crooked nose. Roland jumped up, joining his opponent in a typical fighter's stance as the two circled each other from a distance of ten feet.

"HE'S A WIRY little bastard!"

"Dirty, you ask me. I don't go for all that nut kicking," the gravel voice proclaimed.

Colonel Silver calmly sipped his coffee, watching the two men circle like boxers. "Buhl is well within the rules. Hancock's free to stop him at any time."

The men palmed the glass, staring down, rapt, ready for more.

"YOU DIRTY fighting little asshole, you broke my nose!" Hancock growled, pawing with his left jab hand—the broken one.

Roland danced like a boxer, taking measured steps backward. He glanced back several times, marking his position.

"C'mon and fight you little swisher. Don't know what to do with a man in front of you, do you?"

Roland kept his hands at the ready, backing up each time Hancock moved forward.

"I'm gonna kill you...swear to God...when I get these hands on you. They won't be able to get down here in time to save you."

Having reached the point where he wanted to be, Roland stopped his backward motion, bouncing to the left and right before he popped forward, using a front kick to, again, strike Hancock in the groin area. The big man was ready this time, blocking the kick with his thigh while firing off a right hook and catching Roland in the ear, making him stagger backward. Sensing Roland was teetering, Hancock charged him, bellowing like a bull. He swung with a wide hook, grazing Roland's face with his fingernails, gouging his cheek and temple.

Roland took two quick steps backward, not dazed but acting like it. He wobbled purposefully, knowing that, at some point, the big man's aggression would work in his favor.

The Californian rushed him again.

When Hancock reached him, Roland moved backward with him, grasping the chest of his jumpsuit and falling downward, pushing up with his feet. The effect somersaulted Hancock's 240 pounds, sending both men cartwheeling over the two-foot wall and into the foot-and-a-half of frigid water surrounding the dormant fountain.

Smaller and more agile, Roland was on his feet first, smashing down with his boot, connecting with Hancock's left hand, crushing it further. Roaring in pain, Hancock lurched to get up and that's when Roland straddled his chest, smashing downward with his elbow into the big man's face. He unleashed eight vicious strikes, battering Hancock's face and forehead, making him go limp. Roland then dropped all his weight on his opponent, grasping at his neck and holding him underwater as the larger man, once again conscious, thrashed and flailed.

Barrett Hancock's hands, including the mangled one, locked onto Roland's arms, veins bulging, trying to free himself. When that didn't work, he pushed at the slimy bottom of the pool, trying to heave himself upward. Roland anticipated every move, stopping the drowning only long enough to smash the crushed hand again. As soon as he saw Hancock react, he thrust downward, sending him under again before the man could get a good breath.

Voices from everywhere. Arms grasped Roland, jerking him backward as powerful spotlights bathed the area with light. Two men in Army fatigues waded in and lifted the battered Hancock from the water, beating his back as he began to vomit. Roland was taking enormous breaths, anger still coursing through him as, for the first few seconds after the intervention, he struggled to get at Hancock. As he regained his senses he ceased his efforts, realizing the brass had rushed down the stairs and were now staring at him, stupefied, their expressions somewhere between shock and indignation. The only one who didn't appear surprised was Colonel Silver, standing behind the group, wearing a triumphant look. He dipped his head in a nod. Roland did the same.

The medics dragged Barrett Hancock from the pool, placing him on the elevated side as he grasped his mutilated left hand. He looked at Roland, his mouth twisted in fury. "You sonofabitch! You tried to kill me! You ruined my hand!"

Roland wanted to respond, but fought the urge. Now was not the time to be unprofessional. He turned to the assembled group of men, gathering himself. The man in the front, the one he knew only as Mr. Hale, stepped forward. The man's mouth moved several times, stuttering an unintelligible phrase. He licked his lips, started over.

"Ah, Buhl, that was…well…frankly, that was a bit more violent than any of us had ever envisaged."

Roland took a final deep breath, gathering himself. Wiped water from his face. "Yes, sir. I understand. A situation like that…a competition between two men…it's difficult to recognize the limit."

Another of the suits spoke up. "You went too far, Buhl. Period—the end."

Roland took the rebuke without expression. "I'm certain that it might have looked that way, but he threatened to kill me."

"Indeed?" Mr. Hale asked.

"Yes, sir. Indeed."

Mr. Hale tugged at his collar, glancing back at the group. He turned back to Roland. "Well, regardless of how things transpired, we're not starting a boys' choir here. So please accept my congratulations, Buhl. You will be moving on to advanced schooling before we decide how to, ah, use your unique skill set in the service of this great nation."

Roland dipped his head in acceptance. He stepped forward, accepting a towel before shaking each man's hand. Colonel Silver was last, pulling him close and winking at him. "Good job, my boy. Way to chop down the tree." Silver clapped him on the upper arm before walking away, joining the men as they exited.

As Roland walked from the maze, he looked over at Barrett Hancock sitting on the marble ledge by the pool of water, bent over, shuddering silently with his head resting in his good hand. One of the men in fatigues was cleaning and bandaging his left hand. Hancock must have sensed his presence, glaring up at Roland, his bloodshot, swollen eyes burning hatred through the tears.

Roland walked over and leaned down to Hancock, his voice a whisper. "Hey, Hancock," he said, gripping the forearm of his good arm. "That got a little out of hand. I'm sorry. It's just, well…what you said kind of set me off."

The big man spoke through his clenched teeth. "Go to hell, you redneck sonofabitch. If we did that a hundred times, I'd win ninety-nine. You're the luckiest little bastard on earth."

Roland allowed the insult to sink in. He didn't break eye contact. "You keep thinking that if it makes you feel better." A challenging smile came over his face. "And in the event you ever want to do it again, you know where I'll be."

Hancock dipped his head, propping it again in his good hand. He didn't look back up.

"Thought so."

The man in fatigues, a medic, looked up at Roland. "Maybe you should clear out, sir, so I can finish what I'm doing."

Roland could feel the adrenaline leaving him, as if someone had pulled a drain plug. He needed a shower and a good steak, his mind already preparing for the spoils of victory. He straightened up, using the towel to dab the gouges on his head. "Patch him up good, doc. He's an asset, and in the end, we're all on the same team."

As he walked from the maze, Roland could hear a fresh set of sobs from Barrett Hancock.

TWO

HANNOVER'S DÜBERGSTRASSE was ghostly quiet at three in the morning. Far down the street, a beat cop walked, his feet scraping, twirling his stick like one might see from a stereotypical policeman in a moving picture. Above him, chintzy *Weihnachten* decorations swayed in the frigid wind—Gerhard, upon a moment's almost humorous reflection, was surprised Hitler hadn't outlawed Santa Claus along with every other beloved icon. Somewhere behind the rows of tenement apartments, two cats howled at one another, on the verge of fighting or screwing, an impossibility to tell the difference. A cold winter rain must have just passed through, applying a sheen of wetness to everything in sight. One solitary gas lamp illuminated the street nearly a block away, providing just enough light to see the policeman turn left on Baltesweg and disappear.

Lieutenant Gerhard Faber, dressed in the nondescript utility clothing of a German factory worker, emerged from the shadows, crossing the street and entering the bottom of the dreary stone building. The street address was memorized in his head, as was the apartment number. After finding the heavy bottom door unlocked, he climbed the stairs, stopping on the fourth floor of the eight-story building. Defeating the forty-year-old lock took less than a minute. He used a nail file and a paper clip, afterward slipping inside and standing alone in the apartment.

While the street and stairwell had been somewhat dark, the apartment was still and black. Faber stood motionless for a full five minutes until his eyes adjusted as well as they were going to, allowing him only enough vision to see the dim outline of a few shapes. He moved forward, carefully probing with his gloved left hand so as not to disturb anything, or to make noise. He was able to see down the faint outline of a short hallway. There were three rooms: one on each side, one at the end. A scant amount of light spilled from each room, most likely from the windows. And he could hear the hollow, slow snoring of someone in a deep sleep.

Padding down the hallway, he looked into the room on the right, seeing a bed mounded with what appeared to be neatly folded laundry. In the room to the left, several ironing boards stood beside dual mountains of unironed clothes. Lieutenant Faber reached the end of the hall, peering inside the room, seeing the single bed off to the left. The person was snoring loudly, nestled beneath the heavy blankets. He could smell liquor (*schnapps?*) from the person's breath, imbuing the air with a putrid sweet-sourness Gerhard knew quite well from his former Wehrmacht barracks. The inside of the apartment was as damp and cold as it was out on the street. Either the building had no heat, or the asshole landlord shut it off at night. Lieutenant Faber carefully pulled the door to, easing it shut without a sound.

He made his way back to the kitchen, lighting a solitary light bulb hanging from a wire. Once the room was lit, he silently searched the cabinets and cupboards, finding provisions that would suit his needs: a can of soup, steel wool, and a can opener. He could've brought his own, but in the event he'd been tailed (*maybe the man with the hook nose at the back of the rail car, reading the same newspaper for two hours?*) it would be more impressive to the cadre to see his improvisation skills. Faber poked a center hole in both ends of the steel can, pouring out the watery tomato soup in the sink. Taking his time, he shredded the steel wool, coaxing three full pads into the can after which he dotted the sides of the tube with smaller holes from the opener. Finished, he replaced the can opener, extinguished the light, and moved down the hallway into the room on the right, the one with the bed and the folded laundry.

After closing the door, Faber turned on the lamp and surveyed the room. The window was closed but drafty. He took the laundry from the bed and, piece by piece, began to stack it on the window sill, continuing until it was teetering, stacked to the top of the indented window sill. He held the pile in place, keeping it from falling, until he had wedged in enough clothing so that the pressure from the top of the sill held the stack in place. The window was now insulated by thirty centimeters of sound-dampening, freshly-laundered fabric.

Lieutenant Faber studied the ceiling, finally realizing there wasn't anything he could do to further insulate it without making noise. But the floor was a different story. He carefully arranged the remainder of the clothing on the floor, even finding additional tattered linens in the wardrobe, and spreading them out as well, covering every bit with several centimeters of fabric. When finished, Faber had created a mostly soundproof room. The building was old and sturdy, and he guessed there was at least a half a meter of heavy timber and mortar connecting the floors. Between that and the soup can, he had to hope it would be sufficient to prevent the sharp noise of the pistol from escaping. Faber wedged the soup can over the barrel of the Sauer and laid it on the bed under the pillow.

Flipping the light off, he opened the door and walked back into the hallway. He moved to the bedroom at the end of the hallway, opening the door. The sickening smell struck him again as he stared at the still snoring form under the quilts. Lieutenant Faber closed his eyes, building up his courage for what he was about to do. Killing a person shouldn't be difficult for a man in his position. But the two colonels had known what they were doing, making it all the more difficult by having him kill someone in an apartment, especially with an un-silenced pistol as loud as the blowback-style Sauer. Tremors passed through his body. He felt as if he might be sick. Finally, after several deep breaths, he crossed the room and gently shook the slumbering person by their shoulder.

The person stirred, turning over. It was a woman.

Faber continued to shake her shoulder. "Mother…mother, wake up. Mother it's me, Gerhard."

Like most people awakened at nearly four in the morning, Katarina Faber appeared bewildered. She looked around for a moment, probably trying to decide if what she was seeing was real or imagined. Enough light bled in from outside that she eventually recognized her son, narrowing her wrinkled eyes at him. "What the hell are you doing here?" she hissed.

Gerhard Faber lightly shook his head. *Same old mother, warm as always.* He and his brothers used to have more made-up words for her foul moods than Eskimos have to describe snow. "Mother, get up."

Katarina Faber whipped the covers from the bed, placing her bony legs over the side and switching on the spindly lamp. She wore a long gown, retrieving a housecoat from a peg and wrapping it tightly around her. In a quick motion, she pulled her wiry gray hair into a bun, fastening it. The thin skin of her face displayed the bones of her skull. She had deep set brown eyes rimmed by darkened sockets and thick pouches underneath. Her wrinkled lips appeared parched, but rather than lick them she stood motionless, staring, waiting.

"Surprised?" he asked with a feigned smile.

"Why are you here? You said you were leaving and never coming back."

Gerhard looked around. Bottle and sticky glass on the table by the bed. Next to it an empty packet of headache powder. "So, how are you, mother?"

"How the hell do you think? I'm tired and hung over."

"Are you happy to see me?" he asked.

She ignored the question, taking on a dubious expression, her eyes staying on him. "How did you get in here? I changed the locks."

He shrugged. "Door was unlocked."

She tried to press past him, but he stopped her with a raised hand. "Mother, wait."

"Get your hand off me," she said, spinning her arm to dislodge his. The reality of wakefulness began to show on her face. "Why *exactly* are you here?"

"I have something in the other bedroom to show you."

"Which bedroom?"

"My old bedroom." He turned, walking to the room and stepping through the doorway.

She walked into the hall, her hand nervously squeezing the top of the housecoat together.

"Come in here," he said in a low voice.

"Let me put on some coffee first."

"No, mother…this can't wait."

Even in the dark he could feel her spiteful glare, imagining the amalgamation of hateful curses churning in her mind. When they were children, their father had died from a peculiar fall while working on the railroad. Gerhard and his brothers later guessed it was probably a suicide, to free himself from her. Following his death, she became more vicious than ever, her favorite method of punishment being an old wooden spoon with a tack pressed through the end. She would beat each of them with it until they had a leg full of welts swollen up like those from a bee sting. Sometime after Gerhard, the youngest, turned sixteen—and was too large to beat on—she became exclusively verbally abusive. Gerhard found this worse. Much worse. The woman could out-curse a Schutzstaffel barracks full of drunken Bavarian soldiers. And they weren't just skillful rants like that of a drill sergeant; they were biting, degrading attacks aimed at each son's weak points. The attacks intensified after each son's death, leaving Gerhard as the sole recipient of the full load of Frau Faber's vitriol. It was the chief reason he left. Gerhard had only seen his mother twice since his last brother's death. On his two brief visits, the attacks had abated, replaced only by a hollow maternal glare which knew no love.

The two colonels back in Potsdam thought Gerhard might have a hard time killing his mother. If only they had known her.

"In here," he said, motioning in the dark.

She walked into the bedroom. "What's all this shit on the floor?" she immediately asked.

"Just step over there and I'll show you."

His mother muttered more foul language under her breath, moving to the far edge of the room. Gerhard waited, finally working the old solid state switch, bathing the room in harsh light. "The hell have you done with my laundry and linens?" she yelled. For the first time she noticed his gloves, crooking a finger at them, following him as he stepped to the bed. When he pulled out the Sauer with the field-improvised silencer, a sinister grin came over her sallow face. "Why you little bastard. You've come to kill your old mother, have you? Come to finish off the job all you ungrateful piss-ant men have been trying to do for all these years."

Gerhard stood before her, focusing on the task, forcing himself to remember the nights he'd cried himself to sleep. Recalling the time she'd nearly ripped his oldest brother's ear from his head, pinched between her filthy fingernails. Remembering how she refused to have a funeral for his father because she didn't want to have to converse with all his "drunken cronies and whores" who would probably show up. He thought back to the tack-spoon lashings she gave him, spewing mind-warping insults that should never have been said to an impressionable child, breaking him down instead of building him up.

"Well, do it, you little pussy!" she shouted, her voice rising to a high squeal. She opened her arms wide, snarling at him with the courage of a back-alley brawler. "Big soldier boy now, thinks he's big and brave by comin' to kill a wrinkled old lady. You ain't got the balls and you never did. Just like your whore-mongerin', limp-dicked father who never amounted to—"

He raised his arm and fired.

The gunshot came from a range of two meters, with smoke and orange flame and steel wool jetting from every hole in the soup can.

The improvised silencer stifled the subsonic round, but not so much that it didn't sound like a firecracker in the fabric-dampened confines of the old bedroom. Gerhard was satisfied that some noise would have reached the street, at least enough to mollify whoever had been tailing him. He lowered the pistol. His mother still stood before him, the gunshot having muted her invectives. Both of her hands had instinctively flown to her head, covering her ears. Now they tugged at her hair as she continued to stare at him, wide-eyed.

Gerhard reached inside his jacket. He'd brought nearly all of his savings with him. The money was banded. He grasped her right hand, pulling it from her head, pressing the money between her fingers.

"This is more money than you'll make in two years."

"What the *hell* are you trying to prove, coming in here and—"

"Be quiet for once in your life," Gerhard growled through clenched teeth. He closed his eyes, calming himself. "You were supposed to die just now."

Her nostrils flared as she pulled in air. She didn't respond.

"You will pack a very small bag right now. You will walk down the stairs with me. You will leave through the back by the cellar door. You can never come back here, or even to Hannover. I don't care where you go. I don't care what you do. But if you ever come back here, they will kill you. Do you hear me?"

She stared at the money before looking at her son through slit eyes. "Who?"

"Where do we live?" he yelled. "Who do I work for? Why do people disappear now? We live in madness." He grasped the hand he'd put the money in. "You've got the means now, mother. There's nothing keeping you here but misery. This is your chance. Head north, tell no one your name and buy your way out. But whatever you do, just leave." He checked the time. "You have two minutes. Go!"

She continued to stand before him, but he saw a flicker of interest in her eyes. After a half a minute, she pushed past him.

While his mother was in her bedroom, Gerhard used his pocket knife to puncture his arm. He poked inward, inside the crook of his elbow, where a large blue vein existed over the tendons and joint, creating a centimeter-wide incision. He began to flex his arm, increasing the blood flow, allowing blood to spatter all over the fabric he'd laid on the floor. When he felt there was enough, he pressed his thumb over the puncture, replacing it with a handkerchief and keeping pressure by bending his arm.

It was time to leave.

Despite her vulgar protests that he hadn't given her enough time, he pulled his mother by the arm, making her lock the apartment behind them. They descended to the cellar, standing by the coal bin that was secured under lock and key.

"I want you to walk out that cellar door and get away from here as fast as you can."

He could barely make out her lined face in the shadowy basement, seeing an expression he couldn't recall ever having seen before. Unless he was mistaken, it was hope. Though the sensible portion of his brain was telling him to leave, Gerhard allowed himself to briefly wonder if anyone had ever given his mother a chance. He'd heard from his uncles about the physical and mental abuse his mother and brothers had endured at the hands of their father, which she, in turn, had wrought on Gerhard and his brothers. But now, as large as she loomed in his mind, the old woman appeared quite pitiful.

"I love you, mom."

Her eyes glistened, but again she didn't respond.

Gerhard grasped her arms and physically turned her toward the short flight of stairs that led upward to the cellar door. "Go now. Go, and never look back."

Katarina Faber did as she was told. She opened the door and paused, but she didn't turn. Then she was gone.

Gerhard exited the way he came, easing away from the piteous south Hannover neighborhood, casually walking the ten kilometers back to the bahnhof, stopping only to deposit the soup-can silencer under a pile of refuse. Though he was concerned his ruse wouldn't work, he decided, if it were revealed to him that his mother's body wasn't in her apartment, that he would insist he'd shot her. He wouldn't volunteer the notion that she'd staggered away, only planning to say it was dark. And based on that darkness, he would let *them* assume that perhaps he'd only wounded her. It was a risky move, but the only one he could see to use.

The Security Police sent two detectives to Potsdam to see him two days later. They found him on the obstacle course in Düppeler Forest, during his physical training. Thankfully, no one else was around, and by the way the men danced around when asking his alibi, he could tell they didn't suspect him of anything.

"Commandant Heydte can verify my whereabouts for the past months," he said condescendingly. "And why do you want to know where I've been for the last week?"

They told him.

"She's missing?" Gerhard bellowed.

"Or possibly dead," the taller man of the two responded sheepishly. They obviously knew he was part of a special contingent of soldiers, their out-of-character obsequiousness not fitting their collective reputation as inter-Reich thugs. "There was a great deal of blood in her flat."

"She's old and frail," Gerhard snapped. "There's no way she could live if she was losing blood. What happened?"

Unable to answer, the two men studied their shoes.

Gerhard wiped sweat with his sleeve. "And you don't know why she was bleeding?"

"We've nothing to go on, sir."

"How incompetent can you Wehrmacht rejects be? Find her, damn you both! And if she's dead, find her killer!"

Later that afternoon, Gerhard reported their visit to Commandant Heydte, leaving out the fact that his mother was missing. After congratulating him, Heydte informed Gerhard that he would be transitioning back to Berlin, into deep immersion training for his new life.

"And where will that new life be, sir?"

Heydte clapped both of Faber's shoulders. "Where do you think? *Das Land des Freien, das Haus des tapferen.*"

Lieutenant Faber nodded his head, jubilant that his plan seemed to have worked. His euphoria sent his thoughts vaulting across the Atlantic, like the colonel said, to the land of the free and the home of the brave.

His time was near.

APRIL, 1941

FIRST LIEUTENANT Roland Buhl strode through the stark white hallway in the bowels of the highly secured Fairfax, Virginia building. In what seemed to be standard operating procedure for all non-field grade SGS personnel, he wore a suit, poorly cut, in coffee brown. In his left hand was his fedora; in his right was a packet of sealed documents and medical records with no distinguishing markings other than his last name. He reached the end of the hallway, rapping on the door and standing back. A small slot, not unlike a gun port, slid open, immediately filled by a set of judgmental hazel eyes.

"Herring," came the voice from the slot.

"Waterfall," Roland replied—the countersign. A bar could be heard sliding away. The door opened, manned by a chiseled Marine in his class-b uniform. He looked like a statue Roland had once seen while traveling in Europe. On the Marine's polished belt was an oily Colt M1911. In his hand was a glossy black-and-white photo of Lieutenant Roland Buhl. The guard unapologetically cut his eyes back and forth, no doubt matching facial features and looking for discrepancies.

"They expecting me?" Roland asked.

Apparently satisfied, he gestured with the picture. "Yes, sir. Just go straight, then through those double doors, and you'll see Mister Hale's assistant and his office."

This was his first visit to the nerve center of the SGS, rumored to soon be getting a name change to Office of Strategic Services. The hot rumor also predicted a dumbed-down, pandering public campaign to (gasp, big surprise...) announce the section's very existence.

His footsteps stopped clicking after he passed through the double doors as concrete gave way to rug. It was then that the smell of...was it cinnamon?...and macadamia...and scotch, good scotch...hit his nose. As he walked through the lobby area, Roland Buhl shook his head in wonderment, drinking in the showy offices outfitted by fine furniture, gilded vases, and oil paintings. Someone with a flair for the dramatic—probably Mr. Hale himself—had carefully thought out the radical transition from the cramped, unembellished white hallway to the cavernous, beautifully appointed lobby. It was almost like something a skilled architect would use to create a certain sensation: cold and bleak to sumptuous warmth in a single threshold. The lobby was walled in by handsome oak, the floors covered in rich Oriental rugs of a deep wine color. To his right, he passed a bank of individually showcased paintings, recognizing Matisse and Kirchner. Certainly they were reproductions. Roland stopped in his tracks, eyes narrowed. He moved to the artwork, studying it, his keen eyes scrutinizing the texture of the raised oil, swirled and smudged as the painter had perfectly left it so long ago.

"Originals," Roland breathed to himself, laughing quietly. "American taxpayer money at work." As he pressed forward, he decided he might as well be at the Yale Club, breaking balls through clenched teeth and delighting in the Depression struggles of old moneyed friends.

He passed around a divider and stood before the reception desk manned by a comely woman in her early thirties. "You must be Lieutenant Buhl," she said, flashing a dazzling smile of burnished white teeth.

"Yes, I am," he replied, leaning forward on the desk, supporting himself by his whitened knuckles. "And it's a crime, my dear, that they've tucked you away down here in this garishly decorated dungeon, where the general public cannot be treated to the delicate layers of your natural beauty."

Still smiling, the auburn-haired woman scribbled a note on a piece of buff-colored paper. "I thought you were from hill country," she said, still working on the note.

"This is all an act," he joked. "After a few drinks my hillbilly accent bursts forth." When she didn't respond he said, "I didn't mean to sidetrack you."

The woman stood, measuring the same height as Roland's six feet with the aid of her heels. "It's worth it when my boredom is interrupted by dashing, brave men such as yourself."

"You're a regular Girl Friday," Roland quipped, flagrantly looking her up and down. "And perhaps, after today, I'll be lucky enough to see you again, preferably in the evening hours?"

"Doubtful," she answered, backing to the closed door behind her. "Regardless of the fact that it would be highly frowned upon, I think you're soon to be on the fast train out of town." With a wink, she disappeared into the office, pulling the door closed behind her. She was back in a matter of seconds, all business now, instructing Roland to go inside.

"Good luck," she whispered.

Roland took several deep breaths, striding through the door and pushing it shut behind him. Seated to his right, in a squared-off sitting area, were Mr. Hale and Colonel Silver. Unlike Roland and the rest of the field agents, both men wore tailor-cut suits. They could have easily passed for board members of a top U.S. company awaiting a massive distribution, daintily holding saucers topped by china cups filled with steaming coffee. A murmur of classical music...Strauss...played from some unseen location.

Yep. Yale Club.

"Good morning, Lieutenant Buhl. Please, have a seat," Silver said, gesturing to the sofa across from the two chairs. Since being recruited by him, Roland had pegged Colonel Silver as an alcoholic, with his sallow eyes and ever-present stubble that he missed during his likely labored morning shaves. Despite his addiction, Roland judged him as a good man with an affable, optimistic nature and a quick wit. And today, since he was meeting with "the man," Silver appeared to have put himself together quite well.

Roland sat, placing his sweaty palms on his legs, rubbing his pants. There was a long pause, the only sound coming as Silver sipped his coffee, nodding at it approvingly. Mr. Hale was reading the contents of a folder. He had a distinguished face with distinct vertical lines and a high forehead. Every time Roland had seen him his skin was bronze, the type tanned by years of outdoor sport, probably golf or sailing. Maybe both. Despite his refined features, his eyes were brown. Though he would certainly never admit it, Roland knew this had probably always been Hale's blue-blooded cross to bear. A man like him should have blue eyes, or perhaps green or even gray— something to announce his Anglo heritage. Regardless of his Mediterranean eyes, Hale had still ascended the mountain, a fact he was obviously quite proud of, evidenced by his gleaming Phi Beta Kappa tie clip and signet ring.

As he adjusted himself, the thick starch of his tailored shirt could be heard lightly crinkling. Finally he flipped the folder shut and tossed it onto the mahogany coffee table, pulled off his reading glasses, tucked them into his pocket just below his monogrammed initials. He appraised Roland, shoes to hair.

"So, lieutenant," he said, running his tongue over his teeth midsentence, "do you think you're good enough to go into the belly of the beast?"

"Yes, sir," Roland answered without hesitation.

"How do you feel about working alone?"

Roland poked out his lips and shrugged. "I prefer it, sir."

Hale raised his eyebrow as if Roland hadn't grasped the gravity of his question. "I'm speaking of very long periods, lieutenant."

Roland shrugged. "Feel free to leave me alone for decades, sir. It won't bother me at all."

Hale's face darkened a bit, as if the conversation had taken an unexpected turn long before he'd wanted it to. He shifted in his seat. "And why do you prefer to be alone?"

"Because other people, even in the finest organizations, have a tendency to dick things up."

Hale frowned at the coarse language, turning to Silver, who took the cue. "Lieutenant Buhl, as you already know, due to your unprecedented training performance, as well as the prowess you showed over the last months during the applied skills portion, we've decided to move forward and send you to England. At some point, when the time is right, it's our plan to insert you into Germany, unaccompanied."

"Germany, or occupied territory, sir?"

"Subject to change, Germany."

"And when might that be?" Roland asked, turning to Hale.

"When—the time—is *right*," Hale replied with emphasis.

Silver leaned forward, pouring more coffee from the silver service as he spoke. "When that time comes, you'll have an array of potential contacts, but you won't communicate with them unless it's an absolute emergency. You will act as an independent agent, and you'll be given money and immaculate papers, allowing you to live and travel as a highly-thought-of member of their so-called Thousand Year Reich."

"And you will be given an assortment of responsibilities," Hale added, overdoing the gravitas. "Most of your duties will seem pedestrian and simple, but in the field of intelligence, even rote information, when combined, can eventually paint an indelible picture."

"Like Matisse out there?" Roland quipped, a sideways smile on his face.

Hale stared at him, expressionless. "I sense a cowboy."

"Or maybe an Indian," Roland countered, allowing his crooked smile to widen. Colonel Silver cleared his throat, shifting in his chair.

Mr. Hale crooked a finger at Roland. "Buhl, you just make sure you follow your orders to the letter. No side missions, no freelancing. You recon what we tell you to recon. You meet who we tell you to meet. You check in when we tell you to check in." He pulled in a breath, his nostrils flaring. "And you kill who we tell you to kill."

Roland held Hale's brown-eyed gaze, his tone serious as he said, "I understand, sir. Please don't take my jocularity as an insult. I'm just stir-crazy with waiting."

Hale didn't smile, only dipped his head a fraction.

Colonel Silver cleared his throat, his face growing more haggard as if his hangover was just now taking good hold of him. "As of this moment, you've been promoted to captain. Your next paycheck will include the promotion and as soon as you enter Germany, your hazard pay will begin. We'll accrue your money until you get back."

"And how long will I be gone?" Roland asked, his eyes searching both men.

"Thought you didn't care," Hale remarked.

"It's not as if I'm concerned, sir. I simply want to be mentally prepared."

"You stay until we pull you out."

"What's my cover?" Roland asked. "How will you communicate with me?"

"All of that will be explained to you in England. You'll likely be there for some time before your insertion," Hale said.

"And when do I leave for England?"

Silver stood, extending his hand, pumping Roland's as he stood also. "You leave tomorrow." Roland rubbed his chin upon hearing the news.

"Too soon?" Hale asked, still sitting, staring through narrowed eyes.

"I can leave *right now*, if you so please."

Mr. Hale rolled his eyes and reluctantly stood. He didn't shake Roland's hand, clasping his own behind his back. His expression and tone were weighty. "Just make sure you succeed, *Captain* Buhl. I have great suspicion that, at this moment, our country and our military are being relentlessly infiltrated by German intelligence. We're getting chatter of some sort of specialized school they have near Berlin." He twisted his neck as if it ached. "As embarrassing as it is to say, we're playing catch-up, and it's only the work of capable men who can get us there. We need you to be one of those men."

Roland made his voice hard and even. "I'll do anything you ask of me, sir."

"Good," Hale said with a satisfied nod. "And don't dick up, as you so eloquently said."

Roland smiled, bowing slightly.

Hale moved behind his vast desk, donning his reading glasses, his brown eyes lowering to whatever piece of correspondence sat on top of the small stack of letters. "Dismissed."

Colonel Silver led Roland back into the foyer. They moved away from the assistant. The colonel grasped Roland's shoulders, giving him several shakes as he spoke. "I need your best efforts, Buhl. I've put my neck way out there in support of you."

Roland nodded, maintaining eye contact as he struggled to zone out the pungent odor of Silver's liquor from the night before.

"Your personal things will be taken care of. There's a car out front. They'll get you where you're going."

"When will I see you again, sir?"

"Probably when the coming war is over, assuming you succeed."

"And how long do you estimate that to be?"

"Years. Because once you're in, we intend to leave you there."

Roland inclined his head to the office. "Just make sure that bureaucrat doesn't hang me out to dry."

"We'll make sure you're taken care of."

The two men shook hands again, nodding at one another as men do who have no more words to say. Roland turned to the assistant, staring at her from across the foyer. He blew her a kiss before he turned and walked from the building. Smoking a cigarette in the back of the taxi, he thought about Germany, wondering where they would insert him, and pondering who they would make him out to be.

Nine days later, Captain Roland Buhl arrived in England courtesy of the RMS Queen Mary. The first week of training was intense, almost all of it involving his German cover. He was given two days to memorize every fact from a one-inch binder, the rest of the week spent being grilled, prosecution-style, about those facts. He amazed the military lawyers with his memory, and his ability to improvise under pressure. The following month was much less difficult, reviewing his cover, practicing his German, and mainly just waiting. In the evenings he met a few local British women, one of them actually interesting, while the brass finalized preparations for his insertion into the Reich.

And despite the remainder of the month being easy, and even with his pleasant nocturnal flirtations, Roland was completely on edge. The day of his insertion couldn't come soon enough.

THE SCHONAU Bar was the largest in the Alexanderplatz area of Berlin. On most nights it didn't usually hit its peak until well after midnight, but since this night was a wartime Friday, the place had surged well past the Berlin fire marshal's maximum occupancy recommendation by ten in the evening. Gerhard Faber sat at a back table, all alone, a pack of cigarettes under his left hand, his seventh glass of Pilzen-style beer touching his right. He was using all of his skill and restraint to maintain his temper as assorted soldiers and civilian men brushed roughly against him, moving here and there throughout the pulsating tavern.

"Hey, pal! Let me take a few of these chairs," a Heer lieutenant shouted at him, already grasping two of the empty chairs at Gerhard's table.

Gerhard lifted his eyes, decorated with a lacework of red. He shook his head once. "I don't think so."

"Well, is anyone using them?" the lieutenant asked, appearing genuinely puzzled.

Gerhard curled his upper lip. "What does it matter? I told you my answer is *nein*."

The lieutenant straightened, placing his hands on his hips for a moment before moving around the table, leaning down to Gerhard's ear. "You trying to be a smart guy? I was trying to be nice and ask, but now I'm just gonna *take* the damned chairs."

Gerhard twisted his head to the lieutenant, eyes locked, enunciating his words clearly. "Piss. Off. *Now*." He held the man's stare, watching him process the insult. Fight or flight time. The lieutenant, like most swaggering soldiers, probably didn't think much of Gerhard Faber at first glance, until he got a good look into his eyes. Deep, jade-colored eyes. Eyes that had seen things most men wouldn't even have nightmares about. The lieutenant's prudent psyche apparently decided the flight mechanism was the better of the two choices. He blinked several times, turned and disappeared into the crowd.

After motioning to the accommodating barmaid for another beer, Gerhard noticed an affecting derriere he hadn't yet seen. Standing on the far side of the table, she had backed up to one of the unused chairs the lieutenant had wanted. Her dress was short and tight, covered in red sequins. The outfit scooped low in the back, displaying the taut skin of youth, and leading to a perfect tear-drop ass that immediately necessitated all available blood to rush into Gerhard's penis. He leered at her, feeling his cheeks begin to flush.

The hefty barmaid arrived, leaving a fresh beer and making a tick mark on his paper coaster. She smiled at him and disappeared again.

Gerhard couldn't take his eyes off the ass. "Come to papa, my sweet," he whispered.

Using his foot, Gerhard reached under the table to nudge the chair into the gorgeous sequined tush. He did it twice before she turned, cocktail in her hand, cocking her head at him. He smiled, motioning for her to sit. She shook her head apologetically, saying something he couldn't hear over the music and the clamor. Gerhard touched his ear, shaking his head, intentionally giving a disarming, schoolboy look. Flashing a radiant smile, the girl—she couldn't have been more than twenty—made her way around the table, leaning down to him.

"Thank you for the offer," she said. "But I'm here with my date."

"So what?"

She straightened, laughing. Leaned back down. "Well, that wouldn't be very polite."

"Where is he?" Gerhard asked. "If you were my date, I certainly wouldn't leave you standing all alone."

"He had to go say hello to one of his commanders. He'll be right back." She smiled again, displaying large, straight teeth framed inside the painted rouge lips. Her eyes were large and expressive and cerulean, all set off by her brilliant bottle-blonde hair. Gerhard's under-table erection was so rigid he felt it might split his pants like the erupting beanstalk from Jack's puerile English fairy tale (which he'd been made to learn as his cover, in the ridiculous event he ever had to discuss the literary milestones of his American childhood.)

She moved away, glancing back one time, again displaying the polite smile. The date showed up a moment later, another Heer officer, a tanker. He had that trendy look about him, with the tanned face and the slicked-back hair that would be out of regulation without all the damned pomade. Looked like he just stepped from a racing car at the bloody Nürburgring racetrack. All he needed was a white scarf to dangle behind him. Bastard was trying to be Errol Flynn. Gerhard would lay three-to-one that he owned a silver cigarette holder and matching lighter. His face was thin and handsome, with a Roman nose and finely plucked eyebrows. He was a major, and therefore—even though Gerhard wasn't in uniform—outranked him.

Gerhard hated him. Wished he would drop dead on the spot.

Don't do it Gerhard. You're drunk.

He did it anyway. *Screw it.* Nudged the chair into that sweet ass again. And again. Hard the third time, so the major would see it. He did, turned. Gerhard glared up at him.

The major asked his beautiful date a question, probably "Who the hell is that asshole ramming a chair into your ass?" Nice girl she was, doubtless trying to protect Gerhard, she shrugged. The major looked at Gerhard again. Gerhard continued to glare, brows lowered, snorting through his nose. The major stepped around the table, gripping the back of Gerhard's chair, leaned over. "You got a problem?" he growled.

"No...*I* don't. *I* don't have a problem at all."

"Show me some identification."

Gerhard removed his Wehrmacht identification. The major glanced at it. He leaned close to Gerhard's ear, his voice edgy. "I was over by the bar earlier. I saw you talk to her."

"So?"

"So, I'm your superior. Show me the proper respect."

Gerhard pondered the order, shaking his head a few times before saying, "I want your date."

"Now you listen to me, lieutenant, I don't give a shit about officers being a cut above or any of that nonsense. I'll take you out back and shoot you and claim you tried to kill me first, you got that? She's my girl, *get your own*." The major stayed still for a moment, his burning eyes focused on Gerhard's. Gerhard returned the stare, a hint of a smile on his face. After quite a stare-down, the major moved back to his date, appearing incredulous at such a confrontation.

The girl glanced over one more time, an "I'm so sorry" look on her face.

Gerhard stared at the two of them, thankful...hell...overjoyed at the major's ill-advised and murderous threat. He glanced back over his shoulder, to the WC, a fine plan erupting in his mind. He would simply need to make sure that he timed it—

His sinister intentions were interrupted by the academy's commandant, Lieutenant Colonel Heydte, also in civilian clothes, who slid into the seat next to him. His presence was unexpected and unannounced.

"Good evening, sir," Gerhard said, puzzled.

Heydte scanned the bar area, motioning to the hefty barmaid for a beer, making a motion with both of his hands to indicate that he wanted a large one. He took one of Gerhard's cigarettes and lit it, puffing away as he eyed the crowd. Gerhard watched as the colonel's eyes swiveled around like a tank's turret, eventually locking onto the girl's delicious posterior. Heydte's eyes widened. *Target, dead ahead!* She was still rubbing up against the chair occasionally, knowing what she was doing, allowing the crease of her ass to rest right on top of the chair's back. Heydte produced a handkerchief and mopped his forehead before turning to Gerhard.

"That lucky bastard," he yelled over the din, motioning to the Heer major. "Been years since I've seen an ass that faultless."

"On that point, sir, we finally agree."

Heydte tapped the cigarette in the ashtray, narrowing his eyes, studying Gerhard. "Still got a case of the studs, I see?"

Gerhard sipped his beer, closing his eyes for a moment. He hadn't wanted to get into his frustration. But Heydte was the commander, and he asked. He turned to the commandant, lifting his right hand, balled in a fist. "Sir, I've been here in this hellhole of a city, sitting on my ass for months." Peeled his fingers up slowly...one...two...three. "Can't wear a uniform. Can't go anywhere. Can't do anything other than turn into an alcoholic. A hollow promise here. A hollow promise there. Sorry, Faber, but your cover is taking longer to set up than we thought. Maybe tomorrow. No...maybe next week. No...sorry, soldier...maybe next year." He lifted his beer again, thought better of it, smacked it back on the table. "So yeah, I guess I *do* still have a case of the studs, sir." He crossed his arms and leaned back in the chair, staring into the crowd, angry at the situation. Angry at his insolence. Angry at the cocksucking major standing there with his perfect date.

Heydte was again staring at the girl, seemingly impervious to Gerhard's bluster. He spoke without looking. "Well maybe, young Gerhard, I came and found you because I have some news."

Gerhard turned his eyes to him. Heydte's face twisted into a grin, coming around to join eyes with his subordinate.

"What news?"

"You fly out tomorrow."

"You wouldn't bullshit me."

Heydte shook his head.

"To where?"

"The boys from Berlin have got you on some cloak-and-dagger diplomatic flight. They're taking you to Ireland, then they're going to ship you to Nova Scotia. From that point you'll be in the hands of an asset we've got over there. They'll take you down through Canada, and you'll start somewhere in the northern U.S." A drag on the cigarette, a wave of the hand. "Now don't quote me on any of that."

Gerhard sat up, his heart racing. "Are you completely sure, sir? No jacking around this time…no false alarms?"

The colonel exhaled smoke upward, into the bar's haze, making a "*Himmel Help Me!*" expression. "This one is solid. I'll meet you tomorrow at Schönefeld, in the Schwarze-Grenze Building. Just a short briefing there. The rest will come from your contact across the ocean."

Hyperventilating, Gerhard's head moved side to side as he pressed his hand back through his hair, an unavoidable smile dominating his face. Heydte stood, gunning the beer as he dropped a few reichsmarks on the table. "Gotta get home to the old lady and the kids. Be at the airport no later than ten in the morning. Wear your uniform, and bring a bag with the American clothes you were issued. Nothing else." He pulled on his Homburg and stared down at Lieutenant Faber. "Sleep well, my boy." Gerhard shook his hand and he was gone.

Gerhard settled back into his chair, his mind racing, flooded with positive thoughts because finally, at long last, his true mission would begin. He'd dreamt of it, almost nightly, of being in the mysterious land where every man could own a home and travel at his own free will. What a dream for an operative. And so unlike the myopic wasteland that was the so-called Thousand Year Reich, where you could hardly buy a coffee without filling out a form in triplicate. This trip…no, this *adventure* was going to be like the silent American westerns he'd watched as a boy. Go where you want, do what you want, and make up your own rules while you do it.

Speaking of going where he wanted, Gerhard watched as the girl with the delicious ass yelled at an acquaintance. The two girls made a big show of fawning over each other's outfit, clasping hands like a good game of mercy, the way girls often do. The Heer major, seeing a chance to break away, turned and headed toward the back of the bar, in the direction of the WC. Gerhard rotated his head, watching him go.

Okay, Errol-Flynn-who-threatened-my-life…time for the big show.

He lit a cigarette, counted to ten, and followed the man.

The bathroom was a three-stall affair. The major was in one stall, standing, urinating. Otherwise the bathroom was empty. Gerhard silently slid the bolt closed on the door. He tossed his cigarette in the sink. Waited.

The major finished, shaking it off before zipping up. He exited the stall, frowning at Gerhard. "You?"

"Yeah, me."

The major stepped back, his feet widening a bit. An athletic stance. "If you want to dance, pal, you picked the wrong guy."

Gerhard laughed heartily.

The Heer major mustn't have liked being laughed at. He rushed forward, swinging a looping right that would have knocked Gerhard out had it connected. Gerhard, with several years of boxing under his belt, effortlessly ducked the telegraphed punch. He unleashed a low uppercut into the major's balls, making him yell out as he bent forward. He gripped the back of the major's jacket collar, lifting him and punching him in the face, in his perfect pointy nose, three times in quick succession. The major crumpled onto the shiny tile floor, moaning as blood leaked from his face. Gerhard straightened, catching his breath.

"You shouldn't have threatened my life, *pal.*"

Cracking the door and seeing no one in the narrow hallway, Gerhard executed a fireman's carry. He lugged the major out the back, into the alleyway. Just another drunkard who'd gone too far—a common sight in party-crazy Berlin. He found a mound of garbage, depositing the major at the base and heaping the pile on top of him. The major continued to moan and groan from the bottom of the rubbish, but didn't seem ready to get up. Gerhard gave himself five minutes before the guy would be back in the bar.

He walked back into the restroom, washing the garbage from his hands before heading back into the tavern. Two young sergeants were quickly ejected from his table before Gerhard resumed his admiration for the lovely fanny standing mere meters away. Her friend had departed, leaving her with an empty drink and a puzzled look as she scanned the bar for her precious major.

Knowing he needed to hurry, Gerhard lit another cigarette and ordered a fresh beer. After a sip, he stood and left some money on the table. He walked over to her.

"You know, you deserve better."

"Excuse me?"

He allowed the back of his finger to trace down her bare arm. "Tell me you haven't been dating him long."

"Why?"

"Just tell me," he said, offering a caring smile.

"This is our second date."

He arched his eyebrows, tilting his head as he looked away.

"Why did you make that expression?" she asked.

"I shouldn't," he said. "As your date emphasized to me earlier, he *is* my superior."

"Tell me," the girl commanded, gripping his arm. "I won't tell him you said anything."

Gerhard joined eyes with her, acting as if the revelation pained him somehow. "I saw him, just a minute ago, over by the bar. He saw some dame he must have known. A real busty, whorey-looking gal with a Bavarian accent. She came up and kissed him…really laid one on him. They talked for a minute then left, real quick like."

The girl's hand went to her mouth as her face contorted. She gathered herself. "You wouldn't lie about this would you?"

He opened his hands in a gesture of innocence. "Why would I do that?"

"He seemed so nice on our first date," she said distantly.

His hand swept over the bar. "Have a look around if you like."

She nodded and walked away. She'd be back. Gerhard wiped a thin film of remaining sweat from his brow, leaning against the same chair she had, wondering how long before the major would emerge from his garbage pile looking for the license plate of the Mercedes truck that ran him over. The girl returned three minutes later, a stunned look on her face.

"He's gone."

"He's a tanker."

"What?"

"He's in the Panzerkorps. They're all like that."

"What a complete scoundrel," she seethed, hand on her forehead.

"Yes, what an ass!" he yelled, barely stifling his grin at his clever double-entendre.

They left together. Gerhard walked her around Alexanderplatz, allowing her sufficient time to vent before leading her, arm in arm, down Am Friedrichshain. It was midnight, the city still alive with its seemingly constant buzz of energy. It took him fifteen minutes to master her insecurities, which, by the way, happened to be her semi-poor upbringing and the lack of a formal degree. Coupled with his reassurances of her unequalled beauty, especially after she thought Errol Flynn had walked out on her, she was as pliable as plumber's putty by the time he purchased two bottles of red wine from the nifty street vendor's cart at the corner of Danzigerstrasse.

They went into the sprawling Volkspark. He found a darkened spot between two barberry bushes. Laid his jacket on the dewy grass. Her protests were minimal. She tasted the wine. He tasted her. An hour after leaving the bar, Gerhard Faber was perched on the derriere he so desired to see, hands on her shoulders, giving her everything he had before collapsing on her back, licking her neck as he caught his breath.

Heydte had been correct. Her ass was flawless. Indeed.

After a brief period of rest, Gerhard lifted up, asking her if she could endure his savagery one more time. She giggled. He stared downward, coming to life again, his smile as wide as it had ever been.

Tomorrow, Miss America…I'm coming.

THE NEXT morning, after purchasing a Hitler-branded coffee from a newsstand, a uniformed, sleepy-eyed Gerhard Faber made his way to the bus stop, an overnight bag in hand. There was a commotion by the Schonau Bar, a large group of onlookers framed on both sides by polizei cars and an ambulance. He ambled over, watching as a photographer flashed pictures from behind a section of waist-level yellow rope. Gerhard craned his neck to see what was happening. The police and several hospital personnel were crowded behind the open doors of the ambulance. A man in a dark suit, wearing a party pin on his lapel, barked orders at the group.

"What happened?" Gerhard asked the photographer.

Without looking, camera still popping, the man said, "They just pulled an Army officer out from under the garbage back there."

Gerhard tried to conceal his shock. "Was he drunk?"

"Drunk?" the man asked, turning. "Would I be taking pictures of a drunk?"

"Dead?" Gerhard breathed.

"I'll say he was. I covered Röhm's embalming and Röhm looked good next to this sap."

Gerhard struggled to swallow. "How did the guy die?"

"I overheard them say he was beaten. Bludgeoned, actually."

"Bludgeoned, you say?" Gerhard asked, confused. He'd wrecked the major's nose, but that was the extent of it.

"It's as bad a beating as I've ever seen. Doubt my publisher will dare go with these shots."

As the medics rolled the covered body by, the reporters and photographers yelled for one good close-up photo opportunity. The medics stopped the gurney and turned to a policeman who shrugged then nodded. Gerhard sucked in a sharp breath as one of the medics pulled the starchy sheet back. The only giveaway that the corpse was the same man Gerhard had encountered was the pomaded blond hair. Other than that, he was unrecognizable; the bloody mess resembling a portion of ground beef more than it did the face of a human being. As the cameras popped, Gerhard turned, walking unsteadily away, wondering what could have happened.

His mind awash in puzzlement and regret over what he'd just seen, and with the excitement of his coming mission, he crossed Alexanderplatz and boarded the crowded bus to Schönefeld Airport. Halfway to the airport he made himself drop his concern over the major's killing. He hadn't done it. Maybe the man had gotten up and picked a fight with someone else. Gerhard knew he would never know—and at this point couldn't afford to worry himself over it.

The airport came into view, marked by a silver Junkers Ju 52 roaring into the sky. Gerhard pulled in a long, satisfying breath, allowing himself a moment to relax. At long last, his mission was finally beginning.

PART TWO

Plagued Beginnings

THREE

JUNE, 1942

IF A POLL was taken at the New York offices of Weston Mechanical Dynamics, nearly every employee would have rated Gerald Fieldhouse as one of the military contractor's rising stars. Those who didn't give him high marks would only have done so out of jealousy. He was dependable, cheerful, and had learned the secret to corporate success in the United States—making his superiors look good. In only thirteen months with Weston he had quickly ascended the corporate ladder from his start as a mail clerk to the title he held this day: Senior Associate for Logistics. So it was a complete surprise to everyone who worked with him when, in early June 1942, Gerald didn't show up for work.

It wasn't until late that afternoon, as the employees were gathered around listening to the radio reports from the sea battle at Midway, that one of the mail clerks rushed in and informed everyone about the gruesome tragedy involving Gerald and his wife.

On the day before the fatal fire, Gerald's day was much as it always was. Weston's employees were due in by 8:30 a.m., their entrance recorded by a bear-trap of a time-clock just off the elevator. Gerald exited the elevator at 7:54 a.m., his left-leg limp as pronounced as ever. Under one arm was a copy of the Times; he would enjoy the paper with his lunch, which he carried with his other hand. After retrieving his coffee, black, Gerald was at his desk and working by 8:05 a.m. Before him was a ledger containing entries for munitions shipments, primarily to the west coast. He checked each one, noting all quantities, but paying careful attention to the small-arms shipments.

Susie Haymann, one of the pool secretaries from Gerald's floor, stopped by his office—nothing more than an interior cubby—at 10:15 a.m., just as Gerald was eating his Granny Smith apple. Gerald conversed with her, politely steering the conversation away each time she would take it in the direction of his personal life. An appealing young woman with pale skin and a tight matting of curly brown hair, it had seemed for some time that she wanted something more than a standard office friendship. Susie wrapped up the conversation, crushing out her secret cigarette in Gerald's ashtray, leaning forward so he might have a full view of her bosom.

While she was leaning down, she turned her eyes to Gerald. "Come to lunch with me today."

Feeling panic shoot through him, and hiding it nicely, Gerald lowered his gaze to the floor. "I can't."

"Sure you can." She checked under his desk, making a show of looking at both of his legs. "See, they don't even have a ball and chain on your ankles."

Gerald's gaze was still down. "Susie, I'm married."

"It's *just* lunch…for now."

He looked up. "While I'm certain you're only seeking friendship, my wife Carol Lynn…" (*Always use your wife's Christian name. Always! It personalizes the situation.*) "…might be hurt if she heard I was even seen so much as walking with such an attractive girl as you."

Susie shrugged, her arms pressing her cleavage together. "Then don't be seen with me. Just bring your lunch to my apartment and we can just talk. My roommates work uptown; they won't be there."

Gerald turned away as he briefly pondered such a tempting liaison. With his erection pressing painfully against the zipper of his trousers, he shook his head and offered a polite smile. "Really, Susie, I wish I could, but I simply can't."

Susie tucked her cigarettes back into her handbag, and without another word, hurried away, her hose making a *shh-shh* sound.

He sucked air into his nose, watching her go. In reality, like most men would, Gerald would have desperately loved to have rendezvoused with Susie, exuberantly taking her up on her ribald request. But he *was* married, and married men have responsibilities. Married men who want to continue to ascend at work don't make a habit of screwing secretaries, either. Especially gossips like Susie Haymann. Had he gone with her at lunch, Gerald would have given it until 3 p.m. before the office would have been atwitter with whispers of the forbidden romance taking place under their noses. He shook the thoughts from his head, refocusing on his tasks. After two more hours of working in the ledger, Gerald packed up and headed outside for lunch.

It was a warm June day, but still containing all the hints of the pleasant spring. Butterflies and birds were everywhere. Flowers were still in bloom. The trees and plants were still bright green from the copious May rains. And the sky was a deep blue, not yet the white hot atmosphere of summer Gerald so detested. One would think a place as far north as New York wouldn't get so hot. He couldn't even begin to imagine living in the hellhole that was the American south, offering a murmur of thanks that he hadn't been sent there. After hobbling several blocks south on Second Avenue, Gerald turned left on East Houston, following it all the way to the sliver of a park that separated Manhattan from the East River. He chose one of the empty benches, placing his hat, his newspaper, and his lunchbox across the bench to prevent anyone else from sitting. Situated, Gerald munched his deviled ham sandwich while reading the first several pages of the Times. His eyes occasionally wandered, for long periods, to the Brooklyn Naval Yards directly across the river. Everything seemed to be as it had been the week before. The superstructure on the Missouri was nearly complete, meaning she would be put to sea for trials within the next few months. Gerald glanced at the burgeoning hulls of several other craft, deciding that there wasn't much activity on this day worth his wasting time on. After a check of his pocket watch, he hurriedly ate half of his second green apple before gathering his things and tottering back in the general direction of Weston, munching the apple along the way.

When he was nearly back to the office, Gerald limped into the Holloway Department Store on Second Avenue, pausing to examine a stand of imported ties in the men's department. He purchased two, one for work and one for evening, satisfying the eager salesperson who took his time wrapping the ties in tissue individually. He perused several other departments, glancing around occasionally, before taking the escalator to the third floor. Gerald entered the restroom, making certain it was empty before hurrying to the porcelain sink. His right hand went under the sink, behind the bowl, where he grasped a small piece of smokeless paper held by a gummy substance. He pocketed the paper, this week's instructions, and transferred the gum to a slip of dot covered paper from his own pocket, his work of the last week, reaffixing it underneath the sink. After relieving himself, he washed his hands and went back to work.

His afternoon was normal until sometime shortly after 4 p.m. Bud Narosette, a highly decorated war veteran from the Great War, and Gerald's immediate supervisor, stopped by his cubby and invited Gerald to a hail and farewell for one of the vice-presidents who happened to be reclaiming his commission in the Navy.

"It'd be real good for you to show up," Bud said, sitting on the corner of Gerald's small desk. "Rumor is that I'm probably getting that job, meaning you'll be one of the three candidates for my corner office."

Gerald returned Bud's oh-so manly smile before wrinkling his brow. "Do you think I have a realistic shot?"

"I think so...if you play your cards right." Just like an old warhorse would, Bud roughly clapped Gerald on the back and stood. "Just come along and hobnob and have a few drinks. The old man invited you, by name."

Gerald troubled his face. "I don't really drink, sir. Will that be a problem?"

"Are you kidding?"

He shook his head, making his tone apologetic. "My family, sir...a few drunks on our side of the tree." Certainly not a lie.

Bud rolled his eyes as if Gerald's abstinence was prudent cautiousness gone too far. "Just come to the tavern, order a beer or a cocktail, and sip on it. And yes, it will be a problem if you don't. They'll never promote a panty-waist and besides, a few drinks won't turn you into a lush overnight." He wrinkled his forehead and said, "You with me?"

Gerald thought about it for only a few seconds, giving a resolute nod. "Yes, sir. I just need to make a quick call home to let my wife know I'll be late." After Bud had gone, Gerald stared at the floor, simultaneously soaring over the potential promotion and warning himself on the dangers of drinking and how alcohol typically affected him. *Alcohol makes people do foolish things*, he reminded himself over and over—*especially me*.

He breathed warnings to himself for the remainder of the day.

Due to the fuel rationing, the men walked to Tommy's, a bustling bar located just off of Wall Street. The high prices kept most of the sailors and soldiers away, and the free drinks from the moneyed male patrons kept Tommy's stocked with bountiful young women, looking to change the four-letter salutation before their name to a three-letter abbreviation.

Eight men from Weston were there, including the president, a man who Gerald had only before said hello to. Gerald was the junior-most employee in the group, and as often happens in social situations—especially ones with large quantities of booze—a camaraderie developed, and several of the senior men took a keen interest in young Gerald. He relayed the memorized tales of his background, growing up in Michigan on a farm, injuring his leg on a thresher, thereby derailing his chance to defend his country against the Japanese.

"Show 'em the scar," Bud said, glancing around at the group. "Wait'll you guys see this butchering he took in that wheat field."

Gerald lifted his pants leg, getting the typical male reactions: hoots, curses, winces, and pained smiles. In reality, the grotesque scar had been surgically induced and was largely cosmetic. He had no residual pain at all, but had been instructed in great detail how to describe the pain in order to gain a medical rejection by the draft board.

After the scar story ran its course, he told them his manufactured tale about graduating from a small college before making the leap to New York with only $35 in his pocket. The men liked him, clapping him on the back as his dry wit shone through the twists of the story. He began to get into the spirit of the evening; the atmosphere became rousing. Gerald's single sipping beer turned to five, and that was before the table whiskey bottle arrived. Shots were poured and, around 10 p.m., a group of ladies from the office arrived as if on cue. They'd obviously gone home for a strategic change of clothing, their collective décolletage commanding every male in the bar pay them absolute attention.

Gerald's heart red-lined when he noticed Susie Haymann among them. She stared at him, without ice or heat, turning away as her painted lips gripped her paper straw, sipping her drink and almost imperceptibly tonguing the straw afterward.

Susie knew what she was doing and Gerald, while he knew too, was too drunk not to fall prey to her metaphorical actions. After another round of shots, the men, all married, began to scatter, each of them conveniently pairing up with the unmarried girls from the secretary pool. Bud Narosette noticed Gerald's hesitation, leaning close to speak over the din.

"Just go with it, Gerald. I know you're a bit out of your element here, but this is where the real business happens…this is how you show the big man you're one of us. Don't worry. The office gals know the score."

His fingers gripping the warm shot, Gerald gunned it, pouring another as Bud craned his neck back in hedonistic laughter. Forgetting his limp (as if anyone was sober enough to have noticed) he staggered across the bar, planting his right hand firmly into the small of Susie's back, pulling her close so she could feel the arrogance of his stiffness.

THREE HOURS later, in Queens, as Gerald staggered into the hallway of their small Murray Hill home, he could hardly recall what had transpired since sundown. All he remembered was polishing off the bottle by himself, a fetid lower Manhattan alleyway, lots of protests, cajoling, panting, and moaning— and now he had sticky, soiled trousers and a bloody knee. As his mind began to show signs of returning to a certain degree of the purgatory before sobriety, Gerald felt a great deal of personal disappointment with himself.

You stupid, undisciplined bastard.

At least he hadn't gone through with it.

Just as he was about to drop his keys into the china plate near the door, a voice made his head snap up.

"What in God's name happened to you?" It was Carol Lynn, standing in her summer nightgown, holding the top button shut with her left hand, her right hand across her abdomen. A tall woman, she had a milquetoast, lightly freckled face and an attractive body. Her legs were her best asset, incredibly long and topped by an attractive rear end and hourglass waist. Despite his initial enjoyment of making love to her, a more recent source of tension between them—especially since he'd begun his corporate climb—was her inability to get pregnant and his lack of interest in trying to rectify the situation.

Of course, Carol Lynn had no idea that her husband had been purposefully sterilized by vasectomy in a Berlin hospital months before he traveled to the United States.

She'd been an easy get. Her friends had been marrying as if the preacher was running a special. Just as he'd been taught, Gerald said all the right things, displayed the proper emotions. Her bland face hadn't hurt either. Despite her lithe body, the boys hadn't exactly been beating down her door. They were married mere weeks after their first meeting. And although he'd only married her because she fit the bill, he truly grew to enjoy her company, finding marriage pleasant.

Until now.

Standing there in his unsteady drunkenness, Gerald felt like a child who had been caught in mischief, which wasn't far from the truth. His lips parted as his mind refused to move at the speed he so desired. After blinking several times, he slurred his way through an explanation. "I've had choo much to drink, but ish okay. (*Ish? Sheise! Pull yourself together!*) This ish all a part of the game at work. I'm shtaring a big promotion right between the eyes."

Susie's mouth twisted and trembled. "A promotion? A *promotion*? That's what sends you home slurring drunk, your knee all bloody, lipstick on your cheek, and covered with the scent of some tart's cheap perfume?"

He shook his head, blinking his eyes as if there was sand in them. "No, darling. Thash not a tart's perfume. We were at a bar…Chommy's, down on Wall Shreet. Shum of the men from work have girlfriends…wives. They were there, shtanding closhe by."

"And why wasn't I invited?"

Gerald paused, his mind working just well enough to grind through the gears of deceit, coming back into his character, the one with the short fuse. His bleary eyes joined hers as he wrinkled his brow. "They didn't tell me to invite you becaush I'm the low man on the totem pole, got it? When I'm vyshe preshident you can choosh the damned wine if you want. But until then you get the hell back to bed before I loosh my temper."

Carol Lynn, her lips pinched in a tight walnut of a knot, hurried down the hall, her gown flowing behind her, giving her the image of an apparition. Gerald closed his eyes, rubbing them with both thumbs. He went to the kitchen, remembering the drill from his university and military days, guzzling three full glasses of tap water, following them with a fourth loaded with two heaping headache powders.

Sitting at the kitchen table, staring at the dewy backyard, Gerald's patience allowed his mind to continue to clear. He reached into the inner pocket of his jacket, his fingers moving over and above, to a hidden seam. From the inner, veiled pocket, Gerald removed the piece of dot-covered paper. He held it in his trouser pocket, easing his way to the bedroom, peering into the indigo darkness. Carol Lynn was on the bed, facing away from him. The curve of her body steadily rose and fell. She seemed to be sleeping.

Gerald exited through the back door and went out into the attached workroom, locking the door and pulling the string for the overhead light. From a stack of instruction and owner's manuals, he removed the one for his rotary lawn mower, flipping to the back. Inside the rear cover was an innocuous-looking dot pattern that wouldn't be noticed by anyone, even had they stumbled across it. Just a pockmarked page in a tattered manual. Gerald, his actions still slowed by the alcohol, translated the note from his pocket, writing everything on a sheet of plain notebook paper. Finished, he read the note three times, etching it into his mind so he would remember his instructions when he awoke with what promised to be a milestone hangover.

Satisfied, he went back into the house and lit a cigarette with a match. Using another match, he burned the small piece of paper he'd retrieved from the bathroom at Holloway's. In the light of the moon, he reread the translated note a final time before lighting the bottom corner aflame, tossing it, too, into the fireplace. Gerald staggered down the hallway, entering the bathroom from the hall door. He brushed his teeth and washed his face, eyeing the bleary red lacework of his eyes in the mirror.

What happened tonight is why Berlin insists on all operatives abstaining from alcohol while in the field. Are you really that stupid?

The thoughts from the alleyway flashed through his mind, like snippets from one of those pathetic peep shows on 42nd Street. She'd wrenched his pants down without even unbuckling his belt, trying to create an illicit union due to his unintended, physiological rigidity. Gerald had a faint recollection of her yanking her own blouse open, massaging herself while she tried to coerce him into reciprocating, not unlike the overheated "starlets" in a film reel he'd once paid five phennigs to watch. But Gerald had resisted, going only as far as kissing, using all of his will not to join her in a deed they would both regret.

The unspeakable things she'd whispered as she'd tried, inflamed, to gain his cooperation. Her fingers had roamed expertly, providing Gerald bursts of pleasure in so many secret zones…

Susie…oh, Susie. You'll never attract a husband that way. Someone else's, yes. Your own…not likely.

He'd fallen down when he finally ran away, tearing his pants, skinning his knee. What a disaster.

Gerald ground his fist silently into his left hand, glaring at himself in the small mirror. *Too damned careless!* And now good old Susie could wind up making trouble for him if she so desired. Bud said the secretaries knew the score but Mother Germany would probably rather not risk its future on the opinion of a horny, middle-aged man looking for a cheap lay. It was going to take a deft hand to disentangle Susie without upsetting the apple cart. She'd cursed him as he fled, yelling after him and asking who the hell he thought he was.

"Du bist so dumm," he whispered to his reflection. Gerald flipped the light off and opened the door to the bedroom. The bedside lamp was on.

Carol Lynn was not in the bed.

His eyes scanned the room. The back window was open, the filmy curtains floating in with the breeze.

"I guess you forgot I took four years of German," Carol Lynn said in a low tone, her voice shattering the still night. He whirled around, the purplish light illuminating her tall form. In her hand was the half-burned sheet of notebook paper. She rattled it, tiny flecks of the charred edge floating to the floor. "But it's no great surprise you forgot, Gerald, because you've never paid anything more than cursory attention to me anyway."

Never appear shocked. Remain calm. Admit nothing.

He swallowed, offering a kind smile. "I only burned it because I wouldn't want you to get the wrong idea."

"The wrong idea," she said flatly.

"Yes."

Maybe it was his residual drunkenness, but the gulf between his last word and her next must have been three minutes. She didn't move; neither did he, other than his unavoidable swaying. Finally she shook the paper again, her voice growing shrill. "This is about ships, Gerald, American ships. And about things from your work. Munitions, quantities, destinations!"

Still drunk, but sobering nicely. He held her gaze. Gave a tight nod, a contrite tone. "Yes, it is."

She lifted the sheet of paper between them. "These are exactly the kinds of things they talk about on the newsreel every Saturday. The kind of things people are supposed to watch out for."

Another nod. "Yes, they are."

Her eyes widened. "Well?"

"Well?"

She threw her arms up. "My God, Gerald, can you explain it?"

"Yes, I can."

"Then do it!" she screamed.

He moved his left hand over his eyes, the thumb on his left temple, his index and middle fingers on the right. He took steadying breaths, waiting to see if she backed away.

She didn't.

Damned alcohol. Of all nights to be drunk. Bruising will be okay—it won't show after the house fire—but a broken bone or cracked tooth will do me in if the coroner happens to be circumspect. I can make this punch, if sober, ninety-five times out of a hundred.

Took a peek between his fingers. She was saying something, imploring him to talk.

Drunk or not, there was no other move on the board.

Two more breaths. Easy. Easy. Surgical strike…on the tip of the chin. Maybe five centimeters square.

He lowered his left hand. "I'm not who you think I am, Carol Lynn. I'm sorry for that." And as he finished his genuine (albeit brief) apology, he planted forward with his left foot and stepped his weight into a straight right, punching her chin slightly off center but more than doing the job. She crumpled unnaturally, her right knee and ankle catching under her weight but popping out as if sprung by thick rubber bands.

After viewing her dazed form with a sharp pang of remorse, he went into the bathroom, reaching under the sink, at the back of the cabinet. There, in a hidden cavity at the bottom of a Boraxo container, was a vial of chloroform.

CAROL LYNN watched as he rushed through the house, talking to himself, carrying this and that. She could hear her pulse thudding in her ears and in her aching jaw. Though gagged, she managed to work her jaw, hearing it popping below her ears. *Had he broken it?* She was angered with herself for crying, but she couldn't help it, damn it! A wave of nausea passed through her, making her stomach convulse. Tears of the betrayed flowed down her face on both sides. She took slow, deep breaths, flaring her nostrils. *Slow down. Stop crying, slow down and think.*

She focused as best she could, thinking back through all of the little inconsistencies she'd never allowed herself to pull together, like the pieces of an unwanted jigsaw puzzle. They never went for a visit (*"ever!"* he so forcefully had always insisted) to Michigan because he claimed to have had a horrible falling out with his family: "loafers and deadbeats," they were. And the one time they met an alumnus of Enright College, of about Gerald's age, he cut the man off quickly, telling him he hated his time at that "miserable excuse for an institution." When she occasionally turned the conversation to his childhood, he told her things that often weren't consistent with one another, such as the name of his primary school. And when she brought it to his attention, he simply said he had attended two schools due to the fact they moved, because they had no money, and it was a shitty memory, and would she mind not talking about his shit-ass childhood anymore?

His pain had seemed plausible then.

Then.

Not anymore.

The towel around her mouth tickled her gag reflex. Her physical revulsions were no doubt mingling with the horrid realization of who her husband was—and what he might do with her. Again she fought back her urge to vomit by concentrating on her breathing. Her mouth and nose still tasted of almonds, presumably courtesy of whatever he'd used to incapacitate her after hitting her. She tugged on her arms and legs, turning her head to see the fleece-covered straps securely tethering her limbs to the bed. Squeezing her eyes shut, she recalled having stumbled upon these straps one time, several months before. They were in the attic, wrapped up neatly, in a black canvas bag hidden under a musty blanket. She'd knelt there puzzled, her head cocked. Then, although she'd never seen anything obscene in nature, she recalled a conversation with one of her racier college suitemates. Her husband—fiancé at the time—would often tie her up, tickling her erogenous zones with a feather, licking her, making her beg, that type of thing. Carol Lynn remembered how she had closed her eyes in the attic that day, hoping something like that was what Gerald had planned. She'd even hurried downstairs, laying on the bed and furiously pleasuring herself at the delicious thought. He never did any such thing, and normal life soon intervened; she forgot all about the straps a few days later.

Now, regrettably, she knew what they were for.

Something about the memory made her scream, only an impotent, muffled sound due to the gag. Though certainly not enough to alert anyone outside, Gerald must have heard her cry. He walked into view from the hallway. He had changed clothes, now dressed casually in a dark outfit she didn't recognize. He stared at her for a moment, touched her cheek, allowing his hand to linger there.

"You might as well relax, Carol Lynn. I need to leave now. I'll send someone for you in a day or so, when I'm long gone from here. Until then, there's no point in straining yourself. You're going to be thirsty, but if you don't scream and don't strain, you'll feel much better. And I can assure you that you won't escape, and no one will hear you no matter how loud you try to yell." He shook his head regretfully. "I didn't want this and I truly am sorry."

Though she knew he was a gifted actor, she thought she sensed true remorse.

With a nod of finality he walked away, turning off the bathroom light. Seconds later, she heard the front door close and the bolt click home.

Carol Lynn felt her breaths growing deeper, raspier. Panic arose in her as if overheated by a flame-red boiler. She arched her back and screamed, the damp towel catching much of the sound.

And, as Gerald promised, no one heard her.

IN THE SEAT next to him were the black bag of additional straps and the small box containing the information and implements he'd hoped he never would have to use. But here and now, speeding west on Long Island, the city lights in the distance, Gerald thanked his years of intensive training back in Potsdam. The secret space in his storage shed held his three escape outs; he'd developed them just as he'd been taught to do, each one designed for a completely different set of circumstances. The first, and perhaps the most deadly, situation involved one of compromise by the host country. That particular out required the cooperation of several other operatives and an airplane. For what it was worth, Gerald didn't have much faith that it would work. Too many working parts and trust in other operatives. Rather than help him, they might easily turn on him to save their own ass. "Trust" was typically a field operative's weak point.

The second escape-out was designed to eliminate, or evade, another covert operative. It required several fake identifications and a frame-job involving a criminal group that operated in Brooklyn and Queens. Gerald was quite proud of how he had architected it, and a small part of him wished he was performing it rather than the coarse escape he was executing at the moment.

He cracked the window on the Ford, hoping beyond hope the man (the key component of this, his third out) was at home. If he wasn't, Gerald would have to dispose of Carol Lynn's body, and in short order—probably less than a day—there would be a search followed by a massive investigation. This would be bad…and heavily frowned upon by the moustaches back in Berlin. After he lit a steadying cigarette, he ran his hand through his short hair and murmured a quick prayer that the man would be home.

He caught his eyes in the rearview mirror. "Kannst du sie töten?" he asked himself. Translated, it meant, "Can you kill her?"

Gerald pulled to the side of the road and vomited.

ROBERT WILLIAMS opened his eyes. The old home creaked and moaned on regular occasion, but something else, a different sound had awoken him.

Hadn't it?

Or had it been in my dream?

He sat up, rubbing his eyes, in that familiar fog when a person's mind is still awash in the muddled period between wakefulness and sleep, trying to see if anything was amiss in the gargantuan master bedroom of the ancient mansion. He looked at the windows, seeing only purple light and the shimmering of the leaves on the giant elm.

It must have been a dream.

He turned the pillow, finding the cool spot, and replaced his head, pulling up the extra sheet. The warm June air had cooled rapidly.

The floor creaked.

Robert turned just in time to see the black apparition glide over the floor like a phantom. He yelled, trying to scurry backward. It was too late. As it turned out, the phantom was nothing more than an average-sized man, as Robert quickly noted. It...*he* clamped a hand behind his neck as the other hand pressed something wet over his face.

Almonds...

In the pale moonlight of the room, the last thing Robert saw was the man's eyes—they were very light, either green or blue—glowing with great intensity as blackness enveloped his world.

GERALD WAITED ten seconds after the man ceased moving. He removed the handkerchief, staying over him for another minute, hoping he hadn't put him too far under. He watched...Robert's breathing was deep but steady. Perfect.

From the black bag he removed identical padded cuffs to the ones he'd used on Carol Lynn. After hog-tying the man, Gerald fashioned a gag from the remainder of his bed sheet, tightly binding the man's mouth. He felt his pulse; it was strong and steady. Gerald patted the man between his cinched up shoulder blades. Unlike the inane decrees from the fanatical leaders of the Thousand Year Reich, he had no beef with homosexuals. Provided they didn't bother him, he was a live-and-let-live kind of guy. This one just happened to have the wrong set of dental records and lived all alone.

"I'll try to make it as painless as possible," he said to him.

In the kitchen, hanging from a nail, he located Robert's keys, pocketing them. He would need them later in the morning. A quick check back in the bedroom; Robert was still out cold. On the nightstand, Gerald found Robert's wallet, pocketing the cash and looking for anything else helpful. There was nothing.

He walked into the kitchen, staring at the room, sweeping his eyes over the rows of cabinets. He put on a percolator of coffee, brewing it strong, realizing he was finally fully sober. He rummaged through all of the cabinets, eventually finding a wad of bills in an oatmeal tube. He took the bills, replacing the tube. Gerald hurriedly went through every drawer and nook in the large house, taking all photographs and valuables, to include a moldy snub-nose revolver that he would be afraid to use, even in a pinch. He went to the bathroom, finding a tackle bag, filling it with the man's copious toiletries. He ransacked the man's closet, taking over half of the clothes and filling two of the largest suitcases. He loaded a few of the items in his own car, placing everything else into the trunk of Robert's car, a Mercury.

Gerald walked back inside, holding a fresh chloroform hankie over his unwilling host's nose for ten more seconds, counting aloud. He then hoisted the man, lugging him through the back door and depositing him in the trunk of the Ford. From the box he'd brought with him, Gerald retrieved an envelope and walked back into the kitchen. He sat, reading the contents of the specially prepared note, written by a team of experts back in Berlin. It was addressed to Robert Williams' mother. Last year, with great difficulty, Gerald had intercepted two different letters from Robert Williams to his mother, a low-level socialite in Manhattan. He steamed the envelopes open, photographed each letter, then replaced the original back into the old bat's mailbox on the following day. She never knew the difference. The boys back on Vosstrasse used the high-quality photos to study the particulars of Robert's handwriting and to pick up on his unique writing patterns. They crafted the letter to his mother as a long good-bye, for he was running off with his new "friend" to Argentina.

But don't worry, Mom, I'll keep up with my bills and likely visit in a few months. Make sure you save the rest of my clothes and, unless it's too much trouble, have someone water my plants.

Gerald walked through the mansion, opening the front door and dropping the letter into the mailbox. He raised the flag and walked around back, opening the trunk of his Ford to see the comatose man. Gerald pressed the mug to the man's lips and walked back inside. Careful to save the lip prints, he poured a cup of coffee inside before dumping out half. He placed the mug on the counter and the percolator in the sink. Running through his mental checklist he locked the front door and gave the house a once over. Satisfied, he carefully made Robert's bed and stepped out the rear door of the mansion, locking it and pulling it shut. Gerald cranked Robert's Mercury and drove away, studying the windows of the homes nearby. He saw nothing, no movement, no light. It was too early, and the houses too far apart for anyone to notice anything suspicious. After parking the car near the train station at Greenpoint, he jogged the four blocks back to Robert's tony mansion, cranking his own Ford and puttering away, with Robert in the trunk.

It was nearly 4 a.m. when Gerald crossed the Kosciuszko Bridge. He slowed, tossing the moldy revolver, wristwatch, and two pieces of jewelry between the trusses and over the edge. Gerald nestled himself into the seat, beginning to feel more comfortable that this plan might actually work—if he could go through with it. Twenty minutes later he coasted down his street, lights off. He pulled into his driveway, exiting the car. After a careful inspection of the street and exterior of his home, Gerald carried Robert Williams inside. When he entered the bedroom, he heard the muffled screams, watching as his wife struggled against her padded bonds. Gerald noted with great satisfaction that the padded bindings had prevented any noticeable abrasions on her arms and legs. It was bad enough what he had to do; he didn't want it to be painful.

More important—much more important—would be the coroner's impression of the bodies. While they should be charred beyond recognition, he didn't want some whippersnapper finding abrasions.

The movement had roused Robert Williams who, also, began to thrash about and attempt to scream. Gerald placed him on the bed, on the side where he typically slept, still hog-tied. He went to the kitchen, filling a glass of water and dumping half of it down the sink. He walked back to the bedroom, placing the water on the bedside table. For good measure, he took the novel from beside the bed, opening it and placing it face-down on the sheet between the loving couple.

Gerald walked around the bed, joining eyes with Carol Lynn. Her nostrils flared like an angered bull's. With her best effort yet, she contracted at the abdomen and bellowed loudly, even through the towel. He turned away, unable to look at her.

The plan from here was straight forward. He was to use the chloroform one last time, but only enough to render the couple unconscious. If they were dead before the fire, the medical examiner would fail to find smoke in their lungs, thereby turning a couple of accidental deaths into a murder investigation. If he did things correctly, he'd render them unconscious before removing their restraints. Then he would quickly start a fire in the bathroom by adding a cigarette to the waste basket. To aid in ignition, he would strategically place the wax-coated shower curtain just above it, lighting the bottom with his lighter. By his estimation, the resulting house fire would take ten minutes to produce enough smoke to kill his victims. Beyond that, he needed the fire to be strong enough to char Robert Williams' body. And that's why the plan called for an early hour to ignite the house—because it was unlikely that any of the neighbors would report the blaze until it was far too late.

Gerald's vision was blurry as he smoked a cigarette down. After a few minutes, he dropped the partially-smoked cigarette into the waste basket before he fell to his knees, vomiting into the toilet. Finished, Gerald lay on the cool tile floor for ten minutes, thinking of all the things his wife had done for him during their time together. All the meals. The back-rubs. The notes in his lunch. She'd been so very kind, caring for him, loving him in the exact manner that had been devoid from his life before her. And although he wasn't *in* love with Carol Lynn, he felt he might actually have love *for* her. Such emotions were foreign to him.

Gerald rolled to his back, his breath coming in heaves.

"I'm a soldier," he whispered to the night air. "Soldiers kill other soldiers. Soldiers don't kill innocents."

He recalled snippets of lessons he'd been taught at the academy. "The only thing paramount to survival is your identity. You shall *never* allow it to be compromised," one of the instructors had said, crooking his finger at the room and then booming, "Ever!" for punctuation.

Gerald pulled himself up to the mirror, viewing his bloodshot eyes in the low light. A seed of an idea began to bloom in his hung-over mind. *How can*

I do this without compromising my identity? Is my identity just my name? He shook his head. *No, it's far more than a name. Anyone can come up with a new name.*

My identity is the man I'm looking at right now.

Gerald nodded to himself, a hint of a smile showing on his face. He checked the wastebasket, making sure the cigarette hadn't ignited the tissues. It had not, so he dropped it in the toilet. He walked back into the bedroom, eyes down before he finally looked at Carol Lynn. Her eyes were accusatory.

After licking his lips and struggling to moisten his mouth, Gerald said, "I realize I've put a stain on your life, Carol Lynn, and for that I do apologize. In doing my given job, it's sometimes necessary that innocent people such as you or Mister Williams here become entangled in my mess." He stepped around the bed, taking a sip of the water due to his struggle to speak. "So here's the bottom line: if compromised, my plan all along was to eliminate you *both* by fire. Using the chloroform I've been using, it would make you both fall unconscious, but your actual death would come from smoke inhalation."

Neither Carol Lynn nor Robert Williams made a sound. Both, however, appeared thunderstruck by Gerald's admission.

"I spent a great deal of time finding Mister Williams when we first moved here. We're the same size. His dental records match mine, and his…*proclivities* assured me that the authorities would accept his disappearance at the time I perished in a fire, along with my loving wife."

Carol Lynn yelled through her gag, bucking her body in the process.

"Of course you're angry, and with good reason." He showed his palms. "But I've made the decision *not* to start a fire. I've made the decision to allow you both to live. It was my stupid fault for allowing myself to get drunk tonight, a decision I will probably always regret. But as I went through my preparations tonight, it troubled me greatly to ponder why such recklessness should earn the two of you a death sentence."

Robert's eyes were closed as he exhaled loudly, seeming to relax with the news. Carol Lynn still stared at Gerald with great intensity, but in her eyes was something else—it was the look a wife gives her husband when she's disappointed with him.

And, indeed, Gerald was ashamed.

He wanted to leave her with as much confidence as he could, leaning down and pushing her hair back as he lied to her. "Nothing *ever* happened between me and any other woman, Carol Lynn. Tonight was simply a staggering, drunken episode. There were never other women. Not tonight, or at any time during our relationship. Had the situation been different, had I been American and our marriage genuine, I would have been happy until old age claimed me." He kissed her forehead. "You'll find someone else, and he'll make you very happy." Gerald straightened and stepped to the end of the bed.

"I must go now. While I realize your bonds aren't comfortable, you'll only be there for about seven more hours. Carol Lynn's mother typically comes during lunch, to have sandwiches and listen to their show. She'll release you both."

Having nothing else to say, Gerald—*Gerhard*—turned and walked away. He felt like a rogue. But he also felt awash in relief.

It was minutes before 5 a.m. when he departed, his head throbbing. He checked the Ford for anything he might have left behind. There was nothing. Staying in the dark shadows of the street, Gerald walked to the intersection up at Utopia Parkway and turned around, taking one last look at his home. There was still ample time to go back and set the house aflame.

"No," he said to the night.

A glance at his watch. The first train at Auburndale would be coming through at 5:20. He walked a quarter of a mile to the stop, keeping his head down lest someone might recognize him.

Gerald's limp was gone.

Only two people boarded with him at Auburndale: a half-asleep construction worker and an intense businessman with a heart attack in his future. Gerald didn't know either of them, and neither person took any note of him.

He took the train to the Greenpoint station and drove away into the morning light, settling into Robert Williams' Mercury as he pondered the reception he would soon receive.

IT WAS nearly 9 a.m. when Gerald slowed in front of the elegant Bryn Mawr, Pennsylvania home. He eased into the shaded driveway, under the stone archway, turning right behind the home and pulling the Mercury into one of the stalls of the garage. Gerald exited the Mercury, pulling the levered garage door shut. He lit a cigarette, seeing the shadow of a face behind one of the home's windows. The rear door of the mansion opened. A stern-faced man, well past the mid-point of his life, stepped onto the back porch.

Gerald eyed him.

The man took a deep breath and nodded once. He motioned irritably, saying, "Well, for God's sake, come inside."

Gerald dreaded giving the news, crossing the pleasant yard the way he might trudge through setting concrete. Inside the large home, another man was summoned. He strode down the curved staircase, eyeing Gerald with a degree of shock. The first man led them into a well-appointed living room. Gerald had never been here, but he had met the older man before. He had immigrated to America as a teen and went by the name of Reginald Ivester, an attorney. Back in Berlin, on his infrequent (and well-concealed) trips, Ivester was known in the Reich's intelligence arm, the *Abwehr*, by his Christian name: Wilhelm Bonitz. Bonitz motioned Gerald to sit.

A butler appeared, offering Gerald coffee, speaking native German, the northern accent not unlike his own. Gerald accepted the coffee, taking several large sips. Bonitz and the other man were silent, adjusting themselves in their seats and clearing their throats until the servant had taken his leave.

"Exactly why are you here?" Bonitz hissed, trepidation in his voice.

Gerald took a great breath. "Gentlemen," he said in German, "I am afraid my operation is over. My wife discovered my intentions."

Bonitz leaned forward, covering his face with both hands.

"What happened?" demanded the other one, a man Gerald had never before laid eyes on. He was tall and thin and boyishly handsome in his immaculately-cut American suit, throwing off an arrogant, country-club smugness.

Gerald arched his brows and studied his own fingernails. "What does it matter? What's done is done."

"It matters, buddy boy," the man answered in crisp, northeastern English. "And you *will* answer for it."

Gerald viewed him with unveiled contempt. "Who are you?"

"Marcus."

"Marcus what?"

"*Just* Marcus."

"What's your job, *Just* Marcus?"

"It's well above your pay-grade, I can assure you of that," Marcus snapped.

"Well, *Just* Marcus, do you have any clue what it's like to be out, for years, as someone you're not? Never able to get a good night's sleep. Unable to make true friends. Every time you hear a siren, you think it may be for you. Every shadowy man who glances sideways is counter-intel about to snuff you out." Gerald jerked his pants leg up. "I had to go under the knife of those butchers at Unterreisen. My leg aches every day. While there, they snipped my balls, leaving me no ability to father a child." Gerald shook his leg, allowing the pants to reseat themselves. "So don't sit there and judge me, *Just* Marcus, while all you do is wear forty dollar suits and listen to radio reports in the safety of a comfy office."

"That's enough," Bonitz interrupted. "We're going to have at least a week together, maybe longer. There will be plenty of time for debriefings, accusations, and petty arguments." He pointed to Gerald. "And you, young man…you'd better start thinking of how you're going to explain this to Berlin." He sipped his coffee. "Because I'm sure as hell not going to be the one to do it." Bonitz paused, cocking his head. "I trust you're here free and clean?"

Gerald turned away.

"You used one of your escape plans," Bonitz said with growing concern. "*Surely* you faked your death."

Gerald didn't respond.

"Didn't you?"

After a steadying breath, Gerald looked up. "No, I didn't."

"My God!" Marcus yelled as a stunned grin coming over his face. It almost seemed he was reveling in Gerald's decision. Bonitz sat in stunned silence.

Gerald's hangover pounded his head as he said, "I made my decision, and cannot go back at this point."

Bonitz cleared his throat and said, "But your wife...she knows your secret."

"Yes."

"And you left her unharmed?" Bonitz whispered.

"That's right," Gerald replied, setting his jaw. "She didn't deserve to die, and since my operation there is now over, her knowing what I look like won't matter."

"Her knowing?" Marcus asked derisively. "It won't be *only* her who knows, buddy boy. Since you left her alive she'll tell the whole bloody country. There will be a manhunt like the United States hasn't seen since the Lindbergh kidnapping." Again he laughed—it was a shrill, grating sound. "How on earth could we train a man that could be so utterly stupid to think—"

Gerald was out of his chair and behind Marcus before he could react. He'd snapped his hand knife out, pressing the tip of the razor-sharp blade into the side of his long, thin neck. A trickle of blood appeared beneath the blade, flowing down and soaking into the starchy-white collar of Marcus' handmade shirt. As Bonitz yelled at Gerald to stop, Gerald put his mouth to the terrified man's ear.

"My wife is innocent, asshole. You're not. It will not bother me to kill you, not a bit."

"Please," Marcus rasped.

"You—have—no—idea," Gerald growled, drawing out the words. "No idea what I've been through."

"You're right. And I have no right questioning you." Marcus began to whimper, tears streaming down his cheeks.

After eyeing Bonitz, who shook his head pleadingly, Gerald pulled the blade off of Marcus' neck, removing his handkerchief and tossing it at him. Marcus scrabbled backward, standing behind Bonitz, looking every bit the part of a sheltered man who'd just gotten his first taste of violence.

Deflating like a balloon with a quick leak, Gerald stepped away and paced the fine carpet of the far side of the room. He stopped at the large, white-paned window, staring out at the manicured front lawn, watching as a nice looking young mother pushed a stroller down the sidewalk, blissfully unaware at the tension inside the mansion—tension between a trio of German spies. He turned.

"Will they recall me?"

Bonitz nodded. "Almost certainly."

"Are you going to contact Berlin?"

"Tonight."

"Fine," Gerald said. "Tell them to contact Lieutenant Colonel Heydte at the academy. Tell them to inform him that I'm enacting *Operation Wolf*. He'll know what that means."

Bonitz appeared nervous as he weakly objected. "But you're not at free-will to do as you please. Furthermore, while here you fall under my supervision. They'll blame me."

"I'm not staying here," Gerald replied.

"I'm afraid you don't understand," Bonitz said. "I'm in charge of *all* intelligence assets in the United States, not just this region."

"I'm not staying in the United States," Gerald clarified.

Marcus, holding the handkerchief on his neck, asked, "Where will you go?"

"I'm going back to Europe. Just tell Heydte about Operation Wolf—it was my thesis...my idea. He knows the rest of the plan."

Exhausted, Gerald made his way up the stairs, finding a couch in a sitting room. After locking the door and affixing a chair behind the knob, he slept on the couch, his knife in hand.

FOUR

TURBULENCE.

The rickety Army Air Corps C-40 felt as if it were on the verge of a midair break-up. The rain sounded like someone was battering the skin of the struggling aircraft with buckets of gravel. During the occasional lightning strikes, Roland glimpsed the wing, watching it bend unnaturally as the extreme forces of atmospheric nature were applied to the aircraft, making him wonder if the designers had any possible way to simulate such extremes on the airframe.

Probably not.

He leaned his head back, allowing his leather football-style helmet to chatter against the rib in the center of the fuselage. Roland closed his eyes, trying to picture his childhood home, set back into the woods. He recalled the serenity of the trickling creek which he had dammed so many times, audible all the way up at the house after a rain storm. The large ash trees had been there on his last visit, many of them still holding rotting boards that had once been his tree-houses. On the back side of the property was the dilapidated old barn, where he would do his chores and hold secret meetings of the club he and his pals had formed—until each of his friends' mothers would scream their name in a shrill voice. It had all been so recent.

So how, in such a short span of time, had the world gone mad and placed him fifteen hundred feet above terra firma, somewhere over the land of his ancestors?

Roland thought back to his U.S. Army enlistment in '38 and how, after being sent to officer candidate school late that year, he endured the newly-named Ranger training under British commandos in Ireland. How he finished with incredibly high marks and, just as he had hoped, a solicitous man in a crappy blue suit had come to see him.

The SGS.

The man's name was Matthew Silver, Colonel. After poring through Roland's military records and his background, he championed Roland all the way to the end, when Roland proved his mettle against the big Californian who was now pushing pencils somewhere in Scotland.

And after all that, here he was being dropped inside the borders of Nazi Germany, into the state of Hessen, near the industrial city of Giessen. He'd gone over everything hundreds of times, perhaps thousands. Once he integrated with the Germany citizenry, his first mission was quite simple by SGS standards. There was a Luftwaffe base near Giessen. Every time an Allied sortie passed nearby, the allegedly Giessen-based ME-109's would hunt down the Allied bombers like a pack of starving wolves. But the pilots and bombardiers in the second wave could never find the damned base from where the Germans had originated. It had gotten so bad that the brass estimated the fighters (that had to originate somewhere near Giessen—calculated by their range) were causing over half of the casualties on bombing flights terminating anywhere near central Germany.

Roland was tasked with locating the cloaked airbase and determining how in the hell the clever krauts were masking it. The common thinking was a grass-strip, but Roland had argued against it. Sure, intel said the 109's could work from grass, but a squadron requires support, fuel, maintenance. As many times as Giessen had been flown over, someone would have seen something.

Think about the Luftwaffe later. Focus on the jump.

The jump master, a cigar-smoking Irish bulldog of a man, stood from his crouch just behind the pilots. In the reddish night light of the C-40, he turned and, holding the taut jump cable, took a few steps toward the aft web bench where Roland sat. Roland could see him shaking his head and simultaneously making a slashing motion across his throat.

"What?" Roland screamed.

The jump master unsteadily made his way to the rear, dropping onto the bench and clapping Roland's leg. "They're bagging it!" he yelled. "This pea soup's so thick we lost our escorts."

Roland felt his heart thudding in his chest. "Have the escorts already turned back?"

"Negative. They gotta make the rally point before they make their turn. S.O.P. on a night like this. Those Brits could be a foot off'a our wingtip for all we know. We go making a turn right now, we might all just become lawn darts in that rich German soil."

Roland banged his helmet backward against the skin of the aircraft, his eyes closed, his teeth gritting. Sitting on his ass in England for over a year…one can only train so much! Each morning he would arrive, bright-eyed and hopeful that his orders had come down—and each morning it was the same. A shake of the head. Maybe the wag of a finger. Go away, Buhl, we'll tell you when we're ready. And then, as if by magic, a week ago he received the green light, unable to keep himself from dancing a jig in front of his superiors.

Here I am now, he thought, *over Germany—over my destiny.*

Roland would be damned if he was going to give up this chance—all because of some rain—to be forced back to playing solitaire in the barracks. As if spring loaded, his eyes flew open and he grasped the jump master's leg strap.

"Tell 'em I'm going anyway," Roland yelled.

The jump master shook his head, shouting over the din. "No way, hoss! Word's come down from on high. This weather's for shit. You could get blown into a house, a castle, a lake. You could wind up landing in a damned military compound!"

Roland stood, grasping the jump cable. He put his face inches from the jump master's, still having to yell over the rush of the wind and the roar from the engines. "Do me a favor. When we're close to the rally point, just nod at me."

It took the jump master a second, but Roland saw the recognition. The man shook his head. "I can't do that, hoss!"

Roland's blue eyes stayed locked on the jump master's. He didn't know him from Adam, having only met him thirty minutes before they left.

But Roland liked him.

He walked his hand down the jump master's arm, grabbing the gloved hand, and gripping it, pulling it up into a handshake. He leaned even closer.

"Just nod, my friend. I'll never tell a soul. Tonight's my night to get down there. I've trained too long, staring at four walls for far too many days. We go back to England, they might change their minds. I may never see this chance again."

The jump master held his gaze for a full half minute. The pitch of the engines changed slightly. In the reddish light, Roland saw the man wink as his mouth displayed the hint of a smile. He turned, sliding his gloved hand on the freshly greased jump cable as he made his way back to the front.

Roland cinched his leg straps tight, feeling the heavy pack between his legs, making them bow out unnaturally like legs on a clichéd old cowboy. He lifted the heavy static line, pulling the safety lever down on the hook, sliding it over the taut, index-finger-thick wire. It had been nearly six months since he'd last jumped, and that was in Northern England, on a cold December day. After murmuring a prayer to the God he rarely spoke to, Roland turned to look at the jump master.

The man was listening to the pilots. Suddenly he straightened, turning his head and nodding rapidly just as the aircraft began a steep bank.

Feeling the familiar hyperventilation he'd experienced each time he'd flung himself to certain death, Roland waddled to the door, taking one final look to the men tasked with delivering him to the drop point. The jump master played the role perfectly, yelling "No!" before he hammered the pilot on his shoulder telling him to slow down. The co-pilot realized Roland was about to jump. He scrambled frantically, trying to get out of his seat, screaming with a raised hand for Roland to halt. Lightning flashed outside of the open door, illuminating the thunderheads surrounding the aircraft like cottony Alps. Roland caught sight of one of the British Spitfires, five hundred feet away and slightly below their level. The Spitfire was well out of the way for Roland to make his jump.

The pilot ceased the banking turn. The jump master and the co-pilot were shuffling his way, and after a quick salute, Roland placed both hands on his reserve. He held his breath and pivoted out the door, yelling, "One-one thousand! Two-one-thousand…"

Gravity and the blast of wet wind did the rest.

When jumping out of a fast-moving aircraft, a person doesn't experience the same sort of falling sensation he or she might if jumping from a stationary object. The inertia of the aircraft, as well as the mass of the jumper, is moving forward, traveling more than a hundred miles per hour. In this particular case, while the airplane had indeed slowed, it was still traveling well in excess of 170 miles per hour.

At its extreme, the 28-foot T-4 parachute was designed for a 140 mile per hour opening.

As Roland was whipped from the aircraft, his body riding the stream of air, his static line pulled the diaper-packed round parachute from the container on his back. Doing exactly as it had been designed to do, the silken parachute freed itself from the bonds of the rubber bands that held it shut, billowing open and slowing Roland's body to a tenth of its original speed in a matter of face-tugging, G-force laden seconds.

In the dark, rainy night, when the roar of the aircraft and the rushing of the air disappeared, all Roland was left with was the whipping sound of the chute above his head and his occasional grunts as he tried to reseat himself in the straps, cutting in dangerously close to his precious male features. A distant flash of lightning gave Roland a brief glimpse of the ground, perhaps five hundred feet below him. He was now below the clouds, descending like the rain.

Just as he had been taught, Roland reached between his legs, finding the claw-clamp and pinching it, lowering his heavy pack to a point twenty feet below him. It was then he heard the ripping sound. Roland gripped both risers, craning his head upward, barely able to see the lighter colored area that represented the silken air-anchor flying above his head.

He heard another rip.

Roland tilted his hands in, wiping the dampness from his eyes as he stared at the disk above his head. It was marked in the five o'clock position by a black triangle, the same color as the menacing sky. He pivoted his head downward, scanning the area where the ground should be. A light burned in the distance, probably from a house. It was rising with great speed.

Roland was descending fast. Far too fast. He whipped his head back up. The dark triangle shouldn't be there. His over-speed departure had blown a hole in his parachute!

Acting on instinct from training, Roland yanked the steel handle under his right hand, unleashing the reserve parachute from his belly pack. The silken mass fell from his stomach, the lines snaking outward. He stared downward, watching as the second parachute began to catch air, filling.

Come on. Fill up! Fill up!

This was new territory for Roland. Like anyone who attended Airborne School, the various types of malfunctions were burned into his brain. Most malfunctions, however, are solved by only two simple ingredients. The first, of course, was ample altitude. A reserve isn't of any value if it doesn't have time to inflate. The second, strangely enough, was the actual usage of the reserve. Roland remembered the instructors telling the tragic tales of students under malfunctioning canopies, with ample time to deploy their reserves, clinging to their risers on their deathly plunge to the ground, too scared to act. Frozen by fear.

Roland, however, had acted as quickly as even the most seasoned jumpers would have. Some might ask, if hesitation is a key reason why so many parachutists die, why shouldn't every jumper *always* deploy his reserve? The reason involves a matter of odds. When a parachutist has two parachutes inflated at once, there is always a chance of entanglement—a sure ride on the fast elevator to death. But in Roland's case, two parachutes, one good and one torn, was a risk well worth taking.

He performed exactly as he should have—his problem, even though he didn't know it on this stygian night, was his lack of altitude. Just as the reserve parachute began to float upward, Roland watched it land on the top of a copse of trees, simultaneously hearing his pack crashing through the branches. Less than a second later, he was next, instinctively preparing himself for a parachute landing fall, a type of controlled crash landing designed to help various parts of the body absorb the coming impact of the ground.

The tree limbs sliced like razors, but were nothing compared to the ground, which he hit at over thirty-five feet per second. His falling speed was somewhere between twenty-five and thirty miles per hour, equivalent to riding a bicycle into a brick wall at downhill speed.

Roland smashed into the ground, the impact with the trees turning his controlled fall into something more closely resembling a sack of concrete thrown from a third floor. The blackness of the sky mingled with the spots in his vision, melding with the horrific pain to create an intense amalgamation of senses he hoped to never again experience. Aware that he had yet to take a breath since he hit the ground, Roland rolled from his side, realizing there was a sharp stick imbedded in his chest. He managed to roll to his back, not sure of what injured part of his body hurt the most. Starting with the good news, his head felt fine. The leather helmet he wore slid right off. He pulled at his curly brown hair, pressing the falling water back as he lay supine, trying to gather his thoughts.

After several minutes of learning to breathe while impaled, Roland pressed his chin to his chest, examining the stick emanating from his chest cavity like his body's own personal banyan tree. It even had leaves still attached to it. The problem, his mind was barely clear enough to recognize, was removing the stick. It was in the right side of his chest, away from his heart. More good news. But, if the stick had penetrated his lung, Roland knew by removing it he could create one of the most dreaded battlefield injuries: a sucking chest wound. He touched the stick, grasping it, wiggling it back and forth. Pain. Intense pain. He cursed.

Another pain, however, seemed to be rapidly overtaking his chest pain. He lifted his head, staring through the scant, rain-diffused light at his lower body. Like any normal man, when he was lying on his back, his right boot pointed upward, canted off to the right. This, like the stick not penetrating his heart, was good. His left boot, however, was twisted backward, causing his pants leg to spiral like the red stripes on a candy cane.

This was not good.

He lifted his leg from the knee, watching as the lower leg pivoted downward, just above the boot, as if his body had magically developed a new knee joint in the middle of his shin. This, however, was far from magic, evidenced by Roland's piercing shriek.

After the brief stun following his fall, all pain receptors seemed to again be fully functioning, and each one of them sent messages to Roland's brain, with an urgent request why theirs was worse than the one before. Like any person who has just been in a serious accident, Roland's brain attempted to process the incoming pain requests until the situation became too dire.

And that's when shock set in.

Having been well-trained in battlefield injuries, Roland knew if he stayed where he was, he would be dead in a matter of hours, if not sooner. He sat up, wincing from the pain in his chest, tugging his pack to him. Once he hoisted the pack beside him, he surveyed his area, looking for something to splint his leg with. Using his fingers for propulsion, Roland dug into the hard mud of the earth, dragging himself around the copse of trees, his leg flipping and flopping like a tennis ball in a sock. With two of the straightest sticks he could find, he created a crude splint, using all of the quarter-inch rope from his bag, wrapped tightly around his leg dozens of times. Oddly enough, when Roland turned the leg to straighten it, the pain had subsided a great deal.

After hastily covering his pack and his two parachutes under a pile of leaves, he began to scoot on his butt—it allowed his lower leg and foot to remain in place—picking a direction in the murky night and sticking with it. Eventually he cleared the stand of trees, coming into what seemed to be a farming field. Roland could tell from the gurgling sound when he coughed that his right lung was beginning to take on blood. The rain ceased. The black night began to display traces of violet, displaying for Roland the eastern sky. Ten minutes later, when Roland was halfway through the field of fragrant yellowish flowers, the light increased enough to display a small wooden home perched on a hill several hundred yards away.

He remembered from studying the region that the crop he was in the midst of was called rapse—used to create oil for all manner of purposes. He continued to drag himself in the direction of the home, correctly guessing that it must be nearing five in the morning. At this time of the year, so far north in the hemisphere, the sun would be fully up by half past five. Assuming they were at home, the farmers were probably already awake, having their coffee and *bröt* and preparing to perform a long day's work.

Roland's clothes were German. Civilian German, made that way in the event of situations like the one he was in. He wore a light sweater with a tan button-down underneath, both now in tatters. His baggy pants were known as motorcycle pants, with multiple cargo pockets. The German joke about motorcycle pants was that they were only necessary when riding British motorcycles, to carry tools for all of the repairs.

At first he considered watching the house to get a feel for the occupants. But that was no good. Roland knew as soon as he stopped moving that things would go from bad to worse. The skin would get cold and clammy. His thirst—which was already bad—would become overwhelming. Hypothermia, even with the warm weather, would set in. And of course, his mental state would degrade and he'd be of no further use to himself. He would have to chance the encounter and rely on his training, and most of all his ability to speak German, to get him through this situation.

In the growing light, just as he was nearing the small porch, the door creaked open and a man of about sixty stood there, staring at him with an open mouth. He must have seen him coming. Or heard the moans and grunts. Roland's head fell back against the hard wet earth, his chest heaving, the upright stick rising and falling from his chest like an obscene joke gone wrong.

This was it. His first encounter in disguise. Certainly not the way anyone had planned. Roland had a decision to make. His life depended on it. He could come clean and, while in trouble, probably get medical attention in a matter of minutes. Or he could stay in character, and try to get through this. He squeezed his eyes shut, deciding.

Deciding.

The latter won out. In German, Roland muttered the phrase, "Helfen Sie mir," over and over.

RECKLESS IS what he had been. He knew it. He should never have jumped. A fool's errand. But through his pain, aided by the woman's schnapps, Roland managed to craft an account about a motorcycle wreck. He'd been enjoying the last few days of liberty, staying too long in Frankfurt, and speeding through the rainy night, trying like hell to get back to Bonn, to his unit before they deployed for France. It was hard to remember exactly how it happened, but he saw a small animal, swerved, and before he knew it he was catapulted into the woods doing well in excess of a hundred kilometers per hour. All things considered, it was a beautiful tale.

"Where were you when you wrecked?" the husband and wife asked simultaneously, both wide eyed and appearing to believe everything Roland told them.

Roland opened his hands as if he didn't know, finally gesturing to the direction he had laboriously scooted from. "I don't really know." Grunt. Wince. "It was a road, out that way somewhere. It was so dark…"

They were inside the home, with Roland on the floor, in front of the dormant fireplace. Rain had dripped into the damper, combining with the ashes to create a smoky-smelling stench. The husband and wife lived alone, their hearts deployed with their two sons, both in their thirties, both serving the Reich in North Africa. The house itself was cozy and simple. It was somewhat dark, made darker by the deep stain on the wood and the woman's penchant for burgundy accents. At some point, because through his pain Roland could hardly remember, the man mentioned something about their location being near Klein Linden, *Small Linden Tree*, wherever the hell that was. Maybe the small Linden was the one in his chest, Roland thought ruefully. After they'd gotten him situated they'd given him the bottle of schnapps, which he'd taken a third of already. Roland stared down at his poorly splinted leg. He could feel the burning moving upward, in his thigh. Not a good sign.

"We need to call the constable," the man said, still kneeling by Roland. "He can declare an emergency, especially since you're military, and have the krankenhaus send the ambulance from Giessen."

"Wait," Roland said, gently holding the man's wrist with his mud-caked hand. "If we do that, I'll be in trouble with my unit. Big trouble. They'll send an investigator and will find I was outside our liberty zone." Roland looked to the house frau, sober enough to put on his sad eyes. "I was seeing my lady. I love her so. Please don't call, not yet. I have a medic friend from my unit. Perhaps I can convince him to come and get me."

The woman of the house, clutching a rosary to her lips, tilted her head at the story. Her husband turned to look at her, and with grim eyes turned back to Roland and nodded.

"Thank you," Roland said. "So you do have a phone?"

"Yes, we do," the man answered with a measure of pride. "For almost five years now."

"Wonderful," Roland murmured. "You're a successful family." He had no choice but to call his contact. It was supposed to be the last resort, but in this situation, he didn't know what else to do. On his mind, far behind the concern for his own injuries, was what his chain of command would do with him now, assuming he ever made it out of here alive. He'd rather face the music for his irresponsible actions, however, than risk being found by the Germans. Roland didn't think, after they extracted what they wanted from his mind, the Germans would have much use for a cripple with nothing else to give.

"Well, shouldn't you go ahead and call him?" the man asked. His tone was helpful, but there seemed to be a sort of guardedness to him. It made Roland worry.

"Will the phone reach?" Roland asked.

"No," the man answered, firmly shaking his head. "Give me the number and I'll call for you."

Roland felt his heart rate spike. He faked a bout of pain, grimacing as he rested his head on the floor and squeezed his eyes tightly shut for a moment. "What time is it?" he grunted.

"About six."

"We'll have to call around eight. They'll be out right now, doing calisthenics. If the watch commander hears me..." Roland covered his face with one hand, not having to work hard to feign disgust with his predicament.

"Could you eat?" the woman asked politely, as if she couldn't think of anything else to offer a guest with a stick in his chest and a shattered leg.

"No, thank you. I'll just nurse this bottle until we're able to call my friend."

Roland caught the man studying him. There was something in his eyes, the smallest of flickers as he stood up, towering over Roland. "Get you anything else?" he asked.

"No, thank you."

The man turned, and without looking at his wife, walked out the door. Through the wooden walls of the farmhouse, Roland could hear his feet scraping across the rain-soaked drive. He looked to the woman.

"Where's he going?"

She placed her rosary back in her apron and walked around Roland, peering out the window. "He's walking out through the field. I can see where you dragged yourself through the rapse. I guess he's going to check on your motorcycle."

Roland had been trying to sit up, but upon hearing this news, the news he feared, he lowered his head to the floor again, his filthy nails clawing at the floor. *No. No. No!* The field was wet, the flowers matted down. He'd walk right to the parachute—a blind man could follow that trail. There was a thumping as Roland repeatedly banged his head backward.

"Mein Herr," the woman whispered, pulling the rosary out again, no doubt concerned by his actions. "Are you well?"

He allowed a long silence to ensue as he thought through the machinations that would likely occur. "Frau?" he asked gently.

"Yes?"

"What is your last name?"

"Bradenhauer."

"Frau Bradenhauer." Roland forced a smile. "How far is the nearest telephone, other than your own?"

She knitted her brow. "In town I guess."

"And how far is that?"

"Four kilometers."

"Do you have a barn?"

She stepped closer, looking down at him. "Yes, a small one…a shed really…on the other side of the house. You wouldn't have seen it from the direction you came."

"And does Herr Bradenhauer have a gun in the barn? Any kind of weapon?"

Frau Bradenhauer narrowed her eyes, tilting her head. "Why do you ask?"

Roland faked a chuckle. "Oh, he just seemed a bit leery of me and I wanted to make sure I wasn't about to get shot. My father was a farmer, you know. Loved his rifle but was suspicious of others."

She laughed, nervously. "My boys are cautious like you are, especially of those of us born before the new century."

He smiled indulgently, allowing it to fade. "So does he?"

"Does he what?"

"Have a gun in the barn?"

She was silent for a moment, her smile fading to caution. "Yes, he does. Ordered it from a catalog. Keeps it for the rats and rabbits."

Roland nodded, grinding his teeth, faking a smile. *Stupid, nosy old bastard! Why couldn't you just have stayed here and been a good little German?*

His right hand slid into the cargo pocket of his pants, from which he retrieved a compact Sauer 38 pistol, keeping it under his leg. Without looking he fingered the piece, adjusting it into the proper position in his right hand. He'd probably fired it a thousand times in England, as familiar with its action as a member of his own body.

He took several bolstering breaths before he elevated his hand, aiming the pistol at her chest. Frau Bradenhauer's eyes went wide as she stared at the compact weapon of death.

Roland inclined his head, holding his left hand behind his neck for support. "I'm so sorry, Frau Bradenhauer. I can tell you and your husband are good people, but he's out there nosing around, and he's going to learn my secret. And no matter what, Frau Bradenhauer, I can't allow my secret to get out, even at the expense of kind people like you."

All that escaped her mouth was a whispered "*nein*".

"My presence on this earth could save thousands of lives...hundreds of thousands."

The woman lifted the rosary to her mouth as tears filled her eyes.

"I cannot believe I have to do this," Roland said with a croak. "I'll try to make it painless."

He fired the gun, the bullet impacting the woman in the dead center of her forehead. She was still for a moment, as if she were deciding whether or not to die. Then the rosary tumbled from her hand just before she crumpled to the floor, only feet from where Roland lay. He stared at her, his physical pain subsiding for a moment, replaced by the ache over what he'd had to do. Frau Bradenhauer's dead eyes were wide with shock. He reached over, lifting her jaw to close it, then he closed her eyes.

Roland banged his head into the floor, again and again.

GÜNTHER BRADENHAUER jogged back through the field, klaxons blaring in his head. The parachutes, the bag of implements—the wounded man had fed them nothing but lies! He was exactly what the good people of Germany had been warned about. Günther, a good German who would've made a fine soldier, had suspected it from the moment he saw the snake slithering through his rapse field. *They'll sneak into your house and kill your children*, the poster by the train depot read. Günther had seen the notice a hundred times, never stopping to imagine its realism. To him such notion as parachuting spies had always seemed like fantasy. He paused outside of the barn, his chest heaving as he recalled the most recent notice from the

Enlightenment & Propaganda Ministry. In the poster, done up like the advertisement for a moving picture, a dark haired, swarthy man was depicted ready to slice the throat of a tow-headed child. And in the background, sliding through the night sky, the spy was shown as an eerie shadow, floating to the ground under a parachute.

He swiveled his head to the house. *A spy, in there with my Susa!*

There was no time to go to town. The fastest way there was by truck, and since it was parked right outside of the house, the spy would hear him and would certainly bring harm to Susa. No, the best option was to go straight in. The spy was in bad shape. Günther could simply hold him under guard until the constable arrived—let him sort it out.

He retrieved his Rheinmetall side-by-side 12-gauge shotgun from the barn, breaking it and jerking out the rock salt shells he used to kill pests. From the worn leather bag, he fingered the shells until he found the buckshot he was looking for. Günther clicked the shotgun closed, turning to the house and licking his lips.

ROLAND HAD managed to drag himself to the other side of the living room. The bleeding from his leg had long since soaked through his leggings and pants, leaving a trail of black blood across the dark floor. It looked like an oil slick. Between the loss of blood and decreased oxygen to his brain, Roland knew if he didn't get help soon he would be joining Frau Bradenhauer in purgatory far above where he'd just descended from.

And God, how he hated what he had to do here. This wasn't his plan. He was supposed to slip into Germany like a cat burglar, leaving no one the wiser to his scent. Upon reflection, his decision to jump had been foolhardy—and he hoped, perhaps more than at any point in his life—to be made to answer for it. Because that would indicate survival, and at this moment he felt his odds were below half and decreasing by the minute.

And how would the brass react to what he'd done on terra firma? He would, of course, tell them he had no choice. It was either him or the Bradenhauers, wasn't it? No, not true…he could have just come clean right off the bat. Told the farmers everything. The brass certainly wouldn't view that as a viable option, but to a man who is mortally wounded, it was damned well worth considering. But, had he done that, he would now be in German hands. They'd have gotten him stable, shot him full of sodium pentothal and wrung him out like a sponge. Ten or twelve men, smoking, making notes, whispering to one another. It would go on for days until Roland repeated all his information three or four times, delirious from the drugs and lack of sleep. And that, in Roland's mind, would have been the end of it. They would attach electrified alligator clips to his nipples and balls, screaming for more. When a decision was made that he'd given them all he had, some swarthy SS would slit his throat, whispering invectives as Roland's life spilled out on the interrogation room floor.

Roland nodded to himself. *What's done is done. The die is cast. Now make the best of it.* He bit his lower lip, waiting.

There was a click outside, in the distance. *The barn door?*

He raised the Sauer 38, holding it as steadily as he could. He waited. Footfalls on the porch. Roland took a great breath and held it. The door squeaked as it opened, spilling lemon-colored morning light in the darkened room. Herr Bradenhauer stepped inside, his malicious intent scattering like a flock of birds as he straightened upon seeing his wife on the floor.

"I'm sorry," Roland said in German.

Herr Bradenhauer turned, his face drawn down as if pulled by numerous fishing weights. The shotgun he had been carrying at the ready was no longer in firing position. Tears welled in the man's eyes, making Roland's heart ache as he imagined what must be going through the man's mind. He might be recalling when he met his wife, perhaps at a dance, their courtship lasting a short time before he went to her father, hat in hand, to ask for her hand in marriage. Those first carefree days before children, when they would make love with the sun shining, taking time to learn the other's body as well as the needs of their own. Perhaps he was thinking of her gripping his hand like a vice, her legs glistening with water as the midwives delivered their firstborn. And the simple things, like the way she would kiss him on the cheek each night as she placed his pork and potatoes before him.

Roland saw all of these things dance across this man's aching eyes, and just as it had when he'd had to eliminate Frau Bradenhauer, his remorse burned in his stomach like a fiery coal.

"You saw my parachute." It wasn't a question.

The man's jaw trembled before finally closing. He swallowed. In a cracking voice he said, "You killed my wife."

"I certainly didn't want to." As the man was about to speak, Roland held up his left hand, cutting him off. "Does anyone else know I'm here?"

Herr Bradenhauer shook his head.

"Thank you for trying to help me, sir. But I wish you would have just stayed in the house. This could have been so much easier."

The same eyes that had displayed such heartache seconds before now blazed forth with a new emotion. A man who loved poker, Roland, for a split second, knew Herr Bradenhauer would have never been any good. The German's expression turned to a snarl before he acted, and despite the pistol aimed squarely at his chest, he managed to get the shotgun up with surprising speed.

Roland, his own reflexes dampened by his condition, squeezed off a round, striking the man in the chest just above his heart. At nearly the same time, the shotgun roared, a cone of white flashing from the barrel. The buckshot yanked Roland backward and to his side, almost knocking him off of the table that he was perched upon.

He watched as the farmer fell to his back and expired in the door's threshold in a matter of seconds. From his mouth came a sound like the last bit of water exiting a bathtub. The gun had fallen on top of him, and the old German's gnarled fingers scratched at it a few times before he became still.

Roland touched his own right arm, twisting his head down to look at it. The buckshot had caught the loose fabric from his shirt and sweater, spinning him, missing his upper arm by inches. Behind him, a grouping of white holes in the dark wooden wall stood out like brightly burning stars on a moonless night. Death had missed Roland by a whisker.

But death still might have its way if he didn't take quick action.

Roland lowered himself to the floor, his actions growing clumsy. He watched aghast as his lower leg again twisted in an impossible direction despite the makeshift splint. The burning sensation in his upper leg had now reached his groin. He screamed out as he clawed his way across the floor, coming to the small kitchen and frantically searching the walls for a telephone.

The phone was ten feet away, on the wall next to the rough hewn kitchen table. His contact, who wasn't to be called unless of an absolute emergency (if this wasn't it, Roland didn't know what was!) was allegedly stationed somewhere between Giessen and Frankfurt. Roland could easily die while waiting for him. He continued to agonizingly labor through the farmhouse, looking back to see the ghastly, sticky trail of blood his ruptured leg was leaving. He glanced down at his chest, which wasn't bleeding nearly as much, the green stick providing a decent seal. Each time he took anything more than a shallow breath, he could feel the stick poke the back side of his lung. Just hours before, Roland's body, the physique of a young and able man, had worked perfectly. He knew, even if he were to survive, it would certainly never work the same again.

Pulling himself up on one of the chairs, Roland grasped the earpiece and paused, his tongue hanging over his lower lip as he realized he'd never been so thirsty in his entire life. He touched the back of his hand, pinching up on his cool and clammy skin before letting go. Rather than snapping back into place, the skin stayed up. Roland knew this was due to his massive loss of blood. The body, requiring blood, begins to rob every organ of fluid, creating quick and deadly dehydration. Once this occurred, things would begin to deteriorate. Roland knew if he didn't get liquid soon—*and hold it down*—the chances of death would rise exponentially. On the center of the table was a powder blue vase, loaded with handpicked wildflowers. Roland used his free hand to jerk them out, turning the vase up and tasting the cool, grassy tasting water. He guzzled every bit, feeling lightheaded for a moment. Then he heard the voice. It was coming from the earpiece. He stuck it to his left ear, just realizing the ear, too, was somehow injured.

"Hallo?" he asked in German. He cleared his throat. "Sorry, I wasn't paying attention."

"Number?"

Roland paused, washing through the haze of his brain to recall the number he'd recited to himself a million times. "J-three-two-seven-eight." *Use any phone you like,* the voice in his head said. *They don't keep records of phone calls, except to certain numbers, and your contact is clean.*

Supposedly.

There were a series of clicks. Something that sounded like a bad ball bearing whirring, another click.

"Ja?"

"This is Michael," Roland rasped in German. "Michael Dingledey, from Cologne." The code.

"Sonofabitch! Why are you calling me?" the man seethed, his tone turning to near panic.

Roland took deep breaths, feeling nauseous. "Have I called the right number?" he finally rasped.

"Herr Dingledey, this is Fritz Hüttenberger. It's, ah, well…it's been a long time." The counter-code, albeit relayed in a stunned voice.

They continued to speak in high German. Roland gave him the abridged version of all that had happened.

"Mein Gott! Where is the farmhouse?"

Squeezing his eyes shut, Roland groaned loudly. He didn't even know the address and hadn't thought of it until this point. Gritting his teeth through the pain, his bleary eyes searched the room. He spotted a stack of papers next to the breadbox. "Wait." Dropping himself from the chair, Roland yelled out as he struggled across the floor, pulling open a drawer above him so he could use it to hoist himself up. In a hail of splinters, the brittle drawer gave way when he was halfway up, making him tumble and causing his shattered leg to break fully free of its moorings. Roland punched the floor, shrieking in pain.

Do this or die, the voice in his head blared.

Roland grasped the rectangle where the drawer had been. He pulled with all his might, struggling to a standing position on his right leg, the room spinning. He rifled through the papers, leaving bloody fingerprints on each one. Near the bottom, he found the address on a postcard. It was from one of their sons. Roland made his way back to the phone, reading it off.

"It'll take me at least an hour to get what we need and get there. Will anyone see your parachute and equipment?"

"No idea." Roland let out a long breath. "It's in the woods." He peered around the walkthrough, seeing the Bradenhauer man in the threshold. "How will you hide the people?"

"There won't be time. I'll probably just have to burn the house. They'll realize the people were shot, but by that time, we'll be long gone. Provided we get your parachute and equipment, the locals will be none the wiser as to who committed the crime."

"And me?"

"I'll need to see what kind of shape you're in. As soon as humanly possible, assuming you live, I want you out of here." Roland was surprised to hear him talking to someone else in the background. "I'll be there as soon as I can. Get the place locked down and try to control your bleeding." The line went dead.

It took Roland ten minutes to get back into the living room and to pull Herr Bradenhauer inside enough to get the door closed. *Please, oh please, let there be no visitors! Especially not some nosy old lady from church.* He lay against the old farmer, resting his head on him. After taking a deep breath, Roland decided that the bleeding in his lung didn't seem to be worsening. That was the good news. But his leg, because it was so mangled, continued to weep blood. That was the bad news. On his back, staring at the ceiling, feeling oddly detached from reality, Roland made a decision that he knew was going to be made anyway.

In his mind, it was his only avenue to life.

After dragging himself back to the pallet Frau Bradenhauer had made for him, he used his Boker knife to cut away the useless remains of the splint and the pants leg underneath. His leg was worse, far worse, than he had expected. The sharp impact with the ground had pile-driven his tibia and fibula up into his knee, and the weak points, just above his boot line, had given way and snapped, grinding together like two sticks mashed together at their tips. What was left looked like two splintered tree branches sticking from the gashed remains of what was once his functioning leg. From the upper edge of the gash, Roland watched as his heart burped out a teaspoon of blood with each pump, trickling from what must have been his tibial artery.

"My God," he breathed, his stomach convulsing. Deep breaths. Deep breaths. Huge gasps of air. The spinning subsided.

He reached backward, jerking a lamp from a table, turning his head as the glass from the bulb and diffuser shattered. Roland dismantled the wooden lamp with his bare hands, yanking out the cord from the inside. He laid the wooden stem to his side and grasped the electrical cord. After wrapping it twice around his leg, just above the wound, Roland used the stem of the lamp as a lever, inserting it into the cord and twisting. He shouted in pain as the tensioned cord seized around his leg like a boa constrictor. The trickle of blood ceased immediately.

The tourniquet was in place. He began to feel a tad better—although the benefit was probably just mental—now that he'd turned off the faucet.

Then it hit him. Now comes the fun part.

Knowing his lower leg was forever useless, Roland let out low bellows and grunts as he began to saw the sinewy flesh and tendon holding the battered leg to the rest of his body. He'd hoped the nerves would no longer be functioning—it turned out to be just the opposite. The injury seemed to amplify the sensitivity in the remaining scrap of leg, and with each cutting and sawing motion, deep waves of bowel-watering pain shot through Roland as he ground his teeth together, nearly shattering them under the pressure.

Numerous times he raised his head and shrieked.

Water poured from his head as if someone were holding a running hose in his hair.

A job he thought might take two minutes took fifteen, each more excruciating than the last. With a renewed vigor, Roland sawed through the final tendon, as thick as the lamp's cord, holding his free lower leg above him when he finished. He fell backward, the surprisingly heavy boot-encased leg resting on his stomach. Through his delirium, Roland was surprised over what the human body—his human body—was able to endure. A fierce wave of nausea passed through him, making him turn and vomit some, or perhaps all, of the flower water onto the floor. The room began to spin again before all became black.

HIS CONTACT arrived forty minutes later, driving the Mercedes behind the farmhouse. He exited, standing perfectly still, only his eyes moving, surveying. The man rotated, his feet a whisper on the still damp hard-pack, looking for anyone, listening for anything. There were no sounds other than the birds. He opened the rear door of the large car, spreading several old quilts over the back seat. Finished, with his hand in his pants pocket gripping his compact Walther, the man took short steps to the farmhouse door. He knocked. Knocked again. Nothing. The man turned the knob, pushed the door open.

The darkness of the room was the second sensation. The first was the smell of blood. Coppery. Acidic. Otherworldly. Rather than grip the Walther, he pulled his handkerchief from his other pocket, holding it over his nose and mouth. When the door was halfway open, the man felt the soft, leaden resistance that could only be a body. He slid through the opening, seeing an old man on the floor, his body twisted, a shotgun lying over him. Roland's contact allowed his gaze to slide across the room, drinking in the other two bodies. It was the most gruesome sight he had ever seen, and that included a year in the trenches during the Great War. He rushed across the small room, pressing his hand to Roland's neck, feeling the pulse, weak but steady. In his chest was a stick, rising and falling, and just below that, his severed leg, covered by his still-laced boot. Roland's splintered bone emerged from the leg, like the handle from a state fair corn dog.

Taking a packet from his pocket, the man dumped the brownish contents into Roland's mouth. The taste awakened him, causing his face to twist. The man held Roland's chin shut until he swallowed. He hurried into the kitchen, coming back with a glass of water. He lifted Roland's head and instructed him to drink. Roland drank the entire glass.

"How long since I called you?" Roland breathed.

"Over an hour." The man traced his hand over the boot. "You cut off your own leg?"

Roland nodded.

The man crossed himself before glancing around the farmhouse.

"You think I'll make it?"

"No idea, but judging by the damage, you'll probably be happier if you don't."

Roland lifted his head, looking down at his body. "And you're just going to burn the place?"

"Sort of. We decided that an explosion might hide the proof of what happened."

"We?"

The man patted Roland's upper arm. "There's more than one of us here, you know. Come on, now." He grasped both of Roland's arms, hoisting him up so he was able to stand on his right leg. His left leg tumbled to the floor. The opium seemed to be seeping into Roland's bloodstream, giving him a glassy look. Placing his shoulders under Roland's left arm, the man took most of his weight as they staggered out of the house. He lowered Roland to the back seat, telling him to rest, closing the door. He watched Roland through the window. He was unconscious within seconds, the opium and shock taking him to a place of twisted bliss.

From the boot of the Mercedes, the man lifted a lumpy sheet, bound at the top, containing ten kilos of TNT and hand-rolled dynamite. He went across the yard into the barn, situating items on a scarred old work-table. He dropped the tattered instruction booklet in a drawer, then drizzled bits of black powder on the table. In a drawer he tucked a roll of fuse behind a number of other implements. Put some glue on a shelf. Several small sticks behind some old cans. When finished, it appeared Herr Bradenhauer was quite the dabbler in dynamite.

After retrieving the shotgun from the farmer, he took it to the barn and inserted two rock-salt shells inside. He wiped it clean before placing it on the rack in the barn. Afterward, hurrying, the man grabbed a bundle of six pre-made sticks, a long fuse emanating from the center, and went back into the house where he examined the stove. The remnants of a coal fire smoldered in the burn pot. From the crib next to the stove, he added several pieces of seasoned wood, watching as they took flame in the orange pile of smoldering heat. He tossed in several lumps of coal, adding even more wood to the top of the pile. Using the hanging oven mitt, he opened the front eye to full heat. From the back of the stove, he lifted the oily iron skillet, wiping it clean with the oven mitt. Placing it on the floor, he curled the fuse from the six sticks of dynamite in the skillet and left it there.

After stepping back to the door, Roland's contact hoisted the old man, bringing him into the kitchen, placing him in one of the chairs next to the stove. The woman was heavier; she weighed at least a hundred kilos. He dragged her in, placing her opposite. After rummaging through the drawers, the man found scissors and knives, scattering them on the table as if the man, like an idiot, had been working on dynamite at the kitchen table. Yes—it would appear as lunacy to the investigators—and there would be no motive why the old man dabbled in dynamite—but it would certainly steer the investigators in a far different direction.

He went back into the den, staring at the scene. The contact replaced the bloody cushions Roland had lain on, hoping the resulting fire would take care of the blood stains. From a rusty nail, the man retrieved a broom, walking outside and whisking the trickles of blood from the dirt emerging from the field. As the morning sun bore down, he could see the trail through the rapse. That, no doubt, would raise the polizei's suspicions, but provided he retrieved the parachute and equipment, they would have nothing else to go on.

Giving the house a once-over, the man went back inside and placed his hand over the hole in the stove. The heat was intense. It was time to leave before some random visitor arrived and spoiled everything. The man lifted the skillet, placing it over the open eye, careful not to disturb the fuse. The long fuse snaked around in the skillet, leading downward to the bundle of dynamite on the floor, sitting almost under the dead remains of the Bradenhauers.

Using one of the blankets, he wrapped Roland's heavy lower leg, carrying it over his shoulder like one might a slaughtered pig.

The man rushed from the house, pulling the door shut behind him.

He started the Mercedes, driving it through the field access, tracking next to Roland's trail through the beautiful yellow rapse. Twice he had to take access trails to the right to follow the diagonal path, each time shaking his head at the resolve of the man lying comatose in his back seat. The trail ended ahead, in a wide stand of trees. The man exited the car, bounding into the woods before he saw the wisps of white from underneath a pile of leaves and pine needles. He grabbed the parachutes and the equipment, using his foot to kick dirt and mud over the small puddle of blood. Seeing nothing else, the man stuffed the chutes and equipment into the boot of the Mercedes (next to the wrapped leg) and hurried back in the direction of the highway that led into Giessen. Just as he was turning onto the deserted road, a shockwave went through the car, followed seconds later by a thunderous boom. The man twisted in his seat, seeing the black cloud and ensuing fireball consume what was left of the little house in the valley.

He leaned back in the comfortable seat of the Mercedes, lighting an Eckstein, smiling to himself as he made his way into light traffic.

Let the krauts chew on that one for a while.

FIVE

GERALD TOLD Bonitz of his plan to travel west, to Pittsburgh, using a white Chrysler Highlander Bonitz had provided him. He would leave the car at the train station and go to the enlistment station with his new identity, also provided by Bonitz. The car would be picked up by an associate in a day or two.

That was the plan. It *was*.

But the associate would never find the car because Gerald wasn't going to Pittsburgh. Sensing a potential reckoning in the air, Gerald drove on, well past Pittsburgh, into Ohio, all the way across the state to Cincinnati.

Would they really kill me? Really…would they?

"Sure they would," he said aloud. Hell, they'd tried to have him kill his own mother. That fact, in his way of thinking, bestowed upon him the justifiable right to change his mind.

He arrived in the queen city late Saturday night. It didn't take him long to find the affluent area, on the northeast side of downtown. He found a phonebook, locating three physicians in the Mt. Adams area. The first one was in a four-story building, heavily fortified with good locks and people milling about—no good. The second was on a shady street, located in an old home that could have easily been in a quiet Hannover neighborhood. E. Weston Hammerwhite, MD. Hammerwhite…probably used to be Hammerweiss. Either an asshole at Ellis Island or an ashamed relative had Anglicized the name.

Gerald parked the Chrysler a block away. It was after midnight. He smoked a cigarette. Eyed himself in the rear-view mirror. Said goodbye to the way he looked. Pulled on his gloves. Exited the car.

The doctor's office was an easy mark. Good side of town. No iron bars. No dogs or night watchmen. Just a tinkling of broken glass and an open window. Took his time, really searched it top to bottom. Copped a scalpel. Box of syringes. Two vials of Amylocaine. Ten of the brand new Oxycodone pain-killer pills, no more. Another scalpel, just in case. A needle and surgical thread. A tiny pair of scissors. Thiomersal and a full bag of cotton balls, gauze…and muslin bandages.

He drove back into the center of the city. More German architecture didn't go without notice. Found an all-night diner on Broadway down near the river. Had coffee while chatting amiably with the tired broad behind the counter. She was in her mid-forties and lonely. He had no doubts she would have been good for an appreciative roll in the hay but he didn't have the time. At nine in the morning, he put the Chrysler into a garage park, paying the attendant for thirty days, telling him he was going on a river cruise and might wind up taking a steady job if he found one. Gave the guy an extra twenty and told him, if he didn't come back, to use the car all he wanted. The attendant didn't argue. Gerald left the garage with one suitcase, walking around the city until he saw a sign on Walnut advertising apartments on a month-to-month basis.

Fedora tilted back, coat over his arm, butterflies flapping in his stomach, Gerald paid two months' rent and trudged up the stairs to the apartment. He carefully unpacked his clothes, placing them on top of the tattered dresser, organizing piles for ease of changing. In each pile was a pair of pants, a shirt, an undershirt, boxers, and a pair of socks. He had enough clothing to change every other day for ten days. He would have to call a laundry at some point, using the phone by the stairs. Gerald decided he would cross that bridge when he got there.

If he got there.

After arranging the clothing, Gerald prepared the bed, tucking the sheets tightly to prevent his rolling over during sleep. He fluffed the pillows, opened the window, placed a glass of water beside the bed. Next to the water he placed two Oxycodone pills. Placed the remainder within arm's reach.

Gerald went into the bathroom, making the sink water hot. He painstakingly shaved his face, stroking it downward first, soaking it, afterward shaving upward for maximum closeness. Then, for the first time in his life, Gerald shaved his eyebrows. He pulled the skin taut, working the safety razor in all directions to remove every trace of hair. He soaked his face in a hot towel for ten full minutes, patting it dry and staring at the structure of his mug in the medicine cabinet mirror. Again he said goodbye.

Then it was time.

He smoked a third of a steadying cigarette, dropping it into the toilet after one final drag. A deep one. After scrubbing the tub with a washcloth and his shampoo, Gerald dragged the spindly coffee table into the grimy tiled bathroom, placing it just next to the tub, leaving himself enough room to get out. From the doctor's bag, he arranged the medical items on the coffee table in the order he thought he might need them. Gerald unscrewed the small mirror from the wall above the sink, placing the screws inside the dirty medicine cabinet. He then filled the tub with six inches of hot water. After removing his clothes, Gerald stood in the water and opened the small square window high on the bathroom wall. The occasional horns from the midday Cincinnati traffic floated up. Gerald took great breaths of fresh air, wincing as he lowered himself into the scalding water.

He lifted his knees up, perching the mirror so he could see his face. Gerald soaked a gauze pad in the rust-colored Thiomersal, rubbing his face all over, paying particular attention to his nose and eyebrows. The antiseptic burned his freshly-shaved face worse than aftershave ever had. As it dried, he jabbed a syringe into the first vial of Amylocaine. More deep breaths. He touched the needle to the side of his lower nose, in the crease where it met his face, and pressed it in until he felt it touch bone. Struggling not to flinch, Gerald backed it out a hair and injected a quarter of the syringe. Tears trickled from his eyes. He repeated this action on the opposite side, already noticing the numbness.

Refilling the syringe, he carefully inserted the needle into his brow line, where he had just shaved his eyebrows, pointing it straight up and watching the needle's girth burrow under his skin like a worm. Just as he had his nose, he injected the left side of his face first, followed by the right. His face now fully numb, inhibiting his ability to make any type of facial expression, he shot two syringes into his knee, massaging it to distribute the liquid. Gerald repositioned himself and gripped the scalpel. After dousing it in the Thiomersal, he leaned his head back, again tilting the mirror so he could see it. He took several giant breaths and, with one finger in his nostril pulling outward, Gerald began to cut the side of his nostril from his face. He cut from the bottom, from the nostril opening, up to where the nostril flare ended. The line was clean and smooth, and bled profusely. Gerald ignored

93

the blood. He made his second cut, almost along the same line, outward by roughly one-half a centimeter. Wincing slightly because of the cutting noise, he sawed upward, satisfied when the triangular piece of skin fell onto his chest.

He twisted the mirror, viewing the left side of his nose. It was nearly hanging open at the bottom, but Gerald had performed the removal exactly as he hoped. Moving faster, he cut away the right side, almost exactly the same. He placed the two surprisingly thick pieces of flesh on his rising and falling stomach, satisfied at their mirror image. Gerald packed two pieces of cotton into the gashes and went to work on his left leg.

He chose the already mutilated skin because, if he were ever examined, it would be doubtful anyone would notice. After two quick stabs of the scalpel, Gerald cut away a ragged rectangle of thick leg skin from just above the knee. When it was fully removed, he placed it back onto the spot from which it had been cut, hoping that the contact with his blood would keep it viable as long as possible. Moving more quickly, and feeling slightly emboldened, Gerald made deep lateral incisions along his brow line, where his eyebrows had once been. Several times he had to wipe the blood to keep it from his eyes. Next, he cut the thick skin from his leg into two wide ovals, approximately an inch wide by a half-inch in height. Using the scalpel, he scraped the skin side of the ovals until pinkish bloody flesh shone through. Gerald pulled open the flaps above his brow line, stuffing each of the ovals inside, working to make sure they were flatly seated beneath the skin, uniform on each side. The gooey, smacking sound of the incisions opening and closing worked on his gag reflex. Twice he had to stop and gather himself before continuing.

After allowing himself to relax and take several deep breaths, Gerald threaded the needle through his brow line, making tight, tiny stitches, three across on each incision. He wiped both with the Thiomersal, sucking air as the burning somehow defeated the local anesthetic. The scars would certainly be noticeable, but once the eyebrows grew back, Gerald didn't think they would be visible to anyone. He studied his lower forehead. It was hard to tell with the cuts and minor swelling, but he felt once everything grew back that the newer, heavy brow would markedly alter his facial structure.

Gerald reached over, soaking two cotton balls in the Thiomersal. After wiping all around his still gushing nose, he wrapped the muslin bandage tightly around his head, pressing the nose back onto his face. He had to adjust it several times, but finally managed to seat the cut sections of his outer nose onto the area where the triangles he had removed had once been. He couldn't stitch this area, and figured it would take at least a week for the new union to take hold.

The last items on the coffee table were his cigarettes and lighter. He placed a Lucky in his mouth, lit it, leaning back and holding it in place with his trembling hand. His lips were too numb to even feel the cigarette. He sat there for a full hour in the cooling, blood-colored water. Gerald allowed two bouts of faintness to pass before he unsteadily toweled off, always holding something as he made his way back to the bed. He swallowed both pills, dribbling water as he washed them down. Wedging himself under the tight sheets, Gerald eased his swollen head onto the pillow and closed his eyes, considering the events of the previous seventy-two hours.

He didn't fear his motherland, and would still do all he could to be of her service. But they had his picture, and at some point, they might decide he was a loose cannon, or that he knew too much. And that was a risk Gerald couldn't afford to take.

Operation Wolf was underway, and he would perform it all alone.

Gerald slept. And slept.

WEEKS LATER...

THE ARMY recruiter had been impressed by the sharp young man from the hills of Kentucky. He was healthy, with a thin build, possessing a rugged bulldog of a face. Most of the hill people were of Scottish origin, but this one probably came from Irish heritage. Or at least his pug nose did. The nose was slightly misshapen, leaving the recruiter with no doubt that...what was his name?...he riffled through the day's enlistment papers...there it was...*Garland Felton*...he had no doubt that Felton wasn't a stranger to a back alley brawl. Tested high on the Army's IQ test. Damn high. Especially for a hill kid. Wanted straight infantry, insisted on it...which was good, mainly for the recruiter's quotas. Too many kids wanted to enlist to be a bombardier or something sexy (and unrealistic) such as the journalism job specialty, thinking they had a shot at being a field reporter. But old Uncle Sam could always use a grunt. And so could the recruiter.

Injured as a young private during the Great War, the recruiter was a thirty-year man, a staff sergeant, stationed at the downtown Cincinnati Army enlistment station. He tucked Garland Felton's papers back in with the rest of them, double checking that he had the stack in alphabetical order. The namby-pamby college-boy captain up in Columbus would have his ass if he didn't. He used a wet sponge to seal the back of the envelope before folding down the brass brad as an extra measure. He dropped the envelope in the secure pick-up box, locked the door and limped off down Race Street, whistling as he jangled his keys.

As he made his way past 9th Street, he saw the olive-green Army bus turn his way, belching smoke as the driver rumbled up through the gears. The Felton kid, sitting alone near the front, waved at him. Two of the recruits in the back shot him the bird and laughed together at their crude attempt at humor. The recruiter shook his head, smiling at himself. *Poor bastards. Don't have a clue what they're in for.* That old government jalopy would take four hours to get to Fort Knox, and the recruiter would lay even money that the drill sergeants at the reception station would keep the new "cruits" up all night.

The bus turned the corner, disappearing from sight but still audible, grinding up through the gears as it headed toward the Roebling Bridge over the Ohio. The recruiter adjusted his garrison cap and picked up his pace despite the grating of bone on bone in his lame leg. Hinder's had a draft special on Thursday nights until seven. If he hurried, he just might make it.

PART THREE

Reconciliation

SIX

SEPTEMBER, 1944

THE SOLDIERS were instructed to come forward in pairs. Being this close to graduation, many were brash and salty about such a simple exercise, while others acted as timid as if preparing to handle dynamite or a poisonous snake with his blood up. Roland had worked extra hard on this day, and on the days prior, for it was soon to be a special occasion. Most of the trainees of class 44-Delta probably saw him as nothing more than a crippled captain with the yellowing, sallow face of a terminal drunk. And they would be correct. But that would all soon change. Purpose was on its way. A reason to live.

"Let's go, you fire-pissers!" he yelled with uncharacteristic gusto. "You're about to be one step closer to matriculation, and then you can stop pretending. Uncle Sam's gonna put a rifle in your hand and send your ass across the pond where you can legally kill a kraut or a Jap…if they don't kill you first. C'mon 'cruits! Who's first?"

The first two soldiers shuffled forward. Roland was paired with Staff Sergeant Jennings, a good sort of fellow he might have actually gone skirt chasing with before that disastrous jump more than two years before. Jennings held the handset, his other hand on the battle book as he explained the straightforward simulation to the two soldiers. Several hundred yards away, and hidden behind one of Camp Gordon's many fire-ant infested sand dunes, was an identical Galvin handheld radio. One soldier would stay here with Captain Buhl, the other would go with Jennings behind the dune, and the two would converse, using the phonetic alphabet and all of the radio procedures they had been taught during their two-week block of commo instruction.

Once Jennings had finished his spiel, he and the other soldier hustled off at double-time in the direction of the dune. The soldier who stayed, a private first class—meaning he'd had a few years of college—stared down at the wooden lower leg protruding from Roland's boot. His mouth trembled, but he managed to speak.

"Sir, may I ask you a question?"

"Parachute accident," Roland said with a knowing grin and a twitch of his cheek.

"Were you one of the jumpers in North Africa, or did it happen—"

"Yeah…Africa, something like that," Roland answered, cutting him off. "Doesn't matter, 'cruit. What we're here for is *your* training." He patiently gave the young soldier a few final tips. In the distance, Jennings and the other soldier disappeared behind the small hill.

Roland listened for a moment as the two trainees began their stilted back and forth exchange. Rather than military, it sounded more like some slapstick comedy routine one might hear on the radio. Better yet, it was comparable to an on-stage skit put together by the USO to make an auditorium of soldiers roar at the two biggest imbeciles ever to serve, tantamount to something in the Sad Sack comic strip that appeared in the Stars & Stripes. Like everything Roland was now forced to deal with, the radio drill felt silly and trite in light of his extensive training. As his soldier (sweating profusely) focused on the exchange, Roland produced the black flask from his utility pants, swilling deeply on the cheap Kentucky bourbon, allowing it to burn into his throat, giving him a medicinal response.

It was nearly noon. His last drink had been…when was it? 0200, maybe? Roland wasn't completely sure. He'd been down on Reynolds Street, arguing Civil War with a southern-fried lieutenant from Alabama who thought the South would surely rise again. Why couldn't they have at least stationed Roland somewhere with people of his intellect? You take one of the Army's most highly trained men and stick him with a passel of commo trainees? It was like pairing filet mignon with cotton candy and soda pop. And, as he took another hard pull on the flask, Roland excused what he was doing to his liver, justifying that the Army's hiding him here was what caused him to turn to the bottle. After the injury, during the months in the hospital and the year it had taken him to learn to use the prosthetic, he'd managed to abstain from alcohol. But once they'd planted him down here, tucking him away like something they were embarrassed of, the bourbon was the only thing that ever did him any good.

Except the occasional woman for hire, he reasoned, *but that was a physiological necessity. And there weren't too many dames out looking for one-legged men, even in Augusta, Georgia.*

He allowed the sun to bake down on his face, tilting his head back. Roland pulled a satisfied breath in through his nose, feeling the temperate air matching the warmth in his gullet, courtesy of the bourbon. Everything was going to change here in…he glanced at his wristwatch…about an hour. He leaned back again, feeling as good as if he were sunning himself on a beach.

"Sir?"

The recruit was looking at him expectantly. The radio was silent.

"Sir? How did we do?"

Roland hadn't even paid attention after the first few exchanges on the script. Reaching for the paper sticking from the elastic band around the kid's M-1 helmet, he scribbled his initials down the sheet by each block and patted the kid on his back. When the private first class scurried out of the sandy bunker, hurrying to compare his bolo card—essentially the Army version of a report card—with his battle buddy, Roland again leaned back against the dune and took a final swig from the flask. He closed his eyes, dreaming of getting into the action, to the front of the line. He wanted to smell the sulfur and cordite, to be in the map tent during tense planning sessions, to hear the clicking of rounds in the clip followed by the satisfying clank of a rifle's bolt ramming forward, seating a small lead dart of death in the chamber. He wanted to bitch about the rancid k-rats and to smoke incessantly, with trembling hands from the numerous shellings. He wanted to feel the loamy European soil under his one good foot and to make a difference in something that mattered. Roland Buhl simply wanted to be normal again.

When Staff Sergeant Jennings finally appeared, Roland was ready to go. "Drive me back to the unit," he said with a toothy smile. Jennings, as always, offered a hand to Roland as he struggled out of the pit. Roland knocked the hand away, grunting as he finally clamored out, having to straighten the half-ass prosthetic afterward. He walked with a heavy hitch, having to lift his left leg at the pelvis and sling it in front of him to create a modified walking motion. The prosthetic was attached from the knee down. The doctors had first left Roland six inches below the knee but, due to infection, twice they had to amputate the remains of his tibia and fibula, finally coaxing the injury to heal enough to accept the rounded cap of the wooden leg.

The September weather in Augusta was more like July in most places, but the wind from the open Jeep felt good. Roland shirked regulation by removing his helmet, allowing the wind to blow over his face and hair, leaning his head back and again accepting the sun's rays, hoping for some color before he was due to travel. The six or so shots of bourbon he'd just ingested made him feel decent again, the way most people feel after a good night of sleep and a hot shower. But Roland's well-being was made all the better by the release he was about to be granted. The release from his personal prison. The release back to Europe. Back to the War.

"COME IN!" yapped the high voice on the other side of the chintzy wood and smoke glass door. Roland stood, combing his freshly dampened hair down with his fingers. His chest swelled with a great breath as he winked at Staff Sergeant Jennings.

"Good luck, sir."

Roland shook his head. "Luck won't have anything to do with it. He promised me." And with that, he twisted the knob and tottered into the commander's office.

Waymon Creel, U.S. Army Major, sat at his wide oak desk staring at a grouping of reports. Perched on his button nose were his reading glasses. He traced his finger under line after line, pausing to grunt once. Finally, after more than a minute, Creel looked up, expressionless. He was quite short, with a round face and a balding head, made all the more ridiculous by the long strands of hair spread out on his pate, glued in place by some sort of pasty hair oil. His skin was permanently splotchy, the flushing seeming to alternate between his cheeks, his neck, and his ears—all depending on the relative stress of the situation. Creel's background was in the Army's school system, a career track that, while necessary, wasn't exactly respected by the men and women in combat units. In a similar manner, Creel seemed to resent the combat arms, criticizing their members as boors and dimwits at every turn. From the day Roland had arrived, the aversion between him and Major Creel was palpable to anyone within fifty feet.

"Well?" Creel asked, opening his hands, irritation in his voice.

"Sir, Captain Buhl reporting as requested, sir." Roland barked his report, fired a crisp salute and waited, mildly piqued by how long Creel took to return the salute.

"Shall I get you a chair, captain? I'm sure, due to your infirmity, that standing is a nuisance." Creel's voice dripped with unnatural empathy.

"No, I'm fine," Roland answered, purposefully leaving "sir" out of the sentence.

"Well then, you requested this meeting," Creel said with an effeminate fluttering of his fingers. "Get on with it. What do you want?"

Roland's lips parted slightly as his heart rate hammered his head with pressure. Creel had better be just sweating him. If he wasn't…he cleared his throat. "Sir, I'm here because the final class of this cycle just finished. You told me at the end of the cycle you would get me back to Europe, back to the…back *into* the theater."

"Hmmm," Creel mused. "I guess I did tell you that, didn't I?"

"Yes, sir, you *did.*"

Creel removed his reading glasses, folding them and slipping them into a crease in his breast pocket. Cleared his own throat. Cleared it again. Added a pinched little smile. Smoothed the long pieces of hair. "Well, captain, since I told you that, there have been some changes."

"Changes?" Roland growled, his eyes narrowing.

The major stood, placing his stubby arms behind his back as he meandered across the office, staring at the platoons practicing drill in the scorched brown grass of the square. Roland took note that Creel never allowed him to stand at ease, making him remain at attention. More important to Roland, though, were these so-called changes Creel was speaking of. The major was taking his time, staring out at the square. Finally he broke the silence, jabbing a sausage finger at the moving platoons.

"See those soldiers there?"

"I'm at attention, sir."

"Then *stand at ease* and look."

Roland did. "Yes, sir. Drill practice."

"Drill practice, yes, but what I see is a bunch of greenhorns who aren't yet ready for the absurdities of combat. As much as I don't care to admit it, they need a man like you. A warhorse, if you will."

Stay calm...talk it through. Don't act, not yet. Roland gave an exasperated shake of his head. "I'm afraid I'm not following."

Creel thoughtfully pulled on the turkey gobbler that hung below his chin. "Due to an influx of new recruits, due much in part to Ike's request for a final mass push, our down cycle has been cut in half. This, as you know, won't give me time to find and train a suitable replacement for your billet. If I had the normal—"

"Suitable replacement?" Roland yelled, breaking with military courtesy and turning, his arms gesturing. "I could find a suitable replacement in that green platoon of 'cruits we just sent through!"

"Watch your bearing, captain," Creel warned, twisting his pear-shaped body and lifting the sausage finger again.

"Sir," Roland said, pausing to calm himself. "You promised me this transfer. All you have to do is make one call. *One call*, sir."

Creel pulled his lips together, as if he'd just tasted something sour. He stepped back behind his desk, opening an oaken box, producing a cigarette and his lighter. Once his cigarette was lit, he smiled thinly. "Captain Buhl, I'm doing you a favor. Here, at our training battalion, you're somebody...a big man. The kids see that little Ranger diamond, they see your jump wings, they see your wooden leg, and they feel like they're standing in the presence of a pirate of some sort...of Blackbeard himself. You're like some grizzled old character from a moving picture." Still standing, he took a drag of the cigarette, blowing a line of smoke across the desk. "But if I send you back to Europe, to the line, you'll be nothing more than a nuisance to anyone who has to command you, or even associate with you. No one will want you because no one wants a...and I'm not deliberately trying to be cruel when I say this...but a cripple." Creel's smile approached sincerity but fell short. He furrowed his brow. "Now, I don't know what strings you pulled to prevent being thrown out of this man's Army after losing your leg, but as far as I'm concerned, you will finish your career right here at—"

For a man with only one good leg, the leap Roland was able to manage was impressive. From his standing position, he was able to launch himself onto the shiny slick desk, his arms outstretched so that he and his 190 pounds would have sufficient momentum to take the corpulent Creel down with ease. It all worked to plan as the two toppled over behind the desk, sending two glass commemorative plates crashing to the floor. Rather than strike the hapless man, Roland clamped his hands around the major's well-padded throat, clamping down for only a few seconds. And for those few seconds, the fear in Creel's beady little eyes was real. Fear he would never experience commanding classroom soldiers. Fear his simple life—every single day going home to his flabby wife and three chubby kids—would never produce. Fear a man could only get when another man is doing his dead-level best to kill him. When the body's fight or flight mechanism kicks into overdrive and every hair stands on end, and every pore begins to burn with adrenalized sweat.

Roland, still holding on to a modicum of sanity, released the death grip after a few seconds.

Creel skittered backward, banging his head against the oak-paneled wall, his small mouth open wide. Staff Sergeant Jennings, hearing the commotion, rushed into the room, standing beside the desk in a ready position, appearing stunned and bewildered about how to intervene in such an unprecedented incident.

Finally, after producing a handkerchief and wiping the drool which had burst from his mouth, Creel screamed in a high-pitched voice for Jennings to arrest Captain Buhl at once, and to call the MPs, and to hold him down until they arrived. From down the hall a lieutenant arrived, as well as a master sergeant, both of them frozen, shocked at the scene, just like Staff Sergeant Jennings. As Creel continued his tirade, demanding the arrest of the crazed captain who tried to strangle the life from him, Roland rolled over on his back, staring at the ceiling, his hand massaging his forehead.

In his mind he asked himself the same question he had at least a thousand times before: *Why did I jump?*

"What in the billy hell is going on in here?" an authoritative voice bawled. Roland didn't move a muscle. He knew who it was. The voice...the commanding, thunderous voice was distinctive. Inimitable. And it belonged to Colonel Tyron Taylor, the brigade commander. His office was at the end of the hall, and he surely heard Creel's shrieks through the five walls that separated them. Years before, a sergeant in personnel noticed the colonel's middle name was Nelson, and since that day, never to his face, everyone who served under the man referred to him by the meaningful initials of TNT. Due to his booming baritone voice and legendary temper, it was a fitting sobriquet and a tidy double entendre. A man who would have surely made general in a combat theater, he was allowed to live stateside due to his long-dying wife. Rumor had it she was down to her final weeks, though one would never know it when viewing the imposing man who never wore a single furrow of what looked like sorrow.

The colonel stepped around the desk, nudging Jennings and the two other men out of the way. He stopped, hands on hips, drinking in the bizarre scene.

Creel pointed an accusatory finger, his voice not unlike a miffed (and sheltered) child on a playground. "He tried to choke me, sir. This...this crippled drunk of a captain who should have been put out to pasture years ago launched himself over my desk, hooligan he is, and tried to *choke* the very life out of me!"

TNT swiveled his head to Roland, arched his eyebrows. Roland, propped up on his elbows, twisted his mouth and nodded.

Taylor's eyes were hawk-like. They darted back and forth, emotionless, before his chest hitched and something akin to a chortle came from his mouth. He eventually uttered two words, aided by a pointed finger. "My office."

CREEL SAT in the chair next to TNT's desk; Roland stood at attention, again, his stump aching from the leap. For five minutes Creel described the incident in fantastical detail, even telling the colonel that he hadn't fought back for fear of injuring the lower-ranking, already crippled man. TNT listened to the entire story with the face of a person who'd just ingested several tablespoons of castor oil. A large man with short steel-gray hair, his long, lantern-like face fit well on his body suitable for a Texan rancher. He steepled his sun-baked fingers in front of his face as Creel wrapped up his story.

"And why did he attack you?" he asked, when Creel finally paused for more than a second.

The question seemed to throw Creel, who added dramatic pauses between the words of his question. "Does—it—matter—sir?"

"I just asked the question, didn't I?"

Major Creel cut his eyes at Roland before looking back at the colonel. "Captain Buhl has been unstable since day one. There's no telling what his delusion of the day is."

"Bullshit," Roland interjected.

"Captain, no one told you to speak!" Creel shouted, standing.

"Shut up, Creel!" TNT yelled, sending a look of shock over the major as if he'd just been slapped across the face. "Sit the hell down and be quiet. Lord knows you've talked long enough." He turned to Roland, exhaling loudly. "Okay, captain, your turn."

Roland paused, gathering himself. "Major Creel promised me, after this cycle, that he would secure orders for me to transition back to Europe. I realize, because of my injury, that I might be limited, but after doing my time here, I want to serve on the line, even if it kills me....sir." Knowing how TNT valued brevity, especially after Creel's painfully long, overly dramatic monologue, Roland zipped his lips.

The colonel turned to Creel. "Did you promise this?"

Creel's mouth moved like a fish out of water before the words caught up. "Well, sir...yes and no. I mean...we had a conversation once...but I don't know if *promise* is the...the...operative word I would—"

"Bullshit," Roland said again.

Creel's bloodshot eyes shot daggers at Roland, but this time he remained quiet.

TNT had seen enough. He went into a file cabinet, producing two folders, laying them on his desk and placing his gargantuan right hand on top. "So, major, exactly why can't we assist Captain Buhl in getting back to the war?"

Creel stuttered. "Sir, we need *able*-bodied fighting men at the front."

TNT rubbed his eyes. "Did you ever play a sport?"

"Sir?"

"A sport. A sport. Bats. Balls. Hoops. A damned sport!"

"Well, back in school we played several games like badminton and—"

"A team sport Creel, a violent one. Like football?"

TNT's words were coming machine gun-fast. Roland could tell he was setting up for the kill.

Creel shook his head. "No, sir."

TNT eyed Roland for a moment. Cut his eyes back to the major. "In a rough sport like football, by the fourth quarter, everyone's beat to hell. And just in case you don't know it, we're in the fourth quarter of this war, and rather than Uncle Sam needing able-bodied men, he needs willing, *convicted* men, like Buhl here."

"But, sir…"

"Shut up for a minute." The colonel opened the top file and flipped through several pages. He curled his lip and glared at Creel. "Look at this shit!" He lifted a thick stack of white and yellow paper. "You've got more doctor's profiles than any soldier I've ever seen. What…your vagina hurting too much to go fight for our country?"

Creel's jaw muscle ceased to work.

TNT dropped the doctor's notes as if they were coated in fecal bacteria. He stared at the top one, waving his hand over it. "It says here you're confined stateside because of a propensity to diverticulitis and gout?"

"Well…yes, sir, from my mother's side. All of the Reynolds half of the family are prone to—"

"Get out." Straight as a needle on a compass, TNT's arm pointed rigidly to the door.

"Sir?"

"Go! Get the hell outta my office. Now!"

Major Creel hurried to the door, still rubbing his neck. He opened it and paused. "Captain Buhl, come with—"

"Dammit, only you, Creel! *Out!*"

Creel hesitated a minute before gingerly pulling the door shut.

"Get the hell away from that door, Major!" Creel's pear-shaped shadow lurched into motion.

TNT shoved the file off his desk, littering his floor with paper. He stared downward, into his own lap. Roland understood what was going through his mind. They both had their own cross to bear. Roland's was his own physical condition; TNT's was his wife's. Both men shared the same result of having to work in an environment that they both despised. Forced to work with the Creels of the world.

TNT finally looked up, considering Roland for a long moment, finally shaking his head. He stood, telling Roland to stand at ease. He circled him, staring at him from all angles. Finally he sniffed several times before he broke the silence.

"Kentucky bourbon?"

Roland waited, nodded. "Yes, sir."

"Why?"

"I hate what I'm doing, sir."

"Does that mean you hate me, too?"

"No, sir, not at all. I think you and I, while different in some respects, are similar in makeup."

TNT perched himself on the corner of the desk, crossing his arms. "I don't like it here either, Buhl, but I don't drown my sorrows in a bottle. I'm stronger than that."

"Yes, sir."

"Shows weakness."

"Given the chance, sir, I'd pitch the bottle with ease."

TNT moved his boot, toeing the carpet of doctor's notes at his feet. "You know, Buhl, as much as I can't stand that little prick Creel, he's right about one thing. I send you over to England, you're gonna play hell trying to get offa that island and back into the game."

Roland nodded again. "I realize that, sir, but how will I ever know if I don't have the chance?"

"Trust me."

"I don't disagree, sir, but if you get me there, I'll convince them."

"Can you really knock off the booze? Word has it you're an all-day man."

Roland dug into his utility pants. He retrieved the flask and placed it on the colonel's desk.

The colonel picked up the flask, twirling it in his hands. He motioned to the combat patch on Roland's right arm. "You got your combat experience, son. If I were you, I'd stay here, finish out my string, and retire with a pension."

"Would you, sir?" Roland asked, cutting his eyes at the man.

TNT hesitated before he showed a rare smile. "No."

"I don't want to either, sir."

There was a considerable silence before TNT motioned him away. "Go to your quarters and stand by. I'll quash that little incident from earlier, but if you ever attack a senior officer again, justified or not, I'll have you shot. You hear me?"

"I do, sir." And he believed it.

"I'm gonna make some calls, pull some strings, call in some favors that you haven't done shit to deserve."

"I don't know what to say, sir."

TNT gnawed on the inside of his cheek. "Lemme correct something…you haven't done shit *here* to deserve it. Maybe you did elsewhere."

"Maybe, sir."

"I'd get your bags packed if I were you."

"They're already packed, sir."

TNT stepped around his desk and sat. He lifted Roland's file, shaking it so he would see it. The colonel opened the file and wrote something in large block letters, leaving the note clipped to the front of the page. "I just made a note to whomever your new commander happens to be. You're to get no second chances, and just to make sure you don't try to alter your file, I'll be sending it by courier. Understand?"

"Yes, sir."

The colonel nodded to him. "Dismissed."

Roland turned, his leg aching from the incident. At the door, TNT called out to him. "Hang on, Buhl."

"Yes, sir?" Roland asked.

"There's a big blank in this file, several years long."

"Yes, sir."

"I've heard some of the rumors."

"Oh?"

"Back to you deserving it...is it true you had to be extracted due to your injuries from a bad jump into Germany?"

"That's the chief rumor, sir."

TNT lit a cigarette, smoke shrouding his head. "Well then, let's just hope this time turns out better than last."

"Yes, sir. It will." He came to attention and fired off a salute. Three hours later, just before *Retreat* and *To The Colors* filled the humid afternoon air of Camp Gordon, a runner arrived at his door with an envelope.

Roland's orders came through.

SEVEN

PARIS WAS a veritable madhouse. Since liberation day, two weeks before, the city of light had pulsated with as much energy as at any time in its storied history. Between the relieved citizenry ready to claim a new way of life out from under the Nazi thumb, and the shell-shocked liberators eager to taste the variety of Parisian delicacies, one couldn't walk a block without witnessing a scene worthy of stopping in one's tracks.

Staff Sergeant Garland Felton, known to those in his unit either as Garland, or sometimes Felt, had no time to stop and smell the roses. His unit was on a three-day furlough, restricted to the inner-ring in Paris. This was an exclusive club, being enjoyed by only a half-million other Allied soldiers at the same time. As he pressed his way down the sticky Champs-Elysees (made gummy from a variety of substances, all organic) walking in the center of the street due to the fifty-deep crowds outside of the bars and clubs, Garland's mind inventoried "the list" as he thought of it. Since the shooting began, it included nine non-commissioned officers, three of them quite senior, including one sergeant major that essentially ran an entire brigade under a hapless nitwit of a colonel. On the commissioned side of the list were seven officers: three lieutenants, a captain, a major, a lieutenant colonel and one full-bird who'd previously thought he was bullet-proof, creeping too close to the line for his own good.

Operation Wolf was proceeding as planned, probably far better than Heydte and Berlin might have expected. If only they knew. Thus far Garland was the only person who knew about the list. But that could change soon.

Maybe.

At the place de la Concorde he continued straight, dodging the frenzied stream of speeding Jeeps and trucks serpentining through the wide plaza, some heading north, the rest rocketing over the Seine. The Jeeps were adorned with fender-flags, some of them announcing that a colonel was inside, the occasional one displaying a star or two. Most of them were probably rushing off to see some fancy whore, using their influence to act as if they were on some sort of official business. He stopped on the street island in the center of the plaza, leaning against the obelisk that looked like a miniature of the tacky Washington Monument. Behind the statues rimming the plaza, he could see at least a mile of Rue de Rivoli. Garland turned around, the Arc de Triomphe a dominating shape a mile up the street from which he'd come. On the right side of the wide avenue a stream of two-way traffic pressed bumper to bumper, flowing who knows where. Across the Seine, on Quai Voltaire, four lanes of traffic barely crawled. Paris was a VIP stampede.

"Now where in the hell would all those American assholes be going?" he whispered to himself in German. "They're no doubt breaking rules."

Rules!

His thoughts were still so German, he pondered as he laughed aloud. He would be lying if he said he hadn't enjoyed his time in the United States. There was a certain carefree spirit that was just so, well…so un-German. It bothered him at first, seeing people crossing the street without stopping and looking both ways. Or how employees often clocked their friends in when the friend was "stuck" here or there, which probably equaled nothing more than a bad hangover or a piss-poor attitude. But those kinds of things had begun to sandpaper Garland's right-angled Germanic inner-being, smoothing away the sharp edges, bit by bit. Back when he'd been in Manhattan, his leg aching from simply faking the damned leg injury, he began to find himself crossing the street, against the light, when there were no cars coming. It always made him laugh aloud, causing curious stares from the New Yorkers. And why the hell shouldn't he have embraced the Yankee ways of life? If he ever made it back to Deutschland, he looked forward to debating these things over a few hundred pilsners, explaining to his countrymen how their rigidity probably drew a straight line to a higher national incidence of hemorrhoids.

Garland lit a Lucky Strike before he bolted through a gap in the speeding vehicles, nearly getting winged by the mirror from a 5-ton truck, its covered cargo area full of screaming American soldiers, each holding a bottle of red wine, shouting in what sounded like southern American accents. Garland gave them the finger without looking back, entering the long green park known as the Tuileries. He'd been here as a teen, on a trip with his school. The entire trip—greasy food, mind-numbing museums, dirty "character-filled" buildings—had been terminally boring until, on the train ride home, a pimply faced girl whose name he couldn't recall gave him a terrific hand-job under a wool blanket. He chuckled as his feet scraped over the pea-gravel, passing through the tent city of displaced French. Of course it had been a terrific hand-job; at that age, what sexual act isn't terrific?

The sound of touristy Parisian music greeted his ears. This is what he'd been looking for. Up ahead a makeshift restaurant had been formed, with hundreds of tables and chairs scattered on the trampled grass. Set in the middle, and almost in the center of the rectangular park, was a bandstand rimmed by covered wooden pallets acting as the dance floor. Thousands of GIs danced with Parisian women, pressing themselves close, not a one of them thinking of their wife or girlfriend back home. This was Paris, after all, and there was still a war going on.

Most of the American patrons were Army, although Garland did spot the occasional squid or Marine. There could only be one reason for anyone other than Army being on mainland Europe, and it had to do with sitting back in the rear while people like Garland were out front fighting, as was evidenced by their clear eyes and unlined faces. Bastards. But petty grudges were not why he was here. No. He was here to have a meeting, and to hopefully maintain his relative anonymity. Anonymity because he couldn't get discovered, by the Americans, doing what he was about to do. He stopped at the roped-off entrance to the restaurant, watching.

The band was playing a soft number, something Garland had heard before. He didn't know very much about music, and didn't really like what was popular. Especially this stuff. Several times back in New York he'd run across Negroes playing jazz on street corners. The music had penetrated his chest, melding with the thump of his heart. It had soul and feeling and made him want to laugh and cry all at the same time. Now *that* was music. *That* was something a person could move to. This, however, was *sheise*. His distaste for the putrid sounds didn't matter though, because Garland didn't plan on hanging around long enough to hear much more.

A slightly faster number started up. Twenty feet in front of him, a splotchy-faced officer in his pinks and browns stood, offering his hand to the only other girl at the table. He was about Garland's size of six-feet and average build. The woman stood, waiting while the man removed his coat, hanging it over the chair and dropping his hat on the table. They headed toward the dance floor, the man allowing his hand to trace down her back to rest at the swell where her derriere began.

Garland moved.

He stood behind the jacket, making sure no one else from the empty table might be returning from the dance floor. He removed his own jacket and garrison cap, donning the officer's jacket, flexing his arms for fit. A little tight but it was acceptable. After sliding the officer's cap on, Garland carried his own items fifty feet away, tucking the garrison cap into the inner pocket and hanging the jacket on a chair at a crowded table. From inside his jacket he retrieved his Ruby pistol, purchased in a Parisian alley for three packs of Luckys. He slid it into the captain's jacket, situating it so it wouldn't bulge.

After turning and hurrying in the direction of the Rue de Rivoli, Garland slowed, taking the inner path toward the Louvre. He made sure his buttons were straight, cocking the tight-fitting hat to the side in the way most men wore them. He looked at his shoulders, realizing he was now, for the moment, a captain in the 101st Airborne. Two young soldiers, one of them with an eye-patch, passed within feet of him, both of them saluting. Garland returned their salute, suppressing a grin. The courtesy felt somehow…Germanic.

After walking the full length of the Louvre, Garland again dodged the hazardous traffic, bolting across Rue de Rivoli and heading into the 1st Arrondissement, up Rue de Valois, in the direction of the Bourse Metro Station. He patted his pockets to make certain he was carrying no identification. He'd left everything, including his dog-tags, back at the abandoned building his Third Army unit was bunking in until they had to move out again. Leaving his ID behind was a serious breach of regulations, but well worth the ass-chewing he would have to endure in the event he was rousted by the MP's. This would be Garland's first contact in over two years, assuming the contact was still where they were supposed to be. Burned into his brain was a system of twelve friendlies, all a part of his network, situated from Denmark to Liechtenstein to Spain. There had been one in England, in London, but that had been before he'd ever begun creating the list. Garland had seen no reason whatsoever to risk a visit, knowing they might have pulled him out of his mission right then and there.

But now…now that there were tangible results attached to Operation Wolf, Garland didn't think there would be any talk about aborting. Nevertheless, to protect himself, he now appeared to be a captain from the 101st instead of a staff sergeant from the Third Army. The motherland didn't know which unit he was in, and he aimed to keep it that way. Additionally, he was curious to see whether there was a question over the change in his appearance. The loss of twenty pounds was one thing, the flattening of his nose and the thickening of his brow another.

He lit another Lucky, tipping his hat to a gaggle of what looked like whores, listening as they peppered him with the only salacious English words they knew. Garland turned his head away, ignoring them; his mind was up ahead. He climbed the shallow rise, stopping at Rue d'Uzes, feeling his pulse rising. He lifted the hat, wiping his forehead. The September weather was cooler than it had been the day before, yet he could feel the perspiration dripping down his chest and back. The street was narrow and arrow-straight, a city ravine, dominated on each side by crooked three-and four-story buildings painted in the oh-so-French aquas, pinks, and greens. He watched as the numbers decreased, stopping at the building with the black plate denoting it as 71. Garland took the three stone steps to the wrought-iron door at the bottom, prepared to ring the buzzer. He tugged and, to his surprise, the door opened. He stepped inside.

There were four units per floor, two on the front and two on the back. His contact was supposed to be on the top floor, flat 44. He'd thought about this day for months. How would his contact react? What if there had been a compromise? It seemed reasonable, especially after the Allies had so effortlessly liberated the city…

That idiot Hitler! Garland read the papers every chance he got. *What sort of a tactician was he, trying to fight a two-front war? Had he maintained the Russo alliance, or ignored Great Britain and France…for the time…the motherland would be flourishing. But no…he'd had to think with his balls instead of his head. A well-placed bullet to the Austrian's head was the best tactical move any good German could hope for at the moment.*

Back to the moment, damn it!

The smell of garlic assaulted his nose as he climbed, ruefully envisioning what might happen when he knocked on the door. There would be a shuffling of feet, the door would open, a genial looking man of sixty would politely usher him in, whispering good Berliner German, soothing Garland enough to pass the threshold. The door would close behind him and six beefy Americans would descend on him, beating the truth out of him before urinating on his wounds, leaving him to die in a pile of his own teeth, thank you very much.

"Stop it," he whispered, slowly climbing.

He'd tried to come up with a valid reason for an American soldier to be knocking on the door, eventually scrawling a note with the address, writing "pays cash for American cigarettes" below the street address. He'd done it carefully, using his left hand, and was prepared to tell the questioners that this had been given to him by a drunken soldier in the Tuileries. Garland also knew, however, if there had been a compromise of his contact, the Allies would learn that his uniform was stolen, and then the jig would be up. In the end, he had to depend on his countrymen, and that their Parisian agent at flat 44, 71 Rue d'Uzes had *not* been discovered.

At exactly 4:01 p.m., two years and three months since he'd last made contact, Garland Felton rapped on the wooden door with the peeling black paint, reconnecting with the country he loved, only not quite as much as before. He waited, listening, hearing boards creaking. In his left hand was the note, weathered by sweat and palm grease. The door opened.

"Peux je vous aider?" She was in her thirties, quite plump, wearing a friendly expression on an attractive, albeit somewhat strained, face. She cocked her head, viewing him curiously. Garland stood there, unable to speak. "May I help you?" she asked blinking, switching to English after drinking in the American uniform.

He cleared his throat, feeling odd without using a code-word. He said, "I was told, several years ago, that you are a *freund.*" The final word in German, slightly discernible from the English version, was the only clue he was willing to offer.

She wrinkled her brow, pulling the door open just wide enough for him to slide through. "Come in. I may not be who you were told about, but my house is open to any of the brave liberators who look like they might enjoy a cup of tea."

Garland stepped inside.

The woman closed the door, stepping around him, giving him a wide berth. She was heavier than he first realized, but not classically fat. She was simply a big woman. Rubenesque. And just being in the same general area with this woman (any woman) with her wide rear end and enormous breasts, made Garland's pulse race. He studied her face. It wasn't what he would call pretty, but there was something appealing about it, a kindness, a yearning.

Maybe the yearning was his imagination; it had just been so damned long.

She moved into the sitting area, outfitted with antique furniture from the middle or late 1800s. "Please, sit."

"Do you know who I am?" he asked her.

She didn't offer the hint of an expression. She only blinked several times, her brown eyes staring at him intently.

Garland tilted his head. "Have I made a mistake?"

"I'm not sure. With this city's constant upheaval, there are just so many people to keep up with." Her smile was now gone. "Tell me where you lived before joining the Army." He could see her visibly masking her interest, but her eyes told the story. They danced, alight with hope that he could be her contact.

"I worked in Manhattan," he said, studying her reaction.

The woman's chin tilted up before nodding once. "Manhattan, you say?"

"Yes."

She took a step closer. "Mightn't you show me some proof?"

He stood, untucking his pinkish shirt, pulling the shirt and jacket up to expose his chest. The woman moved very close, lifting reading glasses that hung by a chain around her neck. She touched the skin of his chest above his heart, pulling at it, making it taut. On his chest, indistinguishable from a grouping of moles except during a scrupulous inspection, were four tiny black dots. The dots were less than two inches apart, and if connected by lines on their outer edge, would have created a diamond shape.

She disappeared into the kitchen, returning with a metallic canister, on the side in glowing script was the word *Café*. Staring at him, she unscrewed the cap, and then from the cap, she twisted her hand the opposite way, using all her strength before the seal broke. The cap revealed itself as two pieces, and from the small shallow between the two pieces, she removed a glass disc. It was a lens. On it was an etching. She motioned for Garland to lift his shirt again, and when he did, she placed the lens over the four dots, using her thumb and forefinger to rotate the disc. Garland looked down. The etching in the glass of the lens was a swastika, and when the lens was situated perfectly, the four dots matched up perfectly with the tails of each end of the ancient Brahmi symbol. She removed the lens, and her glasses, her face hinting at a smile.

"You are *Nummer Acht*, aren't you?"

"Pardon?"

"Number Eight. You're the one we know as Eight."

Garland shrugged. "I honestly don't know."

"Show me the leg."

Realizing she knew about his surgically altered leg, he unbloused his left boot and lifted the trousers, twisting his leg in the light. She leaned down, running her hands over the scars. "Does it hurt?"

"Not really. Faking that limp back in Manhattan was the most painful part." He took the lens from her hand. "My contact was to have the same markings. Show me."

She nodded. With her left hand, she pulled at the neck of her conservative dress, stretching it downward. He felt a rush of excitement course through him as she nearly exposed the entirety of her massive breast, holding the neckline down unashamedly for him to stare at the four tiny black marks. He placed the lens on her breast—it fit perfectly. Garland's eyes only studied the convergence for a second, magnetically drawn downward by the upper edge of her tan areola.

"Satisfied?" she asked, taking the lens and replacing it in the modern-looking coffee canister.

Garland, his throat too thick to speak, nodded.

"Sit."

He did.

She remained standing, her cheeks flushing pink, her Bavarian German distinct. "Where the *hell* have you been? Do you realize why you're called Number Eight?" She didn't wait on an answer. "You're called that because, when the program began, there were eight altogether. We've got confirmation that half are dead, and of the others we've found, their projects have had minimal success. Some of our other assets have tried like hell to find you, without exposing themselves, and thus far have come up zeroes."

"May I have a drink?" he asked pleasantly, touching his throat.

The woman had been pacing. She stopped, bending at the waist as she glared at him. "Are you not taking this seriously?"

"Of course I am, but I'm parched. And when you get me a drink, I'll explain."

She disappeared, coming back seconds later with an open bottle of red table wine and a small glass. "Am I drinking alone?" he asked.

"You wanted a drink, I got you a drink," she said, her voice cross.

Garland dipped his head in thanks, pouring the red wine and drinking half the glass in several gulps. He stared at it, taking deep breaths. "Two years," he breathed. "Two long years since I've had a taste of alcohol."

"Bully for you. Now please, I have to report in at sunset, and after nothing meaningful in months, it would be well-received in Berlin if I were to tell them *today* of your so-called successes."

He drank the remainder of his glass before pouring another one, emptying the bottle, watching the sediment drizzle into the glass. He produced his GI pack of Lucky Strikes, offering one to her. She declined and fidgeted. He used his shiny new Zippo to light his cigarette, motioning to the chair opposite him. "Please, sit. You're making me nervous."

The woman glanced at the clock, as did Garland. It was nearly six in the evening.

"You've got nearly an hour and a half until sundown. Trust me. I know these things. Night is a soldier's best enemy...or sometimes his worst friend."

"That makes no sense."

"Try coming to the battlefield with me sometime. See how much sense it makes."

"Excuse me for a moment."

"Where are you going?" he asked.

"Might I use my own water closet?"

He waved his hand, settling back with his wine and cigarette, feeling very good with warm alcohol in his veins and a busty woman close by.

THE WOMAN walked down the short hallway, entering the bathroom and pushing the door shut. Her shaking hands went straight to the medicine cabinet, opening it and unlatching the false front, spiriting the small bottle, the pencil, and the notepad from the cavity in the wall. Sitting on the toilet, she scrawled a brief message:

Nummer Acht is here! He is situated perfectly for our needs! Give me until 2000 hours and come up. He is all we hoped and more!

Steadying her hands, she breathed on the note to moisten it before folding it and rolling it tightly. She stuffed the note inside the small bottle, capping it. Behind the toilet was an inconspicuous brown pipe emerging from the floor like an old piece of defunct plumbing. It was capped. She bent over, unscrewing the cap and dropping the bottle inside, satisfied as it disappeared followed by a light plunk. The woman recapped the pipe, flushed the toilet and stared at herself in the mirror, pulling wisps of her hair back behind her ears before tugging at her face, smoothing the age lines.

"A little sex, a little talk, perhaps some more sex, and then we take him in." She grinned at her reflection. The man out there wasn't classically handsome, but there was something quite alluring about him…

With a deep breath, she left the water closet.

LIVING ONE floor below her was her partner, also a German posing as a French citizen. At one time he was supposed to be the muscle of the two-person intelligence team. A long-time closet alcoholic, since the Allied invasion, he'd begun to privately numb the pain of his addiction with opium. In fact, he'd taken a large quantity only fifteen minutes earlier. His once-powerful body lay sprawled on his unmade bed as he breathed deeply. Mere feet from him, sitting in the cavity behind his own medicine cabinet, where the pipe terminated, was the note in the bottle. It had rung a small bell upon its arrival but he'd been far too benumbed to register the sound.

He would not read the note for some time.

AFTER BREEZING back into the sitting area, satisfied as Nummer Acht devoured her with his eyes, the woman sat. She stared at him, pulling air in through her small, upturned nose. "How did you manage to make captain?"

"Blood stripes."

"And how have you aided the Reich?"

Garland pulled on the remains of his cigarette, twisting his mouth to blow the smoke to the side. "Where are you from?"

She rolled her eyes. "Mister Eight, please dispense with your questions and answer mine."

He smiled. "Mister Eight...I like it. Well, Madame, if you intend to hear my answers, you will have to humor me somewhat. As you might imagine, the life of a dog soldier is very lonely. All the more lonely when surrounded, day in and day out, by one's adversary."

"What's your new name?"

His smile turned wry. "For now, I think Mister Eight will be fine."

"I certainly won't have a hard time remembering it." She inched forward in her seat. "Your given name is Gerhard."

"Perhaps."

"It is. Gerhard Faber, *aus* Hannover."

"That's unimportant. Back to my question," he said.

There was a long pause before she threw up her hands. "I'm from Rosenheim."

"Ah," he said, dropping the cigarette in the empty wine bottle. "I should've known...a mountain girl."

"Now answer mine."

"My name is of no concern. And regarding your first question, I've aided the Thousand Year Reich by eliminating Allied soldiers of influence, thus far Americans only, doing so at critical times, weakening their leadership as well as their decision-making ability."

She greeted his answer with a lapse of silence. "Who were they?"

"My turn. How long have you lived here?"

One eyebrow went up. She seemed impatient, but Garland could see the faintest flicker of interest in him, in his queries. "Since thirty-eight."

"You're officially a Parisian."

"In some ways, yes," she allowed.

"Are you married?"

"No."

"Ever been?"

A thin smile creased her lips. "Tell me who you've killed, Mister Eight."

Garland sipped from the glass, nestling back into the poorly padded chair, making it squeak in protest. "Do you want the list in chronological order, or by rank?"

"As you wish."

He placed the glass on the coffee table. "The first was a talented sergeant first class from Omaha, Nebraska, ironically on a beach the Allies code-named Omaha. He was doing a fine job instructing those pesky American grunts against our boys." Garland closed his eyes, conjuring the image. "When he moved forward to a dune, I shot him in the back. No one was ever the wiser in all the commotion." He opened his eyes. "It's a damned wonder I made it off that beach."

"Did you come in with the first wave?"

"Tail end of it. Didn't matter, though. The beach was a zoo, lead flying everywhere, bodies clogging the intakes of the landing craft. Hell on earth."

The woman remained silent. Garland recalled several private moments before lifting his eyes to her. "The second one on my list, the very next day, was a major. I didn't know him. He and a few other officers were inspecting the empty German bunkers for intelligence. The bunkers had already been cleared by the engineers, so I pinned a grenade and left it under a stiff German officer. When the major began searching him for intel, the grenade blew him ten feet backward." The memory made him queasy. He stopped talking, his green eyes locked on her brown. She was listening intently.

"What are you thinking?"

"I think I want to hear the rest." She turned, her eyes narrowing as if something struck her. Her eyes came back to him. "The patch you wear is the Hundred and First."

He felt his pulse quicken a tad. "Yes."

"The Hundred and First jumped inland."

"So?"

"You just said you killed that man on the beach."

Garland took the accusation without much emotion. Among other things, liars talk too much. They over explain. They react dramatically. He simply lifted his eyebrows and tilted his mouth.

"Did you hear me?"

"Sure, I did."

"Am I correct?"

"Mostly."

"So how did you happen to land at Normandy?"

"The division didn't land as a whole, but some units did. I had no choice in the matter but would have rather jumped."

Appearing satisfied with his lie, she nodded. "Tell me about the rest."

"In due time. The list is acceptable, but once we move from Paris, it will grow dramatically. I've got a plan to eliminate some of the Americans' most senior officers."

She looked down to the floor.

"What's the matter?" he asked, seeing her expression change.

"You've long since been recalled. When I tell them you're here, they're going to want you back."

"Why?" he asked, struggling not to sound panicked.

"I don't know exactly, but there's much chatter that we're planning a massive counter-offensive now that the Allies are pushing through France. If so, they'll want to know everything you know."

"But why stop me now? I could do more good by telling you what I know, and then resuming my operation."

"I doubt they'll think that having a man in the military, assassinating officers, is going to do much good. Not this late in the game. They'll likely move you into strategic planning and mine your brain for all you know."

He fingered the glass, spinning it. While trying not to appear upset at the news, inside his stomach churned and his mind raced. After all he had done, and all he had accomplished, finally getting promoted to staff sergeant, gaining the favor of his commanders—a recall was simply unacceptable. Each and every day he had risked his life, not only as a saboteur, but against his own countrymen. Did the assholes back in Berlin realize what a delicate balance it was trying to appear successful without actually shooting German soldiers? He looked up, forcing a hopeful expression.

"Perhaps when they hear my full report, *through you*, they will decide to let me stay?"

She was chewing on her fingernail. "I can tell by your face how much you hope that to be true, but I have my doubts. This recall was demanded with an iron fist."

He allowed that to sink in. Time to change tack. Garland tilted his head, drinking in her form. He allowed a smile to creep onto his face as he sipped the wine.

"Are you done telling me about the list?" she asked.

"For the moment." He stood and moved across the room, sitting beside her on the sofa so their legs touched. "You're beautiful."

She turned away, shaking her head, a knowing look on her face. "I've been described as many things, Mister Eight, but never as being beautiful."

Garland placed his left arm around her, pulling her to him. She turned. He kissed her cheek, moving his mouth to her lips. She gently pulled away.

"I can't."

He could hear the yearning in her voice. This woman, hidden away by the Reich, needed love like everyone else. And here, sitting in her flat, was a man of her same age, well-built with a handsome enough face. An expert at reading people, he could see the dilation of her pupils; he could hear her shallow breaths; he could see the palpitations of her pulse on her flushed neck and chest. And he could imagine the rapid dampening in the treasure between her legs.

"Please, go sit back over there," she asked with no conviction whatsoever.

He grasped her right hand, moving it to his rigid prick, held down by the woolen pants leg of his uniform. Garland listened as her shallow breathing became ragged; he could see her neck hitching as she struggled to swallow. She turned back to him, her lips swollen and pouty. "Stop it, please." Her hand remained where it was.

Garland leaned forward again, kissing her gently, at first just on the lips. As she turned her head, he kissed her more passionately down the length of her neck. The woman's hand began to move on his erection. She stopped, pulling back. Her mouth hung open as she panted like an overheated German Shepherd.

"We shouldn't do this. They'll know."

He wiped saliva from his mouth with the back of the captain's sleeve. "Don't tell them you found me."

"I must."

"You don't *have* to."

She leaned closer, obviously wanting him to continue, her voice nothing more than breath. "If they found out that I knew you were here, but didn't report it...they would kill me." Her hand moved quickly, roughly stroking him through his pants.

The woman's eyes were dreamy pools of desire, staring at him as if he were the only male left on the face of the earth. Years before, at university, when a coed's good-girl barrier would abruptly disappear in the span of hours, Garland had heard that she was likely ovulating, craving what only a virile man could provide her. Just like this one, they would get that pouty, doe-eyed look, and their limbs would become sticky, as if trying to entangle the object of their affection like a spider in its web.

He unbuckled his trousers, watching as she hurriedly unzipped his fly and wrenched his pants down. "They circumcised it," she whispered, rubbing him painfully.

"When they worked on my leg," he answered, wincing from the friction.

She dove forward, taking him in her mouth, humming as she went to work. Garland leaned backward, closing his eyes. *If this woman doesn't make her report to Berlin, would they have any way of knowing I was here? How would they? There*

126

are a half-million occupying Allies, and even if there happened to be a second operative watching her visitors, the Germans would find themselves looking for a captain with a screaming eagle on his shoulder. And while Berlin didn't know the exact military unit of Mister Eight, in the event they ever found out, they would realize he's not in the 101ˢᵗ, and therefore not the man seen at their agent's flat. Yes, holding back her report was indeed the way to go. He lifted the woman by her shoulders. Her hand automatically took over where her mouth left off.

"Listen," he said, his face cloudy, "I'm having a tough time concentrating. Are you a hundred-percent certain they'll recall me?"

Her lips were bright red, her lipstick smeared outward onto her pale skin. She nodded. "It's not a bad thing, you know."

"Why?"

She smiled, her great bosom bouncing as she chuckled. "Herr Acht, you will surely be hailed a hero for all you've done."

Garland's mind was moving at great speed. He leaned his head back, easing her back down, allowing her to finish. It didn't take long, and he managed it with only a few sharp grunts. She rose up and smiled awkwardly, holding the back of her hand to her mouth as she disappeared down the short hallway.

He sat there, drained and thinking, staring at the orange and purple September sky as the sun began to set over the dingy Parisian rooftops. Being on the top floor, the tall window in the living room was gabled from the roof, the windows opening inward, the shutters facing out. A pigeon could be heard roosting somewhere just out of sight, cooing distinctively. Such a pretty view, along with a powerful climax, cleared his mind. The woman reappeared, beaming.

"I've just had a thought."

"Oh?" he asked.

"How long are you on furlough?"

"Two more days."

"Do you have to go back tonight?"

"No. I doubt anyone will."

She resumed her place next to him, sidling up close. Like old lovers reunited, she leaned over, licking his neck, nuzzling, whispering. "I'll report that you're here tonight. But I'll tell them you have to go back to your unit to collect some final intelligence. This will buy us a day or two before we send you back to the Reich. And until then, you can love me, over and over. Do with me as you please…I'll try anything." Her hand pressed inside the captain's jacket, tickling at his ribs.

The prospect of the recall had ruined everything. Garland forced a smile, using all his skill not to seem annoyed as he asked, "When do you have to call in?"

"Anytime now. If I wait too long they may send someone."

"Who? You're the contact here in Paris."

"Do you honestly think the Reich would tell me who else is here? But there *are* others, believe me." Her eyes were cast downward as she spoke.

He lifted her chin, kissing her cheek before pulling away, a hopeful look on his face. "I'm so very close to achieving what I have labored so hard to set up. With the trust and influence I have gained, I will be able to kill generals in the coming days. *Generals*. Do you absolutely have to report our contact?"

She listened intently, instantly gnawing a fingernail when the question was out. After a pause she nodded. "I have no choice. If I don't, they will make me wish I was dead…"

"They won't know."

"They will."

"They *won't*," he said sternly.

She rubbed at her neck, her eyes drifting down the hallway, to the water closet. "They were most emphatic with this order. *All* contacts are to be reported in, immediately, without question."

He leveled his gaze. "And nothing I say can sway you?"

"I'm so sorry, Mister Eight, but I cannot go against orders, even as grand as your plans sound."

He nodded solemnly, wondering where her radio was. "Then go ahead and make tonight's report. As you said, I will stay with you until tomorrow."

She clasped her hands together, her face radiant. "It's so nice to have a military man here—a real man in my home." Her expression grew demure. "Though it's not very ladylike, I must say I can hardly wait for more."

He faked a smile. "Me too. I want to feel you under me."

"And you inside me," she said breathily, the way an over-acting stage performer might. She pecked him on the lips, her hand squeezing him one final time. She went into the kitchen, removing pots and pans. He closed his eyes for a long moment, filled with dread, already warring with himself over how to do it. He stood, carrying the ashtray, which contained only the ashes from his cigarettes, dumping it out the window. He stared outside, taking great breaths. Thoughts of his mother, of Carol Lynn. The sounds in the kitchen ceased. He stood aside as the woman swept back into the living room carrying the radio. Mounted on a painted board, it was black, made of metal, covered in wires and tubes and copper helixes. She attached a threaded wire to a hidden piece of wire leading outside of her window. Garland moved to the window, glancing upward, seeing that the antenna was cleverly mounted to the slate roof, leading all the way to the top, extending only a few centimeters like a stubby lightning rod.

The radio hummed after she plugged it to the wall. Just as the woman was about to make her report, he stopped her, grasping her buttocks and kissing the back of her neck. She moaned with delight, kneeling forward and placing the handset of the radio on the coffee table.

"Right here," he commanded, pushing her to the floor.

"Shouldn't I make my report first?"

"Let's do it once before. Just in case they have someone close by." His hand reached under her skirt, making her eyes clamp shut as her mouth fell open. He rubbed several times before quickly removing his hand.

The woman lowered herself to the throw rug as he pulled the shutters to. Garland crossed the floor, watching as she hiked her dress up over her wide hips. He stood above her, staring down before moving astride her, lowering himself down to sit on her stomach. She licked her lips, tugging at him, eager for what was to come.

Garland cracked his knuckles, pondering strangulation. His train of thought was shattered by his conscience:

You can't kill this poor woman. She's no different from your mother or Carol Lynn or the homosexual man. Even if she is aiding the Reich, she's no soldier. Killing sergeants and colonels is one thing…killing citizens, even ones such as this, is another. You're a spy, not a murderer.

But if you leave her alive, you risk getting caught, his mind countered, warring with itself.

As his thoughts raged, he touched her upper chest, allowing his fingers to trace feather-light patterns over the pale, freckled skin. She took his hand, pulling it to her mouth, fellating the fingers. If he were to attempt to kill her, it probably wouldn't be easy. Garland guessed her weight to be at least as much as his own, which was nearly two hundred pounds.

Pounds!

Funny, he'd been acting like an American so long, he was even thinking like an American, using their bungling weights and measures instead of the tidy metric system. Years before, back when he was living with Carol Lynn, his thoughts had gradually transitioned from German to English. Shortly after running from his life in New York, when he had assumed Garland Felton's identity and attended basic infantry training at Fort Knox in Kentucky, his dreams began to occur in English. And long before either of those events, during his psychology training in Potsdam, Garland remembered the perverted old psychologist teaching him, warning him, that dreams were the acid test. "Be careful how much you give in to the American way," the crotchety old relic had warned, crooking his finger, "lest you want to become an American. First comes the dreadful language, then the dreams, then you start enjoying that damned sophomoric, rugby-style game they misguidedly term football." He remembered the old buzzard whacking the lectern with his stick and yelling, "Where your heart and mind lie, so lies your loyalty!"

She reached between his legs, stroking him, opening her legs wider.

Garland knew he should kill her. If she were left alive, regardless of his subterfuge involving the captain's uniform, Berlin would have a tighter bead on his position.

Don't do it! You can still leave here without being caught. How will they find you in this madhouse that is Paris?

Despite his distracted thoughts, her ministrations were effective. He slid forward as the woman guided him in, both of them moaning when he pushed all the way to the hilt. They lay still for just a moment, each of them paralyzed by the pleasure of the moment.

"Love me," she whispered.

Carol Lynn used to say the exact same thing.

He clenched his eyes shut. There was no killing this woman.

Although he desperately wanted to complete their union, Garland pulled away.

"What's the matter?" his contact asked, reaching for him.

"Give me just a minute," he said, faking a smile. He stood, tugging his trousers upward. From the captain's jacket he produced the Ruby pistol, aiming it at her.

The woman was still on the floor, eyeing the handgun with a look of shock. She closed her legs, pushing her dress downward. "Mister Eight," she breathed. "What are you doing?"

"You know what I'm doing, Madame. And by doing it this way, I will prevent your getting in trouble with your superiors."

"If you believe that," she said, scrambling to her feet, "then you're the most naïve man in all of Paris. They will kill me."

Irritation growing, Garland swept his free arm to the window. "Then I suggest, after I take my leave, that you do the same. There's a half-million Allied soldiers out there, all desperate for a lovely woman like you. Certainly you can use your skills to find one that will take you someplace safe." He wagged the pistol to one of the chairs. "Sit right there."

Moving his back to the wall so he could keep his eye on her, he unplugged the radio before grasping the antenna and yanking. It whipped from the roof as he reeled the rubber-coated wire inward. He closed the windows and the shutters, switching on a lamp in the nearly dark room.

"Are you going to kill me?" she asked from the chair.

He stopped what he was doing. "No. I know I probably should for my own self-preservation but…"

"But what?"

"You remind me of someone I once knew. And you don't deserve such a fate." He took the sash from her drapes and used it to gag her.

"Do not move," he warned, stepping back to the radio. After disassembling the components, he used the power cord to tie each of her ankles tightly to the front feet of the chair. With the other sash he bound her wrists in front of her, and with the long antenna cable he secured her torso to the chair. Satisfied her bonds would hold her, Garland prepared to leave. The woman was trying to tell him something.

He walked into her small kitchen, pouring a glass of tap water. He pushed her gag down and held it before her. The woman drank half the water before pulling her head away. As Garland lifted the gag, she asked him to wait.

"What is it, Madame?"

She was on the verge of tears. "Please, Mister Eight, don't do this."

"My doing it is no longer a question."

"They will order you killed upon first sight."

Garland made his smile rueful. "I'm not certain they wouldn't kill me if I went in right now." He moved in front of her and squatted. "And they will never know I was here unless *you* tell them."

Her eyes darted away. It was as if she knew something he didn't.

"Am I wrong?" Garland asked, sensing her trepidation.

She shook her head. "No, Mister Eight, you're not wrong. I have no way of telling them." She eyed the radio. "Are you taking that with you?"

"Of course."

"Then you leave me with two choices. I will either stay and be forced to tell them when they come. Or...I will do as you suggested and disappear."

Garland patted her knee. "No matter how successful my operation turns out to be, because of that fool Hitler choosing to fight dual fronts, I give the Reich only a slim chance of winning this war." He stood. "And to me that means you have no real choice."

A tear ran down her reddened cheek. "Why don't you want to go back? If what you've told me is true, if you're still acting on behalf of the Reich, why are you so adamant not to be taken in?"

He stiffened, cocking his head. It was a very good question, one he wasn't quite ready to fully examine. Knowing nothing else to say, he said, "I don't want to go back until my operation is complete."

He was preparing to slide the gag over her mouth but she stopped him. "As you said, I have no choice in my decision. So would you mind loosening my bonds just a bit?"

"You're going to leave?"

"Yes, I am."

After replacing her gag, Garland made her leg and hand bonds very loose, estimating she'd be free in a half hour at the most. In her bedroom, he rummaged through her things until he found a grip large enough to hold her radio. Wiping each piece carefully, he placed the radio, disassembled, into the grip. As he readied himself to leave, Garland stood before his contact and said, "I'm sorry for involving you in this mess. But my mission is not yet done. Perhaps the Reich thinks I would be better used in their bosom, but I respectfully disagree." He leaned forward. "And, Madame, I desperately wish I could have stayed the night with you."

After finding the woman's key, he pulled the door shut, locking the flat, carrying the grip and the wine bottle. Rue d'Uzes was dark by this time. Garland turned right before ducking into a southbound alley, nestling the wine bottle into a garbage can. Once he'd negotiated the shadows of two more neighborhood streets, he emerged near the Bourse metro stop. Garland pressed his way into the crowded station, teeming with Allied soldiers and civilians, using his captain's rank to push his way into the next train headed for Gare du Nord. After the overcrowded, humid ride, he emerged into Gare du Nord's cavernous platform area, wandering for twenty minutes until he saw what he was looking for. A sign marked *Valises mal Placées*, meaning "displaced luggage". He followed the stone stairs down under the station, seeing five lines ten deep, all containing irritated, yelling passengers who'd become separated from their goods. A cigarette clamped in his mouth, Garland pressed through the back of the throng, moving around to the right. He pushed forward, handing the suitcase to a dark-skinned man shuttling cases to and from a cavernous warehouse.

"The engineer up top told me this goes in here," Garland said, speaking slowly. The man nodded, chucking the case into a mountain of others.

Smiling, Garland Felton walked back upstairs and took the metro back to the stop at Tuileries. With his Ruby pistol hidden in his trousers, he dropped the jacket and hat in a chair across the dance floor from where he'd taken them, donning his own staff sergeant's jacket with the Indianhead 2nd Infantry Division patch. Garland pulled on his garrison cap before turning and sliding the pistol behind his back—to a more comfortable position. He began to walk, heading back in the direction of the Arc de Triomphe, back to where his unit was garrisoned.

He stopped.

"I'm on furlough," he said in English. And it was only ten in the evening. Garland turned and walked back to the bar, taking a seat and ordering a glass of beer. Taking deep breaths, he prepared to ponder his day, casually wondering if his contact would run, as she said she would, or make contact with her superiors. Having been in Paris all this time, and all the while maintaining her loyalty to the Reich, Garland felt she would probably get cold feet about running away. He would bet that she would grudgingly report his contacting her, then claim he overpowered her.

If she did that, he pitied her for the interrogation she would endure.

Just as Hernán Cortés had done in Mexico more than four centuries before, by contacting her, Garland had metaphorically torched his ships. There was no turning back now.

When one beer turned to three, he noticed a buck-toothed French girl batting her fake eyelashes at him. Wrapping up his train of thought, he knew his best course of action (his only course) was to press on with Operation Wolf. If he were to create mounds of good news for the Reich (such as the killing of a few generals,) perhaps they would view his freelancing in a different light.

But the true question, the one he wasn't quite yet ready to face, was what his contact had asked him earlier. Why was he so adamant about not going back?

Was it because he was fearful they would kill him over his actions in the United States?

Or was it because he was revolted by the prospect of resuming his life as a Nazi?

It was a question he would deal with in due time.

Garland downed his third beer in several gulps, ordering another and pointing to the girl with buck teeth. "And one of whatever she's drinking," he told the elderly barkeep.

EIGHT

ABOVE THE Hole, as it was unofficially known to those who worked there, London's traffic and citizenry scurried about, unaware that six feet below them existed a cavernous underground warehouse. A military sweatshop, long and narrow, it was jammed with serried ranks of haggard men and women hunched over poorly-lit work tables, scrutinizing data, reports, death certificates, award certificates, pay forms, and anything else which could be recorded on paper. If any less-than-top-secret document existed in Allied Europe, it eventually filtered through the Hole.

The Hole itself was nothing more than a basement, situated underneath, and extending away from, a centuries-old building used by the Allied Logistical Command. It probably contained more invalids than any hospital in all of England. The soldiers who worked there were missing eyes, arms, legs, feet, hands, fingers, and even a few other (depending on who one might be talking to) nonessential body parts. There wasn't a person there who hadn't had their own personal battle to simply stay in the Army, so the atmosphere—even in the smoky, stuffy, overheated basement—was always lively and full of energy. The men and women who worked in the Hole lived in a tent city squarely next to the River Thames, and the Hole itself was located to the south and east of the center of London, off of Belvedere, near Jubilee Gardens.

A foghorn blast from a passing barge made the shell-shocked members of the Hole jump. Roland Buhl, even while sober, didn't flinch. He was sitting with a first lieutenant, poring over reports from Normandy and the subsequent Third Army engagements throughout northwest France. The lieutenant's name was Simon Jericho. His right arm was missing, blown off at the shoulder. When Roland arrived on the previous day, the officer in charge, a lieutenant colonel, paired Roland with Simon, making all manner of bad jokes about their missing limbs. "Combined together, you two might make a helluva soldier," he'd said. Simon was following behind him, making a masturbating motion as the senior officer spoke. Roland immediately liked Simon.

They'd been at it for hours, in the intel section, neither man knowing what he was reading. Just searching for searching's sake. "Read until something jumps out at you," the colonel had instructed them." When Roland had asked what that might be, the colonel had answered, "Boy…how the hell would I know that? That's why I'm telling you to read the reports."

So that's what they did, smoking and reading and chatting. Making notes here and there. Dog-earing papers, creating their own little system. Most everything they found seemed highly irrelevant, but at least it would show they'd made an effort.

"You know, I met Patton once," Simon said as he used his one arm to retrieve a sheaf of papers from the bin behind them.

"Yeah?" Roland asked, still feeling the want of alcohol, but doggedly pressing through his tenth day of sobriety. He grabbed the top piece of ledger paper, transcribing an insignificant morsel of information, looking for inconsistencies in the poorly written battle report.

"They brought him in after we landed, when we were pinned down in all those mazes of hedgerows. When he took over, he pushed the Nazis straight back, led those guys outta there."

"Those guys?" Roland poked his pencil into the paper, holding his place. "You weren't with them? Is that because you lost the…" he pointed, "…you know, the arm?"

Simon nodded, a grin forming. "Don't worry, pal, I already made peace with it. To be honest, it took me a few months, but I finally decided, like being dealt a pair of deuces in the big game, it's all about how you play the hand." He shrugged. "You can be pissed about it, fold right then. Or you can stay in the game a bit, let people worry about what you might be holding."

"So you're staying in the game?"

"I'm here, ain't I?"

Roland leaned back, studying Simon as he went to work on his own stack of papers. He was a few inches shorter than average, with stringy black hair and a skeleton-skinny face. His nose was rather large, with a hump at the bridge, his eyes smudged dark underneath from a lack of sleep. Roland had never heard an accent like his, Maine, and decided within a few hours that a "Mainer" accent was the most unique in all the United States. When angered or excited, Simon had a tendency to throw his father's Yiddish in as well. It was quite unique.

"Simon."

The lieutenant lifted his head, his brown eyes narrowing as cigarette smoke shrouded him. "Yeah?"

"You didn't finish the Patton story."

"Oh yeah....sorry. So I'm in the field hospital, right? It was set up back at the beach, back where we had first landed. So all hell breaks loose in that medical tent, right? I'm laying there in my bed, in jo-jeezly pain, watching this tube comin' outta my shoulder dripping blood and some kinda greenish fluid, when all of a sudden I see more brass than you might see layin' next to a spent Howitzer, and then I look up and see *him*...standin' right there in fronta me."

Roland lowered his pencil. "Patton."

"Damn skippy, Patton. Hands on his hips, grippin' one of those short horse-whip things like he's ready to pop off at any moment."

"What'd you say?"

"Nothing at first. My mind was working faster than my mouth could react."

"And you were no doubt thinking about that deal that happened in Italy, when he slapped the shit out of some Sad Sack in a medical tent."

Simon lit a cigarette and tossed the pack across the table. "Damn right, I was. So I'm looking at him, and he just looks like any old man, and I do mean *old*. His face has got age spots and lines all over it, and he's not as big as I thought he woulda been, and he's just standin' there, starin' at me."

Roland was transfixed. "So he just stood there?"

"Just starin' at me. Not sayin' a word either."

"Then what, who broke the silence?"

"I finally got my mouth moving and told him I'd gladly salute, but my right arm was somewheres back at the front line, in a hedgerow somewhere."

Roland laughed, motioning for him to continue.

"So that old buzzard chuckled at my attempt at humor. He tells his entourage to scram and sits down on the corner of my bed, and we talk about Maine a bit, and hunting, and then he catches me staring at him…studying him, you know?"

Roland had pulled a cigarette from the pack, holding it, unlit. He was frozen by the story. "Then what?"

"Old Patton asks me why I'm starin' at him like that." Simon pulled on his cigarette, his eyes staring up at the damp ceiling, recalling the story. "Now you gotta remember, they got me hopped up on morphine so I'm kinda loopy."

"He asked why you were staring at him…"

"Yeah! So I looks up into those baby blue eyes o'his and I tells him, 'Sir, no offense, but if you slap me like you did that putz in Italy, I'm pretty sure that even with the one arm I can whip your old ass.'"

Roland's palms slapped the table as his face registered appropriate shock. "My ass you said that!"

"Sure as shit! I can barely remember it, but it was all my bunkmates could talk about for weeks."

"What did he do?"

"He loved it! Slapped me on the knee…not the face…and laughed so hard I thought he might fart." Simon's expression changed, his smile faded. He allowed the silence to come back, finally saying, "Patton looked at me after that and asked me if I wanted to stay in the Army."

"What'd you say?"

"The hell you think? I said yes and he asked the doc for my orders. Changed them right there on the spot. It's why I'm here today."

Roland leaned back, finding the cigarette that had tumbled to the ground and lighting it. The two men allowed their own silence to mingle with the din of the Hole. Finally Roland spoke. "You happy here, Simon?"

"I guess."

"Seriously. Are you happy?"

"Happy? No, but I'm glad I'm not back home. Be kinda tough loggin' with just one arm. After goin' years with hardly a bite to eat, I'm just glad not to be a burden on my old man."

Roland nodded thoughtfully. "I'm in a similar boat. The hell am I gonna do with a peg leg?" He stared hard at Simon for a full minute, making the thin man turn away several times.

"You okay?" Simon finally asked, tilting his head and appearing puzzled.

"Just measuring you."

"Measuring me for what?"

"My plan."

"Yeah, what's that?"

"Before I tell you, I want to know if you're in with me."

"I don't know the plan yet."

"In or not."

Simon shrugged. "Unless it involves you and me sharing your fart-sack and whispering in each other's ear, I guess I'm in."

Roland chuckled. "It's a plan involving our pitiful little careers."

"What've I got to lose? I'm already in the Hole. Tell me."

After a pull on the cigarette, Roland leaned forward. His voice lowered. "Somehow, someway, me and you need to come up with something so worthwhile, so meaningful, so utterly earth-shattering that it'll cement our future in the military long after this war is over."

Simon leaned forward, crushing out his own cigarette. He appeared nonplussed.

"You get me?" Roland asked.

"Not really."

"With all that's happened over there on the continent, you would think, somewhere in this building of paper, that there is a colossal story to piece together."

"I'm not following."

"We just have to use our minds to put the pieces of the puzzle together."

Simon laughed. "Who're you, Philip Marlowe?"

"Seriously. Don't you think, somewhere in all this data, that there's something critical the brass has missed?"

He blinked several times, finally nodding. "Well, you would think."

"It's up to us to find it. They've already got us in intel, so we've got access to everything."

"What do we look for?"

Roland touched the stack of papers before motioning to the mountains of boxes behind him. "If you and I work hard...really bust our collective asses, rack our brains, challenge each other...I believe we'll find it, whatever *it* is. But when we do, we need to keep *it* to ourselves, and use *it* as our own personal stack of chips to get ourselves back in the game."

Simon's brow lowered. "Again, cap'n, I'm afraid I don't follow."

Roland nodded as if this were the expected response. "Somewhere in this room, Lieutenant Jericho...somewhere in this mountain of paper is a story. I don't know what it is yet, in fact, I've got no inkling as to which direction to even take. But if we can find the right kind of evidence, maybe of poor leadership, or of a pattern of some sort, or maybe a crime that's taken place...we can use that as our leverage to snag a promotion, to make a career in the military so we can both get full- retirement and not just cripple-pay...and maybe to even get back to the front line."

Simon's left arm crossed his body, massaging the lump where his right arm would be. He grimaced before his thin face twisted into a smile. "You know what, sir? I think you're crazy."

Roland dragged on the cigarette before speaking. "Of course I'm crazy, lieutenant. Jo-jeezly crazy."

LATER THAT night, just after midnight, Roland lay alone in the officers' tent, his arm crooked back under his head, a heavily-ashed cigarette dangling from his lips. A solitary yellow bulb hung from an extension cord behind his head, illuminating his forty square feet of personal space as he viewed a picture book about Germany. The pictures had all been taken in the 30's, before the war, each of them probably scrutinized by Hitler's maniacal propaganda people, showing only cherubic children, beautiful, baby-bearing women, and handsome, Nordic men, none of them a hair less than six feet in height. In nearly every photo, somewhere conspicuous, was the Nazi flag or a handsome soldier in uniform, and in every description it seemed careful attention had been paid to portray their "Thousand Year Reich" in the best light.

Roland dreamed about Germany. Not every night, and the dreams had become less frequent, but they still pressed into his mind like a tidal wave, flooding the recesses of his brain with the gruesome memories of his forty-eight hour trip behind the lines. In the dream he didn't always saw off his leg. Sometimes he managed to save it, and the woman he had killed—Frau Bradenhauer—helped to patch him up, caring for him, mopping his feverish head with a lemony smelling washcloth. But then, without warning, he would kill her anyway. The husband wasn't always in the dream, but every single time he'd had the dream, in some gruesome fashion, Roland would always murder Frau Bradenhauer in the coldest of blood. Often times she would raise up afterward, and displaying the hurt of a mother betrayed by her own son, she would ask why he had killed her. And that would bring the end of the dream. Always. Roland had never had a chance to tell her, even in his dreams, that he was only doing his job. That had her nosy husband not gone traipsing off through the rapse field to find his parachute and pack, he could have bid his farewell without anyone ever being the wiser.

Yes, he felt a tremendous amount of guilt over what he had done. When he pondered the guilt in quiet moments such as this, Roland was able to validate his actions through the soldier's ever-present shroud of duty. Had he not taken action, he would almost certainly be dead. No matter what he might have told the Gestapo who would have come for him—even given the fact he had been able to speak fluent German—once they discovered his pack and parachute, they would have unmercifully interrogated him before allowing him to succumb to his injuries. But because of Roland's deadly decision that day, he was whisked back to Frankfurt, patched up, and taken out of the country through a network of friendlies, at one point even traveling by cargo train in a specially constructed coffin.

He lifted up on one elbow, taking a final pull off the nub of a cigarette before crushing it out. He unscrewed the cap of his canteen, taking a swig of the brackish London water. Roland dropped back to the cot, pressing his head back into the homemade pillow, placing the open book over his stomach. He was happy to finally be in England, but knew his good cheer wouldn't last for more than a week or two. There was talk of a major push through western France, a German-style blitz through the thick forests that would lead the Allies into Germany. A push back to where he'd had the accident. Roland wanted to be a part of this battle. He wanted to go back to Germany. Because this time, if given the chance, he would get it right.

He used a rag to unscrew his hot light bulb and feigned sleep when Simon stumbled into the tent, mumbling on and on about some loose WACs who had just arrived for a two-week stay. Roland squeezed his eyes shut, struggling with the bizarre phantom pain of his foot that was no longer there. As Simon immediately (and thankfully) slipped into his alcohol-induced coma, Roland prayed silently, praying for a return to Germany, and praying that someday his recurring nightmare would cease forever.

THE FEMALE Parisian agent's given name was Christina Döller. True to her word, she was from Rosenheim, in southern Germany. Once dead, her body had been loaded into a plain panel van and driven to a crematorium where it was burned until all that remained was less than a pound of ash and marble-sized chunks of stubborn bone. While her family had not spoken with her in years, they would receive no notice of death from the German government. Except for the few people who knew what happened, like so many others during wartime, she simply ceased to exist.

Her interrogation had taken two hours. Cigarette burns were used at first. When she insisted, between her shrieks, that she was telling the truth, they made certain by pulling several of her teeth with a pair of pliers. Still, through her tears and cries of pain, Agent Döller maintained she had told them everything. At the end of the second hour, in a show of skewed benevolence, she was given a cyanide capsule with a glass of water. Her coma occurred six minutes later—death, two minutes after that.

Döller's partner, despite his dope addiction, was still alive. His name was Klaus Langen, chosen to be her backup due to his French language proficiency and circus strongman's body. He sat at a weathered table, a gently swaying light bulb above his head. His hands were below the table, clamped to his quivering legs. His shakes didn't go without notice to the three men who had questioned him for the last hour.

The room was in the basement of an abandoned building owned by a sympathizer. The walls were slick with dampness as water from the rain-soaked earth seeped through, puddling in the low corner of the subterranean room. The man behind Langen was a semi-intelligent thug recruited from the ranks of the SS. The interrogators were two men from intelligence. The first was Josef Penner: a thin, bookish type in a dark suit. The other was Gerhard (currently Garland) Faber's former commander, the recently promoted Brigadier General (*Generalmajor* in German) Emil von Marburg—the man who signed off on Gerhard's killing his mother as a show of loyalty. Both men wore civilian clothes, their presence in Allied occupied Paris a closely guarded secret.

Von Marburg leaned on the table, supporting himself by his knuckles. "And you are one hundred percent certain you never saw Nummer Acht, Gerhard Faber?"

Langen's shirt had been ripped open and, as he shook his head, the flabby skin of his once powerful chest undulated and rippled like that of a Shar-Pei. "No, sir. We never had contact with him...not a single time before his alleged visit."

"Never before? Never saw anyone who could have been him casing the building, waiting for you to leave?"

Langen's bloodshot eyes whipped upward. "If I had, I *never* would have left her."

"But when he decided to show himself...assuming the note is genuine...you say you were at the market?"

He lifted the glass of water with a trembling hand, drooling some of it as he gulped. He paused a moment. "I'm sorry...I'm very nervous."

Penner stood in the shadow of the corner. In his hand was a file, the pages open about halfway. He tapped the paper. "It says here you've always been unflappable, even in survival training. Why are you so jumpy now, Agent Langen? Hell, you're shaking all over."

It almost seemed as if two people were too much for Klaus Langen to deal with. His head jerked back and forth between Penner and Von Marburg. Several times his mouth twisted, as if tears were hovering just below the surface. He screwed his eyes shut, audibly grinding his teeth.

Von Marburg spoke loudly. "Klaus Langen, do you think the note is genuine? Our man says it's her handwriting, but it could have been forged by the Allies in the event they managed to flip Nummer Acht and send in their own man."

Langen quaked in his seat, eyes still clamped shut. He didn't answer.

"Agent Langen!"

His eyelids sprung open, red-tinged eyes bulging from their sockets. "S-s-sir?"

Von Marburg turned to face his associate in the shadow. He looked behind Langen at the third man, standing several feet behind the failed security agent. His eyes drifted back to Langen. Von Marburg's voice was a whisper. "Pull up your sleeves. Show me your arms."

Langen sucked in a great quantity of air. He just sat there, taking deep breaths, his head shaking back and forth, staring into some faraway place. Light sobs could be heard from deep in his belly.

The general pinched his lips together, stepping back and leaning against the wet wall. He looked to his left, looked across the room. "Do it."

Both men lurched into action. The one behind Agent Langen levered his arm around his neck in a chokehold, squeezing tightly enough to control him. Penner grasped Langen's right arm, muscling it to the table and yanking his sleeve upward. Hundreds of reddish dots and small scabs marked the pathways of Langen's veins like a roadmap.

"Damn it!" Von Marburg yelled.

The men released him as Langen began to moan and mumble his apologies. He went on and on about the years of undercover isolation and something about pain from losing his sister years before. Penner stepped to Von Marburg, whispering in his ear.

"Sir, I dealt with this same thing in Spain. We'll need to clean him up properly, in a hospital. It could take weeks but his information could still prove to be—"

"No," the general said in a steely tone, cutting him off. "I will not deal with an addict…the weakness…the whimpering." Von Marburg then made a dismissive gesture, saying, "And it's obvious to me, drugs or not, this dolt doesn't know a damned thing about anything."

Langen's tremors stopped. He looked at Von Marburg before turning to Penner, his face matching his pleading. "No. Wait. I can be of value. I can help you find Nummer Acht!"

"That time has passed," Von Marburg said icily. He looked to the man standing behind Langen. He closed his eyes and nodded.

The man donned a pair of work gloves and squatted to the floor, lifting a coiled section of rubber-coated wire. He wrapped the wire around his hands as Langen turned to look at him. The former SS soldier lurched forward, snapping the wire around Langen's neck and clamping down with a loud grunt. Langen, though firmly in his addiction's grasp, still had a survival instinct. He tried to stand as the chair clattered backward to the wall. The two men went to the floor as the wire constricted around Langen's neck, making him gurgle and flop around like a fish on a hot wooden dock while the burly SS man hung on, laughing maniacally, challenging the dying man to struggle harder. A grinding, popping sound indicated something—probably Langen's trachea—had crushed like a glass bottle.

Von Marburg and Penner watched the scene playing out before them. Penner shook out two American Lucky Strikes, handing one to the general and lighting them both. By the time they were both puffing, the struggle was ending, as only occasional twitches came from the wasted body of Security Agent Klaus Langen.

As the SS man came to a sitting position, taking enormous breaths, Von Marburg curled his upper lip and massaged his eyes. "Mein Gott," he whispered.

"Quite amazing to see how even a fruitless addict can struggle," Penner said academically. He puffed thoughtfully, nudging Langen's body with his loafer before turning to the general. "Do you think it was truly Faber who visited Agent Döller? Or do you think the Americans are onto us and sent a fake?"

The general puffed his cigarette, having turned away, staring at the brick wall. He reached into his suit pocket, removing the note. He held it in the light:

> *Nummer Acht is here! He is situated perfectly for our needs! Give me until 2000 hours and come up. He is all we hoped and more!*

Von Marburg thought back to the first time he met Nummer Acht—Gerhard Faber—in Potsdam. Unremarkable in appearance, the man willingly killed his mother without any more compunction than one might show when ridding himself of an annoying insect. He remembered the story Faber told him about his brother, killing his other brother over a measly portion of food. Unless he was an actor of the finest caliber, Faber's coldness—combined with the grisly killing he'd just witnessed—shook the general to his core.

"Sir?"

"Yes, I *do* think it was Nummer Acht."

"But why would he have left her alive?"

Von Marburg hitched his head. "He's obviously not yet ready to come in, just as she said."

The SS man, having recovered his wind, stood. He removed the gloves and rubbed his reddened hands. "Leave us now," Penner commanded. The man exited, leaving his superiors with the oozing sounds and rancid smells emanating from the warm corpse of Security Agent Klaus Langen.

Von Marburg placed the note on the table, smoothing it. "Nummer Acht is out there somewhere," he said, touching the yellowish paper and making sure his tone was one of assurance. "If, as this note says, he's situated perfectly, we still need him. The Rhein Offensive is on the board and his knowledge could be the difference between success and failure." Von Marburg dropped the half-smoked cigarette to the damp floor, grinding it underneath his polished shoe.

"Should I put on a full effort to locate him?"

A sober nod. "Absolutely. Get all of our assets on it." Von Marburg grasped the man's sleeve. "And Josef…"

"Yes, sir?"

"Find him, Josef. Find him, and find him soon. Because if you don't," he nudged Agent Klaus Langen with his Brogue shoe, "we'll wind up just like him."

FOR THREE days Staff Sergeant Garland Felton bided his time. His traitorous thoughts weighed heavily on him, and he needed a way to expiate his actions. To free his mind. To move forward. To be a German once again.

The skirmish they'd gotten into the day after decamping Paris had turned out to be brutal. What had looked like a simple German patrol wound up being a battalion-strength column, hidden amongst the cozy cottages and hay bales of postcard-worthy western France. Garland had been riding in an M-3 half-track when the shooting began. The yells of "Incoming!" were exceeded only by the screams of those who were mortally wounded by the vicious first volley. The soldiers of the 23rd Infantry Regiment, 2nd Infantry Division had boiled out of the vehicles like angered ants, pressing forward against the Hun. For an hour, German bullets whizzing by his head like hornets, Garland thought his time had finally come. He wondered, were he to die, his corpse strewn among the serried rows of bodies, if anyone would ever learn his secret. Probably not, he decided. They would bag his body with the rest of them and continue forward. Some Kentucky coal miner would get a death notice of his infant son who had died nearly thirty years ago. But much more important would be the $250 life insurance check the man would be holding. It was highly unlikely that he would scream, "There's a mistake, he couldn't have been the real Garland Felton!"

Those fruitless thoughts ceased when the shooting intensified. This was, by far, the worst firefight he'd been in since Normandy. Garland realized, Germans or not, he was going to have to kill or be killed. A bullet struck the mound in front of him, sending dirt spraying into his eyes. He leaned his back against the ditch, wiping his eyes and looking to his left. A private he'd only first seen in Paris—a replacement—had skittered next to him. They were hemmed in, stuck in a half-full drainage ditch, their boots and asses submerged in murky pasture water. One German crew with a towed machine gun was keeping them pinned down from the left, and from their two o'clock, a Panzer was firing in the opposite direction with its main gun while one of the crew members was working on Garland and his new battle mate with the top-mounted machine gun. Mercifully, the towed machine gun and its crew were taken out by what Garland correctly guessed to be an American mortar. Garland watched as the two-man gun crew flew lifelessly through the air, arms and legs splayed like DaVinci's Vitruvian man.

"Bastards," Garland growled through clenched teeth, his venom directed at the Germans as well as the unseen mortar crew who might have just saved his life.

A fresh round of bullets spewed overhead, causing both men to momentarily submerge in the manure-imbued water. When they came up, Garland gestured to the east, screaming at the private to move. Staying out of vision, they repositioned themselves as the Panzer turned its full attention—and its 75 millimeter gun—to their former position. Garland knew, even burrowed several feet under the lip of the Frankish ditch, that once the tank unleashed its round remotely close to their location, he and the private would be killed by the high-explosive round's devastating impact. He grabbed the soldier by his combat suspenders, screaming inches from his face.

"Get out of the ditch and run that way," he said, pointing again to the east. "Count five and dive back in the ditch and don't be a second late!"

The soldier, who would have made a fine German due to his immediate and unflinching adherence to orders, did exactly as he was told. He jumped from the ditch and sprinted, arms flailing in a mad dash, covering forty yards in his life-or-death five second sprint. His action had the prescribed effect on the Panzer crew. Garland peeked up enough to see a crew member inside hurriedly rotate the hull-mounted Mauser machine gun, lighting up the ground as he tried to track down the fleeing American. Like Superman at the American matinees, the private leapt with both hands out, somersaulting back into the ditch.

Without hesitating—knowing this was a survival moment—Garland lifted his M1 and deposited two rounds squarely in the tank commander's chest, sending him flailing backward. The gunner, who must have had a good line of sight from his hatch, whirled the main gun back around in Garland's direction. Knowing he had but a second to act, Garland scrambled to his right, keeping himself down in the filthy water, invisible to the crew of the tank.

The Panzer unleashed a round where he had just been.

Even from fifteen feet, the impact of the high-explosive projectile lifted Garland from the ditch. While the explosion still thundered in his ears, he felt a burning in his left calf. Ignoring it, he yelled for the private to run. Garland jerked a grenade from his pistol belt, snatching out the pin as he sprinted to the back of the tank, outrunning the turret rotating as fast as it could. Either the driver or the gunner recognized Garland's flanking maneuver, because almost immediately Garland saw the man pop up to try and commandeer the more agile, top-mounted 7.92 millimeter machine gun. Knowing the Panzer full well, he placed the grenade atop the rear sprocket of the tank, making sure the spoon unseated itself. Garland rushed around the tank, just gaining cover from the tank's hull when the grenade went off. He glanced around the rear, satisfied when he saw the track unrolling from the rollers. The tank was now crippled.

The soldier in the cupola saw Garland when he popped up, whirling the machine gun around for another go. Garland yanked his remaining grenade, pulling the pin and skittering around the tank below the tanker's line of sight. He reached the other side, watching as the German frantically scanned the opposite direction for him. Garland leapt onto the back of the steel gray war machine, releasing the spoon and tossing the grenade in next to the tanker, who he shot with his M-1. The German crewman, even while shot in the back, was able to scramble off the tank before the grenade exploded inside, killing whatever occupants remained. Garland, who had leapt from the tank a second before the escaping crewman, had his M1 at the ready. As soon as the crewman began to stand, holding his hand over his right chest where Garland's first bullet had exited, Garland shot him in the heart, dropping him instantly.

The tank's crew was vanquished. The engine had ceased running. It sat quietly, blue smoke drifting from the hatch.

Garland drew several great breaths before sidling next to the hot tank, staring upward and waiting for any residual explosions. There were none. The grenade must not have created enough of an explosion to have any effect on the tank's rounds. He looked all around him. Across the ditch, the majority of his unit was working in unison with an armored unit, pressing forward toward the town of Morlaix. Above his head, sounding like a bed sheet being ripped in two, mortars and heavy artillery sped unseen through the sky, their explosions in the small town visible many seconds before the sound wave arrived. The Germans were retreating, and the Panzer Garland stood beside was one of many smoldering behind the forward-moving line. Bodies lay scattered through the freshly cut field, most of them German. Some squirmed about like an earthworm cut in half by a shovel. Medics moved amongst the Americans, providing what treatment they could. Garland could see a chaplain gripping a man's hand, praying over him as his life slipped away.

He hoisted himself up onto the searing deck at the tank's rear, inventorying the strapped-on equipment. Seeing nothing he could use, Garland glanced around before he lowered himself into the tank's belly, waving his hand to clear the acrid smoke, wincing when he saw what remained of the grenade riddled bodies. The sight of bloody death was worse than if someone had thrown a stick of dynamite into a butcher's cooler.

Garland vomited two times before he was able to bolster himself enough to search the blood-coated tank.

It had been years since he had familiarized himself with the inside of a German Panzer. After opening two hatches, he found the tank's rounds, fed by a gravity hopper, next to the gunner's space. As the swirling wind cleared away more smoke, Garland worked a heavy hasp, opening a compartment next to the track commander's platform. Inside, he found extra small arms rounds and exactly what he was hoping to find: two S-mines, known colloquially by the Americans as the vaunted "bouncing betty". The mines were in their familiar olive musette bags with a shoulder strap. Each mine, including the fuze, was slightly smaller than an American football.

The bouncing betty was probably the most feared of all small German battlefield weapons, mainly due to its maiming nature. Most conventional mines, when triggered, explode and kill anyone within a certain radius. The S-mine, however, leapt into the air before detonating. The explosive core was surrounded, typically, by steel balls. Other variations, depending on place and time of manufacture, used steel rods or even shards of rusty scrap metal. Not only was it destructive, but because of its ingeniously malicious design, it had morphed into an effective psychological weapon. The bouncing betty wounded more soldiers than it killed. Oftentimes the mine would bounce to a height of three feet, ripping Allied soldiers to shreds at genital level. As one old master sergeant told Garland shortly after landing at Normandy, "You see one pop up, you better hit the deck and hope she misses you altogether or kills you. Ain't no good in-between with a bouncin' betty."

He took one of the mines, slinging it over his shoulder. Reaching up, Garland un-holstered the Luger from the track commander's belt, dropping the beautiful pistol into his cargo pocket. He exited the tank and began to hurry forward, catching up to the advance. Halfway back to the front line, Garland located a dead German medic. He stopped, lying prone next to the medic's body. Garland dumped half of the implements from the medical bag before shoving in the bouncing betty, concealing his deadly find underneath the plethora of medical supplies. By the time he reached the town of Morlaix, the Americans had just dispatched a rooftop sniper and the Germans were in full retreat.

The different units of the 23rd Infantry Regiment were relieved by their compatriots from the 9th. Garland's company mustered on the western edge of town, the weary men propping their feet up, lamenting the dead, telling of their individual exploits and, of course, comparing injuries. Using his Ka-Bar, Garland dug the nickel-size piece of shrapnel from his left calf. After holding his knife in a nearby flame for a full minute, he cauterized the gash, biting down on a bandage from the medic's bag. Two of his buddies, both sergeants, watched him in fascination.

"You oughta use that injury to get a few more days back in the rear," one of them said.

Garland winked at him afterward, offering a wry smile and lifting the medic's bag. "Nah. Took this off some dead kraut back there by the ditch. I'm like a walking hospital now."

The other sergeant, wincing from a flash burn on his arm, asked if there was any morphine in the bag. He made a move for it. Garland yanked it away.

"Damn, Felton," protested the injured NCO. "What the hell?"

Garland turned his eyes away. "Just don't want you turning into a hop-head…seen it too many times before." Moving the bag to his far side, so they couldn't see inside, he searched and found the pocket full of morphine stick-vials, tossing only one to the sergeant. "Let me know if you need more."

As the sergeant jammed his thigh and found temporary nirvana, and the other sergeant smoked while rereading a tattered letter from home, Garland tilted his helmet forward over his eyes, his right arm resting on the German bag. He was comforted by the feel of the bag, but far more by what lay hidden in its center: his very own bouncing betty.

THE TWO bodies moved together at a frenzied tempo. The German agent's hands held the woman's shoulders in a death grip. Her legs were locked behind his back. They were in an old hotel in a standard chamber, the sheets and coverlet on the wooden floor beside the bed. High above the street, their window was open, the filmy curtain swaying inward with the night breeze.

The man was on top of her, sweating, grunting with each thrust as if he were in an athletic competition. She gouged his back with her lacquered nails, clenching her teeth, her eyes shut as she unsuccessfully tried to find her own release. His grunts became louder. Faster. He finished and collapsed in a heap on top of her, much to the woman's frustration.

The German agent rolled off and sat on the side of the bed, drinking from a bottle of cheap wine. "That was nice...damned nice. Thank you."

She pressed her head back into the pillow, a hand on her forehead. Her eyes were closed.

"What do you have for me?"

She snorted. "Romantic, aren't you?"

He grabbed his pants, laying them beside him. "You suggested this, not me."

She sat up, placing a hand on his shoulder. "As I said earlier, it's imperative we find Nummer Acht, given name Gerhard Faber, probably using an alias beginning with the same initials."

"You have no idea of his name now?"

"Just the initials, and that's only a maybe."

"That doesn't help me."

She stood, brazenly posing in front of him, unashamed of her nakedness. She removed an envelope from the inner hem of the jacket she had been wearing and handed it to him. "Inside the envelope you'll find the intel regarding his supposed location as well as his background. There's a service picture in there too, the last one we have of him."

"Why the sudden rush to find this guy?"

"Two reasons...first, because of his placement in the invasion force, and our embarrassing lack of intel on their tactics and intentions, he can aid us greatly in the planning of a coming operation, perhaps the most important of the war. If we don't succeed..." she said, her voice trailing off.

The male field operative finished the wine, tossing the bottle into the metal pail with a loud clunk. "And the second?"

"Through several stateside channels, we've already learned the Americans are scouring their military for German spies. Several of the men who came through the same program as Faber have disappeared...Berlin thinks they may have been found and eliminated." She took a step closer. "It's only a matter of time before someone in their Army becomes suspicious of Gerhard Faber...or whatever name he goes by now. They *must not* find him." She stepped even closer, her mound inches from his face. "But *we* must."

"Is there a chance that the man who showed himself in Paris is actually an American?"

"There's always a chance, but leadership thinks it was actually the genuine Nummer Acht. He killed both of our Parisian agents."

"They think he's gone rogue?"

"Yes."

The man placed the envelope on the table and touched her in a particularly sensitive spot. Her breath hitched and her knees nearly buckled. "I need to get back, but perhaps I have time to enjoy you once more."

She stepped back, pushing his hand away. "You *must* find him before the Americans do. I cannot put enough emphasis on this."

"I got the message." He grasped her, pulling her to the bed. The woman twisted, pressing him downward.

"I'm on top this time."

Their second effort was longer, and better.

NINE

IT DIDN'T take very long before Garland found an opportunity to use his bouncing betty. On a rainy morning, with a cold storm pressing in from the Atlantic, he scurried around outside of Bravo Company's command tent, organizing the next guard force. Although they were well behind the forward line, guard—known to the soldiers as "O.P.", a dreaded Army acronym for Observation Post—was still quite important. Not a week went by without another story about a German soldier, overlooked somehow, behind the lines, shooting Americans in the back. Garland directed the privates here and there, checking out the phone in each hole, confirming that their firing stakes were set properly, making sure the soldiers had food. Just as he was finishing at the last observation post, several Jeeps arrived on the soggy trail from regiment.

The second Jeep contained a VIP, denoted by the new canvas roof that none of the normal Jeeps had. Garland stared from a distance as it splashed to a stop. Soldiers scurried from the Jeeps and the command tent. Garland moved closer. Even through the heavy rain he saw the single shoulder star of Brigadier General Kagan as he exited his Jeep. A short man with a heavily-lined, sun-battered face, the general took his time before heading into the tent, ignoring the driving rain, slapping soldiers on the back, telling them to keep up the good work. His trademark (all generals try to develop one) was the candy he kept in his pocket. Garland thought it made him come off like a perverted old uncle, but nodded his thanks as the general stopped in front of him, pressing a red cinnamon disc in his hand.

"Where you from, son?"

"Kentucky, sir."

"Kentucky, huh? Been there more times than I can count. The gateway to the south…and great turkey hunting." He cocked his head. "Where in Kentucky?"

Garland paused for a fraction of a second. "Flemingsburg, sir."

"Never been there."

Major Rezeldnik, from regiment, stepped forward, grasping Garland's shoulder. "Sir, this is one of our finest young NCOs. Just a few days ago, when we were on rotation, Sergeant Felton took out an entire Panzer on his own, from foot. He took fire from its main gun before charging the tank. Killed the track commander, an officer, and then dropped a grenade inside. One tanker made it out, and Felton shot him on the spot."

The general had hands on his hips, water cascading off of his helmet. He rotated back to Garland, a smile creasing his face. "God, how I love hearing stories like that." His face beamed as he drank Garland's image in, looking him up and down. "Congratulations, son…you're a real-life American hero."

For killing Germans…

Garland shrugged. "I don't feel like it, sir. Just doing my job."

"What you did saved American lives. You prevented plenty of American mamas back home from getting a dreaded telegram."

And caused undeserving German mamas to receive one of their own…

"Thank you, sir," Garland mumbled, eyes downward.

The general looked around at his entourage, nodding to them as he spoke. "I'll see that you're put in for an award." A toadying major, who was almost touching the general he was so close, scribbled a note despite the rain.

"Again, sir, thank you," Garland breathed.

"And depending how your command writes their portion up, a medal such as this one could be a biggie. Just need to make sure we can get enough accounts of what happened."

Garland said nothing.

"What do you think about that, sergeant?" Kagan asked, raising his head as he tried to make eye contact through the rain.

Garland didn't smile, just nodded.

Brigadier General Kagan crossed his arms. "Killing a man, especially up close, is tough business." He inched closer, lowering his voice. "I can sense your pain, son, and that's okay. War is hell."

Garland stared.

"But remember this," he glanced around, "those were piece of shit, baby-killing krauts. All you did was rid the world of a few more rats. Trust me, son, I've seen the intel…those people are savages. I wouldn't shed a tear if they were all vaporized tomorrow."

Garland's mouth was dry. He breathed through his nose, eyes locked on the general, his mind reversing itself to that morning in Potsdam, listening to two officers demanding that he kill his mother. *This one was no different, other than his uniform. You put a shiny little accoutrement on a man's shoulder and all of a sudden he thinks he's God?* Still unable to speak, Garland held the stare, his cheek twitching.

"Well, again, thank you for your service, son. A few more fire-pissers like you and this war'll be over by Thanksgiving." The general shook Garland's hand. Garland squeezed very hard.

The brass, all of them, disappeared into the tent. Garland listened to the sounds escaping, hearing the general offering up all of the same greetings, fake little bastard that he was. His head jerked to the right, to the path the Jeeps had arrived from.

Yes…

He made sure each of the guard posts were situated, knowing his personal mission would take at least an hour. Went back to his base vehicle, slung the medic bag over his shoulder. Found the hidden Luger, twisted it a few times, scrutinizing. No markings. Just another Pistole '08 manufactured by the reliable Mauser-Werke in Oberndorf am Neckar. Garland dropped it in his cargo pocket and began to ruck his way out of camp, using a blind spot he'd noticed when setting the guards and taking further advantage of two soldiers hunkered down due to the weather. They never saw him.

Pouring rain, gray rain, everywhere, coming in at a stinging slant. Artillery in the distance. They were many kilometers behind the forward line, a kilometer from the town of Morlaix. The road heading west was crammed with American vehicles. Numerous soldiers, like Garland, walked on the side of the road, not of a high-enough rank to warrant a ride on four wheels.

The rain intensified. It'd be hard to make someone out from ten feet.

Baby killers...

He reached Morlaix, now firmly in the breast of the Allies. Probably had been a beautiful little town at one time. A group of soldiers off to the left were tending to an American soldier that had fallen from a building. Probably found some wine, got drunk and fell. Garland shook his head. "War is hell," the general had said. He walked past; the medics lifted the wounded soldier. His arm was shaped like a Z, bone protruding from two places.

"Dummkopf," Garland muttered.

Pressed toward the center of Morlaix, scanning. *Most of the residents are gone. Water rushing ankle deep through the streets, carrying cigarette butts and the sediment of smashed buildings. Bricks and stones covering the sidewalks. Soldiers everywhere, from brigade and division headquarters. Assholes. Wouldn't know the front line if they walked up on it.* Even with the maelstrom, Garland noticed their clean uniforms and unlined faces.

Assholes indeed.

He stopped, looked to the right. Antennas. A forest of them.

Rats...savages...

Garland walked in that direction, acting like he knew what he was doing. Saw a lieutenant in a bombed-out building, sitting in a dry area writing something. The lieutenant paid him no heed, never looking up. Behind him was a relatively untouched building with blown-out windows. Just outside, hidden from the horizon, were the mass of hastily erected antennas. Garland stood across the street, looking inside. It had been a restaurant, now acting as brigade headquarters. Several officers could be seen working the radios. Two maps were strung up, lit by portable lights. The sound of generators echoed between the buildings, providing the headquarters with power. Someone had gotten a fire going in the restaurant's fireplace. The place looked cozy. He moved around the building.

Standing guard on the far side of the building were two soldiers. Through the rain Garland couldn't see their rank. Their sergeant-of-the-guard had placed them on the two corners on opposite sides of the street. Both were trying their damndest to huddle under the eave of their respective buildings, and since Garland was already inside their inner perimeter, they never looked back in his direction.

Garland turned around, wondering where the rear guard was. Staying put, after several minutes he saw the fellow, tall and hunched, emerge from another bombed out building. The soldier adjusted the zipper of his soaked trousers a few times. Bathroom break. General Kagan and his entourage were out and about, so obviously everyone's guard was down a notch or two.

The entrance to the restaurant consisted of one flagstone step up into a shallow portico. From his position across the street, Garland studied it through the driving rain. He saw no other way in or out. Dotting the street and narrow excuse for a sidewalk out front were mortar craters, each no more than a half meter wide. Typical of the low impact rounds, they had done nothing more than crack and slightly depress the concrete-and-macadam finish.

He looked in all directions. As they were trained, the trifecta of guards were still gazing out, not in. What few officers there were in the restaurant headquarters were busy, and from where he was headed, wouldn't be able to see him. In a period of intense rain, Staff Sergeant Garland Felton moved across the street, pawing at the craters. The one just to the right of the door was perfect. He knelt there, quickly removing the bouncing betty and concealing it under the bag. From his pocket, he removed his captured Luger, placing it next to him. Garland lifted a pie-shaped piece of concrete, using his hands to scoop out the muddy gravel from underneath. He armed the mine and, holding his breath, wedged it into the hole while keeping the trigger depressed, covering it with sand and mud. Garland put the Luger next to the betty, wedging it under the loose concrete so that only the barrel would be trapped by the lid of the booby trap. Carefully, he replaced the pie-shaped piece of concrete, pressing downward to take the mine's trigger pressure, and wedging the barrel of the gun under the piece of concrete.

Garland stepped back, doing a full turn. No one was nearby. No one was looking. He walked into the street, staring at his personal subterfuge. It wasn't his best-ever work, and anyone with half a brain would immediately wonder why no one had seen the Luger before. But oftentimes soldiers—even officers—have less than a half a brain. Especially the ones that are tired. Cold. Battle weary.

I wouldn't shed a tear if they were all vaporized tomorrow.

Garland's mouth ticked upward. Cinching up his gear, he walked back the way he came, staying on the same side of the street as where he'd seen the hunched-over guard appear. The guard turned, watching him as he walked.

Shit! This could ruin everything.

Garland tried to appear relaxed, wiping rain from his face. He approached the guard with a steady, confident stride. The guard stared at him, his M-1 still slung, more bored than curious.

"Where the hell were you earlier?" Garland asked, stepping nearly chest to chest with him, seeing that he was a private E-2.

"What do you mean, Sarge?"

Garland gestured to the avenue. "I came through here, walked right to H.Q., never got a challenge from a guard. Where the hell were you?"

"Had to take a dump. Was an emergency, Sarge, but least I waited 'til the general was away." Calling on his auto-didactic training on American accents, this one sounded like a Texan, or perhaps an Oklahoman.

"Did you find a latrine?"

"Water don't work, but it's dry and pretty clean."

Garland glanced around. "Show it to me real quick." Usable johns were right up there with liquor and fresh food as scarcities to be treasured.

He followed the private through the rubble-littered building. It had once been someone's home, the tenants long gone. Smashed furniture had already been picked over. Glass everywhere. Water poured in through various holes in the ceiling. Garland stopped at one point, able to see the steely gray sky through a massive hole reaching through all three floors.

"Back here, Sarge," said the private, gesturing through an arched alcove.

Garland hesitated, closing his eyes and taking deep breaths. "He's a soldier, Gerhard," he whispered to his real self. "He's not some innocent civilian. He's out here to kill you as much as you are to kill him."

"Sarge? You comin'?"

"Think about General Kagan," Garland continued to whisper, his voice drowned out by the pouring rain. "Kagan's no different from Von Marburg or Heydte."

"Sarge?"

"We're all killers," Garland said with a nod. Bolstered, he followed the private, unsheathing his Ka-Bar and concealing it in his right hand, the blade tilted upward under his sleeve. It was cold and hard against his skin.

The private gestured to a closet-like room with a slanted ceiling, under the stairs. "Thanks," Garland said. He lowered his brows, cocking his head, staring at a spot under the private's arm, in the rib area.

"What's wrong, Sarge?" the private asked, following his eyes.

"Did you get shot or something?" Garland asked, staring puzzled.

A trace of alarm passed over the private's face, like it would any person's. But then, a second later, good sense kicked in and he smiled. "Naw, Sarge. Why?"

"Then what's all that coming from your back?"

The private lifted his left arm, pulling at the soaked jacket, pressing his chin down to his chest. "Don't see nothin', Sarge."

Garland twirled his left hand. "Turn around, I'll show you."

Privates do as they're told, especially when instructed by friendly, seemingly helpful staff sergeants. They don't expect, however, to have a six-inch hardened steel blade jammed into their lower back, at kidney level. The private lurched forward, falling, making a guttural sound unlike anything Garland had ever heard.

Garland dove forward, jamming the knife in two more times before finding the sweet spot in the back of the private's neck, just a millimeter from his spine. The young man went limp.

Acting quickly, Garland hefted the private before the blood could hit the floor. He pulled him into the small bathroom, depositing him on the toilet. The soldier's eyes were wide as he stared, paralyzed, at his killer. The last stab must have severed his spinal cord. He sat slumped, no longer breathing or making noise.

Garland had to look away.

It only took another moment before the kid's life escaped him. Garland closed the private's eyes and leaned him back, watching as the blood poured to the floor. He stepped out, swinging the door all the way around, pressing it shut. Cautiously, Garland made his way back to the front of the building, peering out into the rain. He saw no one. Turning left, he hurriedly made his way back to the center of town, relaxing once he was among the throngs of soaked soldiers, each heading in different directions.

On the road from Morlaix, Garland stepped aside as the two Jeeps sped by, back into town. Salutes were not to be proffered during battle conditions, the theory being that any nearby snipers would then know who the higher ranking official was (as if their arrogant fender flags didn't tip them off.) So instead, Garland simply stood in the small ditch to the side of the battered road, standing ankle deep in water, his head down anonymously as the general and his entourage sped by. Through the pouring rain they wouldn't have been able to recognize him as the hero from earlier.

Garland resumed his spot on the road, increasing his pace back to his camp which lay several hundred meters ahead.

Other than the private he'd had to kill, Garland's only regret was not being able to watch.

IN THE LEAD Jeep was a driver, a buck sergeant. Next to him the general's aide-de-camp, a youngish, battle-promoted major who had worked mere blocks away from Garland on Wall Street, prior to his joining up in '42. In the back of the Jeep, hunched over, smoking, the brigade sergeant major. He flicked the driver's ear, telling him to slow down as they drove into Morlaix, glancing at the major who was busy reading reports of some sort. The two vehicles rounded the final turn.

"Stop the Jeep!" the sergeant major yelled. The sergeant obeyed, tires scuffing to a stop on the wet street.

"What is it?" the major asked, turning his head in obvious irritation.

"Where the hell's my rear guard?" the sergeant major asked, peering through the opening on the right of the Jeep. There was a crate, and underneath it the guard phone. Black commo wire led into the building.

"Probably trying to stay dry," the major answered disinterestedly, going back to his report.

The sergeant major pressed forward on the driver's seat, unwedging himself and stepping out into the pouring rain. He leaned his head back in and said, "Major, wait here a minute." The major grunted.

He walked behind the vehicle, holding his hand up in a stopping motion to the general's Jeep, then extending his index finger. Halt for one minute. General Kagan adjusted himself in his seat. The sergeant major tossed his now soaked cigarette, looking up and down the street. Through the rain he could see the two dark figures on the far end of the avenue, the two forward guards. Behind him, soldiers and Jeeps hurried about on the main Morlaix thoroughfare. So where was this guard? He removed his .45, holding it down beside him, picking his way into the rubble-strewn building. Behind him, the major in the front Jeep opened the door and waved his arm forward. Both Jeeps revved and accelerated down the street to headquarters.

"Stupid-ass major," the wizened old NCO growled. He had been through the previous war, and had seen enough death to know that it was always there, lurking, just below the surface. Like a man walking a wide ledge of a high building, eventually a soldier begins to relax. But it only takes one slip-up, one little mistake, and down you go. Gravity and the ground don't give a shit how long you walked that building. The same could be said for the unforgiving nature of warfare. Death, like a dangling two-ton safe overhead, could care less about your pay-grade.

He moved through the building, seeing the commo wire that had been laid, leading to the rear of the building. He followed it, down a hallway, seeing the closed door. A latrine. The sergeant major gripped the knob, swinging the door out, hoping to find the kid relieving himself so he could deliver an ass-chewing and be on his way.

He stared inside, eyes widening.

Gripping his .45, he turned and sprinted from the building, yelling. Yelling as loud as he could.

"YOU COULD stick a lump of coal in the sergeant major's ass and be rewarded with an instant diamond," the major said, closing his report book and opening his door even before the sergeant got the Jeep stopped.

"The hell was all that about?" General Kagan asked as everyone exited the Jeeps.

"Sergeant Major wanting to keep you waiting because his guard disappeared. I think he just wants attention," the aide de camp said conspiratorially. "Once I get us some tea I'll help you disseminate that new intel, sir." They turned and headed into the converted restaurant.

From General Kagan's Jeep emerged the driver, a staff sergeant, and a lieutenant colonel. The driver from the major's Jeep stood by his vehicle, waiting, as the train of staff made their way in. He turned around upon hearing something from the way they had come. A soldier, a tall soldier, was running and shouting something. The major brushed past him.

"Will you look at that?" the major said, kneeling.

"Get your asses back!" bellowed the command from the rapidly approaching sergeant major.

In the last few moments the rain had lessened considerably, and now the general heard the sergeant major, whirling to him before turning back to his aide, seeing what he was doing. He was kneeling, lifting a piece of concrete under which appeared to be wedged a pistol. "No!" General Kagan yelled.

Like something from a child's toy bin, the mine popped, no louder than a cap-gun, springing into the air. It only took about a second—ample time for everyone nearby to clearly see what it was. Each man, other than the dumbfounded aide, instinctively turned and hunched as the mine reached its zenith at four feet of height.

Death, that dastardly dangling safe that existed overhead, was paying them a visit.

The next explosion was far more than that of a cap-gun.

THE SERGEANT major slid to his stomach when he saw the bouncing betty. There was nothing else he could do, and being forty meters away, hitting the ground was his only choice. The mine reached its apex, and in the quickest prayer of his life, the sergeant major prayed for a dud.

The prayer didn't work.

The explosion and resulting flash momentarily blinded him, and when he turned back, what he saw sickened him. Each man, other than the driver pinned against his Jeep, had been blown back by at least ten feet. The lieutenant colonel, the farthest from the mine, writhed and yelled on the pavement, holding his shredded hands to his face. The major was sprawled forward of the Jeeps, headless. And the general lay against the edge of the building, water pooling against him, turning crimson downstream.

Soldiers began to appear from everywhere. The sergeant major, his ears not working well after the blast, stood and instructed a few sergeants to begin a search for Germans, and to kill anyone looking half the part. As he pointed, he realized his own hands were bleeding, having taken some shrapnel from the destructive German S-mine.

As the soldiers rushed off, each more desperate than the other to find the German saboteur, the sergeant major sucked on the wounds of his hand. He watched as medics tended to the men. The lieutenant colonel would make it, minus his eyes. The sergeant was dead, the other one—the staff sergeant who was the general's driver—was remarkably barely hurt. The major, the *dumbass* major who had fallen for the booby trap, had been cleanly decapitated, and the general, luckily, still had a pulse.

The sergeant major shrugged off medical attention, watching as the medics worked on the general. The rain ceased; the generators were turned off; and the resulting quiet was made all the more eerie by the frantic voices of the men trying to save their leader. One medic laced his hands and began to pound on the general's heart. The other medics screamed, telling him to hang on, *hang on!* Someone had a pair of bloody forceps, trying to get something from his neck.

Simultaneously, each medic stopped what they were doing. Their heads dipped. People mumbled curses, lit cigarettes. No eye contact was made. The sergeant major bit his lower lip, cursed the dead major, cursed the dead private, cursed this damned war and the men who started it. He found his Colt .45 on the wet street and, after making sure there was a round seated in the chamber, went and joined the search for the German sonofabitch who did this.

TEN

ROLAND'S SHIFT was ending just as the news came in. The day had been quiet up until then. As he'd predicted, the newness of being in London was beginning to wear off. Unable to find anything to advance his position, a pall began to creep in, making him crave alcohol to deaden his depression. But on this day, his break finally came.

He and Simon were tidying up their workspace when a flurry of activity occurred up at the communications desk. The radio operators scribbled frantically, bursts of chatter coming in over the radio and the code machine. The operators sent messengers running with wax-sealed envelopes. It had to be big news. Roland and Simon watched the commotion for ten minutes. Finally, they walked to the desk, finding the two 2nd lieutenants huddled, whispering excitedly.

"What was all that?" Roland asked.

The short lieutenant, who bunked next to Roland and liked to read Descartes and Comte, curled his lip. "Sorry, field-grade eyes-only traffic for the brass."

"Don't be a cock," Simon said, leaning on the desk with his one arm. "What was all the hot news?"

The other lieutenant, the taller one, turned back to his radio, speaking with his back to them. "A general officer died this afternoon."

"How?" Roland asked.

Silence.

"How?" he growled.

The lieutenant sighed as if explaining was of the greatest inconvenience. "A mine…a bouncing betty. They think some Germans were left behind the lines and set a trap."

Roland's eyes widened. He and Simon shared a glance. "What unit?"

The lieutenant turned. "Why do you want to know?"

Roland hobbled around the desk. The shorter lieutenant quickly stood in protest. Roland shoved him back into his chair. He leaned over the taller one, grabbing him by his collar, growling into his ear. "Why do I want to know? Why do I want to know? Because I wanna win this damned war, that's why I wanna know! And the last time I checked, a captain outranks a piss-ant butterbar." He released the collar but didn't move from his spot.

The lieutenant sat back, his nostrils flaring before he took on a resigned countenance. "It was Brigadier Kagan, Second Infantry, one of the brigade commanders. He and his aide and a sergeant. A lieutenant colonel got torn up pretty bad, too."

Roland straightened, smoothing the lieutenant's collar. "See now, was that so hard?" He patted him on the back and turned, quickly adjusting his wooden leg. They went back to their table. Roland motioned for quiet, chewing on his fingernail. His mind was racing. He nodded, his hand moving as if he were writing on an imaginary tablet. Nodded again. He turned to Simon, who was watching him with a type of concerned interest. "I have a plan," Roland said.

The next shift arrived, a sergeant first class with the shakes and a captain with stitches all the way around his head like Boris Karloff in Frankenstein. "Take this shift off," Roland commanded. Simon whipped his head around at Roland.

"S-s-say wh-wh-what, s-s-sir?" the sergeant asked.

"We got it covered. Go drink some of that red ale they serve around here. We'll take your shift."

"Wait," Simon said to the men as they were hurrying away. "Are you serious?" he asked Roland. Roland winked at him.

"But I need the alcohol!" Simon protested. "It's how I came off the morphine, plus…and you know this…I'm from Maine."

"Then go get a flask," Roland said. He turned to the two hopeful men. "We're good here. Go."

"Will you tell the duty officer?" the stitched-up captain asked.

Roland hobbled over to the desk on the opposite side of the room. A dozing major, recovering from burns, looked up, listened, shrugged, resumed dozing. Roland came back. "You're good to go, gentlemen." Even in their condition, like soldiers of any rank, the two men knew a good deal when they heard it and didn't want to hang around in the event the decision was somehow reversed. They turned and disappeared like thieves.

"What the hell're you doing?" Simon asked, taking his chair. Roland moved to the wall and rolled over a library cart full of casualty registers, parking it next to their table. He ran his hand over the spines of the binders, selecting four of them, each several inches thick. They contained the casualty reports of the Third Army since D-Day. He dropped the binders on the desk, drumming on the top.

"We're getting ready to crunch some numbers."

"What numbers?"

Roland lifted the top two binders and placed them in front of Simon, resting his left hand on them, his right on the two in front of his own chair. "Go through those two and note every single death, by *unit*, that occurred. Put an asterisk beside every officer and senior NCO, but the most important thing is to categorize the death by unit."

"How're they currently filed?"

"By date," Roland said.

"But this'll take days," the lieutenant protested.

"Yes, it will. And make sure you leave out any death that resulted from a distant weapon—bombs, artillery...get it?"

"How about snipers?"

"Sniper deaths should be recorded." Roland pointed to Simon's two binders. "You up for this?"

Simon lit a cigarette and flipped open the first binder, staring at it the way a student looks at algebra homework. "What do you think we're gonna find in here?"

"We won't know until we dig in."

"And my flask?" Simon asked. Roland nodded and hobbled away. Five minutes later he returned with an ornate gold and silver flask engraved with words foreign to both men.

"The hell'd you get this?" Simon asked.

"I'll bet you a pound it's vodka."

"Whose is it?"

"You know that hard-boiled Russian liaison who sleeps in our tent? The one with the huge mole on his forehead…"

"Yeah."

"Well, he's passed out cold, as usual. I'd advise you slide it back under his bunk after our shift."

Simon stared at the flask, unscrewed the cap, swigged. He screwed up his face. "Paint remover!"

"Shall I take it back?" Roland asked.

Simon's hollow eyes moved from Roland back to the flask. He took one more swig and pocketed it.

The two men worked until the shift change at midnight. They were able to complete half of the division's deaths. Following six hours of sleep, the men continued their research over barley coffee the following morning.

THEIR MOVE back to the front was indefinitely delayed, most assuredly by a bouncing betty straight up Uncle Sam's ass, Garland decided with mixed feelings, nestling back onto his cot. He'd worked his shift until well past midnight, afterward successfully stringing together five hours of sleep. After a half-decent breakfast at the company goulash cannon, Garland lay outside the tent, one arm crooked under his head, a passed-around week-old Stars & Stripes on his stomach. Before he read the twelve-pages of American propaganda, his mind went over the list. What he'd added yesterday was most certainly the pièce de résistance. He knew, right now, he could simply gather a few of his things and deftly pick his way through the battle line and back into the bosom of his countrymen. The front line officers would listen skeptically before shuttling him this way and that, probably eventually getting him to some forward *Sicherheitsdienst* outpost. It'd be there that some thunderstruck SD standartenführer would listen to his tale, mouth hanging limp, before personally escorting him back to Berlin for about a year of harsh debriefing.

He could hear the standartenführer now, standing in front of Schepmann or maybe the Führer himself, speaking solicitously. "This fine young German specimen has single-handedly disposed of nineteen senior men—leaders—of the American Army. His prowess weakened their Second Infantry Division so greatly that we are currently beating them back to the Atlantic."

"Yeah, right," he whispered to himself.

As vapor rose above their still-soaked position, Garland stretched out and allowed the morning sun to warm his face, pondering the situation. He lit a cigarette, his other hand fingering the Stars & Stripes. His plan was fraught with weakness. First and foremost, how could he prove the things he'd done? Oh sure, he had enough faith in the motherland that somehow, someway, they could confirm the deaths that he listed for them. But—after leaving Carol Lynn alive, and disappearing the way he had—Garland expected a great deal of scrutiny from his chain of command in Berlin, and downright skepticism from the leadership in Berlin. That was the first problem...how to prove the list.

Second, and quite ancillary, was the number itself. Currently, after the bouncing betty, the list stood at nineteen. Ten NCOs, nine officers. The private he'd gutted in Morlaix, due to his low rank, didn't count as someone in leadership. Being a good German, Garland didn't like the uneven number, especially when twenty was so close. Worse than the uneven number was the commissioned officer total being a lesser number. Although NCOs wielded more power, more influence in the American forces than they did inside the militaries of the Reich, Garland still expected the brass to turn their collective noses up at his ten dead NCOs.

"Nine officers," he murmured, exhaling a stream of cigarette smoke into the still morning air. "Nine men who had a mom, and a dad, and maybe a kid sister. Some of them had wives and kids...kids who might be crying for their papa right now."

He kicked his legs over the side of the cot and sat up, running his hand back through his hair, feeling the strain on his face and neck. "Weak thoughts," he growled. "You were doing your job." Garland closed his eyes, calming himself with a brief moment of meditation. Getting back to his original train of thought, he laid back down on the cot.

The third problem, one that was quite clear to him, was the fact that the Germans were getting their asses kicked. Forget the fact that Hitler had blundered more times than Garland could enumerate, but somehow he just couldn't envision a parade being thrown for his paltry list of assassinations that had yielded no tangible fruit.

The fourth problem, and perhaps the biggest one of all, was Garland himself. Was he ready to go back? Did he *want* to go back? Were each of these objections simply ways to prolong his being an American? The killing of General Kagan didn't bother him so much. The man was a warmonger, no different from warmongers of Germany, of Russia, of Japan. It was the private Garland had killed—that killing bothered him a great deal.

Don't start in on that again, he thought.

There were voices to his left. Garland propped himself up on his elbows as he watched the company commander and his XO leaving the perimeter, beginning a hike straight down into the damp wooded valley below the company position. On the opposite hillside, sitting above the valley's fog, was the regimental headquarters, hidden under the canopy of trees in a mass of tents. His jade-green eyes alternated between the regiment and the two officers as they disappeared down the hillside.

The area at the bottom was perfect for an ambush. Narrow. Confined. Hidden.

He stared a moment more before he made a mental note and began to read, quickly realizing that five hours of sleep hadn't been enough. Like all of the soldiers in the mainland theater of battle, he probably needed a week of sleep just to catch up. As he read, the words jumbled together, making sense about half the time. The headline involved a Pacific battle at Morotai. To the right of that, in typical Stars & Stripes fashion, was a human interest story, this one involving some bumpkin who was fortunate enough to get a kiss on the puss from Betty Grable at a USO show in Paris. *Lucky bastard.* Shaking his head, Garland's eyes moved to the small story on the bottom right of the front page.

Rumors Abound Regarding German Camps

Are the Nazis guilty of murdering innocent citizens?

For years, Allied Intelligence has known of the various detention camps strewn about Adolf Hitler's criminal empire. In the waning days of the previous decade, German diplomats brushed them off as prisons, places where convicted criminals were sent for reform. German newsreels backed up this claim, showing clean-shaven men doing calisthenics and contributing to society by learning a trade or craft to ply after their sentence.

But in the past year, the U.S. State Department, as well as their British counterparts, have grown mum on the subject. This, coupled with numerous alleged escapees who have made their way out of Hitler's Reich, has led to a growing suspicion among many scholars that the camps are actually nothing more than a front to exterminate the Jewish population.

New "work camps" have been reported in places such as– (cont. on page 4)

Garland bolted straight up, his fingers pulling the paper taut. *...to exterminate the Jewish population.* He blinked, his gaze turning to the filtered sky. "Mein Gott," he whispered. If this was true about the Nazis deliberately killing the Jews—and having seen many racially-explosive incidents back in Germany, he had little doubt that it was—then Germany *couldn't* win. There was absolutely no way. Having lived in the United States for such a period of time, seeing the vast resources and the power the Jewish community wielded, Garland knew, even in the event of a peaceful cease-fire, that the Americans wouldn't allow Germany any latitude if their governing body had committed such an atrocity. As was his growing ideology, killing during wartime was one thing, but exterminating innocent civilians was quite another. He shook his head, opening the paper to the continuation of the article.

"Hey, Sergeant Felton. Talk to you?"

Garland looked up. A private stood there, his face bright white and dotted with patches of peach fuzz. Like the private Garland had fought alongside before taking out the Panzer, this one was part of the group of new arrivals that had come in from the Repple-Depple back when the 23rd was garrisoned in Paris. There were about twenty of them, all of them still firmly on the outs with the salty dogfaces that had fought since Normandy. It'd probably be Thanksgiving, or at least three more firefights, before the newbies were half-heartedly welcomed into the fold. Garland had seen this one before, ordered him here and there, that kind of thing. He'd never had to actually converse with him. He folded the paper over and stuffed it under his sleeping bag, rubbing his heavy brow where his leg skin now flourished underneath. "What do you need?" he asked, using a purposefully curt tone.

The private motioned a bony finger at the cot. "M-m-may I, Sarge?" Garland thought he saw the kid's lip quivering.

With closed eyes, a breath escaping audibly, Garland sat up and told him to sit. The private did, and that's when he began to shiver. The kid buried his face in his hands and shuddered, seeming to do his best not to cry. Garland cocked an eyebrow, glancing around to make sure no one was witnessing this awkward scene. He let the kid gather himself for a minute before patting him on the back.

"C'mon, private, pull it together. Don't start crying. Get it together before someone else sees you. Crying won't do you much good with this bunch, trust me."

The kid lowered his hands, sucking in great breaths through his nose. He produced a tan handkerchief and dabbed at the tears that had welled in his eyes. "Sorry, Sarge."

"What's the problem?"

"My...my...mother..." The tremors started again. While stuck on the words, the kid reached into his jacket and pulled out a small, stiff envelope. Garland had seen plenty of these, Army telegrams. He pinched it between his fingernails and slid it out, reading quickly. The kid's mother was on her death bed, cancer.

"Read the date, Sarge," the private whispered. Garland did. It was two weeks old.

"She's probably *already* dead," the private blurted, dropping his face back into both hands.

Garland lit another cigarette, watching the kid as he sat there, the picture of despair. Two soldiers, corporals, walked by. Garland hitched his head at them, a sign for them to keep moving. When the private finally lifted his head, Garland said, "Take it easy, pal. I know it's hard, but there's nothing you can do about it from here."

"But that's not why I'm upset, Sarge. Not because she was dying or probably already died."

"Yeah?" Garland asked, surprised. "Why, then?"

The kid sniffed a few times, his face growing stolid, his gray eyes staring down, into some unknown place.

"Out with it."

The gray eyes flicked up, coming back to present. His voice was monotone when he spoke. "What has been upsetting me the most is that I never loved her."

Garland studied the kid. "Why do you say that?"

The change in the conversation's direction seemed to solidify the private. He turned, picking a twig from the ground, breaking tiny bits from the ends. "My mom never loved me or my two sisters. I don't think she was capable of loving anyone."

His mind jumping to his childhood in Hannover, Garland said, "It probably wasn't that bad."

The kid's voice turned shrill. "It was. It was worse! She was mean as a snake. I mean…how does a woman care for you but still hate you? How's that possible?" He dipped his head again.

There was a long pause as Garland's mind flashed like a moving picture through snippets of his own life, seeing his mother's familiar disapproving faces, her sneer. "Do it, you little pussy!" had been one of the last things she'd said to him, wanting him to kill her. Daring him. He looked back at the kid, understanding his angst.

"It's all just bullshit," the kid said, his voice somewhere between anger and crying.

"What is?"

"Life, Sarge! I'm supposed to care about her, but I feel even worse because a huge piece of me—as sick as it sounds—hopes she *is* dead." Lip quivering, the kid took a few bolstering breaths. "But the other part of me is sick about this telegram. Sick about the prospect of her dying." He shook his head. "Does any of that make sense?"

"It does, believe me," Garland said in a low voice.

The private turned his head to Garland, his gray eyes pooling with tears again. His voice was that of a child, pure and clear. "In the end, she's *my*

173

mother, Sergeant Felton. No matter how nasty she was to me and my sisters, she clothed us, fed us, got us off to that damned school, and tucked us in at night. She kept a roof over our head and tended to our cuts and bruises. Nothing she could ever do, no amount of love she *never* gave can take any of that away."

Garland struggled to breathe.

"She didn't love us, Sarge. That was a fact. But why am I such a sick bastard that I don't love her neither?"

Garland looked away.

At least half a minute of silence floated between them before Garland handed the telegram back. "When are you on guard?"

"I'm on your shift, I think, late this afternoon."

"You'll feel better if you get some sleep," Garland said dismissively. As he watched the skinny private walk away, head downward, kicking at pebbles and sticks, Garland's mind was awash in too many emotions to categorize. He swiveled around to lie back on the cot, and surprisingly, with all that danced in his mind, managed a long nap.

EACH MAN had filled ten sheets of ledger paper. Top to bottom, left to right, nearly every block of the paper was penciled in with information. As they worked, the two men developed a system of categorization. NCOs were underlined, officers circled. Above the subset a numeral was written, denoting the rank. A major is designated an O-4 by the military, so in the event of a major's death, it was marked by a circle with a 4 at the top. The two men were calculating their totals, having never stopped to do so. This filled an additional ledger sheet and, once it was complete, Roland smoothed it out on the table and stared at his partner.

"Ready to compare?"

Simon sipped his ersatz coffee, wincing as he did after every taste. He put the cup by the sheet, tracing one of his five fingers over the ledger paper, tapping each unit with a large number of senior NCO and officer casualties. Roland did the same, standing back, his excellent vision enabling him to see the differences from five feet away. The sheet was broken out by the order of battle, starting with the Third Army at the left, then moving downward to divisions, brigades, regiments, and battalions. Simon tapped the 2nd Infantry Division, known as Indianhead due to their large unit patch displaying the profile of an American Indian in full headdress.

"Second I.D. seems high."

"Mmm-hmmm," Roland hummed, stepping forward, crushing out his cigarette. He picked up his own untouched cup of ersatz, stared at it, curled his lip, put it back down. "Go to the right." He watched as Simon traced his finger over the paper to the 23rd Infantry Regiment.

Simon lifted his finger before poking it back down with force. "This unit's got double the numbers as anyone."

Roland peered at the numbers. Since D-Day, there had been eighteen NCOs killed in the 23rd, six of them senior NCOs, meaning E-7 and above. Among the other similar units, discounting artillery fire or bombing, the closest number was four. The 23rd had lost fifteen officers versus a high of nine from the next-closest unit.

"And these don't include the men killed yesterday from the booby-trap," Simon said. "They were from the division, too."

"Wait here," Roland said. His heart was racing; he could feel his pulse stoking in his neck as he crossed the Hole, moving to the map boards. A captain was using a blue grease pencil, making changes on the Belgium map. On the board, in various colors, were all manner of lines, boxes, circles, X's, hash marks and Roman symbols. Each had its own meaning to a trained set of eyes.

"Griffin," Roland said. The captain turned. He and Roland had met a few times and were on friendly terms. "Do me a favor; point out 2nd I.D.'s location to me, their H.Q."

"Okay." The captain turned, sliding the maps left and right, each hanging from strung wire. He finally located one displaying western France and the coastline. He moved his finger in a wide circle, finally stabbing the map a short distance inland from the northern coast. "They're right here, at Morlaix. This is where the general got hisself killed yesterday."

Roland nodded, faking a thank-you smile. "Now show me the division's 23rd Infantry Regiment."

The captain turned, scratching his head before he touched the map, moving his hand in tight circles away from Morlaix. "No. No. Wait…no." He tapped it. "Here they are, a few klicks to the east."

"A few klicks, you say?"

"If that."

"Are they on the front line?"

"Nope. Looks like they're back a bit. I can check their rotation if you like, see when they go back up front."

"That'd be great." Roland produced a fresh pack of Lucky Strikes, shaking one out, proffering it. "Thanks for your help, Griff."

Captain Griffin took the cigarette, placing it on his desk. "What's this about?"

"Who the hell knows?" Roland said, turning to walk away. "All I do is what the old man tells me." He walked back to Simon, his heart soaring. He reached the table, sat down, pinching his lips together in a smile.

"What is it?" Simon asked.

Roland looked around. The tables next to them were full of other soldiers. He stood, donning his jacket, grabbing his hat. "Come on, and bring the binder with the Second Division's casualties." They went outside, Roland returning a few salutes as they walked. They crossed the muddy lawn, hunched over from the mist, to the canteen by the Thames. Simon tried to talk to him the whole way, Roland waving him off each time, doing his best not to lose his left leg in the suction of the London mud. They wiped their boots on the brushes outside of the snack bar and went inside. The canteen was quiet this early. Roland motioned to the Chinese man behind the counter. "Two London Prides…we'll be over there in the corner."

"Are you nuts?" Simon asked, whipping his head around. "They see us drinking now and we'll get written up."

"Quit being a pussy and sit."

The canteen was a converted fabric warehouse, old and shadowy. Made of old brick, the wooden floors soft from age, it had been mothballed several years earlier, now serving the Allies as the evening watering pub for the cripples from the Hole and the Royal Air Force pilots billeted on the next block. It even had a pool table, replete with as much slope as a Scottish links course. Those who learned its undulations could stay on the table for hours at a time. The beers arrived.

"Wait five minutes and bring two more," Roland said, handing the Chinese man two pounds and telling him to keep the change.

"Thought you quit drinking," Simon said, holding his beer and glancing around.

"Special occasion."

"Yeah? What's that?"

Roland sipped his beer, tasting it, allowing it to rest on his tongue. He held it in front of him, staring at the red ale for a moment. Swallowed, exhaled loudly. "Damn, that's good." Another sip and he placed it on the table. His face widened with a smile. "Twenty-third infantry regiment has a saboteur, my friend. A wolf in sheep's clothing."

Simon blinked a few times. "That thought crossed my mind too, but it could just be a coincidence."

Roland shook his head emphatically.

"You can't be sure, can you?"

Tapping the binder, Roland said, "Read 'em to me."

The lieutenant thumbed through the binder, licking his finger, found the first page. "A sergeant shot in the chest is first." Flipped a page. "Same day, a sergeant first class shot...in the back."

"In the *back*," Roland emphasized, copying Simon's Maine accent. "Where were they?"

"Omaha Beach, Normandy." Simon shook his head, a skeptical look overtaking his gaunt face. "C'mon...he could'a simply turned around to yell at his men and got plugged by some kraut's Mauser."

"Yeah, or he could'a been clipped by one of his own men in the back. Keep going."

Simon flipped the page. "The next day, a major, the S-three, got whacked by a booby-trap grenade on the same beach."

Roland had already read this one, but for Simon's sake, told him to read aloud.

"Says they got careless searching for intel. Said the major shouldn't have been in there, but was trying to instruct his team on how to do it. Two others got injured and the major got his head blown off."

"German grenade?"

Simon's head swiveled back and forth as he read. Eyebrows shot up. "First guys on the scene said the frags looked like they came from our pineapple variety."

"Yep."

"C'mon cap'n, you and I both know, especially in a zoo like Normandy, that everyone pilfers weaponry off'a all the dead bodies. There'd be *humdingah numbahs* of weapons layin' around all over the place."

They drank another beer as they went through every single death. By the time they were finished, seventeen of the deaths occurred from circumstances which, while individually explained away in wartime, when put together formed an ominous pattern of bad luck for the senior men of the 23rd Infantry. Simon flipped back and forth, reading to himself. He shook his head as he sucked in a long breath.

"You believe me now?" Roland asked him.

"But what about the general and his crew? He's not in this regiment."

"I checked it on the map. Division's just a few klicks away. The sonofabitch walked over there, I'd bet my life. And yesterday, remember…we saw all the Brylcreem Boys hangin' around here because they were grounded…awful storm over the mainland. Bet you the killer used the shitty weather as his cover."

Simon drained the remainder of his beer. "How can such a thing happen? How could an enemy soldier get into our military?"

Roland shrugged, waiting as the Chinese bartender cleared the bottles. He gave him a few shillings and asked him to bring some peppermints. Looked back at Simon. "The saboteur isn't necessarily an enemy soldier. Hell, it could be some American kid that hates our country, or maybe just hates the Army." Simon was about to speak, but Roland cut him off. "But what I do know, after reading these reports, seeing who he has managed to kill, assuming he offed the general yesterday…I know that he's good." Nodded. "Yeah. He's damn good and he's getting bolder."

The peppermints arrived. Both men untwisted one each, placing it in the side of their mouth. "So what do you aim to do?"

Roland swished the peppermint around, bit down, chewed quickly and swallowed. "I aim to get us off this island and over there to the Second Division…over there to find that sabotaging sonofabitch." He untwisted another peppermint, popped it in his mouth.

Simon waited a moment, crunched his own peppermint, leaned forward. "How are we gonna do that?"

"Eat that other peppermint and I'll show you."

ELEVEN

THEY WENT back to the officer's tent to change into their best uniforms. In case the OIC wondered where they were, Roland instructed one of his bunkmates, a lieutenant, to tell him that they were instructed to go see the commander. With Simon following, mumbling about the trouble they were going to get into, the two men headed out.

The walk to the command offices was lengthy, across the partially damaged Waterloo Bridge over the Thames and into the Covent Garden area near the center of the city. The heavily diffused light from the sun was nearly down, and although the bombings had long since ceased, a blackout was still in effect. A few citizens scurried about, long since adjusted to the war, hurrying home to do whatever it was they did at night. Roland tipped his cap to an elderly woman as he explained his plan to Simon.

"I don't see how the hell that'll work," Simon complained.

"Maybe it will…maybe it won't," Roland said crisply, "but it'll get us noticed. Every time something like this happens, we'll be over here acting the squeaky wheel."

"Won't that piss the old man off?"

"I sure as hell hope so. Because eventually he'll send us over there with the hopes that we get killed."

Simon tossed his cigarette into a barren flower urn. They turned up the steep cobblestone mews, Roland slowing considerably as he labored to hitch his leg out and around to keep it from dragging on the slope.

"Cap'n, I just don't understand why we don't show 'em the ledger and go through those death reports. Once he sees that, just like we did, he'll be convinced of the same thing."

Roland stopped, closed his eyes for a long moment. *Patience...* He opened them. "You're right, Simon. He *would* see the correlation and it *would* move him. Most assuredly."

"Right."

"But that's no good."

Simon opened his one hand. "So what's the problem?"

"Colonel Sealock's back here, stuck running logistics in London. You think he wouldn't kill to produce such a statistical story as the one we've unearthed?" Roland turned, bumping up the hill again. "Damn right he would. He'd take it from us, pat us on our collective heads and send us straight the hell back to the Hole to keep on crunching numbers. Sure as we're both missing limbs, that's what he'd do."

"So if we don't get to leave...by using your method...aren't we hurting our country by not reporting this? The saboteur could kill other people because of our selfishness."

Roland stopped again. Didn't turn. Blinked a few times. Simon was right, in theory. He started moving again. "Let's just see what happens before we start making moral decisions."

The division headquarters was located in a long row building inside of Covent Garden's pedestrian-only area. Of course, the no-vehicle rule had flown out the window when the American Army arrived, and now Jeeps and motorcycles whizzed in and out of the sloped cloister so quickly that a military policeman had to be stationed there at all times to keep someone from being killed.

The MP waved the two wounded soldiers across, staring at them curiously. The casualties from the Hole didn't normally make their way up to division, especially ones missing limbs. Hesitating, he saluted, cocking his eye at Simon.

"What, you never seen an officer salute with his left hand before?" Simon growled as he passed the MP.

The levity was brief. Roland tensed his jaw as he entered the cool lobby of the building. They passed by another MP, evidently passing his eye test.

Simon and Roland walked down a long corridor loaded with individual offices. Painted lettering on the doors announced such offices as G-2, G-3, S-1, Procurement, and Displaced Citizenry. They didn't see anyone in the hallway below the rank of lieutenant colonel. Each time they passed one of the field grade officers, staring at the two of them as if they were the Swiss ice comics Frick & Frack, Simon would quickly whisper, "I'm tellin' ya, this is all wet!" Roland loped to the end of the hallway, pushing past a cluster of senior sergeants and captains to the commander's door. One captain stopped him, gently holding a hand to his chest.

"Where the hell do you think you guys are going?"

Roland gripped the captain's wrist and moved it. He stood toe to toe with him, glaring. "We're going in to see Colonel Sealock."

"He's in a meeting. A very *high-level* meeting."

Roland twisted his head to Simon before turning back to the captain. "And who do you think they're meeting about? You think I lost my leg, and L.T. here lost his arm, playing cards down at the canteen?" He pushed past the man, pressing the door open, entering the anteroom outside of the colonel's office.

Sealock's administrative assistant, a staff sergeant who was certainly used to seeing much higher ranking officers than a lieutenant and a captain, barely looked up over his thick glasses. He pressed them back onto his nose, turning his eyes back to whatever it was he was working on. "What do you guys need? Big meeting going on in there." It was the same tone someone might use to greet an unwanted door-to-door salesman.

Roland didn't say a word.

Simon, probably sensing Roland's silence, stepped forward to speak. Roland lifted his hand. *Silence.* Simon backed up. The staff sergeant eventually looked up. Roland's face was stone, his eyes boring into the NCO.

"Is there a problem, *captain?*"

It was the way the little prick said "captain," like somehow, simply because the staff sergeant worked for Colonel Sealock, he, too, was above Roland's rank. Roland glanced at Simon, grinned. He turned back to the NCO, dissolving his smile. "Get on your feet," he rasped.

"What?"

"Get on your damned feet when you speak to me!"

The sergeant popped up, stunned, cocking an eyebrow.

"And stand at frigging attention, too! I'm a commissioned officer in this man's Army, and while I don't cotton to ridiculous, ego-boosting requests for courtesy, I will be damned if I stand idle while some four-eyed staff sergeant, who, by the way, wouldn't know the working end of an M-1 if it shot him in the balls, sits there and ignores my rank and how I bled for it!" Roland's nostrils were flared wide. His steely gaze beamed pure electricity at the staff sergeant, who seemed to be at a loss for words.

The door to their left opened. A major stood staring at them. His face and the side of his head were horribly disfigured, the skin stretched and smeared like it had been made from a child's putty. He considered Roland and Simon a moment, stepped through the door, pulled it shut behind him. Pinched his lips. They were not as wide as normal and somewhat diagonal. "What's going on here, and what's all the yelling?"

Roland turned, swallowing a few times. "Sir, I'm Captain Buhl; with me is Lieutenant Jericho. We're here to see the colonel about the deaths over in Morlaix yesterday. We have some critical information for him."

The major narrowed his eyes. "Was he expecting you? Because if he was, I should certainly know about it." The sergeant grunted. Roland swiveled a warning eye his way. He turned back to the major.

"No, sir, but I can assure you he'll want to hear what we have to say."

A quick shake of the head. "If you'd like, I will be happy to meet with you tomorrow. If what you say has credence, then perhaps we will meet with the colonel together. But until—"

Roland raised his voice. "Sir, all due respect, but I insist that you—"

The door behind him opened. A large figure stepped through, the dual eagles on his shoulders gleaming. Roland felt it was the most handsome insignia in the entire American military, especially at this moment. Wearing the rank was Colonel Sealock. Roland had seen him before, walking through the Hole, clapping the soldiers on their backs, playing politician, trying to keep the morale of the cripples up. His face, at this moment, wasn't as jovial. A tall, lanky man with a high forehead and perpetual five o'clock shadow, he narrowed his eyes at Roland and Simon, looking them up and down. "Who the hell was that screaming and yelling here, in *my* office?"

The major placed his hands behind his back and stepped aside. Sealock stayed in the wedge of the partially open door, staring, waiting.

Roland cleared his throat. "That was me, sir. I would apologize, but I'm afraid I cannot. This…" he thumbed with his right hand to indicate the sergeant, "…staff *sergeant* acts as if he's wearing your rank, sir. He disrespected me and Lieutenant Jericho, and while I hate I interrupted your meeting, I'd do it again, sir, for the corps of commissioned officers."

Sealock blew out a breath, displaying trumpeter's cheeks. He looked back into his office, speaking to someone. "Be right back." Pulled the door shut behind him. Walked around the desk to the staff sergeant.

"Sergeant Boyd, did you disrespect these officers?"

Old Boyd was certainly at attention now. Two times he started to speak, fumbling on his words. Finally he got it out. "S-s-sir, perhaps disrespect was perceived, but it certainly wasn't intended. All I was trying to do was to…well…protect you from an intrusion by…well…"

Sealock was shaking his head, eyes closed. "Shut up, Boyd. Just shut up. Jeez, Lord, just once could ya send me an NCO worth two nickels?" Opened his eyes. "Sergeant, get your helmet on, and your combat suspenders. Fill the canteens full…and I mean full. Grab one of those dummy rifles from the parade room and get your ass out in that plaza and run around the outer edge thirty times."

Staff Sergeant Boyd's mouth opened and closed like he was testing his jaw muscles. He appeared to be trying to say something when Sealock cut him off.

"Move your ass, Boyd, or I'll have you shipped over to the front line to clear mines! Think I'm shittin'. Major Torres here'll be watching you out the window, counting laps, so don't even think of taking a damned shortcut."

Evidently Boyd didn't think he was shittin'. He hurriedly gathered up his gear, disappearing into the crowded hallway. Sealock groaned, massaging the back of his neck. "Guy's been in the Army a year and a half and he's already a staff. This damned war…too many people dyin'…moves these guys up way too fast." He looked up, studying the two men before him. "Now…why are you two here?"

Roland tilted his chin upward. "I want to discuss what happened to the general yesterday, in Morlaix, to him and his men. I think we can help, sir."

"Morlaix, huh? That's what we're in there discussing right now."

"Then can we come in, sir?"

"I don't think you want to do that," Sealock said with a chuckle. "Major Torres here can meet with you later."

Roland took a step closer, his fake leg thumping on the floor. "Two minutes, sir. Just two minutes. You don't like what I have to say, throw me out."

A smirk came over the leathered colonel's face. "You really want to go in there?"

"Yes, sir." Roland looked back at Simon, baring his teeth.

"Yes, sir, me too," Simon echoed.

Colonel Sealock nodded once. "Very well, gents, two minutes." He turned back to the major. "Torres, show these men inside."

The major twisted the knob, opening the door, motioning them inside the way a butler might. Sealock walked in first, moving to the sitting area to his right. Roland motioned Simon in, following behind, thumping over the hollow floor. He watched as Simon surveyed the room, swiveling his head back as he walked. His eyes were so wide Roland could see the whites above and below the brown.

Sealock's voice was authoritative. "Gentlemen, welcome our visitors. Captain, lieutenant, present yourselves."

Roland surveyed the men in the room, seated comfortably to the right in high-back chairs and on leather sofas. In addition to Colonel Sealock, there was another full-bird colonel, a brigadier general, two two-star generals, and seated all the way to the right, his three stars shining like the sun, Lieutenant General George S. Patton, staring at both of them through slit eyes.

After all this time, hearing all the stories about him, Patton, right there. The world-famous Nazi insulter, mere feet away. And here Roland was, on a wooden leg, working in a paper factory, still trembling from two years of alcoholism. He felt naked.

"Just a précis. We don't have all day," Colonel Sealock said.

Roland couldn't take his eyes off of Patton—the man people either loved or hated. No middle ground. He struggled to speak.

IT WAS A GLORIOUS September evening near the coast of France. There had been no shellings all day. Men had actually gotten more than a half-hour of sleep in one stretch. Garland, after his five hours in the evening, managed to get another two after his odd talk with the milk-white private, he of the unloving mother. The weather was cool and overcast and the evening breeze brought with it the rich, salty smell of the ocean. Garland situated his guard force, paraphrasing what the company commander had said earlier about the German, or the saboteur, operating behind the lines.

"Anyone comes near the perimeter or this BAR," Garland said, kneeling in front of the two privates, his index finger raised for punctuation, "you issue the challenge. If they don't know the countersign, if they freeze and don't say shit, you light 'em up."

"I've had that happen with our own guys, Sarge," said the muscular, Italian-looking soldier.

Garland nodded with a knowing grin. "I'd say Lieutenant Yaupon made it pretty clear earlier that every soldier, from private to general, better know their signs and countersigns. If they don't, hell, maybe they deserve to get shot." He made them recite both, several times each. The privates asked several more questions before he felt confident they could get through their four-hour shift without making an egregious error. As he began to leave, the other private, the despondent one from earlier, stopped him.

"Ask you something, Sarge?"

Garland hoped it had nothing to do with the kid's mother. He'd managed to tamp down his own feelings. The last thing he needed was the kid roiling them up again. "What do you need?"

"Over there, Sarge." The private turned back to his guard mate. "No offense."

Garland told himself to be patient, leading the private away from the observation post bunker. They stood in a small copse, Garland's hands on his hips. "What's your name anyway?"

"Holder, Sergeant."

"Well, Holder, I'm not trying to be harsh, but I don't want to talk about your mom anymore. You've got guard tonight and, as cold as this sounds, you just need to suck it up."

Holder nodded. Looked down.

"It's for your own good. People with the blues don't think clearly, and that's a good way to get killed out here." Garland simulated a punch to Holder's chest. "You hear me, pal?"

"I hear you, Sarge."

"So what'd you need?"

Holder's eyes came up. "Just wanted to thank you, that's all. You're the first regular around here who actually listened to me."

Garland nodded his thanks, feeling like a heel. He changed tack, asking, "Are you comfortable with guard?"

"Yeah, Sergeant, I feel pretty good about it."

"Were you in the firefight right after Paris?"

"No, I just missed it. I was in the group of three that arrived after that."

Garland pinched an unlit cigarette in his mouth as he spoke. "When we get back into some real action, simply follow your gut. If we're in a firefight and you feel you need to move, then move. Think you see someone in a tree line about to shoot, even if they look like a shadow, then take their ass out." He began to move away. "The American soldier is supposed to be skilled as well as having the ability to take over when needed. You need to listen to your NCOs, but don't be afraid to *act* when you think the time is right."

Holder stood still, adjusted his stance.

Garland stopped, removed the cigarette. "Did any of that make sense?"

"Yes, Sergeant. Just standing here, kinda burning those things into my brain."

"Good, but do me a favor…burn 'em into your brain back in that hole. And welcome to the Twenty-Third, Holder." His helmet tilted back, Garland walked back to the platoon tent, feeling better for having imparted wisdom to the grieving kid, even if, technically, the private was the enemy.

Outside of the tent was a basin that had been set up for shaving, filled with milky water. Garland went into his bag, located his razor, and set about sharpening it on a strap. Months before, he'd gotten a medical profile from the doctor for ingrown hairs, adding to his disguise. Per regulation, he was allowed to keep a short beard, but was required to keep it trimmed. After trimming his beard with a small set of scissors, he pulled the skin of his neck taut, creating a hard line of hair between his chin and Adam's apple. When he had half his neck shaved, the platoon leader, Sergeant First Class

Whitcomb, ambled over. The previous two lieutenants in Whitcomb's billet had been killed (one of them thanks to Garland,) leaving the former squad leader to jump two spots, now occupying the officer's billet. Whitcomb swigged from his canteen and wiped his mouth with his dirty sleeve.

"You got any ideas on how that booby trap could'a been set yesterday?"

Garland pinched the cigarette in his mouth while he shaved upward on his neck, going against the grain. He dipped his razor in the basin, swishing it. "Like the commander said, they found the rear guard dead. Rain storm like that, the kraut most likely killed the guard, snuck up there, set the betty, disappeared."

"I get all that," Whitcomb said. Took another swig. "But Morlaix is six, seven klicks behind the line. How did the kraut get all the way back there without being seen?"

Garland stopped what he was doing and straightened. Pinching the cigarette between his wet fingers, he narrowed his eyes before shrugging. "Maybe he took a uniform off of a dead GI."

"Gotta be that," Whitcomb said, nodding thoughtfully. "You know, those officers that got killed could have been any of us." He stared off into the darkness of the trees, the day's light nearly gone, leaving a patchwork of indigo through the twisted blackened branches. "It's hell enough havin' to die from an arty blast, or from getting pinged in the neck by some sharpshootin' kraut's bullet, but to have to worry about dyin' in the relative safety way behind the damned line…it's just too much."

An agreeable silence came between them as Garland kept shaving. "Just met one of the 'cruits…kid named Holder."

"Yeah, I think the company got three or four newbies when we came offa the line."

"Kid doesn't know his mouth from his asshole."

Whitcomb grunted. "Seems we're scrapin' the bottom of the barrel for bodies now." Another silence. "But if that's bad, think about the krauts. Fightin' a two-front war like they are. Bet their new recruits are certifiable limp-noodles, not that their regulars are much better. Buncha cowardly bastards."

Garland felt his heart rate increase as he scraped the last of the hair from his neck, trimming a small amount from his cheeks. "You really believe that?"

"What?"

"That their regular soldiers—not their leadership, but just their grunts like me and you—are any different from us?"

"They're baby killers."

Garland stopped shaving, cocking his brow. "Did you see that in a newsreel? Hell, I saw three American GIs havin' their way with a French gal back in a Paris alley, and believe me, she didn't look like she was into it."

"Spoils of war," Whitcomb said with a shrug.

Garland knew he was walking a fine line. "All I'm saying is that the kraut soldiers aren't all that different than us. Hell, a third of our guys are second-generation kraut."

"Guess so," Whitcomb replied. "But they just seem more savage than us."

Though he didn't agree, Garland nodded. "You stayin' up tonight?"

Whitcomb slipped his canteen into its cover before unbuckling his combat suspenders. "Hell no. A few of the fellas are over at the mess tent. Someone *acquired* a case of wine from a local farmhouse cellar. They'll be up a while." He stepped away. "Me…I'm gonna take this chance to snooze. We're rollin' tomorrow sometime, back to the front."

"Any idea for how long?"

"No, and that's why I'm thinkin' a good damned night of sleep's in order. I'm hearin' two different things about how the war against Jerry is going. I heard Duncan from battalion say that Hitler'll be dead by Thanksgiving, if not sooner. He said if we can take Berlin earlier, they may have to put that Oktoberfest of theirs on just for us."

Garland snorted like any skeptical NCO would. "And the other?"

"It was Lieutenant Yaupon. Said he saw a West Point buddy from one of the armor units. Said the damned Fritzes are dug in but good in these Franco forests and it's gonna be hell to unseat 'em…maybe even undoable."

"So I take it, if you're going for the benefit of a good night of sleep, that you're siding with the plebe who says the Germans are going to be a bitch?"

Whitcomb's smile was evident even in the scant light. "Like I said, I still believe the krauts are a buncha cowardly bastards. Even still, in case it is tough row to hoe, why take the risk? I almost feel for these drunkards...rollin' forward with the hangover they're gonna have tomorrow." He removed his helmet and disappeared into the tent.

A half-hour later Garland stood quietly, like a shadow, leaning on a knotty tree. He watched an anonymous soldier pass through the company area, lugging something. Somewhere a guitar strummed, playing...*Stille Nacht?* He could live in the States a hundred years, but Garland felt he would never truly understand the American free spirit. Christmas carols in September...

He padded across the company area, coming up behind the mess tent. The men were using an illicit, highly-forbidden candle to illuminate what looked like a raucous game of Spades.

"Got the damned ace down in your crotch, you sumbitch!"

"T'hell you say."

"Right there!"

"Don't be reachin' for my dick!"

"Then put that extra ace back in the second deck, ya cheatin' bastard!"

Four players and about ten onlookers, each of them holding a plain bottle, swigging regularly. The smell of grapes, and plums, and currants wafted by. Garland looked around. Other than the card game, and a few rogue wanderers, it seemed everyone in the company had bedded down. Except for his soldiers stationed around perimeter on guard.

The company leadership was across the ravine, up at regiment. They'd been there for a half-hour, probably eating a hot meal and having a nip or two with their commissioned brethren.

His regretful thoughts flooded his mind. Again he thought about the men he'd killed, about their children. He shook his head back and forth. Violently.

"Do your job, Gerhard," he breathed, imagining what would happen if he crossed the battle line tonight, without taking Operation Wolf any farther.

"Vy didn't you go for twenty, Gerhard? Vy stop at nineteen? It doezn't zeem believable, Agent Nummer Acht. Added to zat, zee mercy you showed your vife and zee homosexual man...vee zink you are too zoft, and zis iz vot vee do vith zofties, Gerhard."

He stared across the ravine.

Just one more. One more good one and then make the decision.

Garland rubbed his temples.

But think about that kid you killed yesterday. Think about how it made you feel.

He closed his eyes, remembering Sergeant First Class Whitcomb's words. *The krauts are baby killers...a buncha cowardly bastards.*

That did it. Feeling his jaw muscles tighten as his molars ground down on each other, Garland slinked back through the perimeter, back to his pup tent, the one he was sharing with Sergeant McQueen (the one who'd had the ace in his crotch.) From the bottom of his rucksack, below the seam he'd painstakingly cut out, Garland removed a spool of what looked like thread and an extra Mk-2 grenade, allowing it to fall down into his undershirt. The unit had been re-supplied upon reaching rear garrison, and if this were to work, Garland knew the first thing to occur would be an inventory. If someone was short a grenade, they would be the prime suspect.

Most of the men carried spare weaponry, the large majority of it being German, primarily kept for souvenir purposes. Everyone, of course, wanted a shiny Luger to take back home (sometimes at the risk of eating a bouncing betty.) The Luger was so prized that it wasn't uncommon to see American officers wearing one, even over the reliable Colt .45. Garland had even seen Major Haag, in the middle of a firefight, carrying a Luger in his right hand, his Colt still in the holster. This grenade, however, was of the common American pineapple variety. Garland had taken it off of a dead American soldier back during a skirmish outside of a hamlet called La Chapelle-Neuve. Lightly loaded with the extra grenade, his combat suspenders, and his rifle, he eased to the southernmost point in the perimeter, low-crawling between the two observation points. After a hundred meters of downhill crawling, Garland stood, slowly picking his way down toward the stream.

There was hardly any light remaining and no moon on the rise. The forest had little undergrowth, the ground covered by years and years of pine needles. The breeze was intensifying, promising one of the evening storms which frequently blew in from the foamy waters of the Atlantic. Like slowly advancing artillery, it would first be announced by strobes from the distant lightning. Then by thunder. And then, each and every time, some soldier would say, "I think this one's gonna pass us," just before the bottom fell out. Amazing how that always happened.

Garland padded several hundred more meters down the hill before he stopped, leaning against the trunk of a colossal pine. He waited, allowing his eyes to adjust to the dark. Garland could hear the trickle of the brook below him. He stared across it, up the hill on the other side, his eyes swiveling back and forth. After three solid minutes, he saw it, at his one o'clock. Someone was being careless, lighting a cigarette without hiding the flame. He marked the position, burning it in his brain. That would be the regiment's headquarters position.

He moved again, carefully picking his way down the remainder of the slope. It was steep at points, with exposed roots that could grab a boot like a hand. At the bottom of the cut, standing by the brook, Garland studied the terrain, able to see just enough. Directly above him was the regimental headquarters company. Behind him, equidistant to about four-hundred meters, was his unit, Bravo Company. What he needed now was to determine the crossing point. He crept up and down the stream, finally seeing a set of smooth stones situated in such a way as to make a fine crossing. That had to be where the officers had been traversing stream— there was no other place suitable. Garland reached into his pocket, retrieving the spool of cutting-edge monofilament nylon. He placed it by the brook and set about feeling the bank, looking for several good-sized sticks. Once he found them, Garland waded into the chilly water, straddling the center stone, ankle deep on his leather boots. The largest of all the rocks, it would make the perfect spot to stop and gather oneself during a crossing. He jammed one of the sticks into the sand on one side of the rock. From his shirt he removed the grenade and, firmly holding the spoon, pulled the pin, thereby straightening it. Biting on his tongue, sweat dripping into his eyes, Garland focused to reinsert the pin, finally finding the hole and slipping it through. Prepared to throw it in the event the spoon somehow fell off, Garland released the tension, satisfied when the spoon held tight.

After letting out a long breath and wiping sweat from his face, Garland tied the monofilament to the first stick, jamming it back in the sand so that the knot was just under water. He painstakingly threaded the wire through the loose pin, tying the other end to the other stick, jamming it, too, in the sand on the opposite side while perching the grenade beside the rock in several inches of water. Garland stretched the loose monofilament across the rock, using the last stick to elevate it several inches above the rock. After retrieving pine needles and some leaves, he covered the line just enough to break the outline. He stepped back, squinting in the dark to admire his work. It was rudimentary but invisible—an effective tripwire.

The water would likely dampen the grenade, but probably not enough to prevent it from being fatal as someone picked their way across the brook. But, here in the dark, he couldn't be sure if his concealment would pass the smell-test in the light of the day. Being deep in the ravine, and from their vantage point, Garland didn't think either unit could see what he was about to do. He leaned over the rock, striking a match and studying his handiwork. Knowing there was a live grenade inches away, Garland carefully stacked a few extra leaves over the wire before dropping the spent match into the water. He began to back away from the trap when he heard a twig snap behind him.

Garland's heart lurched up into his throat. His eyes focused on the area from where the sound emanated. He crawled up to the bank, grabbing his M-1. Controlling his breathing, he stared into the darkness, raising the rifle to his shoulder.

The match. The damned match! If there was someone out there, they had just seen everything.

Garland stopped breathing, his ears perked to any sound, the rifle at the ready. He scanned the woods, a shape here, a stump there. His eyes stopped moving. A sliver of something of a lighter color. Was it a bush, or a person? He aimed the M-1 at the shape, waiting.

Waiting.

The shape burst into motion.

A person! He pitched up, fifty feet away, and began to run back towards Bravo Company, skittering up the steep hill.

Giving the grenade a wide berth, Garland splashed through the water, scrambling onto the bank, clawing in with his fingers, moving as fast as he could.

No! Nein! Nein! Nein! He wasn't ready for this to end.

Garland ran with toes barely touching the ground, a survival sprint. While his body recruited every muscle fiber of his person to close on his quarry, he suddenly had an epiphany regarding his going across the lines.

With the jolt of an amperage-heavy current of electricity, Garland realized he wasn't ready to be a Nazi again. Not now, not ever. And he finally admitted it to himself.

But if he didn't catch the person in front of him, he knew he wouldn't get a chance to stay or to go back to Germany. He'd face a military tribunal followed by the firing line.

Garland chided himself as he pressed up the hill, getting close enough to hear the grunts from his prey. Why did he do this? The list was already impressive enough. And if he had no desire to go back, what was the point in the first place? Was it guilt over wanting to be an American? Was it some sort of Germanic loyalty to duty, unavoidable despite the yearnings of his heart?

Or was it because he was a truly screwed-up individual?

No matter the reason, Garland knew he'd been careless. This stunt was too damned close to the killing of the general, which should have been his coup de grâce anyhow. But, no, he'd had to give in to the famous Faber desire and greed. His mother's was a desire for control, wrought by cruelty. His was a desire to impress, but who, now, was he trying to impress?

He bit down on his lip as he ran, jinking in and out of trees, biting so hard it drew blood.

His secret could not get out. Not tonight. Not ever.

With a final burst of speed, Garland closed the distance quickly.

TWELVE

AT THAT same moment, 295 miles away in London's Covent Garden neighborhood, Roland tried to gather himself, making eyes at Simon who was still staring back at him. Roland did a right-face, standing at attention, swallowing a few times. "Sir...I mean...officers...I'm, uh, Captain Buhl. An-an-and this is lieutenant...this is lieutenant..."

"Jericho," Simon whispered from the corner of his mouth.

"J-J-Jericho."

Patton chuckled a few times. "Get these two," he said, grinning to his cadre. He turned back, gesturing with his swagger stick. "So which one of you dropped the grenade?" A chorus of laughter went up.

"Sir?" Roland asked.

"You've got no damned leg, he's got no damned arm. Hell, it seemed the logical assumption."

Roland managed to force a laugh. "Oh, I get it, sir. It was separate accidents, actually."

"I said *two minutes*, cap'n," Sealock said in a friendly-sounding warning tone.

"Yes, sir," Roland answered, nodding. Took a chest-expanding breath. "To get right down to it, I would like your permission, sir, to leave here and go to France, to the Second Infantry, and assist them as they move forward."

"Assist them?" Sealock asked.

"Yes, sir."

"In what way?"

"Sir, when General Kagan was killed yesterday, and the others, it was obviously done by a German who'd gotten behind the lines."

Patton leaned forward. "The kraut-bastard also killed a major, a staff sergeant, and gutted a shit-ass private who, had he done his job, would have prevented all those deaths."

Roland made sure his tone was even and confident. "Well, I can prevent it from happening again, sir."

The other officers fidgeted. Patton's eyes moved down Roland's uniform, eyeing the blue and yellow Ranger lozenge patch, darting over to the Expert Infantryman Badge, the jump wings.

"How exactly can you help them?" asked Colonel Sealock.

"Sir, I was part of the OSS...the SGS it was called at that time...trained to be dropped behind the lines and to live amongst the Germans. I'm fluent, and from German blood. I know their ways, their methods. I also have extensive knowledge of guerilla warfare, which, by the way, is what doomed the general."

"Some suspect it was an inside-job," one of the other generals said. "Done by a flag-saluting Army soldier. One of our own."

"I respectfully disagree, sir," Roland said boldly, even though he completely agreed with him. "The killer could have certainly confiscated a uniform, but I don't think he's actually in our military."

Sealock shook his head. "Listen, captain, I just don't—"

Patton lowered his tea, cutting Sealock off. "Did you say the SGS was going to drop you behind the lines?"

"Yes, sir."

"And when was this to be?"

"June of forty-two, sir. I actually made the jump...that's when I lost the leg."

Patton's face had clouded but brightened. "I thought so." He glanced around at the seated officers, a sideways smile crinkling his face. "You guys read about this?" All heads shook no. "Well, and correct me if I'm wrong Buhl, but it was like this...this fella here is on-board a blacked out jump plane, over Germany, primed and ready to bail out, but the OIC radios in to wave it off because of weather. Am I right, Buhl?"

Roland, gnawing his lower lip, nodded. "You are, sir."

"So our young captain here tells the pilot and OIC to go to hell and he jumps anyway, into a helluva storm, right Buhl?"

"Yes, sir."

"Ballsy as it was, it wasn't too bright of a move." Patton grunted as he stood, walking to Roland. His voice was louder than the most boisterous of men, yet somehow didn't come across as classically obnoxious. It was as if he felt it was his duty to entertain those around him—and it worked. On his right hip was his Colt; on the left, his famous Smith & Wesson .357, forged of blued steel. Both guns were equipped with pearl grips. Patton eyed him a moment, using the swagger stick to tap Roland's prosthetic.

"Buhl's chute blew out due to the jump speed and he shatters his leg to bits upon landing. Then, half in shock, he drags his ass...how far, Buhl?"

"About a mile, sir."

"About a mile to a pig farmer's house, kills the resident Herr and Frau, calls his handler to get him out, then..." Patton's brown teeth glistened as his smile grew. He squatted down, made a sawing motion with his hand across Roland's knee, "...young Buhl here cut off his own damned leg to save himself from dying."

The officers whooped and hollered. Sealock grinned, wincing at the same time. General Patton straightened, adjusting his gun belt, his hands resting on the pistols as if by habit. "They talk about you at West Point, son. Kind of an example of what misguided balls can do to a man." He took Roland's hand, gripped it firmly, pumped once. "Damned glad I met you." The smile faded. He turned to Simon. "Do I know you?"

Simon took a moment to get it out. "Sir, I did actually meet you once, in a medical tent near Normandy, after I lost the arm."

Patton rubbed his chin, squinting. Looked up at the ceiling before his lips parted. His head snapped back, eyes glaring. His tone was challenging. "Knew you looked familiar, with that ghostly face and those blackish eye sockets. You threatened to whip my ass that day, didn't you?"

Silence. Stuttering. He finally got it out. "That's what my pals said, s-s-sir. I was on m-m-morphine."

Patton turned his head to the group of officers. They fidgeted uncomfortably until Patton began to laugh. "I'm not shitting you, he really did." There was more laughter. Patton shook left hands with Simon. "Good to meet you soldiers, it really was." He turned, walked back to his chair, talking to himself. "What a coupla characters. Uncle Sam's got a ragtag bunch…" He sat, made a dismissive motion. "All yours, Sealock."

The colonel looked at Roland and Simon, shook his head. "Captain, lieutenant, I appreciate your willingness, and we all appreciate this entertaining little diversion, but I think we're all better by your serving Uncle Sam right here in London. Your request has been duly considered and denied." He stood, motioning for the disfigured major to open the door. "Dismissed, gentlemen."

"Sir, if I may," Roland implored.

"That's my final decision, captain," Sealock said firmly, using his warning tone again, this time without the friendliness.

Roland looked at Simon who offered a minuscule shrug. He surveyed the senior officers, some of whom were already talking amongst themselves. Patton, however, had just lit a bratwurst-thick cigar, puffing on it as he stared at Roland, eyebrow cocked expectantly. Roland held his gaze. He couldn't be sure, but he thought Patton offered the faintest hint of a nod.

It was now or never.

"Colonel Sealock," Roland said in an elevated voice. "I disagree and I implore you to rethink this decision. You lose nothing, *absolutely nothing*, by sending us over there, two cripples."

Sealock had been about to sit. He stopped, pushing on the arms of the chair, straightening. A quiver ran through his face as his eyes burned anger. "Okay, son, first you interrupt my meeting, and then abuse my generosity of granting you two minutes' time by questioning my damned judgment in front of my superiors?"

"I'm not trying to show you up, sir, but I cannot tell you how strongly I feel about—"

"Out, captain!" Colonel Sealock bellowed, jabbing a rigid arm to the door. "And bring your ass back here at zero-six tomorrow to get busted to second-lieutenant for insubordination."

Roland ground his teeth together, his breath coming loudly from his nose. He glared at Sealock for a full ten seconds before executing a modified about-face on his prosthetic, followed by Simon to the door. The major opened it, pointing to the anteroom.

A loud voice. "Hold it right there, gentlemen."

Patton.

Roland and Simon stopped, turned to the general.

"Sit down, Sealock. Major, get lost for five minutes." Sealock sat, the major got lost. Patton puffed a few times, spinning his cigar. He blew out the smoke, billowing above him. "You feel strongly about this, don't you, Buhl?"

"Yes, sir, I do."

"And now you're carrying your little torch of redemption after that fouled-up incident I told them about?"

"Yes, sir, I guess I am."

Patton looked over at Colonel Sealock. "The colonel here doesn't mean any harm, and in reality, probably made the best decision by telling you not to go. But I'm going to override him, not because I don't respect Colonel Sealock, but because I can feel how much you want to get back over there, back to the action." He appraised his cigar a moment, his eyes coming back up. "I like that kinda passion. More people had it, we'd be back in the States already."

"Thank you, sir," Roland said, his voice shaky.

The general stood, puffing smoke as he walked, the cigar rigidly leading the way like the main gun of a Sherman tank. He circled the two men, stopping in front of Roland. His voice lowered for the first time, as if the two men were having a private conversation. "You've got balls, cap'n, brass ones. Watching you a moment ago, I felt like I was watching myself." He removed the cigar, moving a fingernail shy of nose to nose. He smelled of good tobacco, and leather, and gun oil. He smiled at Roland, his craggy face splitting wide and displaying his brown, gapped teeth. "They've been trying like hell to hold me back my whole life, kid. Can't do this. Can't do that. And you know what?...I called bullshit on 'em all. My ass, I can't do it." A snort. "I can do *anything*, kid. Any-damn-thing I damn well please." He jabbed the cigar back into his mouth and wrapped his powerful hands around Roland's shoulders, giving them a good shake, his voice modulated by the Cuban. "Go get 'em son. Go find the Fritz who killed my general, rip his guts out and eat 'em with mustard and sauerkraut while he watches you."

He rotated his head around to Sealock, still speaking with the cigar clamped between his teeth. "That okay with you, colonel?"

Colonel Sealock popped to his feet. "Yes, sir."

Patton nodded. Turned and ambled back to his seat. "Good. Now you two broke-dicks get the hell outta here and get your gear. I'll see you tonight at Croydon."

"Sir?" Roland asked.

Patton jerked the cigar out. "Did I stutter, kid? That jump foul up your ears, too? I said I'll see you at Croydon…it's an airfield. You're flying back with me."

GARLAND DIDN'T risk shooting. It was far too dark to get off an accurate shot, and in the event he missed, the person who had spied on him would be long gone and he'd be left to explain a gunshot and a booby trap. He was dodging through the small trees, fleet of foot, getting closer to the person. Up to his right was Bravo Company. The farthest observation point was probably still a third of a kilometer away—too far for them to hear him chasing this person through the rain-dampened woods.

The person ahead stumbled, regaining his feet but allowing Garland to close within two arm lengths. Knowing he had him, Garland dropped his rifle and jerked the Ka-Bar from its sheath, knife arcing through the air as he made a final push. He felt the knife go in and stop when it hit bone, causing the runner to tumble to the ground with Garland on top. He could tell by the feel of the uniform and combat suspenders that it was a soldier. He pulled the knife out, stopping himself before he jammed it in again. Squeezing his eyes shut, Garland lowered his head to the now-still person, hating himself for setting the grenade, hating himself for stabbing whoever this was.

He stayed that way for a moment, finally pushing up. The person below him moaned, and that's when Garland heard yelling and crashing behind him. A person, maybe more than one, was rushing through the inky forest.

"I heard it!" a voice yelled.

"Tell him to halt!" roared an authoritative voice.

The person underneath him moaned again. Garland whipped his head around, judging the advancing voices to be no more than a hundred meters away. Then came the explosion.

The grenade!

Gunfire erupted, tracers flying all over the ravine as his own guard force began to light up the valley. Fearing he'd be seen, Garland dove off the soldier and raced up the hill, going wide of the gunfire, using the sound as his cover. He could see the closest observation point firing away with their BAR, and in between bursts could hear someone in the ravine screaming for a cease-fire. Garland stayed well to the left of the observation point, dropping to his stomach and skittering into the perimeter. It was a madhouse. Soldiers ran everywhere, half of them drunk, smashing into trees and each other, the other half still dazed from the rude awakening of their gloriously deep REM sleep.

Garland doubled back, coming up from behind the southernmost observation point, yelling the countersign in the event the two privates had itchy trigger fingers. When he dove into the freshly-dug hole, one of the privates was fumbling with an ammo can, trying to feed a new belt into the Browning. The phrase "cease fire" was being bellowed from the ravine now by a chorus of voices. Suddenly, lights began to bathe the area as the men in the ravine broke with regulation by using their flashlights. Garland peered downward to see someone flopping around in the water of the ravine. His eyes shot to the right of where the grenade had exploded, scanning for the soldier he'd just knifed. He couldn't see him.

"Medic! Medic!" came the shouts from the ravine. Other men began to race down the hill and soldiers from headquarters could be seen bounding down on the other side, everyone now using their flashlights.

"I didn't know I was shooting at our guys, Sarge!" cried the muscular private manning the Browning. "I heard an explosion and then everything went to hell. People were shooting, screaming...I thought we were under attack!"

Garland held up his hand, telling the kid to relax. As pandemonium ruled inside the perimeter, he walked over to the face-wash, dumping water onto the Ka-Bar and wiping it with a paper towel, which he stuffed underneath trash in the refuse container. After wiping considerable sweat from his face, he hurried back down the hill, jumping into the water so his wetness from setting the booby-trap wouldn't arouse any suspicion. Now seeming to be part of the group that had stormed the ravine, he helped the two sets of medics carrying the litters as they struggled to climb the hill under a heavy load.

The muscular private was still perched on the earthen mound at the front of the hole. "Where's your other guard?" Garland asked as he stepped away from the litters, head whipping in all directions.

The private turned, opening his hands. "He went out a little bit ago."

"Went out where?"

"That's why I was shootin', Sarge! Holder went down there, into the ravine, and it wasn't long after that when I heard some yelling, then I saw the explosion."

Garland tilted his head back to the heavens. *Das ist so Scheisse!* He'd probably knifed the private from earlier...Holder...the kid with the unloving mother. He rushed to the medical tent. Men shone lights on the ground in front of the two teams of medics, illuminating their passage to the medical tent.

On the first litter was Lieutenant Yaupon, the company commander. He'd been the one hit by the grenade, evidenced by his left ass cheek hanging from his body like a disjointed Sunday pot roast. Garland moved closer as the litter went by, seeing a protruding lump of bone from his hip socket as well as the back half of his pelvis. A few flecks of blood peppered his back, nothing else. Yaupon was steadily streaming curses, typically a good sign that an injured man would live.

The other litter approached, the soldier unmoving, eyes closed. "Who's that?" Garland yelled at the front medic. "Who the *hell* is that on that litter?"

"New kid," the medic answered. "Don't know his name. The sonofabitch who set that booby trap down there must'a knifed him."

"What booby trap?"

"The XO says they heard something off to their left. Went to cross the crick and the commander set off an explosion of some sort."

Garland made sure his face registered the appropriate shock and anger. "Is the newbie dead?"

"Not yet, but he took a long knife right into his back," the medic answered, rushing past and hurrying the new arrival into the large, rectangular medical tent.

Garland rubbed his face with his hands as some of the other NCOs began to organize squads to go down into the ravine and find the rogue German killer. They promised vengeance and blood, the drunk ones sounding much more savage than the ones still trying to wake up. Their mission was a completely unnecessary exercise, and like Whitcomb had said earlier, they'd all be better off getting a good night's sleep.

Because the Nazi killer wasn't down in the ravine, he was right there amongst them, cursing himself for his sloppy stratagem. He had no desire to join the posse, for his mind was far more occupied by the wounded Private Holder, and whether or not he would survive.

The doc appeared, cigarette hanging from his mouth, gray stubble on his face, hair going every direction, cursing loudly. He'd been sleeping for three days, pulling no guard duty, and having no wounds to patch—still bitching as if he were the busiest man in the unit. He held his hands out while his medic squirted them with a rust-colored fluid. He rubbed them vigorously before going into the tent, yelling for black coffee to no one in particular, wanting to know what happened, wanting to know who was worse off so he could decide who should get cut on first.

And all Garland could do was sit on his ass and wait.

THE EXECUTIVE model of the C-47 was quite a bit different than the last aircraft that had carried Roland over mainland Europe. Instead of olive-green ribs, wires, and steel panels, this one was outfitted with wood-paneled walls, scarlet carpet and gold drapery. Rather than webbed seating, Roland's chair was covered in supple brown leather. It was bolted to the deck by a swivel, in front of the fold-down oak table that held his dinner. The dinner, too, was held down by an ingenious section of clips made into the table. The special plates and glasses clipped to the table so as not to spill during flight.

Not counting the pilots, there were only five people aboard the aircraft, as well as Patton's white bull terrier Willie. A heavily armed staff sergeant, also with a Ranger diamond, sat on a fold-down jump seat behind the pilots, facing the rear. There was Roland, Lieutenant Jericho, Colonel Weston—one of Patton's aides, and the General himself. When Roland and Simon had boarded, there was already food on the table, sitting under a silver service. A staff sergeant in white mess had boarded last, going to the rear of the plane and fiddling about with additional platters and drinks. Willie slumbered on a stuffed pillow beside the general.

"You there," Patton had said after greeting his two guests. The mess sergeant turned, wide-eyed. The general made a shooing motion. "Take the night off, son. Go out in London, have a billy time, dip your wick if you can find a willing dame."

After struggling with his words, the sergeant said, "But, sir, I was assigned to fly with you tonight. If I'm not here, no one will be able—"

"We'll figure it out! Shit, Ike's setting this Army up to create a bunch of pampered pussies. Like I can't pour my own damned tea…"

That had been an hour earlier. They were now out over the Channel. Every few minutes the co-pilot would call over the intercom, letting the passengers know that there would be heavy banking due to storms in the area, making Roland's mind hearken back to his near-fatal jump. Patton sawed on a piece of rare beef, jabbing it into his mouth and chewing with his hind teeth.

"Might as well be eating this chair leather. Damned Brits know less about food than the Krauts." He laughed. "Hell, at least the fritzes have figured out how to make sausage."

"And beer," the colonel quipped.

Roland barely listened as Patton went on and on about a bevy of subjects, crowing about how the Germans were more scared of him than any other commander, about intercepted communiqués of German field marshals discussing his tactics. While Patton was initially entertaining, Roland could see how one might quickly bore of his unbridled braggadocio. "I did this," and "I cut their ass off stone-cold," and "I told him that." *I did…I am…I will.* He peered over Patton's shoulder at the two pilots, a colonel and a light colonel. Both wore side-arms. The co-pilot seemed to be doing the flying, twisting the yoke to the left into a steep bank as the aircraft began to hit turbulence, making it sound like a rickety truck going down a washed-out road. He pulled the napkin from his collar and looked at his fellow ranger, listing back and forth in the jump seat with heavy eyelids. It was after midnight, after all, and the droning of the Pratt & Whitney engines did become hypnotic.

"The hell you staring at them for?" Patton asked, jarring Roland's train of thought. He buttered a roll, stuffing half into his mouth and washing it down with a gulp of ice tea. "So, when we land, what's your plan?"

Roland was caught off guard. *Plan?* He cleared his throat, buying a few seconds. "Will I have any assets at my disposal, sir?"

"You can have a Jeep, a driver. Maybe the colonel here can rustle up a few pistols. After all that huffing and puffing you did back there, I figured you'd have a plan laid on."

Roland nodded as if he'd thought everything through. "I do, sir. I want to go to the Second Infantry—Indianhead—to their H.Q. at Morlaix. I want to see where the general was killed."

"And?"

"I'd like to speak to the soldiers who were nearby and study how far back from the line Morlaix is, look at the local area, that type of thing."

Patton cocked an eye, leaning forward, elbows on the table. "Yeah, I caught that line of bullshit you were feeding us. Those rubes back there in London might have bought it, but dispense with the purebred bullshit when you're talking to me, how 'bout it?" Patton dragged the remainder of the roll through the pool of bloody liquid, sopping it up before he ate it.

Roland turned his eyes to Simon. True to his usual form around ranking officers, the lieutenant had been very quiet. Roland made a questioning face. Simon nodded. Roland agreed. He reached inside his jacket, removing the ledger sheet, spreading it on the side of the table. Roland stood, leaning against the table for support. He indicated 2nd Infantry with his finger, then traced his hand to the 23rd Regiment.

"Sir, the Second, and specifically their Twenty-Third Regiment, has had twice the categorical deaths of officers and senior enlisted than anyone in your Third Army."

"Categorical?"

"Meaning, by means *other* than certain German influence."

Patton's eyes moved up from the sheet.

Roland clarified. "Death from things like grenades, mines, booby traps, snipers shots."

Patton sawed another piece of the tough beef, chewing it before he twirled his fork. "Unlike the colonel here, I have an incredibly high IQ. Speed it up."

"Well, sir, when we went back through the death reports, we determined that the 23rd has had an unusually high occurrence of these types of deaths. In fact, their total stuck out like a sore thumb."

Patton struggled with the piece of meat, chewing loudly, holding his hand up for silence. He managed to swallow it, drank the rest of his tea, and jerked the linen napkin from his collar with a huge exhalation and a clap of his belly. "So you think, instead of some Kraut sneaking around behind the lines, that the Twenty-Third has someone working from the inside?"

The two lower-ranking men locked eyes again. "We do," they said simultaneously.

"Yet, earlier, when General Clovage suggested that exact thing, you disagreed with him, damned vehemently if I recall."

Roland pulled in air through his nose, holding the general's gaze. "I didn't want anyone to steal this from us. Neither of us is of much use anymore, unless—"

"*Unless* you can produce a Fritz who's been killing GI Joe every day from behind the lines. I get it. Pretty devious, but effectively pulled off. Touché." He reached to his jacket, hanging on a peg, retrieving a leather pouch. "Cigar?" Roland and Simon declined; the colonel partook. Patton pulled two out, prepped them, lit his and the colonel's with matches, leaned back and puffed. He stared at Roland for a long moment as the engines whirred.

"So why, gentlemen, should I not pour every investigator and MP I've got into that regiment and roust out the German by force?"

Roland's head shook back and forth emphatically. "All due respect, sir, but you'd never find him. He'd simply clam up and look like any other soldier."

"But what if he's a German plant?" the colonel interjected. "Intel would figure that out."

"Not in my opinion, sir," Roland countered. "Though we don't like to admit it, and though they've spent far more time working in England, the German network in the United States is very good. It's likely they would have used a U.S. citizen. Hell, a third of our country is from German heritage."

"And what makes you the expert?" Patton asked.

"I was trained in doing exactly this, sir…assimilating. Whether or not we like him, whoever this asshole is, he's damn good. To kill senior officers like this, under everyone else's noses, takes skill. We go in there and upset the apple cart, all he'll do is go to ground for a bit and know we're onto him."

Patton looked skeptical. "So how will you do it?"

"I'm going to trick him."

"Thought you said he was damned good."

"I'm better."

As he puffed his cigar, Patton said, "As long as there isn't a parachute involved."

"Touché back to you, sir."

Patton stared at Roland and Simon for a long moment. He leaned down and patted Willie, who didn't budge. Then he turned to the colonel, nodded, turned his head back. "I'm going to give you two the authority. Go where you want, do what you want. You need something, you find the colonel here and he'll let me know. And don't tell anyone what this is related to. Some smartass commander starts asking you questions, you show 'em the orders and tell 'em to find me. That'll shut 'em up lickety split."

"Orders, sir?"

Patton snapped his fingers. From under the table, the colonel produced an envelope with a red twist string on the back. Roland opened it, unfolding the crisp white paper on Patton's personal Army stationary, holding it so Simon could read it too.

September 19, 1944

To: Third Army Personnel
From: General George S. Patton
Order: 032707

This is to certify that I have deputized Captain Roland Buhl (left leg lost) and First Lieutenant Simon Jericho (right arm lost) to investigate enemy activity behind the Third Army lines of demarcation. They are to be given full access to personnel, unit activity areas, and anything else they deem fit. Their mission is of the highest priority, and any resistance by Third Army personnel will be considered a direct affront to me. I will deal with that person, or persons, myself.

This order stands effective until midnight (zulu) of September 30th, 1944.

My two deputies report directly to me. Victory.

Gen. George S. Patton

kd/GP

Roland swallowed twice as he quickly reread the order. It was exactly what he had dreamed up when he first met Simon, when he first went to work in the Hole. Damn if that didn't seem ages ago. Now he had a purpose again, and authority. Much like before the accident, Roland Buhl was now in charge of his own destiny.

And this time would be different.

Patton took the paper, accepted a pen from the colonel, and signed it in black ink. He capped the fountain pen and handed the paper back. "There now, that paper'll be a brand new set of testicles for you both."

Roland thanked him, folding the orders back into the envelope and tucking it into his jacket. "Where will we land, sir?"

"Near Morlaix at…" he turned.

"Ploujean," the colonel said, using a decidedly American pronunciation.

Patton nodded. "Right, *Plow-gene*. You can proceed at first light."

"I need you to hold the Twenty-Third back, sir."

The general ground his teeth. "How long?"

"Twenty-four hours? Forty-eight tops."

"Why so long?"

"We'll move as fast as possible, sir."

Patton closed his eyes for a moment. "Done."

"Thank you, sir," he and Simon said at the same time.

"Thank me by producing this kraut on a stick." He eyed Roland, then Simon, then changed his tone completely, morphing back into the entertainer. Patton gave the colonel the nickel version of Roland's story. He then listened intently to Simon's story of Normandy, interrupting several times to take the talk down a rabbit trail about the Nazis, somehow always coming back to himself. Roland's mind was elsewhere, racing, computing possibilities he hadn't yet even dreamed. The engines slowed, the aircraft descending through smoother air. Roland, still zoned-out of Patton's bombastic tales, was looking over the table, down at the grips of Patton's two protruding pistols. On his right hip was the beautiful single-action Colt .45. On his left side, in a custom holster, was the famed .357 Roland had seen earlier. The bluing of its steel shone under the amber lights of the cabin. Patton was leaning on the table, resting on his elbows, cradling the cigar in both hands. He stopped what he was saying and followed Roland's eyes downward.

"She's pretty, isn't she?"

"Beautiful, sir."

"You like to shoot?"

"Yes, sir."

"You any good?"

Roland shrugged. "I think so."

"Ever competed?"

"When I went through the SGS's program, I out-shot the former leader of the San Francisco Police's marksmanship team."

Patton laughed a wheezy laugh. "Kinda like me sayin' I outran a one-legged man."

Roland forced a laugh, nodding. He pointed at the .357. "May I hold her, sir?"

Patton's smile faded. There was a long, pregnant pause. Simon's eyes went down. The colonel shifted in his seat. Patton leaned forward, his face stony, shaking his head. "No one, in all my time as a general, has ever been brassy enough to ask to *hold* my personal sidearm."

Roland's heart hammered in his ears. He swallowed. "I like to be first in everything, sir."

It took a moment, but Patton's harsh gaze gave way to his trademark leathery grin. "Smart bastard, aren't you?" He bit down on the cigar, unclipped the holster, jerked the .357 from the belt. He flipped the gun around, handing it over in the proper way.

The colonel moved his hand to intercept the weapon, carefully taking it from the general. He flipped the cylinder out, emptying the gleaming rounds on the white table-cloth before flicking it back shut. He handed it to Roland.

Roland frowned at the colonel. "What do you take me for, sir?"

The colonel looked at Simon's shoulder, where an arm should be. He craned his neck, looking down at Roland's prosthetic leg. "You two seem to be a bit accident-prone. I didn't want to take any chances."

Roland held the pistol, his mind on the orders in his jacket pocket. He looked up at Patton. "Thank you, sir."

"As I said, thank me by bringing that sonofabitch back to me, dead or alive."

After Roland had handed the pistol back, Patton snapped his fingers, waking Willie and slapping his leg so the dog would place his paws in his lap. He fed him the remnants of the bloody beef as the aircraft made one final turn. Minutes later, the landing gear barked as the C-47 Executive rumbled onto the tarmac at Ploujean.

Following a short drive to Third Army's headquarters, Roland and Simon had a three-hour nap in the seat of their brand new Jeep. When they awoke with the sun, both men were shocked to find real, genuine coffee at the mess tent. After drinking more than their share, they loaded up with implements and sped off in the direction of Morlaix.

PART FOUR

Doppelgänger

THIRTEEN

THE SECOND Division was all but gone. Pigeons, hundreds of them, probably conditioned to being fed scraps from restaurants, milled about, cooing loudly, taking great hunger-motivated risks as they looked for any edible handout or crumb from the few humans remaining in Morlaix. The Jeep was parked in the middle of the five-point intersection in front of the restaurant that had doubled as Division Headquarters. Roland had gotten out and crossed the intersection, yelling up to a master sergeant overseeing the removal of antennas and communication wire. The master sergeant came down a shaky ladder from the roof and showed the two officers where the bouncing betty had killed the general and members of his entourage.

"You can see where the clean-up crew put gravel in the hole there. That's where the mine was hidden." The master sergeant was no less than fifty. Tall and impossibly tan, his eyes a translucent hazel, Roland assumed he must have American Indian blood in his veins. His hair, peeking out from under his helmet, was black, flecked with gray around the sideburns. The master sergeant's face was narrow, with high, prominent cheekbones and pencil thin eyebrows. And unlike nearly every soldier in theater, he didn't have a single whisker on his face, giving him a pulled-together, almost aristocratic look. He waited patiently while Roland drank in the scene, staring at him as if he was somehow listening to his train of thought.

Roland studied at the building, looked at the hole out front. He imagined the heavy rain, the explosion, the terrified screams. He didn't have to imagine the smell of death. He knew it well, his mind hearkening back, as it often did, to that coppery-smelling farmhouse in Germany. They were currently standing only a couple hundred miles from there, from the copse of trees, from the rapse field, from the killing ground. He closed his eyes, the thoughts dizzying his mind.

Simon broke the silence, slowly turning in a circle as he spoke. "Which way did the Jeeps come in from?"

The master sergeant turned too, lifting his arm to the narrow street behind them. "They'd just driven in from the east, straight down this road." He walked past the crater. "They stopped right here, and that's when someone…I think it was the major…set off the mine."

Simon lit a cigarette. The master sergeant accepted one from him. Simon offered one to Roland, but Roland didn't respond. He didn't hear him.

His eyes drifted over the buildings to the sky. The warm breeze cleansed his mind, pressing the memories of the farmhouse mercifully away. It was a beautiful September day near the coast of France, with mild temperatures and cobalt blue skies, interrupted only by a few cottony clouds, drifting off to the west. And while Morlaix was a shadow of its former self, what with the rubble and destruction, the hard rains followed by the crisp, dry air gave everything a linen-fresh feel, as if nature had decided to scrub away the death that had occurred here. A breeze blew from the east, carrying with it the clean, fresh smells of the surrounding fields and evergreen forests. Overhead, engines could be heard droning.

Roland shaded his eyes and looked in the direction of the sun. B-17's, in formation, headed north. Back to England, fresh from destroying German industry, and probably several hundred souls. With air superiority achieved, arrogant daytime raids were now the norm.

But even with air superiority, the war wasn't yet over. Not by a long shot.

Roland refocused. He walked to the crater and knelt, moving his hand over the packed wet gravel. Using his fingernail, he pried out a piece of metal, blowing on it, wiping it on his trousers. It was a ball bearing from the bouncing betty. He held it up. There would have been hundreds of them, flying at well over a thousand feet per second, ready to rip through and savage bodily tissue of anyone standing within fifty meters. He'd been trained on the betty, knowing that the cunning Germans who designed it probably did so with its maiming properties in mind. Tossing the ball bearing in his hand, he stood, stepping back to survey the area.

From twenty feet, he could see the pock marks in the mortar of the building. The walls were painted pink, dotted every few inches with tiny craters where the ball bearings had found no target. Most of the pock marks fell between two to six feet above the ground. He turned to peer down the street, again using his hands to shade his eyes. He spoke for the first time since the master sergeant's arrival.

"Show us where the guard was killed."

The master sergeant took a final drag on the Lucky, flicking it to the sidewalk and stepping off at a brisk pace. At the end of the street, in a rubble-strewn building, he turned left, picking his way inside.

Simon followed, with Roland going third. He was too busy looking around, wondering if the building had been destroyed by the Americans or the Germans. He didn't notice a tilted section of floor, and when he stepped on it with his bad leg, it caused the prosthetic to buckle, making him fall down.

"Sonofabitch!" he growled. The fall had made him instinctively reach out with his right hand. With no time to react, he jammed it straight onto a nail that happened to be sticking up through a piece of slat board. Roland pulled his hand back slowly, watching with fascination as the nail withdrew back through his hand.

"You okay?" Simon asked, hurrying back to him.

His hand dripping blood, Roland reaffixed his prosthetic—it had popped off his knee—adjusting and tightening the straps. The master sergeant stared at the fake leg in a type of transfixed distress—a "that could easily be me" look—from the hallway on the far side of the rubble.

Simon helped Roland up, removing a wad of wound dressing from the small pack on his suspenders. Roland gripped it in his fist, shooed his partner away, mumbled a few practiced thank you's for his concern, and told the master sergeant to get on with it.

"Sir, are you sure you're okay? That hand injury looks as bad as a bullet hole, and the nail was rusty."

"I'll live. Show us where the guard died."

The old NCO turned, opening the door to the water closet under the stairs. A blast of flies flew out, followed by the same pungent smell from the German farmhouse.

Enough light shone through the blown out building to illuminate the dark stains from the dead guard's blood. No one had bothered to clean it up. Simon peered in briefly, holding the inside crook of his only elbow over his nose and mouth. "Oh, man," he said, sounding as if he were talking into a pillow. More pale than normal, he scurried away and sat on the rubble, finishing his cigarette, leaning back and resting his head against a fallen timber.

The old master sergeant ingested the smell with a great breath, seemingly impervious. With a grim nod he stepped aside, allowing Roland to drink in the gruesome sight. All of the blood in the guard's body must have spilled out in the bathroom. It covered the floor, still sticky because of the sheer volume. Roland could see where his legs had been on the toilet seat, with blood all around their impressions. He stepped back, looking back to where the guard had presumably stood on the street.

"Let me reconstruct this thing." He snapped his fingers. "Simon, find your balls and get out on the street. Sarge, forget rank, okay? We're all old friends here." They picked their way back through the rubble, back into the clean brilliance of the noonday sunshine.

Roland stood in the street, turning, getting his bearings. He was about to speak when a question popped in his mind. "Where were they coming from?" he asked the master sergeant.

"Who?"

"The Jeeps."

The master sergeant pointed east. "They came from that way, then veered down this street here."

"But where. Where had they been?"

"East of here, at the Twenty-Third Infantry."

Roland rotated his head to the quickly-recovering Simon. The Twenty-Third. Both men nodded.

"I miss something?" the master sergeant asked.

"We're about to find out." Roland snapped his fingers at Simon. "Unfold that map. We looked at the locations before, but now that I'm here on-site, I need to see it again. Show me where the Twenty-Third is."

Simon opened the folded map, roughly orienting it. From his pocket, he removed a compass, flicking it open. "Gimme a hand here, Sarge. I'm working with only one arm." The master sergeant held the map taut as they made a few small corrections. Once square with grid north, he laid the map on the ground, weighting it with his compass and canteen. Simon stabbed the map with one of his five remaining fingers. "Us." His finger jumped two grid squares to the east. "Twenty-Third."

Roland knelt down awkwardly, using his arms to muscle his prosthetic into a suitable position, not wanting it to buckle again. He hummed as he traced his finger from the 23rd's location to Morlaix. "So our guy has to get from there to here." He looked up at the master sergeant. "Squat down here, Sarge. Don't be shy." He did. "So, three or four days ago when the general died—"

"Two," Simon corrected.

"Two days?"

"Right-o."

"Shit. That's what a lack of sleep will do to you. So…the day before yesterday, it was raining, correct?"

"Like a sieve," the master sergeant answered.

"Would there have been much traffic between the units over here," he said, touching the map, "and here at Morlaix?"

"That was the main supply line, so yes, a great deal. I drove it myself two or three times that day, and it was loaded with vehicles and soldiers on foot. We actually had a kid from one of the support companies get struck in the back of his head by a truck mirror. Lucky he didn't die."

"Uh-huh," Roland muttered, nodding. He stood, pointed to the east. "So our guy walked. He wouldn't have taken a vehicle. Too conspicuous. He comes in from the east, head down, the rain keeping him anonymous. Just another dog soldier, miserable in shitty weather like everyone else. The main road is one block north, so our killer turns down this way, all alone." Roland points to the street corner. "The guard's right there. Holds his hand up, tells him he can't pass. No one from Division H.Q. is outside, because it's raining so hard."

The master sergeant inched closer, transfixed by Roland's recreation. Simon watched through narrowed eyes, hanging on every word.

Chewing on a fingernail, Roland thought it through and eventually nodded. "Okay, the guard died in the shitter. Our guy probably walks up and gets buddy-buddy with him, you know, offers him a smoke and commiserates with him…screw the Army…screw your platoon sergeant for sticking you on this sopping guard…screw your old lady who's cheating on you back in Des Moines or Wichita or Charlotte with the plumber and his partner and maybe even your brother…and then, when the guard's comfortable, our killer tells him he's gotta take a dump and does he know where a nice latrine is." Roland stabbed a finger to the water closet. "The guard, like any soldier would, gladly takes the smoke and even more gladly walks our killer down that hallway, because it's dry. So they're smoking and joking and having a good old time when our killer rams his Ka-Bar into the poor sap's gut. He calmly spins the guy around, deposits him on the toilet for one final time, then walks back out to place his trap."

Roland began to limp down the street, his loud voice echoing between the buildings. The pigeons followed him, cooing and clucking as they alternated between walking and flying short distances.

"So, as I understand it, the sergeant major stopped the two Jeeps because he saw no guard."

"That's right, sir," the master sergeant said. "But for whatever reason, while he was looking for the guard, the Jeeps drove on ahead, and that's when the mine went off."

"Some impatient dickhead," Simon muttered. "Maybe the general himself."

The master sergeant shook his head. "Doubtful. He was a good man, smart too. I'd guess it was his aide. Hate to say it about the dead, but he was a real prick."

Roland nodded his understanding as he stopped at the crater again. He looked down, looked at the pock marks, studied the ball bearing from his pocket, then pointed his finger back up the street. A faint smile came over his face. "Damn, this guy's good. The general and posse were at the Twenty-Third, which, Sarge, is where we think the killer came from. So he knows when they get back to Division they're most likely going to be the ones who find the bouncing betty. He hauled ass all the way over here to Morlaix, walks into town, sees the guard, knows he's gonna be trouble so he does him…right there in that bathroom." Roland raised his hands to the sky, lowering his wriggling fingers like a maniacal piano player, causing the bloody gauze to tumble to the street. His voice was edgy, excited. "Rain coming down in buckets. The other guards too far up the opposite streets to see him...or care even if they did. Remember, they're simply trying to stay dry and warm." He moved directly over the crater. "Our boy hurries down *la rue* here, sets the S-mine...hauls ass. The general and his posse arrive a short time later. Bright sergeant major stops everyone, as is S.O.P., because he can't find the rear guard. Impatient general's aide, probably irritated with said bright sergeant major, moves them forward. One of them, the major you say...probably the same one who had been impatient...triggers the bouncing betty." Roland clasped his hands in front of him before jerking them outward. "Boom!"

Roland, finished with his improvised recreation, looked at the two men with raised eyebrows.

"Not sure what's more scary—what actually happened or your little soliloquy," Simon deadpanned.

The master sergeant removed his helmet and rubbed his ragged, close-cut hair. "All due respect, sir, but you talk about this bastard almost like you admire his sorry ass."

Roland stood blinking for a moment, letting the accusation hang in the air. "No, Sarge, I hate him. I want his head on a spit. But, years ago, I was trained in many of the same disciplines, trained to do just this type of thing. And no matter how I feel about him, when we looked at the numbers he's achieved, especially now that I've seen his handiwork, it only bolsters my notion that he's incredibly dangerous." He tapped out a cigarette and gestured to the master sergeant. "So I can still hate him while appreciating his skill, can't I? The same way you might admire captured German communication equipment? Just because you like their gear doesn't make you a Nazi, does it?"

"No, sir, it doesn't," the master sergeant replied.

Roland could tell by the master sergeant's tone he still didn't agree with all the praise.

"Thanks for your help, Sarge. We're going to head over to the Twenty-Third." Roland reached into the Jeep and tossed the master sergeant a pack of Chesterfields before climbing in the driver's seat. They did a full-circle in the five-point intersection and headed east, to the 23rd Infantry Regiment.

As the Jeep bumped along, leaving Morlaix and crossing the buttercup splashed dike in the stark sunshine, Simon leaned over, speaking over the rush of the wind. "Like I asked you before, you sure you're not Philip Marlowe?"

"What the hell are you talking about?" Roland asked, leaning his own head out into the warm breeze.

"Seriously…before you were commissioned in the Army, were you a police detective?"

Roland grinned, swishing his head in the current of air.

"You ain't gonna answer me?" Simon persisted.

"No, I wasn't a detective," he replied over the rushing air.

"Then how the hell did you know how that killing went down?"

Roland pulled his head back in and turned to him. "Because it's exactly what I would have done."

ACROSS THE ravine from where an anxious staff sergeant awaited news from the medical tent, a Jeep arrived carrying two officers, each missing a limb. Upon successfully giving the countersign, they were allowed to proceed, coming to a stop outside of the regiment command post. Roland Buhl and Simon Jericho exited, walking to the entrance flap of the tent. Simon stopped him.

"You really think, somewhere in this regiment, is our saboteur?"

"From now on, let's privately refer to him as the assassin." Roland put his hand behind Simon and nudged. "Just follow my lead."

The regiment headquarters tent was a frenetic traffic pattern of soldierly activity. Maps hung from the tent poles on all sides, illuminated by hanging lanterns and small, portable spotlights. Sawdust had been sprinkled on the dirt floor to prevent the ground from turning to impassable mud. The cedar smell of the sawdust mingled with the resident body odor and cigarettes to create a tangy miasma that was without comparison but known to soldiers the world over. No less than fifteen men scurried about in the cramped space, all of them yelling, carrying radio handsets and grease pencils, marking maps, elbowing their way to each one. Roland saw a major, sitting on a crate, screaming into a Graham-11 radio. He jammed the receiver back down on the radio and ran his fingers through his sweaty black mop of hair. The major took a sip of what looked like ersatz from his canteen cup and looked up, his eyes sleepily drifting over Roland and Simon before going back to the floor.

"What the hell do you two want?"

"To speak in private, sir."

"In private about what?"

Roland took a step closer, bending over from the waist. "It's important, sir. Very important."

The major shook his head. Back expanding several times as he took deep breaths. Looked up, eyes bleary. "Important, huh? Well...you two're not in my regiment, and at the moment my regiment's in crisis. We *were* due on the line right-damned now, but I'm held up because Third Army put the skids on me, and right about that time one of my commanders lost half his ass to a booby-trap grenade, and the only one who mighta seen who did it took a knife to the back."

Roland whipped his head to Simon, sharing an electric glare. He turned back. "Sir, *when* did this happen?"

"Just this morning," the major answered. "Few minutes before first light."

Simon spoke up. "We hadn't heard about it, sir. But it's exactly why we're here."

The major screwed up his face as he stood, towering over everyone, his nest of hair touching the six-and-a-half-foot tent ceiling. "Well, if you hadn't heard about it, lieutenant, then how the hell are you here *because* of it?"

Roland gestured outside. "That's what we're here to explain to you, sir...in private."

"Here from where?"

"Third Army, sir," Roland answered. "Captain Roland Buhl. This is Lieutenant Simon Jericho."

"My name's Haag." The major looked down at Roland's leg, Simon's arm. Cocked a bushy caterpillar of an eyebrow. Sipped his ersatz, winced, wiped his lips with his sleeve. Checked his Bulova Army wristwatch and puckered out his lips. "You've got five minutes. My tent. Right now." He turned to the chaos. "Back in five mikes!"

The major led the way, crossing the shadowy forest floor. Roland turned his head as they walked, seeing a large group of soldiers, standing in a circle, talking excitedly about something. Major Haag saw it too, stopping short of the rectangular T-323 tent, motioning a sergeant over. "Get over there and clear up that damned gaggle, sergeant. I realize we're in the rear, but one good arty round would wipe out half my regiment."

They entered the eight-by-ten tent. On one end was a standard Army cot topped by a rumpled sleeping bag. The major extended the wick of a lantern, filling the space with auburn light. Next to the cot was a book, *The Razor's Edge*, by Somerset Maugham. The major followed Roland's eyes to it.

"Read that one?"

"Yes."

"What'd you think?"

Roland tilted his head sideways. A long blink. "The beginning was entertaining, but in the end it was all communist bullshit, sir."

The major snorted. "You missed the point." He unfolded two squat stools and placed them across from the cot. "You boys lose those limbs in combat?"

Roland sat. "He did. Mine was an accident of a different nature." Not wanting to get into the story, he quickly produced the envelope containing Patton's orders, handing it to Major Haag. "Sir, I believe this will help you with why we're here."

Haag shook the inner paper out and held it near the lantern, squinting his eyes to read in the dim light. He refolded it, thoughtful, finally looked up. "What's all this?"

"You've a killer on your hands, sir."

"He's out there somewhere."

"No, sir," Roland said. "He's in here somewhere."

"In where?"

"He's an American soldier."

"Not in *my* regiment," Haag said, his lips tightening over his teeth.

Roland's retort was respectful but firm. "We believe he is."

The major pulled in air through his nose. "Explain to me how in the hell you didn't even know about one of my commanders getting fragged, but now you're here to tell me I've got a subversive on my hands?"

"Perhaps it would be easier if we showed you." Roland turned to Simon. Flicked his eyes to his satchel. *Show him the stats.*

The lieutenant removed a small notebook. They had condensed the spreadsheet to raw numbers, showing the average lives lost per unit within the Third Army in comparison to Haag's regiment. They allowed the major to drink in the numbers before turning the page, displaying average deaths by means which could have been carried out by an assassin, the number being double. Haag stared at the book wide-eyed.

"Sir, I have no desire to try to drag you or your unit through the mud. General Patton knows about this, and no one else. He wants to keep it that way, as do I."

The major listened to this before digging into his jacket, retrieving a flask. When Roland and Simon declined, he took a swig before sliding it into his sleeping bag. The smell of bourbon, charred and oaky, filled the tent. "So what do you intend to do?"

Roland leaned forward, elbows on knees. "For starters sir, I want to know about this incident with the grenade. And did you say there may be a witness?"

Haag stared at the spot where he'd slid the flask. He chewed on his lip, then set his head with one nod. "Bravo Company is across the way," he said, pointing. "All three companies are spread out around us. We had a staff meeting last night, and when Bravo's commander, Yaupon..." he turned to Simon, "...a kid of a lieutenant younger than you...when he and his XO walked back, they crossed the creek and that's when Yaupon took the grenade's explosion. Luckily, it seems the water may have sapped some of the grenade's effectiveness."

"And the witness?" Roland asked, wetting his lips.

"All hell broke loose, as you can imagine. The kids out on O.P. thought there was a firefight, so they started lighting up the valley. When the dust settled, we found one of our new arrivals upstream, a deep knife hole in his back."

"What was he doing down there?" Simon asked.

"He was on O.P. His fellow guard said he thought he saw something and went down into the woods to have a look."

"Dumbass," Roland muttered. "Outside of the perimeter, all alone?"

"That's what I said. Fresh off the boat, too. Kid was still in high school a year ago, and now he's in a morphine coma with a punctured lung."

Roland allowed the conversation to grind to a halt. He took the journal from Simon, closing it on his finger. "Sir, we believe General Kagan was killed by your guy as well."

"That was way the hell over in Morlaix!" the major protested. "You shitbirds trying to end my damned career?"

Roland put his palms up. "Not at all, sir."

Haag reached under the sleeping bag and stood, uncapped the flask, thought about it, recapped it, tossed it on the cot. Paced in the cramped space. "Statistics can be helpful, but they can also be utter bullshit...you been around long enough so you oughta damn well know that." He came back to the cot, sat, steepled his rigid fingers. "Did you know we've had more time on the front line than any other regiment in the entire division? Who's to say that those numbers aren't because of that?"

Roland nodded with closed eyes. "And they very well may be. That's why we wanted to speak with you in private, sir."

Major Haag chewed on his thumbnail before spitting in the corner. "I just cannot...will not...believe that I could have a Trojan horse here under my command."

"We hope not, sir," Simon offered. "But in the event you do, wouldn't you like to know it, especially before it gets out?"

The major stared at Simon with a cocked eye. He looked down, again running fingers through his hair. His voice was half-groan. "So what do we do first?"

"First, sir," Roland said, "we keep this quiet. No one needs to know who we are. No one at all. If any of your staff ask you, just tell them there could be some leftover Krauts behind the lines and we're talking to all the units. That type of thing."

"Like the Army makes a habit of sending two broke-dicks out looking for rogue Germans," Haag said with a snort.

"Or I could just call the general," Roland said with a thin smile.

The major stared at Roland with leaden eyes. "What was the other thing?"

"Take us down to where the grenade went off."

"What the hell's that gonna tell you?"

"Maybe nothing. Maybe everything."

Haag stared at the flask again before tucking it under the sleeping bag. He led them outside, motioning with his hand to follow him. The walk took ten minutes, primarily due to Roland's difficulty negotiating the steep hill. At the bottom of the deep cut was a trickling brook straight from a painting. The water negotiated itself down a steep drop, probably still runoff from the heavy fall rains. Even in the warmth of the day, a slight fog gathered in the ravine, giving the area a hint of softness. At any other time, Roland thought, it would be a nice spot for a picnic with a pretty girl.

"Where did the grenade go off, sir?" Simon asked.

Haag walked up and down the brook, finally pointing to a spot. "There's the blood." On the other side, boot prints and streaks of mud could be seen where the lieutenant was dragged from the water. Next to the mud was a steady stream of black. Roland stared at the spot for a long moment, holding up his hand for silence. This area was the killer's canvas. Some artists worked in charcoals, others in oil...this one specialized in death. The smell came back again, the same one from the bathroom back in Morlaix...the one from the farmhouse in Germany. Grinding his teeth together, Roland eased himself into the ankle-deep water, crossing the brook and thankful the bottom was sand and not mud. He studied the bank, lifted a twig. He rotated it in the light.

"Dried blood, all right." He turned, looking at the stones in the river. Some appeared normal; others were algae side-up, still damp. Roland hefted one, turning it over. It was heavily scarred.

"This one took a shitload of the frag." He placed it back down, surveying the area. Picked his way carefully downstream. After twenty feet, Roland pointed to something floating by the bank. It glinted as the murmuring water moved it. Simon and Major Haag walked above the object on the bank. Roland stepped into a deeper pool of water, leaned over, retrieved it. He dangled it in the light. It was a shimmering piece of ultra-thin wire. On one end, a splintered twig. On the other end was a pin from a grenade. He held it up in the diffused light before tossing it up to Major Haag, who held it directly in front of his eyes, pulling it taut.

"Monofilament," the major whispered.

"The grenade wasn't thrown," Roland pronounced. "It was set. And that pin is from one of our grenades. Whoever set it knew where your officers would cross. And that kid, the one who got knifed, probably did see the killer screwing around down here in the creek, setting a trap. Most salty soldiers would ignore such a thing, but the newbie thinks he's GI Joe, wades right into the situation, and takes a knife because of it."

Major Haag tugged on his ear as he stared at the tripwire. "Okay, *assuming* he's here, how do we catch this sonofabitch?"

"I think we should start with each of your company first sergeants."

Haag's head jerked up. "You think it was a first sergeant?"

Roland shook his head no. "Didn't say that. I think we should start with them, with a few questions."

"Questions about what?"

"You want to know what a company is capable of, you go to the commander." Roland gestured for Simon to lend him his left hand, struggling to pull himself up on the bank. He wiped his hands on his uniform and said, "But if you want to know what a company is *made* of…want to know its people…you go to the first sergeant. Let's go back up to the tent." He craned his head to the west, marking the sun's position. "We've still got three, four hours of light. This won't take too long."

"TOP, I NEED you to provide me with a listing of everyone who meets a certain set of criteria."

"Roger, sir. Anything you need."

"Have a seat right there. Good, now, just relax. No one, not even your company commander, needs to know about this, got it?"

"Yes, sir."

"I mean it, Top. *No one* at all. Don't say a damned word, not even over a nip."

"I'm hearin' you five-by-five, sir."

"All right, Top…here, speaking of a nip."

"Ahhh…thank you, sir. Kentucky, isn't it?"

"You know your bourbon."

"Unfortunately. Figured this war'd make me quit drinking, but damned if I haven't drank more here than when we was trainin' back in Derry. If'n I make it home I'll have to dry out. My wife and her family are Methodist, you know."

"I'm sure you will. All right, Top. I need a list of your company men, officers—which isn't likely, because I think they're all newer arrivals—and enlisted who made it through each one of the battles I've listed on this sheet."

"Okay, sir…so basically, let me look at this here, yeah…purdy much everythin' since we crossed the Channel."

"Right, but make sure you eliminate anyone who was injured and sent back to the Repple Depple during any of those battles. Second, I want you to eliminate from the group anyone who's not a model soldier. The fellow I'm looking for will have advanced rapidly, and is the type of guy you would turn to when you want the job done damned right. You follow?"

"Roger that, sir. I know what you mean."

"*Squared away*, Top. The kind of fellow who just knows things. Capable and adept in battle as well as back in the rear…never gets in trouble either…that kinda guy. The one you call on in a pinch."

"I gotcha, sir."

"About how many soldiers in your company would fit this bill, just guessing?"

"Well, sir, maybe…I dunno…this is just a guess, but maybe two or three…four at the most."

"Good…good. And I need it quickly, real quickly, so run back over to your company and check on the medical files. And remember, not a—"

"Not a word! I got it, sir."

Major Haag stepped from the tent, watching the first sergeant scurry away. He walked to the Jeep parked on the other side of the perimeter. The two officers were sleeping, snoring loudly. He rousted them.

"That's it, that's all the first sergeants."

Roland rubbed his eyes, smacked his mouth together. He looked around, squinting. "It's still light? Feel like I was asleep for hours."

Simon rubbed the stump where his arm had been, groaned. "Felt like about ten minutes to me."

Haag removed his helmet, smoothing the mop of dark hair backward. "All of them are getting me their lists. I should be hearing back soon."

"Sir, could you just wake us up when you get all of the lists back? What we're going to do will probably take all night." Roland repositioned himself and closed his eyes.

"Sure thing, *cap'n.* Don't let me disturb you." Grumbling to himself, Major Haag crossed the perimeter and entered the command post. He shooed everyone out, telling them to wait outside. Ignoring the company radios, which were droning about a general shortage of supplies, he picked up the radio on the far right, the one that was rarely used, keying the mic. "White-six, white-six, this is orange-six, over."

"Orange-six, wait one, over."

Haag lifted someone's half smoked Chesterfield, tapping off the long ash, pulling hard on the butt while the radio operator at brigade rousted Colonel Duggan. *Madness is what this is, utter madness!* Haag had been a part of some ridiculous wastes of manpower in his day (who in the Army hasn't?) but holding up an entire infantry regiment—and a damned good one—during wartime to go on an ill-advised, penny-ante witch hunt for a vapor-like saboteur who probably didn't even exist took the damned cake. And in the event it was true, how in the hell was this going to affect him when the promotion list came around? Would this hold him back from getting his O-5? He could see the promotion board now…*Okay, who's next on the list? Major Haag, huh? Let's have a look at the file. Okay, says here he had a German spy in his regiment for six months and was none the wiser while the kraut picked off half of his men. Yep…that's what it says right here. See for yourself. That's not exactly what I would term as knowing one's men. I'd say we pass on him, what do you boys say? And while we're at it, call the general and make sure Haag gets a dishonorable discharge. Done? Good. Now then…on to this next guy…a good-looking major named Kissassalot.*

Had Haag fought the draft and stayed home, he would have been on track to be assistant superintendent by now. He'd already been the best school principal in the whole damned county. But Uncle Sam had come calling by post. Haag remembered standing by the mailbox, staring at his draft card, never once thinking about trying to get an exception. He believed in the war, and in his country. He thought back to the day he heard about Pearl Harbor, learning a few days later that his nephew was missing. They found his body later, along with hundreds of others, jammed into a forward compartment of the Battleship Oklahoma, sitting on the bottom of the shallow Hawaiian Harbor.

The whole world's gone mad.

The radio crackled then chirped. "Orange-six, white-six here, over."

"White-six, the two oscars from Great Big Six are in my A.O., taking a bit longer than we thought, over."

"What two oscars?"

"I don't want to put it out over air, but they have good orders from Great Big Six to do as they please, over."

A pause. "How long before you can un-ass, over?"

Haag rested the cool radio against his forehead for a moment. "You tell me. You're the one who put us on hold."

"That hold expires at zero hours zulu. How long from now 'til you're ready to move?"

"Twenty-four maximum, hopefully sooner, over."

The speaker buzzed as Haag could hear Duggan let out a breath, making the radio squelch with feedback. "I'll pass that on to Great Big Six. Call me at first light, out."

Haag slid the receiver back into the hook and checked his watch. The initial first sergeant he had spoken to should be back any time now. He didn't know what the two special investigators were going to do with these lists, but he couldn't say he wasn't curious.

He stepped out of the command post, sending the gaggle of officers and NCOs back inside before making his way across the rapidly darkening perimeter. Yeah…assistant superintendent by now, chief superintendent of the Laramie County schools in another five years. He would have done ten more years after that, then been set for life with a nice government pension and a small boat up on Lake Solitude. But not now. No…he had to beat the draft and join post-haste only to wind up with a damned Nazi spy in his regiment! It would deep six his career! Hell, he might as well end up like his nephew down in the bottom—

"Take it easy," he breathed to himself as he pushed his way into his own tent. Haag found the flask and took a few nips. Took a third, a big one. Would need to refill soon. He read two pages of his book (and it actually *was* starting to become "communistic bullshit"...) before he took a nap, a brief one. Brief because the first sergeant from Alpha Company was back a half hour later. His list had only three names.

And, oh, how he hoped those two limbless assholes were wrong.

FOURTEEN

GARLAND HAD been told to clear the hell away twice, both times the wizened old doctor exited for a smoke. From all he could glean, Lieutenant Yaupon was doing fine, stable and sleeping on his stomach, his ass cheek freshly stapled back onto his body. Garland had heard the doc speaking to the other doctors who showed up from division, telling them that he'd have some recovery to do, but that the buttocks was a huge muscle and, with good circulation, typically healed nicely. But Garland wasn't concerned with Yaupon. It was the private, Holder, he was concerned about. Not only was Garland upset over knifing the kid, even worse was the fact that Holder knew his secret. *Damn, why did it have to be him?* Each time he caught a glimpse of the doctors looking at each other, their expressions were grave; they would give that fatal little shake of the head meaning, "He's a goner." While it pained him to think that he might have killed the kid, Garland was almost equally relieved to keep his secret intact.

"Garland Felton! Staff Sergeant Garland Felton! Anyone know where the hell he is?" It was a voice, a loud one, bellowing from the area over by the command post. Garland took one last look inside the medical tent, seeing Holder's limp body lying there, tubes snaking all around him. He pulled his helmet down, crossing the perimeter and finding First Sergeant Nelson.

"Lookin' for me, top?"

The first sergeant, a pear-shaped man with a swarthy, hound-dog face, turned. He spoke around the clamped nub of an unlit, saliva-soaked cigar. "Orders just come down. You're to get your shit, all of it, and be on the supply truck in ten mikes."

Garland felt his pulse spike. He tried not to show alarm. "Orders? All due respect, Top, but what the hell are you talking about?"

The first sergeant opened his arms and shrugged. "Haag got trumped and division raked off about ten of his soldiers to fill in over to the Sixty-Seventh. They got pounded by arty yesterday and lost a third of their men."

"Fill in? As in, permanently?"

"Shitfire, Felton, you think they tell me that kinda stuff? Could only be a week for all I know, but I'd suggest you plan on longer. They were damned specific that you're to bring *everything*. All gear and possessions." He took a step closer and rested a friendly hand on Garland's shoulder. "That, to me, sounds like you ain't gonna be back anytime soon."

The first sergeant's eyes seemed genuine. He didn't stare too expectantly, like he might if he were a component in a sophisticated trap. Instead he looked and sounded like any senior enlisted man breaking some not-so-good news to a subordinate. Garland nodded, turned. He stopped, turned back. "Who else, Top?"

"Zablonski and Bettencourt from our company. Don't know about the other companies."

Garland blinked, processing. Zablonski and Bettencourt were two damned fine soldiers. Like himself, Zablonski was a staff sergeant; Bettencourt was a corporal who had arrived just before the Channel crossing and had turned out to be a pleasant surprise for everyone.

"Top, not to toot my own horn, but how did division get away with pulling three of our best soldiers?"

The first sergeant snorted, breaking eye contact. "Our regiment's got a major filling a lieutenant colonel's billet. Prob'ly didn't have enough ass to sway the old man. Trust me, I already raised hell about it, but my commander's layin' in there, his ass all blowed up. No one up at HQ listens to a tired old first sergeant."

While he had done a fine job of acting up until then, Garland noticed his discomfort at the question. The first sergeant knew more than what he was letting on, Garland would bet his life on it. Something was going on. Something…

But for now, until he could get a read on it, the best thing he could do was comply. Garland threw off a mock salute and walked to where his gear was stowed. The regiment had been ordered to pack up for the road march back to the front, meaning his gear was already essentially pulled together.

As he lifted his ruck and his gear bag, his mind raced over what contingencies, if any, he should plan for. The bouncing betty and the extra grenade were gone. Garland whipped his M-1 off his back, popping out the cartridge and removing the chambered round, both of which he placed into his ammo box, per SOP. Glancing around in the creeping twilight, he made sure no one was watching him as he slid the Ka-Bar out, studying the blade for blood. It was clean. He worried about any residue which might be down in the sheath, but if there were, he reasoned it would be sticking to the blade each time he pulled it in and out.

You're being paranoid.

Yeah, I am, and paranoid is what's kept me alive this long. Paranoid sure as hell kept me alive in Paris.

Point taken.

As it often did, his mind acted as distinct as two people.

Just remember…you're simply Staff Sergeant Garland Felton of Kentucky. A move like this would tick any soldier off, taking him from the brothers he had fought so diligently aside. Show it to everyone: you're confused, angry, wanting an explanation. In general, you're pissed off and don't care who knows it.

No, Gerhard. Run away. Run away now. Get to the front line and cross—cross back to the motherland. If you don't, you'll be sorry.

Gerhard trudged in the direction of the supply truck, his face grim, his mind answering itself.

I'm already sorry.

IT WAS nearly midnight. Major Haag was doing things exactly as Roland had asked him. The chosen from each company were mustered in a tent inside the regiment perimeter. All of them were now sleeping soundly, none the wiser as to what was going on. After they were finished questioning one, Haag would go get the next one, telling him to get up and bring all his gear. The soldier would enter Haag's tent, meet Roland and Simon, be questioned, have his gear scrutinized, and then be sent to a second tent, which was guarded by two staff sergeants under strict orders to not allow the men to leave. Thus far, everything had flowed as to plan.

Haag entered, followed by a fireplug of a corporal named Bettencourt. Roland studied the face. Bettencourt was likely of Hispanic heritage. While showing signs of fatigue, his face was handsome and tanned, framed on top of a muscular neck and powerful body. While he didn't think this was his man, Roland plowed forward as he had been doing the entire night.

"Corporal Bettencourt, I see here in your file you linked up with the regiment back in March."

The corporal snapped to attention, nodding. "Yes, sir. I joined up last year, was sidelined by something called mono, and then went to basic training around Christmas."

"Where did you grow up?"

"Corpus Christi, sir, in Texas."

Roland flipped to the next page, shaking his head as he looked over at Simon. "Says here that you're ninth of *thirteen* kids?"

"Roger that, sir. My parents were busy people."

"In more ways than one, it appears," Simon quipped.

Roland allowed the clipboard to tumble to the cedar covered ground, yawning as he spoke. "Dump your gear, Bettencourt, and don't hide a damned thing."

He emptied his rucksack first. It contained the normal items such as the Army's standard wool blanket, entrenching tool, extra socks, and rubber boots. Simon had him move the items around, exposing the boots to make sure they weren't hiding something.

"Sir, if I may, what is all this? Why the search?"

"Just routine," Haag said disinterestedly.

Simon. "Now the gear bag."

Bettencourt hesitated, swallowed visibly.

"C'mon, corporal, we don't have all damned night," Haag said irritably. He was sitting behind Roland and Simon, sipping ersatz coffee, looking quite hung over.

The corporal undid the clip on top of the gear bag. He turned it over, gently pouring the contents on the floor. There was a bevy of cold-weather equipment, his shelter-half and accompanying poles, and the large roll that was his sleeping bag.

"Unroll it," Roland said knowingly.

He did.

"Shake it out."

Bettencourt looked sick. Moving as if he were slowed by molasses, he shook the sleeping bag until a sleek, modern-looking pistol tumbled out. Simon leaned over and retrieved it, whistling as he studied it. Haag leaned forward before sitting back, grumbling. Roland took the gun, hefting it.

"You know what this is, corporal?"

"A German pistol, sir."

"Very good, but do you know what's unique about it?"

"Well...yeah. It looks kinda like something from one of those futuristic movies. A buncha the guys have offered me all kinds of things in trade."

"Well, you were smart to keep it. This is a Mauser HSC." He turned it, gesturing to the back of the slide, holding it so all in the tent could see. "It's unique because the hammer is concealed inside the body of the pistol. Where did you get this?"

"Pretty soon after Normandy, sir. We were on a patrol and I found a pilot, dead...in the woods, his parachute beside him. Someone had shot him up on the way down."

Roland's face heated up as his mind went back to his own parachuting incident. He nodded. "Your story checks out. This pistol is only issued to the German Luftwaffe and some of their Navy." He raked the slide, making sure the pistol was clear. He handed it back. The corporal's eyebrows shot up.

"I can keep it?"

"Everyone's had a souvenir so far, Bettencourt. I could really give a crap. Now shake that bag again for me." Bettencourt did. There was nothing else. Roland turned.

"We're done here, major. You can drop him off and get the next one."

"Come on, corporal," Haag said, grunting as he stood.

"Any of them interest you so far?" Simon asked when the two men had exited.

Roland narrowed his eyes. "Before I answer, I might ask you the same thing."

Simon glanced down at his notes, tracing his finger down the page. "Whigham from Alpha Company was a shifty little bastard. He squirmed under questioning, at least so I thought." Flipped a page. "And Enright from Headquarters Company seemed the type to be a cold-blooded killer."

Roland didn't believe they had found their man, but agreed about Enright. "Not too sure about Whigham, but there was definitely something to Enright. I doubt he's our guy, but I wouldn't want to turn my back on him."

The flaps of the tent pressed inward. Haag entered stooped, motioning in the soldier behind him. "Gentlemen, this is Staff Sergeant Felton from Bravo Company. Felton, Cap'n Buhl and Lieutenant Jericho."

Garland Felton was a slender man with a rugged, if not a bit caveman-like, face. He popped to attention, staring straight ahead. "Stand at ease, Felton," Simon said immediately. "Just a couple of questions for you."

Roland studied the man. He didn't seem nervous at all, staring straight ahead with his green eyes. *Jade-green.* Like everyone else, his uniform was filthy, but his hands and face were clean. He hadn't shaved, however, which Roland found a bit odd. There had to be at least a week of growth on his face, neatly trimmed. Being well behind the front lines, nearly everyone in the regiment was clean shaven.

"Your razor broken?" Roland snapped.

"Negative, sir. I caught a skin condition in the bogs and doc told me not to shave for a bit. I've got a profile note in case you want to see it."

Roland ignored the offer, glancing at Simon, arching his brows to show that this soldier could possibly be their man. He turned back to the staff sergeant, studying him for a moment before saying, "Dump out your gear, Felton."

"Sir?"

"Dump it out, rucksack first." The ruck contained all of the standard issue. Simon checked it for additional items. Found nothing. "Okay, Sarge," Roland said, "now your gear bag."

Staff Sergeant Garland Felton cut his eyes down at Roland. He nodded his understanding of the order, but Roland could see something beyond what would be typical irritation over an officer searching a soldier's gear. Behind the veneer this staff sergeant seemed to be working so hard to maintain, Roland could see an emotion like a distant, flickering flame.

The emotion was fury, pure fury.

This was him, Roland would bet his bottom dollar. He looked different from what he could recall of the photo, quite different, but looks could be altered. The items spilled out all over the cedar-covered earth.

"Check it," Roland said to Simon. When Garland turned his eyes down to Simon going through his things, Roland unclipped the leather strap from the stud on his pistol holster.

Simon went through everything, poring over items which could be used to hide something else. He looked to Roland, shook his head.

"Okay, pack it up." The men waited in silence as the staff sergeant put his gear back into the two bags. "I hear you're quite the hero," Roland said after he had finished.

"Not really, sir."

"Major here told me about your brave actions up at Brest, about taking out a tank single-handedly."

Garland shrugged. "Just doing my job."

"Uh-huh. Tell me about your background."

"In the Army?"

"Prior to the Army. Childhood to manhood."

Garland blinked several times. He appeared briefly nervous, but Roland had to give him the benefit of the doubt since it was such an out of place request.

"Grew up in Kentucky, sir, town called Flemingsburg. Had a twin who died at birth. Worked on the farm, graduated high school, worked in the mines for a few years, joined up before I got drafted."

Roland nodded with closed eyes, as if this were a lie he'd heard a hundred times. Simon poured two cups of ersatz from a thermos, handing one to Roland. He topped off Haag's who, obviously not picking up on the electricity of the exchange, was on the verge of sleep.

"So, what about your parents?" Roland asked.

A pause. "They're dead."

"How?"

"Fire."

Roland smirked at Simon. Simon appeared nonplussed. He turned back to Staff Sergeant Felton. "When did they die?"

Another hesitation. "A number of years back."

Roland lifted the file from his lap, shook it. "I already know when, Felton, so prove to me you're not a liar."

The staff sergeant gritted his teeth before responding. "Believe it was the summer of thirty-two."

"Your parents are dead, as is your twin?"

"Yes, sir."

"Other siblings?"

"No, sir."

"No one who can confirm you are who you say you are?"

Felton took a sharp breath before cutting his green eyes away for a split second. The sign of a caught man. He cleared his throat. "I have kin, sir. They're all over the hills back home."

Roland grinned openly at Garland. "Sure, sure. Kin everywhere," he said, holding the staff sergeant's electric gaze. "Just no kin in your immediate family, since they're all conveniently dead."

Roland turned to Simon and Major Haag, made eyes with them both. He then slid his right hand downward, whipping out the semi-automatic Colt .45 General Patton had arranged for him to carry. There was already a round in the chamber. He simply cocked the hammer, holding it at waist level, pointed at dead center mass of the surprised staff sergeant standing before him.

"Th'hell are you doing?" Major Haag bellowed, standing.

"Simon," Roland said calmly. "Take that pair of handcuffs off of my belt and cuff this murdering Nazi sonofabitch." He tilted his head back. "Major, sorry to be bossing you around, but please help the lieutenant. He's a bit limited with the one arm. And be careful." Roland wagged the pistol at Garland. "This *kraut's* very dangerous. After he's cuffed, check his back pockets and waistline so he can't pull a fast one."

Garland stared straight at Roland, never blinking, never breaking eye contact. His face and eyes maintained their intensity. He didn't utter a word as he was stripped of his gear and cuffed.

"Simon, pull that chair under him. There now. Sit down *Felton.*" Garland obeyed.

Haag stood to the side, out of the line of potential fire. His voice was high and tense. "Okay cap'n, you want to explain what the hell's going on here?"

"This is your guy, sir. This is the one that killed your men. He killed the lieutenants, the captain, several majors, and I bet he killed the former regimental commander as well. And I can guaran-damn-tee you he murdered General Kagan and his entourage over in Morlaix."

"How can you be so sure? All I heard was some innocent talk about him being a hillbilly from Kentucky."

Roland broke eye contact with Garland Felton and looked up at the major. "He assumed the life of some long-dead bumpkin from Kentucky. May have even killed someone to do it, right, Felton?"

Garland's jaw flexed once. He didn't answer, just stared.

Simon screwed up his face and looked at Roland, then up at the major, who was shaking his head. "I'm not following," Haag said.

"Me either," Simon chimed in.

Roland nodded patiently, keeping the Colt trained on the man he thought to be the assassin. "It's standard procedure, sir, for an operative who needs to change identity. I was trained the exact same way. You go to an impoverished area where there's no cameras, no photographs, no good records…find a graveyard and copy down names and dates of birth. Then you go to the county office and search records until you find someone whose death wasn't registered. It's really quite simple to do."

Simon gestured to Garland. "But what makes you think that this is our guy? Just the fact that he's from Kentucky and has dead relatives? Hell, that'd mean a third of the people from Maine are spies, too."

Roland's head shook, a thin smile on his face as he held Garland's stare. "That's not what first triggered my suspicion."

Haag. "Well, what else did?"

"What was different about him and the rest of the soldiers we saw tonight?"

"His beard?" Simon asked.

"Not that. Think hard, gents. What did he *not* have that everyone else did?"

"Stop with the quiz, captain!" Haag bawled. "I'll ask the damned questions here."

Roland chuckled at the rebuke. "Alright, sir. Sorry." He pointed at the staff sergeant. "He didn't have a souvenir, sir. Not a single one. Everyone else had Lugers, Mausers, Totenkopfs, knives…this asshole was lily-white, not carrying a damned thing."

Simon and Haag went silent, both thoughtfully looking down at Garland's gear.

Roland's tone was triumphant. "Only a good German, a rule-follower to the very end, would have no interest in a Nazi keepsake."

Garland's flat nostrils were flared wide like an about-to-charge bull.

"You set that grenade down at the creek, didn't you?" Roland chided. "You killed the major and the general and the lieutenant colonel and everyone else around here who died by means other than battle, didn't you, you devious sonofabitch?"

Staff Sergeant Garland Felton's jade eyes were slits, his lips knotted together, white from the pressure. A tremor went through him.

Roland took Garland's combat suspenders from Simon, handing him the Colt. "Keep that on him." Roland slid the Ka-Bar sheath off, pulled the knife out, studying the blade. As everyone looked on, he patiently used the tip of the knife to pop the threads holding the thick leather sheath together. Once he popped three of them, he was able to grasp the thread and pull it out. Finished, he splayed the sheath open, whistling softly as he did. Inside the sheath, at the bottom, was a small quantity of sticky crimson blood.

"Sonofabitch," Haag muttered.

"Yes, sir, he is," Roland said. "Hundred to one this blood matches that of your private over in Bravo Company—the one fighting for his life." He cocked his head. "And also the rear guard that got gutted near where that mine went off."

Haag lurched at Garland. "You murdering bastard!"

Roland caught him, pulling him backward. "Not here, sir," he said in a calming tone. "Not here."

Haag's breathing was ragged as he leveled a finger at Garland. "You're gonna swing for this."

"Not a bad idea," Roland said, still maintaining eye contact with the silent Garland.

Simon held the Colt steadily in his left hand. "What now?"

"We need to move him elsewhere," Roland said while turning to Haag. "Sir, you mind going outside and pulling up our Jeep, real quiet-like?"

"The Jeep, for what?"

"Would you rather this situation become public? A Nazi assassin in your unit all this time?" Roland took a step closer, his voice lowering. "Or would you rather the problem simply go away?"

Haag shook his head. "Tell me this will be reported. My career be damned, I would rather this be learned from than for some other unit to have to go through such a thing."

"Of course, sir. Through the OSS. Trust me, they'll take this out to deep water and make sure it never happens again," Roland said mildly. "But there's no need to alert your chain of command, or to tell your soldiers. Every time there is a strange death, they'd tear each other apart, thinking the other was a Nazi." He turned to Garland. "This bastard's secret is just for us, General George Patton, and the OSS." A grin grew on Roland's face. "Oh, and for you too, *Garland*...or whatever your real name is."

Haag's breathing slowed. After a moment he nodded and exited the tent. Shortly thereafter, the Jeep appeared, idling softly. The three men got in.

GARLAND SAT in the back seat of the Jeep, his mind running through the possibilities, none of which were good. The cuffs behind his back were very tight. He'd already tried to worm a hand out but it wasn't happening. The one-armed lieutenant was sitting next to him, holding the Colt on him with his left hand. The captain, Buhl, was driving. He'd asked the major to sit over in the passenger seat. They were obeying the blackout rules, driving slowly with no headlights. Garland had briefly considered making a scene—

he could have yelled and caused a commotion before they left the regiment area—but quickly decided it would have done him no good. Bringing more attention to what was happening, especially after the captain found the blood on his knife, would have probably only guaranteed a quick death. No, his only hope now was the slim possibility of escape.

His captors weren't talking very much. There was a razor-thin strip of orange on the horizon off to the right, meaning they were heading north. The captain had passed through several checkpoints, getting into it with a pissy lieutenant at the second one before producing an envelope from his pocket. Whatever the envelope contained, a letter or orders, sure as hell got the lieutenant moving. He saluted and...Garland could have sworn he said something about General Patton.

Patton?

Each time someone tried to talk, Buhl asked them to wait. "We'll be there in just a minute," he kept saying. Finally, after a thirty minute drive, the nicked-up cuffs bloodying Garland's overactive wrists, the Jeep squeaked to a stop. The sun was now nearly peeking over the horizon, still off to the right. Waves could be heard crashing in the distance. When they pulled Garland out, he could feel the give of sand under his boots, could see the gray water down below. They were high up on the dunes on the northern coast of France. He looked all around as the captain, struggling to walk in the sand, led him over the dunes and down to the beach.

AS THE DAYLIGHT grew, Roland looked up and down the beach, seeing no one. Several dark shadows existed just above the waterline, a mile out. That would be the shore patrol. Probably highly-mobile PT boats and maybe a sub or two. Allied ships. The Channel was locked down tight and had been for many months. The beach itself was deserted. And on the drive in, there hadn't been a checkpoint for the last mile, with no one visible in either direction at this section of the shore. *Yeah, this is the perfect spot.* He stopped in the hard tidal sand, fifty feet from the lapping waves and the water that appeared to be moving out.

"This'll work," he said, shoving Garland backward.

Simon held the Colt on the prisoner and moved to the left of Roland. Major Haag, looking perplexed, stood to the right of him. Well to their right, the first slice of molten sun appeared, illuminating the beach in a magical auburn glow.

"Watch him closely, Simon. Keep your finger on that trigger. He's thinking about making a break. I can guarantee it."

Haag unholstered his own Colt after hearing this. He pulled the slide backward, chambering a round. "If he tries, he'll have two bullets to contend with."

"I've something to show you both." Roland dug inside his jacket pocket, coming out with a pack of Chesterfields. He unfolded the top of the pack, and using his fingernail, slid out a tattered sepia photograph, small pieces of tobacco flitting away in the breeze. He held it in Haag's vision, then turned and displayed it for Simon. "What do you think?" The photograph was not unlike one from a college yearbook. It displayed a German soldier, wearing his dress uniform and garrison cap, looking at the camera, seemingly devoid of emotion. Roland flipped it over, reading the black cursive scrawl for the first time in weeks. *"Almost six feet, stocky build, jade-green eyes."* He looked at both men. "Well? Can you see the resemblance?"

Simon's mouth hung open. "Where in the *hell* did you get that?"

"I've had it the entire time."

"Then why didn't you show me?"

Haag stepped forward to look at the picture. "What in the Sam Hill's going on here?" He looked down at the photo and then up at Garland.

While everyone stared at him, Garland only looked at Roland.

"Think it's him?" Roland asked.

"I think you'd better tell me where you got that, and why you didn't show me," Simon persisted.

Roland handed the picture to Haag, who held it out in front of him, next to the pistol. "I dunno," he said to Simon. "The damned beard throws everything off, and something about his face is wrong." He flipped it over, reading the notes. "He could have lost weight…that's easy enough. The height and the eyes are spot on."

"The facial features can be altered," Roland said as he walked to Garland. He knelt behind him, pulling the bloused field pants up out of the neck of his left boot. Before revealing the leg, he stared up at Haag and Simon. "Our guy has surgically-induced scarring all over his left leg." He lifted the trouser up, bunching it over the knee.

"Sonofabitch, look at that," Haag muttered. "His knee's all torn up."

"Intel tells me this was medically done in the event he needed to use it as an excuse to pull back. It's all cosmetic, isn't it?" Roland asked Garland, clapping him on the leg.

Garland didn't respond.

Haag was mystified, but Simon was still incensed. "Stop it, captain. Just stop!" Roland stood, wincing as he adjusted his prosthetic. Simon stepped closer, still keeping the Colt aimed at the alleged German. "Why didn't you share any of this with me? You misled me all this time!"

Roland made a calming motion with his hands. "Easy, fella, easy. You've done a helluva job and I couldn't really tell you everything up until now." He paused, took a breath of the salty air. "Told you I used to work for the SGS, right? I still do, though now it's the OSS. And because the organization is still new, and a crossover to the civilian world, old dogs like Patton aren't exactly the biggest fans of what we do. After my injury, they shelved me, sticking me at Camp Gordon as a trainer, trying to spot infiltration agents, like this one, as they came through."

"So *how* did you happen to have his picture?" Simon demanded.

"When I got assigned to England, they gave me two items to help identify the saboteur…the *assassin*, rather…that the OSS felt was working from the American side. They had no idea where he might be, and that's where you came in. It was our work, our keen investigative toiling that found this guy."

Simon blinked rapidly as he ingested the information. "Still doesn't explain why you didn't show me the picture."

"Don't take it personally."

Simon nodded, still appearing puzzled.

"Wait a minute," Major Haag interjected. He tucked the picture into his pocket with his left hand before pointing at Roland. "You said they gave you *two* items."

"Yes, they did." Roland walked to Simon and took his Colt from him. "Keep your pistol steady on him, sir." Using his thumbnail, Roland popped off the textured pistol grip on the left side of the Colt, holding it in his left hand. He looked at Simon.

"Go lift his jacket and his blouse up to his chest."

Simon frowned.

"Trust me."

Simon walked over and stood before Garland.

"Don't move a damned muscle," Roland warned, aiming the pistol at Garland's head.

Simon used his only hand to lift the filthy clothing, grasping the undershirt and rolling both garments upward.

"Higher," said Roland.

He rolled it all the way to his neck.

From the inside of the Colt's grip, in the hollowed area, Roland pried out a small glass disc. A lens.

"Keep that pistol aimed at his head, sir."

Roland stepped to the two men and pressed the lens into Simon's hand, holding the garments upward with the pistol pressing against Garland's upper chest. "If this is our guy, lieutenant, then he should have four tiny black dots—they'll look like moles—on his chest, right there above his heart. Place the lens on them, and then rotate it until the dots match the ends of the symbol."

Haag moved forward, craning his neck over Roland's shoulder. "What symbol?"

Simon, whose breaths were now coming loudly, pinched the lens between his thumb and index finger, holding it up above Garland's shoulder in the growing daylight. Everyone could see the etched swastika.

"Apparently the krauts use this little system to identify their field agents," Roland said, grinning at Garland as he nudged him with the barrel. "But they didn't expect so many of their agents to double. That's how we learned of it."

Simon looked back at Haag then at Roland, who nodded. Haag repositioned himself to the side so he could see. Garland stood perfectly still as Simon placed the lens on his chest, moving it around a bit. "Well, I'll be licked up one side and down the other," Simon said to himself in full Maine accent. Still pinching the lens between his thumb and index finger, he twisted the lens like a watch dial, stopping after a quarter turn as the four dots marked the ends of the ancient symbol. "It matches perfectly."

Simon and Major Haag were thunderstruck. They alternated their eyes between Staff Sergeant Felton's chest and Captain Roland Buhl, smiling triumphantly. Finally Haag broke the silence.

"Why didn't you check his knee back in the tent?"

"Didn't have to," Roland answered without hesitation. "Like I told you back there, I knew it was him."

"Then why did you want to come out here?" Simon asked.

"Because this is the perfect place to dispose of a body."

"You're kidding," Simon said.

"You two men step back, please," Roland said smoothly. He popped the grip back on the Colt, tipping the slide to view the round inside.

FIFTEEN

"GENTLEMEN," ROLAND pronounced majestically as he wagged the pistol at Garland, "I give you German Wehrmacht Major Gerhard Faber, in the flesh. He is a Nazi agent, and killer of numerous American soldiers."

"What's his name?" Simon asked.

"Gerhard Faber, from Hannover. I'm going to be a national hero for finding him."

And then Roland spun to his right, pulling the trigger of the Colt with the barrel mere inches from Major Haag's head. The .45 caliber bullet entered Haag's skull, and with the power of a speeding truck, sent the major cart-wheeling backward over the hard packed sand. There was no doubt that he was quite dead. By the time Haag ceased his tumble, Roland had the pistol aimed at Simon, who was slowly backing up, his face a mask of horror and surprise.

"Simon, mein freund," Roland said, using precise high German, known in his native country as *Hochdeutsch*. He switched to English. "Simon, you are a fine American and have a good mind. I've never been one to hold it against a man for being born the way he is, and in your case, into the bosom of the wretched Jewry. The fate of religions and ethnicities is for men much senior than me to decide." Roland glanced to his right at Garland Felton...*Gerhard*...*Gerhard Faber*...winking once. He turned back. "But, Herr Simon Jericho, while I do not make global decisions, I'm quite capable of making local ones, and I have decided that it is best for our Thousand Year Reich for you to perish."

With an accusatory finger stabbing the air, Simon yelled, "You kraut bast—"

He never finished the binary insult. Not unlike the shot that killed Major Haag, the bullet entered Simon's skull at the forehead, sending him skidding backward on the sand as if he'd been yanked by a rope attached to an accelerating truck. Roland looked around in all directions, seeing only a flock of seagulls scared by the blasts, circling overhead, waiting for the carnage to cease. He holstered the warm .45 and stepped behind Gerhard, producing a key and unlocking the cuffs. He moved back around, staring face to face with his countryman.

"Gerhard Faber, Number Eight, I am Ritter Böhl, Number Four."

Roland Buhl was now Ritter Böhl, his true self. And Garland Felton was Gerhard Faber, though he appeared quite bewildered about it.

Ritter took Gerhard's hand and pumped it. "Your country has been looking—desperately looking—for you for some time now."

Gerhard's lips parted as he rubbed his wrists. He started to speak twice, stopping each time. His chest was heaving. He looked at the bodies, bringing his wide eyes back around. Finally, after a minute of silence, he asked, "You went through the academy?"

"*Jawohl*, in Potsdam, just like you. Lieutenant Colonel Heydte was like a father to me." Ritter jabbed a finger in each ear, wiggling it rapidly as he worked his jaw. "That damned Colt sounds like a black powder cannon. Typical American inefficiency." He searched the ground between himself and the bleeding form of Simon Jericho. "Ah, here it is." He lifted the lens from the hard sand, wiping it on his uniform before handing it to Gerhard. Ritter lifted his tunic and blouse, pulling it above his chest. "See for yourself."

Gerhard eyed him for a moment before placing the lens over Ritter's chest, rotating it. Ritter glanced down, knowing it was a perfect match. The four trails of the swastika lined up in tight German precision over the four mole-like tattoos. Finished, Ritter placed the lens back into the grip of the pistol.

Gerhard massaged his forehead. "This is a bit much for me to take in."

"I completely understand, my friend!" Ritter answered with an appreciative laugh. "You've been in deep cover nearly as long as I have." He gestured to Simon. "That kid there, Jericho, is a Jew." He wagged a finger, saying, "While I will never admit it to anyone in Potsdam or Berlin, I actually enjoyed his company. A fine man and a fine soldier, no matter what the

Führer might say. If I could have let him live, I would. Wouldn't want him dating my daughter, but he probably had a place somewhere in this world."

Gerhard again looked at both bodies. "I don't know what to say." Ritter didn't respond, allowing more time to pass. Finally, Gerhard dipped his head. "I didn't know how to come in, how to break away. I simply kept doing what I was tasked to do. My life has been extremely confusing."

Ritter grasped both of Gerhard's shoulders, giving them a friendly shake. "Everything will be fine once we're back. Even starchy Berlin sympathizes with an agent's oft confusing plight."

Gerhard massaged his wrists again. "Who gave you my picture?"

Ritter's mouth turned upward. "Did you ever meet our London contact? She's there, working undercover as a nurse. Tall, lithe, big head of hair—a helluva lay…from Frankfurt."

"Can't say I did."

"The woman was insatiable and more comfortable naked than with clothes on." Ritter handed Gerhard a cigarette, struggling to get them both lit in the beach breeze. He leaned back, puffing several times as he smiled into the rising sun. "As soon as I got to London I went to see her. Seems this entire program has been a colossal failure, except for you. They didn't know for sure where you were, but they suspected you came in during the invasion."

Gerhard seemed to be eyeing Ritter as he took only a few heavy drags of his cigarette and dropped it into the sand. "Did she mention her counterpart in Paris?"

Ritter tried not to flinch. He kept his face neutral. "Yes, she mentioned that you'd made contact with her. Berlin was fine with what you did…taking her radio."

"Why wouldn't that bother Berlin?" Gerhard asked with narrowed eyes.

Ritter flicked his cigarette away and took a step closer. "There are a few Ritter Böhls like me—poorly positioned spies—interspersed through the Allied militaries…but, again, poorly placed. However, to my knowledge, there are no other Gerhard Fabers. You are a fighting man on the front lines in a key strategic unit. You're a smashing success, Gerhard. You know the American strengths and weaknesses as well as their order of battle, and that knowledge may be *all* it takes to cripple this criminal assault on Europe." Ritter pointed east. "That's why we must cross the battle lines with alacrity."

Gerhard took a half-step backward. "What's the hurry?"

"Absolute desperation, Gerhard," Ritter answered with a wan smile. "If we don't stop the Allies stone-cold, and fast, Berlin will either be shouting praises to Stalin or singing Yankee Doodle Dandy by Christmas." He took a step toward Gerhard. "There is talk of a major counter-offensive from our country, and your knowledge could be the foundation our friends in Berlin are seeking."

Gerhard was silent, standing arms crossed, eyes downward. He looked over at Major Haag and Lieutenant Jericho. "Was this really necessary? I've killed a truckload of men, but this…this ambush-style execution seemed over-the-top. Seems you could have just arrested me and left."

Ritter smirked, recalling what he'd been told about Gerhard's penchant for shows of sympathy.

"Why are you grinning?" Gerhard asked.

"Sorry," Ritter answered with a wave of his hand. "I'm just pleased to have found you. And regarding my killing these two, I had to have their cooperation to find you, and because of the way I did it, they're the only two who knew." He shrugged and said, "Who now, other than me, knows you're a German? We've eliminated the only two, and done so in as painless a way as possible."

Gerhard, gnawing his lip, nodded his understanding.

"After we make contact with our own people…who knows? Perhaps they will send you right back in to feed false information while serving in your unit. That's why it's imperative we maintain your cover on the way out."

Gerhard's green eyes cut away for a moment. "So, what now?"

"Come along. We've much to do."

THEY HAD just dragged the bodies into the dunes, using the Jeep's shovel to cover them in sand. Before burying them, they stripped Simon Jericho of his lieutenant's uniform, shaking off the sand and concealing it in the vehicle. Ritter made sure he retrieved the picture of Gerhard from the major's pocket.

Finally, he lugged the gas can from the Jeep, dousing both sandy graves in gasoline.

"Are you going to burn them?" Gerhard asked, feeling odd speaking his native tongue.

"No, but the fumes from the gas will keep the crabs and gulls at bay for days. No one will have an inkling the bodies are here."

After washing their hands in the water, they drove back by a different route than the one they had come, with Ritter passing through two checkpoints while drawing nary a glance. It wasn't long until they were back near the front, just another Jeep among the hundreds. As they crept along behind a tank column, near Morlaix, Ritter removed the tattered envelope from his jacket and handed it to Gerhard.

"Read that, and hold it tightly in this breeze. It's worth more than even the largest cache of Jew diamonds or gold."

Gerhard's eyes moved back and forth as he read the letter twice, rapt. He carefully folded it and replaced it in the envelope, handing it back. After chewing on his fingernail for a moment's reflection, he asked, "How...*on earth*...did you get that?"

"It was dicey," Ritter answered, smiling proudly. "It all started after I began my initial mission. Like you, at the outset I was placed in the United States, but unlike you, my first mission *was* to join the Army. From what I understand, yours was not."

"Correct."

"Unbeknownst to the sloppy American intelligence system, being a highly-trained commando, I quickly floated to the top of their commissioned officers heap and was chosen for SGS duty."

"But how did you pass the background check?"

"The Army's?"

"No," Gerhard said, making a shooing motion. "Their regular Army background check involves nothing more than a phone call to your supposed hometown. But the SGS is supposed to have an incredibly rigorous background investigation. That's why I never sought after it."

Ritter nodded. "As I said, the plan for me all along was to enter the SGS. The Reich worked very hard in my case to make sure I had the proper elements in my background. There were never any problems."

"So what happened to your leg?"

They entered Morlaix as Ritter told him the entire story of the failed insertion into Germany.

"You killed a German family and *hacked off* your own leg?" Gerhard asked incredulously, switching back to English as they crept through the town.

Ritter placed both his hands on the steering wheel, twisting and gripping as his knuckles whitened. "I'm not proud of it. In fact, it was horrible. Put on a uniform and I have no problem…no hesitation whatsoever about killing you. But they, well…they were just innocent farmers. Good German people." He shook his head. "The man though, he was such a nosy bastard." Clucked his tongue. "A waste, but it had to be done."

After pondering this for a moment, Gerhard asked, "How exactly would our country benefit from the Americans sending you inside the Reich?"

Ritter rolled his eyes. "Do you really need me to answer that?"

Gerhard, feeling his face grow warm, didn't respond.

Ritter's tone was patronizing. "Think about it…it was perfect. I could give them false information and they would have believed every bit of it. Who knows what sort of inane bullshit Berlin would have had me feeding them? And, if and when the Americans ever found out, what could they have done? I would have been safely in the Reich." His smile faded. "But then, when I hit the ground that morning, everything went to hell."

"So why didn't you just call Berlin after the accident? Why did you kill the farmers to go back to the Americans?"

Ritter made a right turn, in the direction of the 23rd. He looked over at Gerhard. "Ah…motivations and reasons…now we're getting to the meat of the subject. These challenges are what I have lain awake at night troubling myself over, and now I can finally discuss them with someone who will understand."

"You could have just told the farmers who you were, called Berlin, and told them that the jump went bad."

"Right, Gerhard…right. I'd have been announcing myself as a legless, *failed* agent. Because that's what I would have been in the Reich's eyes."

"Not necessarily."

"Yes, necessarily. Think of the secrets we both know, Gerhard. It's why you've been hiding all these years. Still doing your job, but hiding nonetheless." They stopped briefly as an artillery column passed. Ritter stared over at Gerhard. "Tell me I'm wrong. Tell me the Reich isn't known to snuff a person out like a match if they have no more use for him."

Gerhard said nothing, his mind drifting back to the order to kill his mother.

"That's why you haven't wanted to come in. Tell me I'm lying."

Gerhard was aware of his pulse, feeling it in his temples.

"My answer, and this is the cold truth, is that farmer would have shot me had I not shot him. But in reality, I'm almost glad he went and retrieved his gun."

"Why?" Gerhard asked.

"It gave me the excuse I needed. It allowed me to keep going." Ritter grinned. "And I'll be the first to say that there is just something exhilarating about living my little lie. Something that gets me up out of bed each and every day because I know I'm living a complete ruse and could be caught at any minute." As they left the town on a much less crowded road, Ritter said, "And you, Gerhard, obviously know the same excitement. That is why you endured cosmetic surgery. Why you didn't want to be found...by anyone. You didn't want to go back any more than me; at least not before you felt your job was done in such a way that they wouldn't dare eliminate you. Especially after..." Ritter's voice trailed away.

"Especially after what?"

"I shouldn't," Ritter said, shaking his head but grinning the way someone does when they own a delicious secret.

"What?" Gerhard demanded.

Ritter turned, his grin turning to a smirk. "The primary reason you have been scared to come in...The primary reason you had your face altered...And the primary reason Berlin wonders if you're thinking of doubling to the Americans, were your overly-lenient, American-style displays of compassion."

"What are you talking about?"

The brakes chirped as Ritter pulled to the side of the road. "I believe, *Nummer Acht*, it started with your mother."

Upon hearing mention of his mother, Gerhard straightened. "What about her?"

"You didn't kill her when you were instructed to."

Gerhard was motionless. *How could he possibly know that?* His heart thudded against his ribcage and his mouth went dry. "Why do you say that?"

"I was briefed about you, Gerhard, in great detail. They've known it all along."

Gerhard didn't respond.

Ritter continued, "And obviously they didn't think less of you, because they still allowed you to proceed into the United States."

Gerhard turned away, eyes on the distant line of forest, wondering where his mother was now. Suddenly, he recalled what Ritter had just said a moment before. He'd said, "*displays* of compassion," more than one. "What else did they tell you?" he asked.

Ritter was lighting a cigarette. He puffed several times and said, "They told me a number of things, like the way you left your wife and that homosexual man alive on Long Island." Ritter made a tsk, tsk sound. "Then you met with Agent Döller in Paris. You tied her up and took her radio, even trying to convince her to go free."

"So, she didn't do it?"

Ritter smiled warmly, seeming to enjoy this exchange. "No, Gerhard, she did not."

Gerhard reached over and grabbed Ritter's collar, twisting it, snarling, "Did they kill her?"

Ritter released the wheel and showed Gerhard his palms. "Easy, boy, easy. You and I are one and the same, so don't kill the messenger. Just let me go and I'll gladly tell you what happened."

Gerhard released him, watching as Ritter adjusted his collar. Ritter found his cigarette from the floorboard, taking a drag before motioning with it to the south, saying, "They interrogated Agent Döller, and then eliminated her."

"Why?" Gerhard demanded, slapping the vertical dash of the Jeep, just above the Willys symbol.

"From Berlin's point of view, think of the greater good. What you and I do has the potential to save millions of lives. What is a single life when there are tidal waves of potential corpses hanging in the balance?" He took another drag, arching his brows as he said, "And that's why they eliminated your wife and that homosexual man, too."

Using his fist like a hammer, Gerhard pounded the dashboard of the Jeep. "What in the hell are you talking about?" he demanded.

Ritter flicked his cigarette away, waiting for a squad of walking soldiers to amble past. He leaned closer, lowering his voice. "The way I understood it, when you turned yourself in to Bonitz, in Philadelphia, he sent someone directly to your home. They found your wife and the homosexual gent tied up, and all the agent did was start the fire. They told me the fire department wrote it off as a genuine fire, and didn't question the homo's body as being your own." He clapped Gerhard on the upper arm. "So, you see, Gerhard, your plan, even though you didn't want to use it, worked beautifully."

Gerhard exited the Jeep, staggering into the high green grass of the adjacent field. He walked for a moment before plopping down on his rear end, lying all the way back to view the blue sky dotted with puffy white clouds. Everything was spinning.

Ritter appeared above him.

"Tough news, I'm sure, but please understand Berlin's reasoning."

"Reasoning," Gerhard whispered. "What do you know about reasoning?"

"Again, don't be angry with me. You can take it up with the leadership when we get back."

"They kill like it's a sport," Gerhard heard himself say, his mind too distracted to control his mouth.

"As I said earlier, Gerhard, we're far too important. Berlin couldn't allow people to walk around knowing—"

Gerhard sat up, his breath caught in his chest. "My mother."

"Excuse me?"

Unsteadily coming to his feet, he stood nose to nose with Ritter. "What about my mother?"

"They moved her to Berlin," Ritter said with a shrug. "I should have told you that a moment ago. They told me she's fine, living quite comfortably as a protected citizen due to your status."

Gerhard studied Ritter's face and eyes. No twitches. No dilations. It seemed he was telling the truth.

"I'm sorry about the others, Gerhard, really. When you reason it out, and when you calm down, you'll understand." He put his hand on Gerhard's shoulder. "But you can relax about your mother. They'd have had nothing to gain by killing her. She's fine."

Taking several steadying breaths, Gerhard eventually nodded. "So, what now?"

Ritter nodded approvingly. "Good question. We're going to go back to your unit and we're going to show my orders from General Patton and we're going to tell the chain of command that you are coming with me to Third Army Headquarters. I will tell them it has to do with the panzer you singlehandedly eliminated...all in the name of publicity back home for Patton." He paused, thinking. "And I'll inform them Major Haag is already on his way there. Any other time they might question this, but when they see these orders, and knowing of Patton's ego...they won't be a bit surprised."

They walked back to the Jeep.

"What about Holder?" Gerhard asked.

"The kid you knifed?"

"Yes."

Ritter cranked the Jeep. "While we're in the perimeter, just go into the tent and hold your hand over his mouth. Given what I heard about his condition, it wouldn't take long."

"It won't be that simple," Gerhard answered, shaking his head. "Before you came and got me, I was lingering near the tent but they were keeping him under close guard."

"Damn it," Ritter snapped, twisting the wheel.

Gerhard allowed a moment to pass before saying, "Perhaps there is a way to do it that will add further cover for our journey back to the Reich."

Ritter's eyes narrowed. "Oh?"

"They think the spy is just some German soldier masquerading around in a pilfered American uniform. They think he's the one that killed the general and his entourage back in Morlaix, and then set the grenade off down in the ravine. They think he's still out there, on the loose."

"And?"

"And I'm going to confirm it for them, by taking out Holder."

Ritter's puzzlement showed. "I thought you just said he was under close guard."

"He is." Gerhard motioned Ritter to drive.

"I'm not sure I follow."

"You will, *Nummer Vier*, you will," Gerhard said with a conspiratorial wink. "Drive on."

RITTER DROVE the Jeep toward Bravo Company, circling around the ravine on the weed-covered road from regiment headquarters. At headquarters, after proudly showing his orders, he had informed the XO that Major Haag was in transit with Lieutenant Jericho to Third Army headquarters and should be back sometime before midnight. Given the broadness of Patton's letter, the wide-eyed XO didn't dare utter a word of question. Ritter then released the mustered soldiers—the ones who, along with Gerhard, had been told they were changing units—sending them back to their jobs, telling them there was a mistake in the paperwork. "Stupid Army bureaucrats! I don't know what they were thinking," he added for a thread of soldiers-are-always-bitching authenticity.

They passed the main observation point, gaining entry to Bravo Company with the day's new countersign. Gerhard told Ritter to stay in the Jeep and to be ready to move. Carrying his rucksack, he first walked to the company command post, distracting the radio operator with a number of questions while studying the company area on the map, marking it to the fourth grid digit, which would be down to the meter. He stepped outside of the tent, scribbling the exact coordinates of the command post on his note pad before pacing the distance to the backside of the medical tent, where Private Holder languished. The guard posted outside the tent, another newbie named Ballew, turned to Gerhard with his basset hound eyes.

"What's goin' on, Sergeant Felton?"

"Just got back. Paperwork screw-up over at regiment. How're the lieutenant and the kid doing?"

"Lieutenant's gonna be fine, so they say. His ass may be a few pounds lighter. Doc says the other guy's gonna be iffy for a while."

"He awake?"

"Naw, been out the whole time."

"Thanks, Ballew. Look alive." Gerhard walked away, staring at the tent, marking *33 meters due south* next to the grid coordinates. He walked to his platoon's tent, not seeing anyone in his chain of command milling about. They'd been on guard all night and, after poking his head in and seeing a bevy of snoring bodies, Gerhard hurried back out to the supply trailer. From the rear he removed a lightweight M2 mortar assembly and plate, sliding them into the shadows under the trailer. He then climbed inside, protected from view by the trailer's canvas and plywood skin.

All alone, Gerhard allowed himself a moment to ponder what Ritter had told him.

They killed his wife, Carol Lynn.

They killed the homosexual man, Robert Williams.

They killed the agent in Paris, Christina Döller.

But, according to Ritter, he of all the sarcastic tones and contemptuous looks, Gerhard's mother was alive and well and living in Berlin.

It didn't make sense.

Gerhard sat silently for several more minutes, his mind racing.

After finalizing his plan, he dug through the accompanying crates, the majority of which were loaded with standard mortar rounds. Finally, at the rear of the trailer, he located the 60-millimeter rounds he was looking for. Gerhard studied the markings of each round in the rectangle of light from the back door of the trailer, taking two. He concealed them in his rucksack, preparing to move.

With the mortar assembly covered in his Army blanket, he lugged all the items back to the Jeep, concealing the weapon underneath the canvas in the back. He took one final look over at the medical tent—the target—before climbing inside.

"You done?" Ritter asked, glancing back at the concealed items.

"Yes."

"What took you so long?" Ritter asked with a sneer.

"Do you want this done the right way?"

Glancing at his watch, Ritter said, "Be right back. I'm going to chat with whoever your acting commander is." Then, currently in character as Captain Roland Buhl, Ritter sauntered to the command tent to excuse Staff Sergeant Felton by using the same excuse he'd used for Major Haag. He was back only a minute later.

"How'd it go?" Gerhard asked, not really caring.

"Milk run. They're down to a butterbar as commander who wouldn't know his head from his left nut. Either way, they now think you'll be gone for twenty-four hours for a 'publicity event with Patton'. That should easily be enough time to do what we need to do."

"Go due east from here," Gerhard said to Ritter as he spread the map on his legs. "Once you leave the perimeter, I'll guide you."

Ritter idled the Jeep back outside of the perimeter, driving east. Gerhard instructed him on where to go—right here, left here, down this ravine and through the creek—picking their way through the French woods on a series of rabbit trails.

As they bumped along, Gerhard removed one of the rounds from his rucksack, cradling it in his hands. It was olive drab and on the side, in sprayed white characters, were the nomenclature and the words HIGH EXPLOSIVE.

"Why are you holding that?"

"The triggers on these things are pressure-activated. You wouldn't want it going off in the Jeep, would you?"

After a full kilometer of careful, deliberate driving, Gerhard instructed Ritter to make his way into a depression that contained a small meadow in the midst of thick woods. There was no sign of anyone nearby.

Hurrying, Gerhard exited with his rucksack and assembled the M2 mortar with Ritter watching interestedly. Upon finding a flat spot and confirming it with the plum-bob and level, he threaded the three leg stems into the base plate, not worrying with the safety pins. After aiming it in the approximate direction, he wiped sweat from his brow and looked up. "Ever fire one?" Gerhard asked.

"Actually, no. Back in the Wehrmacht, I came up through the panzer corps before enduring the academy." He edged closer. "So this is interesting to me."

Gerhard made sure everything was foursquare before stepping to the Jeep to retrieve the map. He slowly dialed in the precise settings based on his plot and the notes from his pad. Finished, he smiled up at Ritter. "The Jeep running?"

Ritter walked over and started it.

"Drive it to the edge of the meadow and be ready to haul ass. I'm going to wait for the next rumble of artillery in the distance."

"Why?"

"Because I'd rather this coincide with many explosions than when everything is quiet. That way, in the event anyone is close by, they won't suspect anything when they hear a nearby detonation and see us driving away."

"And the mortar tube?" Ritter asked.

"You can't see it above the scrub brush. We'll just leave it," Gerhard said.

Ritter lit a cigarette and drove fifty feet away, to the edge of the forest. Gerhard reached into his rucksack, retrieving the hidden mortar round. After fifteen painful minutes of waiting, artillery finally began to rumble in the distance. He gave a final glance back to Ritter who nodded. Gerhard palmed the round in his hand, and, with his eyes closed, dropped it into the tube.

The mortar firing didn't sound like much. Just a punching sound and a whoosh of air, similar to something a person might expect to hear from a powerful piece of hydraulic machinery. The real explosion would occur downrange, on or near the medical tent, where Lieutenant Yaupon and the clinging-to-life Private Holder lay. *And won't they be surprised?* Gerhard sprinted across the meadow and dove into the Jeep, yelling "Schnell!" to Ritter.

Once they were rolling, speeding away, Ritter asked, "Do you think it hit the tent?"

"Within five meters," Gerhard answered, breathless. "Hardly any wind today, and with my mortaring skills, I'm positive the tent received the full benefit of that mortar round's payload." He climbed forward into the passenger seat and caught his breath. Ritter handed him an already lit cigarette, which Gerhard sucked on greedily, gathering his thoughts. "Where to now?"

"Well, with these orders I can go just about anywhere. I need to go back to Third Army to inform them that I and Lieutenant Jericho and Major Haag will be out of touch for a bit. I'll lead them to think we're hot on the trail of our man."

"What about me?"

"Patton doesn't have a clue who you are. And I took care of your whereabouts back at your unit, remember?" Ritter turned his eyes back to the road. "I need to have a look at Patton's tactical map to see the weak point in the line, and that's where we will cross."

"Won't our own Germans on the front line shoot us up?"

Ritter patted his breast pocket. "I have a special frequency, Gerhard. All I have to do is transmit one brief, coded message, and they will welcome us with open arms. We're going to be national heroes, you know."

Gerhard didn't respond. He finished the cigarette as he stared ahead, his mind clearly elsewhere.

Several minutes later, they were once again nearing the main thoroughfare back to Morlaix. "Were you close with that major I killed?" Ritter asked.

"No."

"How about the two you just fired on, the ones in the tent?"

"No."

"Well, I must say you look upset about something."

Gerhard turned to face him. "Not upset, no. But ready for all of this to be over, yes."

Ritter slowed behind a creeping column of engineer tractors. "If you're like me, you don't really enjoy the killing, per se...but rather the precision, and the *satisfaction*, of a good, clean kill."

Gerhard poked his bottom lip out, nodding thoughtfully. "Well put, *mein Kamerad*...a good, clean kill." He studied Ritter a bit. "And you know, as I sit here thinking about it...with both of us loving a good clean kill, and with our similar paths, and even our left legs having such damage...I realized something about us."

"What's that?"

"I realized, as the old German legend goes, you're essentially my doppelgänger."

Ritter turned to him, a stoic expression transforming into a creeping smile before he burst into hearty laughter.

"What?"

The laughter continued—mocking laughter.

"What's so funny?" Gerhard demanded.

The laughter trailed off, turning to poorly-veiled derision. "You've been around the moronic Americans too long, *mein Hohlkopf.*"

Gerhard's brow lowered at the insult. "Yeah, and why is that?"

"A doppelgänger, Gerhard, in its truest definition, is an evil apparition of similar appearance. A spirit…a ghost. The Americans, as they love to do, have twisted the word to make it mean something as simple as one's twin. But such a meaning is completely inaccurate."

"An evil apparition, a spirit, a ghost."

"Yes. Don't make such errors when we get across the line, lest they think you've become impregnated with the characteristic American ignorance."

Gerhard's voice was toneless. "I'll try to remember that."

Ritter entered Morlaix. The battered town was much less crowded than the days before. Several soldiers could be seen here and there, along with a civilian or two, doing their best to clean up the rubble. Ritter drove around the town, finally finding a military outpost located on the opposite side of town from where Gerhard's bouncing betty had done such damage. An engineering battalion had commandeered what had once been a sawmill. After leaving Gerhard in the Jeep and showing his special orders to a major, he learned the new position of the Third Army, memorizing the location from one of the battalion's hanging maps.

He lingered in the dusty command center for a moment, contentedly listening to the frantic bursts of radio chatter about a stray mortar having just landed inside of Bravo Company of the 23rd Infantry. Ritter hurried back to the Jeep and headed out of Morlaix.

"Your mortar found its home," he said, grinning at Gerhard. "The radios are all abuzz about it."

"What'd they say?"

"The radios were going nuts about the mortar. I didn't stick around as if I were listening to a ballgame."

Gerhard straightened the map. "Where to?"

Ritter told him the Third Army's location, giving him the name of the nearest town of Penverne and telling him the headquarters was exactly one kilometer to the south. Gerhard slid his finger over the map, finding the town and moving his finger downward. Giving clipped, concise directions, he navigated his countrymen to the outer edge of where they would find the Third U.S. Army.

They had driven five kilometers, speaking very little. Ritter pulled into the woods about a half a kilometer away from Third Army, edging the Jeep behind a twist of brambles. He left the engine running, turning to his counterpart. "Gerhard, I've not known you long, but I know the human psyche well enough to know something is *indeed* troubling you."

"Other than the fact that I was discovered like some menial amateur?"

Ritter shook the shifter with his hand as he chuckled good-naturedly. "That, I can understand. But you were never discovered by the Americans, and you still haven't been. Your time with them may not yet be over." He cocked his head. "But there's something else, Gerhard. I can tell."

Gerhard focused on Ritter, sharing a charged glare. "That *is* all. This has been an extraordinary day and you will please excuse me if I'm a bit shaken. It will pass."

As was his habit, Ritter showed Gerhard his palms. "I understand." He looked over his shoulder in the direction of the Third Army. "You wait here. It could take a little while. When I return, we will go to our countrymen."

"As heroes, didn't you say?"

Ritter showed a toothy grin. "Goebbels will make a movie about us."

Gerhard nodded. He grabbed his rucksack from the Jeep and took Major Haag's pistol.

"Ah, ah, ah," Ritter admonished, twisting the pistol from Gerhard's hand. "No weapons for you."

"Why?" Gerhard asked.

"As you said, it's been an extraordinary day. I can't have you taking your own life, or mine. Just stay hidden back here and wait for me." He patted the hand he'd just taken the pistol from. "In just a bit we will see what mother Germany has in store for us. Okay?"

Gerhard stepped back from the Jeep, backing himself to a v-shaped double tree. He lowered himself into the wedge, tapped out a cigarette and lit it with his Zippo. He nodded to Ritter. "I'll be here."

Ritter twisted the wheel and drove the Jeep from the thick woods. Once clear, Gerhard could hear him accelerating through the gears on the Penverne road that led to Third Army.

RITTER SLOWED the Jeep, carefully concealing Haag's Colt under his own seat, stuffing his sweater over it. Simon Jericho's uniform was wadded up under the passenger seat, covered by old cigarette packs and other trash. The mess looked completely normal as most vehicles in the theater were a complete wreck. As he worked the clutch with his prosthetic and resumed speed, Ritter Böhl's mind moved with great speed. He didn't trust this *Hannoveraner*, Gerhard Faber, one bit. The man had lying eyes of the worst sort. During pillow talk after their second session, the unquenchable German contact back in London was fairly certain Faber had lied about numerous items during and after his training. *But why? What could he have gained by lying?* Something about him didn't square in Ritter's mind. Had he planned all along on doubling for the Americans, it might have made sense. But there was no evidence of him doubling. In fact, there was airtight evidence (like subsequently killing a brigadier general in Morlaix with a bouncing betty) that he hadn't.

There was a checkpoint up ahead—a large one with several tanks. Ritter lifted his only foot, coasting the rest of the way. As they had a tendency to do, the Jeep's brakes chirped when Ritter stopped at the checkpoint. Two military policemen approached, one to Ritter and the other to the passenger side of the Jeep. The one standing by Ritter issued the challenge. Ritter gave the countersign, produced his identification and the tattered set of orders. The other soldier was on his knees, searching underneath the Jeep. He stood and glanced in the back before stepping away and nodding. The one next to Ritter, a sergeant who looked in desperate need of sleep, asked where he had come from.

"Been all over," Ritter answered. "Mainly near Morlaix."

"Well, sir, the radios are all lit up about a stray German out and about, probably wearing one of our unis. Dickhead fragged a couple of guys and just a bit ago is alleged to have fired a mortar into a company perimeter not far from there. You didn't see anyone out of place, did you?"

"Negative, but that's exactly what I've been working on. As you can see, I'm going in to speak with the general right now."

The MP folded the orders, stuffed them in the envelope and handed them over. "Have a nice day and stay safe."

Ritter showed him the V-sign with his fingers and slowly motored into the command area. His mind went back to Gerhard Faber. The man was a loose cannon. His actions made no sense and that, in Ritter's mind, made him a liability. Therefore, Ritter Böhl had no problem—none at all—handing him over to his German brethren. They would probably interrogate him unmercifully, learning all they wanted to know about the American Army, before executing him for altering his appearance. And for attempting to "turn" their Paris-based agent.

And Ritter, one leg and all, would be hailed a hero for finally producing the rogue operative Germany had so desperately sought. Who knows, with these invaluable orders of his they might send *him* back in a matter of hours to kill Patton. Because Patton would have no way of knowing about any of this. A smile split his face. Ritter stopped the Jeep and clasped his hands in front of him, squeezing them tightly. It was perfect! A perfect plan.

He took deep breaths, steadying himself as a military policeman sauntered over, pointing to his sidearm.

"I need that weapon if you're going in the inner perimeter."

"Why?"

"No one gets near the commander with a weapon." Without hesitating, the policeman stepped to him and held his hand out for the Colt, making Ritter's heart lurch as he thought about the lens. After Ritter handed it over, the MP patted him down, motioning for him to follow. A small locker was set up next to the MP Jeep. He scribbled something and placed the Colt inside.

"It'll be here when you come out."

"Am I free to go into the inner perimeter?"

"Have at it," the MP answered.

Ritter, weaponless, walked inside the strand of black rope. He looked around, watching the buzz of activity, the plan cementing in his mind. To himself, quietly, he whispered in German, "Gerhard Faber, you may be good, but in me you have finally met your match."

SIXTEEN

A BEAUTIFUL bluebird fluttered about, scooting from limb to limb in the tree above Gerhard, chirping frantically. He looked up, watching the bird, turning his eyes to the clump of a nest on one of the low branches. He heard the tiny chirps coming from the nest. Then he realized what was going on— she was the mother; she wanted him to move away. He acquiesced to her agitated twitters, moving to a fallen tree across the protected clearing and watching her as she fed a meal to her offspring. *A little late in the year for baby birds. Winter is coming. Better teach your children well.* He turned his head away, reflecting on his own mother. Though she'd done it without displaying any love, Gerhard's mother had taught him well. What she lacked in warmth she more than made up for in toughness—something she instilled in each of her children.

He closed his eyes, his mind hearkening back. Saturdays were cleaning days in whatever Hannover hovel they happened to be living in at the time. Because she had to bring her work home in the form of laundry, the house was normally a wreck. But once a week, a full cleaning was required. There were no rules requiring Gerhard and his brothers to stay and clean. If they didn't want to help, they could go out and play or, more likely, get into mischief. But if it were raining, or too cold, or for whatever reason they simply wanted to be inside, her apron on, scrub-brush in hand, she would yell at them with the same phrase, over and over.

"Get to working, or get out!"

He could still recall her shrill voice as clear as the baby birds perched ten meters away.

Gerhard removed his helmet, letting out a long breath as he rubbed his beard and shaggy hair.

Next to him was a hollow tree, still upright and rooted in the ground, the opening wide enough to stand inside. Gerhard turned, staring at the hollowed-out cavity. He tapped out his last cigarette and leaned his head back, finding a ray of sun penetrating the forest canopy. The sounds of the birds, the smell of the forest, the feeling of his secret being out—he felt a peace come over him unlike any other time in his life. He was once again Gerhard Faber; formerly Gerald Fieldhouse; formerly Garland Felton. The list, as he'd conveniently termed it, floated into his consciousness, pushing the other thoughts away. In essence, the list was his life's only meaningful work. Some men created cures for sickness. Others simply worked all day to feed their family. His tapestry was death. He wondered, when he was only days old, did his mother look into his green eyes and say, "I want you, my son, to grow up to be a killer?"

His cheek twitched involuntarily as he whispered, "That's all I am...a killer." He pulled on the cigarette, the sun warm on his face as he thought about the list...and the souls it was comprised of.

Just after the Allies had invaded at Normandy, Gerhard recalled the very first man on his list of confirmed kills. He'd been a sergeant first class, from Alpha Company. Gerhard shot him while he was bravely working to direct Allied soldiers on the lead-covered beach. What made the sergeant first class different from a German? The color of his uniform? Was that enough reason to sentence him to death? Gerhard recalled the man catching his eye, encouraging him with the manly smile of a football captain, telling him to move forward to the sand dunes, where the engineers had breached the line. But Gerhard had held back, waiting for the NCO to move forward. And that's when he shot the man in the back of his neck. While there'd been exhilaration at the moment of the killing, he recalled the sickening feeling later that night, when he'd had time to reflect on what he'd done.

As he leaned against the tree, Gerhard looked down at his hand. His fingernails had gouged into the trunk of the black alder, peeling his fingernails back, ripping them from the quick. He pulled his hand away, stuffing it into his pocket.

The list was comprised entirely of Americans—Americans who were simply doing their jobs, serving their country and their loved ones back home. For sake of personal transparency, he added the private he'd gutted after setting the bouncing betty, making the dead an even twenty, or possibly twenty-one, depending on whether or not Holder had yet expired. But unless the mortar round had fallen directly on his cot, it certainly wasn't due to that.

Gerhard stared at the other tree, at the hollow. He thought about his little trick with the mortar round, wondering if Ritter yet knew. He whispered a prayer that Holder might make it, that his disgusting list would remain at twenty.

Ritter had said Carol Lynn was dead, as was the man, Robert Williams— the one he'd kidnapped and brought to his home that night when he'd planned to set the fire. Even though he'd tried to spare them, they died anyway, and they, too, belonged on the list. Because, whether or not it was his intention, they'd died because of his carelessness.

As did the agent in Paris.

He dabbed his last cigarette to his tongue, taking the burn without a flinch. He would save the last few puffs for later. Gerhard tucked it back into the pack and placed it in his pocket. He removed his shiny silver Zippo, staring at his own reflection. The beard. The heavy brow. The flattened nose. He held the lighter in front of his face to gaze into his jade-green eyes. They were still the same, the window into his soul.

His hollow soul.

He remembered concealing his identity in Paris, telling himself it was because he wanted to finish his work with the list. Trying to convince that woman he could be more effective in the field. Telling himself that Berlin would want an even number.

All lies.

He didn't want to be found because, in his heart of hearts, Gerhard had no intentions of ever going back.

"All those people, dead because of me," he said aloud.

His hand massaged his chest. He felt a strange ache all over, wondering briefly if it was sorrow. *No*, he decided. Though he didn't feel it very often, he knew what sorrow was. This emotion was different. Gerhard peered through the trees, into the heavens, and that's when it hit him. The emotion tightening his chest, affecting his body, coursing through his veins…

It was disgust.

Disgust and self-loathing.

His voice was a whisper, flat and even. "Get to working, or get out." That's when it all came clear to Gerhard.

And for the first time in several days, Gerhard suddenly felt quite good.

After dragging his rucksack next to the hollow tree, he unlaced his boots…

GENERAL PATTON was taking a much deserved shower, so Ritter was told. He waited outside of the command tent, sitting on the stump of a freshly-cut tree. In his bandaged hand were the orders. He'd just showed them to a group of self-important senior officers he'd never seen before. They demanded to know what the orders were all about. Ritter stayed mum. "If you want to punish me for withholding information, then do so after the general has returned. I will let him know that each of you insisted upon knowing what exactly he was up to with this decree." That shut them up. They milled about in a knot the way soldiers of every rank do. Smoking. Breaking balls. Making trashy jokes. Glowering at him.

After ten minutes, Patton strode across the trodden French soil, his skin pink and freshly scrubbed, wearing his familiar summer tan riding breeches with the chocolate field jacket. His brown boots gleamed, matched by the shining leather of his gun holsters. Next to him, bounding playfully, was his dog Willie. He was carrying a large bone.

Smelling of peppermint and spicy soap, Patton came to a halt before Ritter, staring at him with squinted eyes. The other officers rushed over, eager to shield him from an unwanted interruption.

"Sir, does this captain have business here?"

"General, this peg-leg is carrying a set of purported orders that could be a sham."

"Sir, I can deal with this insolent underling if you'd like."

Ritter, Captain Roland Buhl to Patton, stood quietly at attention. Patton turned to the assembled group of knee-suckers. "All of you piss off! And while you're at it, why don't you do some damned work? We're at war last I checked!"

He turned back to Ritter, waiting until the others had dissipated. "Th'hell happened to your hand?" His voice was curt. Edgy. He wasn't putting off the cocksure air of the times before.

"We've turned France upside down looking for the kraut. In the process I fell on a nail."

"Well, have you found him?"

Ritter stepped closer, his voice a whisper. "We're on his trail, sir."

Just below the two men, growling lowly, Willie began his work on the bone.

"You're on whose trail?"

"The German, sir. The assassin."

Patton paused for a moment. "Where?"

"He's going to try to cross the line, sir."

"Where?"

"I can show you. Can you take me into your map tent?"

Patton considered this before nodding once. They crossed the muddy clearing, the general waving officers off with his swagger stick. A military police staff sergeant stood outside of the rectangular tent. All Patton barked was, "No one comes in!" when he passed him. Willie must not have counted, because moments later he appeared and nestled onto a throw rug in the corner of the tent.

The tent was well lit, dominated in its center by an expansive sand table. The sand table even had terrain features, displaying the relief between the high and low grounds of the rolling countryside. Patton moved to the right, tapping the table's edge. "This is south." He leaned his swagger stick against the wall of the tent, trading it for a red-tipped pointer stick. "Us," he said, pointing to the area below Penverne, represented by a block with the Roman numeral III. He moved well to the right, tracing a diagonal line from northeast to southwest. "The front line. Where we stand we're about a klick out of reach of their best artillery, even with a tailwind. The line's been pretty solid for about a week now. Damned krauts have stiffened up a bit, but we got something for 'em in a few days."

Ritter studied the front line, memorizing it. The line was marked by units covering nearly the entire expanse, all except one area near the northern end, possibly due to bogs or swamps. *And that's where I will cross! Thank you*

General "Arshloch" Patton. After quickly memorizing the hamlets of that area, Ritter pointed to the opposite end, an area heavily defended between two armor units. "There, sir. That's where he's headed."

The general snorted. "Well he better be a mole if he plans to slip through there. I've got a tank idling every fifty meters."

"He's good, sir, and in uniform. Can you concentrate your efforts of finding him there? Perhaps for five klicks in each direction. I can give you his description to a tee."

Patton stepped back, smacking the stick in his hand. "Before I do anything like that, how do you know for sure that you're following the actual assassin?"

"We first spotted him across a field, moving like a fox, darting in and out. He was all alone and had no business being out there by himself. We lost him but kept watching the field and not long after we were stunned when we saw him pop up and fire what appeared to be a mortar."

"*He* fired the mortar?" Patton yelled. "Are you sure?"

"Yes, sir. It was a mortar all right. Jericho's still back there chasing him with a major we picked up along the way. That kraut fired it and hauled ass, and Jericho said they've since spotted him on and off to this area," Ritter said, again pointing to the heavily fortified area on the map."

Patton eyed Ritter for a moment before turning back to the sand table. He tapped the map at the 23rd. "That bastard's mortar landed here, smack dab in the middle of this unit."

Ritter fought to suppress a smile. "Yes, sir, that would make sense since that's where he set that grenade." He leaned over the table. "We saw him here," he said, pointing to the clearing where Gerhard fired the mortar. "And then he sped here, and here, and here," Ritter lied, pointing to the southern area of the sand table. "Even with help we haven't been able to catch him. The man is a true commando. That's why we need you to focus your efforts on that end of the line, sir."

"Well, he ain't all that smart," Patton said, the wisp of a smirk on his face.

"Sir?"

"The mortar he fired."

Ritter had no idea what Patton was about to say, but he felt as if someone had just lit a blowtorch under his feet. "Yes, sir?"

"It was a frigging Willie-Pete round." Upon hearing his name, Willie stop gnawing on the bone for a moment, cocked his head, then quickly resumed his feast.

"Willie-Pete, sir?" Ritter breathed.

"Willie-Pete…white phosphorous. Your *expert* German assassin fired a *smoke* round into that infantry company. Scared the shit outta everyone, but that's about it. You ever seen a Willie-Pete mortar round, Buhl?"

Ritter was struck dumb. He simply shook his head.

"It's longer than a high-explosive round, but the dead giveaway is that it's white with bright yellow letters announcing what it is. You'd have to be a complete lummox to confuse the two."

Ritter's eyes drifted to the right, images flashing through his mind as things began to come clear. Gerhard had shown him a round marked high-explosive.

Gerhard had deceived him.

Ritter struggled to swallow, feeling his good leg wobble a bit.

"You okay, captain?"

Leaning a hand on the edge of the sand table, he managed to wet his parched mouth. He could feel his heart thumping in his chest as blackness crossed his vision several times. *Gerhard damned Faber!* Ritter took deep breaths, regaining his composure, straightening. "Sorry, sir. It just occurred to me that I haven't eaten in many, many hours. Got a little dizzy."

"Well, grab some chow and we'll get my XO in here to formulate a plan. We can use a couple'a light companies and surround this kraut like a noose. Then, everybody moves in at once and he's trapped. An old Indian technique and damned effective for ensnaring a slippery bastard."

Ritter licked his lips. "I'll do that, sir. Can I get a good half-hour? That'll give me time to radio Jericho and the major who's helping us, then I'll feed my face."

"Where was he last spotted?"

Ritter pointed to the map, ten kilometers from the front line.

"That'll take him hours in that wet terrain down there." Patton stepped to the folds of the tent. "I want to catch this prick, son, more to hurt him than to see what the hell is going on with the krauts. But they're stiffening up more than I thought they possibly could, so the intel we get from him could be invaluable. You come to the command center when you're ready."

The general left, barking orders the second he left the tent. Willie quickly followed. Patton's voice trailed away.

A smoke round! He fired a damned smoke round at the medical tent. He's an infantryman. Infantrymen know mortars. And not only is he an infantryman, but one of the most highly-trained commandos to exit the academy in Potsdam. Surely he would know the difference between a smoke round and the high-explosive version.

Ritter straightened. He used his handkerchief to wipe the growing sweat from his brow and around his eyes.

Eyes.

Gerhard's jade-green eyes.

Lying eyes.

He'd lied about the kid, Holder, the one in the tent. He'd lied for a reason. But what was the reason? Ritter squeezed his eyes shut, forcing his frenzied ruminations into a singular train of thought. The cosmetic surgery. His attempt to turn the Paris-based agent. And now this fiasco with the smoke round.

His eyes sprung open.

"Gerhard *is* going to turn!" he said in a loud whisper. "He wasn't completely sure before, that's why he went ahead and killed the general. But he's sure now." His eyes danced around the tent before he nodded with finality. *Sure as shit, he's going to turn and that bastard is going to use me, his supposed ally, as his bargaining chip.*

Ritter punched his bandaged right hand into his left palm, grinding his teeth. He limped away from the tent, walking outside of the inner perimeter, retrieving his Colt. "Where's the supply area?"

The MP pointed to the far edge of the outer perimeter, near the checkpoint with the tanks. Ritter drove the Jeep there, ordering the clerk to take him to the armorer. After finding the man, a staff sergeant, sleeping in a chair, Ritter produced the tattered orders and demanded to be outfitted with a particular weapon. Tolerating the sleepy sergeant's grumbling as they walked the rows of rifles, Ritter accepted the weapon, looking it over and signing his American name on three sheets of paper.

"Don't load it 'til you get past them tanks," the armorer warned. He handed Ritter a box of ammo.

Outside of the main perimeter, Ritter drove the Jeep into the woods, halfway to the copse in which he had deposited Gerhard. After loading the weapon, he slid the handle of the bolt forward and down, locking the round home. He caressed the rifle, holding its cold steel to his face as he kissed it. Then, with his set jaw, he exited the Jeep, creeping into the thick forest.

"We'll see who is whose pawn," he whispered.

FINISHED WITH his work, Gerhard heard the chirp of the Jeep's brakes.

Ritter Böhl.

Gerhard took a deep breath. He was ready.

THE WEAVER sight mounted atop the Caliber 30 bolt-action rifle allowed an above-average shooter to eliminate the enemy at a range of up to 600 yards. Ritter Böhl could have easily been classified as a skilled sniper, but on this day there was no reason for such certification. Prosthetic and all, he had crept through the damp forest with nary a sound, situating the rifle in the V of a small tree at a range of no more than fifty yards. Settling in with slow movements, he adjusted the scope, eliminating the halo of fuzz around the image of Gerhard Faber. In no rush to complete his action, Ritter watched him for at least ten minutes. Gerhard was facing Ritter, casually sitting on a downed tree, a placid expression on his face as he waited.

"Cocksucker," Ritter whispered, using the English version of the word. He would lay ten-to-one odds that, had he tried to take Gerhard across the line, once they were in the vehicle and driving, Gerhard would almost certainly have tried to incapacitate him. Because that's when Ritter would have been the most vulnerable. Assuming Gerhard was able to gain the upper hand, his first order of business would have been to secure Ritter, probably with rope or wire from the Jeep. He would have then immediately tried to learn of Private Holder's condition. If Holder had died of his knife wounds, it wouldn't be out of the realm of possibility for Gerhard to simply kill Ritter and take him back to his unit, fabricating a fantastic tale about Ritter being the German spy. Haag and Jericho's bodies, dead by Ritter's Colt—as well as a deep study of Ritter's background—would have more than clinched it.

But if Holder's condition had improved, Gerhard would then be forced to admit who he was and cut a deal, using Ritter as the leverage.

Either way, Ritter would have been the pawn.

He lifted his eye from the scope, shaking his head. There was one thing bothering him, gnawing at him. No matter which way he sliced it, it never added up. Why hadn't Gerhard fired the correct mortar round at Holder? As Patton said, he would have certainly known which one to use. Even if he planned on turning to the Americans, it would make no sense to have left Holder alive. Hell, Gerhard could have blamed all of it on Ritter with Holder out of the picture, including Holder's death.

Something was wrong.

Using the scope, he peered at his contemporary again. Sitting there on the downed tree, Gerhard tapped out a stubby cigarette and lit it. With the cigarette pinched in the corner of his mouth, he smiled broadly, staring straight at Ritter.

What in the hell? There was no way he could see Ritter, nor could he have heard him coming. The brush was quite thick, and Ritter had slithered into position with all the sound of a shadow. He focused on him again, smoke from the cigarette lacing around his head in the still, thick forest air. Still sitting there, a smug smile on his bearded face. His green eyes were focused directly on Ritter.

Ritter felt his blood begin to boil. Something was amiss and this prick Gerhard was grinning about it. Well, Ritter intended to find out what it was. And besides, if he arrived in the arms of his countrymen with a wounded Faber—especially given the man's bizarre actions—he would be more than justified to have shot him.

Jawohl…it is time.

Ritter Böhl took a deep breath, letting half out slowly. He aimed at Gerhard's right shoulder, a fist-width in and a fist-width down—just above the lung—certainly a non-fatal shot to a healthy man. The weapon wasn't zeroed to Ritter's shooting style, but with the permanent scope and such a finely milled rifle, he didn't expect to be more than a centimeter off in these ideal conditions.

He added pressure to the trigger.

Pressure.

Pressure.

Crack!

The 30-06 jacketed bullet hurtled through the sky at better than 2,800 feet per second, meaning it struck Gerhard Faber almost instantly. Ritter didn't move, watching the round knock his countryman backward, off the log, out of sight.

Ritter stood, grunting from pain in what remained of his bad leg. The long, silencing suppressor on the front end of the rifle did its job. The bullet was supersonic, and had certainly made a sound on its short trip, but wouldn't have been loud enough to draw anyone's attention unless they happened to be nearby. And no one was. He left the rifle behind, unholstering his Colt and carrying it aimed forward, at the ready. Picking his way through the thicket, Ritter arrived above Gerhard a minute later.

Gerhard's breathing was quick and shallow. He lay on his back, one of his legs still propped up on the fallen tree where he had sat. His right shoulder was a deep red, the uniform slick with blood. While obviously in pain, Ritter was surprised when Gerhard managed to muster the same smile again, his teeth clenched at the same time.

It was a knowing smile.

It was a smile of what looked like retribution.

Ritter held the Colt .45 steadily at Gerhard's head, his eyes narrowed as he couldn't get his contemporary's peculiar actions to make any sort of sense. And nonsensical behavior, to a good German, is maddening—especially when paired with a smile that promised some sort of unpleasantness. After licking his lips, Ritter asked one simple question. "Why did you shoot a smoke round at the medical tent?"

Grunting, Gerhard held his grin as he replied, "Because that was my plan."

"But you showed me the round in the Jeep," Ritter protested. "It was clearly marked 'high-explosive'."

Gerhard's immediate laughter was nothing more than several loud breaths from his nose. "So you figured that out, did you?"

"Damn it…*why*, Gerhard? Why would you do something so stupid? It makes no sense!"

Gerhard squeezed his eyes shut for a moment, appearing to be in great pain. The aggrieved expression washed over his face, taking the smile with it. He opened his eyes again, a sadness clearly visible in their jade-green. "I killed people, Ritter. A lot of people. And even those I didn't kill…my wife…the homosexual man…our agent in Paris, they died because of me."

"Killing is your job."

"Job or not, Ritter, it was all shit. And, like a pile of shit, it just kept adding up. The kid, Holder, the one I knifed…he put me over the top."

Ritter shook his head. *Gibberish. Pure gibberish. More rubbish from a crazy man.* "Gerhard," Ritter said patiently, still holding the Colt on him. "You're a German, a Nazi. All of the American soldiers you killed *deserved* to die. Hell, the ones in that perimeter up the road are actively trying to kill you and me and our friends and our women and our children."

"I'm not a soldier, Ritter. I'm a murderer. As are you."

Ritter felt his ears get hot. "Now is not the time for weakness, Gerhard. You'll realize later why I shot you, which…by the way…was only to incapacitate you because of this bizarre behavior." He took a step closer, keeping the pistol steady on the downed man. "When we are in the bosom of our Nazi brethren, perhaps you can regain your senses."

Gerhard lifted his right hand, weak and shaking from the gunshot. His index finger wagged back and forth in a correcting expression. "No, Ritter…I *was* a Nazi. I'm still a German, but not a Nazi. There's a big difference."

Ritter arched his eyebrows, twisting the pistol. "I know what you are, Gerhard, you're absolutely bat-shit crazy…but more important, you're also my prisoner, and you're coming with me."

Gerhard laughed a low, menacing laugh. "No, Ritter."

"What did you just say?"

"You heard me. I'm staying right here, and so are you."

"Right, Gerhard…you're lying there with a hole in your chest, yet you're still in charge."

"Just try to move me and see what happens."

Ritter snorted as he stared off beyond Gerhard. Though he was trying to maintain his bravado, he was actually crestfallen. With a sobering dose of disappointment, he decided it would be best to just kill Gerhard now. He'd obviously lost his mind, and trying to drive to the front line with him still alive was going to be a liability. There would be checkpoints to pass—too much risk.

His anger coming up, Ritter said, "Do you remember a tussle you had with another officer at the Schonau Bar in Berlin? It was the night before you departed for the United States."

"Yes," Gerhard replied, a gurgle sound coming with his voice.

"Commandant Heydte told me all about it during a clandestine rendezvous we had before my fateful jump. He said you beat the man but left him relatively unharmed, even when the man had threatened your life."

"How would he have known that?" Gerhard asked.

"Because Heydte sent one of his thugs to follow you that night. And his thug went into that back alley and beat that officer to death." Ritter snorted. "He did your wet work for you."

Gerhard blinked but made no sound.

"They framed you for it, Gerhard. Even though the case has since gone cold, I'm sure they will reopen it very soon."

"It won't matter."

"Oh, and speaking of wet work…there's one other thing, Gerhard," Ritter said with growing magniloquence. "About your mother—"

"I know she's dead, Ritter. I'm sure, had you been in Germany, you'd have been honored to have done the killing."

"Bravo," Ritter said, clapping his left hand against the Colt. "I'm impressed you figured it out."

"It wasn't that hard," Gerhard said, coughing a quantity of blood from his mouth. "Once you told me about the others, I knew they had killed her, too."

Still angry about having his grand plan ruined, Ritter said, "Oh, and you're correct, Gerhard. Had I been there, I would have *loved* to have killed your mother."

No sooner had Ritter spoken about his mother when Gerhard's leg dropped off of the fallen tree. With little resistance, Gerhard's boot slid off, tumbling to the ground. Ritter frowned, glancing at the stray boot before cutting his eyes back to his prisoner. There were no laces on either of his boots.

"What did you do with your boot laces?"

Laughter. Weak. Breathy. But growing in intensity. It grew so much Gerhard began to cough loudly, sputtering blood after each hack. When he recovered, he lifted his left hand from underneath the pine needles and leaves. Tied around his fingers was a boot lace. Ritter followed the string as it came up. It led to the hollowed out tree trunk ten feet away, holding a skinny twig in place. Above the twig, rigged to his other bootlace—which was vertical and appeared very taut—was a mortar round. On the projectile the white stenciling of HIGH EXPLOSIVE glowed like neon in the murkiness of the hollow. Ritter knew enough about artillery rounds to see that the fuze had been removed and was hotwired with two green wires to the bottom, to the percussion primer. At the bottom of the contraption, sticking straight up, was the straightened spring from one of the clips on Gerhard's rucksack. An improvised firing pin.

"If you shoot me, Ritter, I'm willing to bet that my body will contract and down that round will come. And that's no smoke round in there." A laugh and a wet cough. "No, sir. As you can see, that one's high-explosive. In other words, it's the solution for you, and for me."

Ritter, eyes wide, lowered the Colt, holding his left hand up at Gerhard in a placating gesture. "Hold on, Gerhard. Hold on. Listen to me. I shot you because I knew you had turned on me. But look! I didn't kill you. No. My aim was true and I spared you because I want to take you across the line and get you some help."

Gerhard spasmed in laughter, his right hand clutching his stomach. "Help. Help. He wants to get me help. As the Americans say, 'That's rich'."

"Gerhard, please. Deep cover can wreck your mind. You're not thinking clearly."

Gerhard's laughter intensified. He managed to say, "Oh, but I am!" between chuckles. "In fact, I'm thinking more clearly than I have in years."

"Why are you doing this?"

Again the smile disappeared. "That soldier I knifed, he could have been me as a youth. And I should kill him…rip his life from him only because he saw me setting a booby trap?"

"But you've killed dozens of men."

"And you…watching you kill the lieutenant, your supposed friend, and the major in such cold blood…it sickened me."

"But you've killed in the *same* cold blood!"

"And I sicken me!" Gerhard thundered, blood spurting from his mouth.

Ritter was silent as his pulse thudded in his ears.

"Do you remember when I said I always felt good when I killed someone who deserved it?"

"Gerhard, please."

Gerhard brought his left hand all the way up, tightening the tension on the bootlace. "And this will, most assuredly, make me feel *damned* good."

"But you're not mortally wounded, you fool! You'll kill yourself, too!"

Gerhard nodded. "Exactly, Ritter. Exactly! And we both deserve to die. Can't you see that? We're disease…fungus on this earth. We're like whatever rotted that hollow tree out. And the world will be better, much better, without either of us." The smile again. Jovial. Maniacal. Exultant. "So for the absolute split second, Ritter, between my jerking this string and both of us being blown to bits, I'll feel so very good."

"You're insane!"

"And what was it you said, Ritter, about an apparition? Not a twin, but a spirit? A ghost?"

Ritter took a step backward, preparing to make a break for it and mentally cursing his limitations caused by the prosthetic.

"Remember that, Ritter?" Gerhard laughed one final time. "Well, now we can both be a doppelgänger."

He yanked the bootlace.

The 60-millimeter mortar slid down the five-foot long zip-line in a half-second. It was just enough time for Ritter Böhl to scream an insult before the accelerant flashed, simultaneously igniting the single pound of TNT in the body of the mortar.

The mortar would have killed a man thirty feet away. The two Germans were less than ten feet from the explosion. Death was violent and instantaneous for both operatives.

A LITTLE over a kilometer away, General George S. Patton's head, like every other head in the perimeter, snapped around to the sound of the explosion. Patton looked to his XO and said, "That sure as hell came from the wrong direction. You sure we're outta range?"

"Damn right we are," the XO answered. "And that wasn't an arty round. Sounded like a mortar to me."

The Jeep was discovered first. The remains of the bodies, along with a tattered prosthetic, ten minutes later.

SEVENTEEN

GENERAL PATTON listened intently as one of the Army's top intelligence men read the report aloud to him and two of his inner circle. They sat in a commandeered mansion, abandoned long before by a French land baron. It was exactly one week later. The war was progressing as planned, the front line having moved ten miles to the east. Only a handful of people knew about the explosion, fewer still the about the discovery of the bodies of Major Haag and Lieutenant Jericho.

The man before him, a brigadier general, summarized the four-page report he'd just read. "Roland Buhl and Garland Felton were, most certainly, both planted in the United States by the Nazis. We found the remains of the worksheet Buhl showed you, the one with the list of the dead, as well as a list of German radio frequencies." He chewed on the stem of his reading glasses for a moment. "Perhaps most damning was a lens, cleverly concealed inside the pistol grip of Buhl's Colt forty-five. It was etched with a swastika. We've heard of this identification system. The lens matches up over tiny tattoos on the body. Unfortunately, their bodies were far too mangled to confirm it."

"I issued him that Colt," Patton said monotone.

"Precisely, sir. So he must have hid the lens afterward."

Patton nodded. "Go on."

"We suspect these two were part of a larger network. Several sources have told us this network was unsuccessful. Additionally, in the past months, since the invasion and the German realization that we're going to win this war, we've had two highly-placed spies come forward, turning on the Nazis. Both reported similar training to the other, meaning they were compartmentalized, and both had the lens and the tattoos. It's likely that our two dead ones were given the same training." The general dropped his glasses on the mahogany table, lacing his hands over his stomach. "For whatever reason, Felton's background in the States was sloppy. It took two of my men only a few hours to crack his manufactured identity."

Patton tapped his cigar in the ashtray. "And Buhl's?"

"His took a great deal of research. In fact, some of his past is what we would call gray. There's really no way to prove it didn't happen, but no way to prove it did."

"Conclusion?" Patton asked.

"It seems Buhl was acting as he was probably ordered. Based on his performance in the Army, and subsequently in intelligence, he likely came to us as a ready-made, highly-skilled commando. We failed in realizing this." The general shifted in his seat. "Felton joined the Army in Cincinnati, Ohio, purportedly hailing from Kentucky." The general lifted the photo displaying the Wehrmacht soldier. "Our analysts think the photo we found in the Jeep was indeed Garland Felton. While his body was ripped to shreds, the medical examiner was able to find evidence of what appeared to be crude cosmetic surgery on his face." He slid the photo halfway across the table. "We think Buhl actually was desperately seeking Felton for quite some time."

Patton reached across the table and took the frayed photo, staring at it a moment before passing it around. "So you think this Felton kid may have been off the reservation. And the reason Buhl came to me with his suppositions was partly true, because he...and the krauts, were trying to find him."

"That's what we think."

"So why the smoke round?" Patton asked.

The brigadier opened his hands. "No one will likely ever know." He straightened his papers and tucked his glasses inside his coat. "As you know, sir, we've now got many assets inside of Germany. In fact, not a day goes by when we don't get another senior officer willing to turn on his country in return for clemency. I will see to it that we put the word out—along with photos of the corpses—that two of their prized operatives are dead as doornails."

Patton barely nodded, staring off in the distance. After a moment, the meeting began to break up. Men lit cigarettes, shook hands, donned overcoats. The door was opened.

"One moment, gentlemen!"

All eyes went back to Patton. He wore a mischievous grin, making them wait in anticipation. Finally he asked a single question. "Did you say you have a number of assets in Germany?"

"Yes, sir."

Patton's index finger tapped his weathered lips. "The truth hurts, but sometimes a deception hurts even worse."

The brigadier general narrowed his eyes. "Please forgive my thick-headedness, sir, but I'm not sure I follow."

Patton's grin again creased his face. His blue eyes twinkled. "The message I want you to give them is simple...real simple. Grab a pencil and paper."

NEARLY A month later, as a cold wind whipped the war-torn citizens of Potsdam, warning them of the sharp teeth of the coming winter, General Emil von Marburg strode the final two blocks from where he had exited the military bus. Petrol was in such short supply that even a general didn't warrant a personal automobile anymore. Von Marburg didn't really care anyway. He'd lost all hope on the war several months prior. Now, instead of placing his full attention and efforts on his intelligence division, his days were spent trying to set himself up for a life after war. Between burning files and manufacturing intelligence, he hoped to create a story that would elicit sympathy from the coming Americans and their allies.

He stopped on the stoop of the three-story mansion, turning, pinching his overcoat as he watched a scarlet Nazi flag whip in the frigid wind. Even the flag was tattered, something Hitler and his minions wouldn't have stood for a year ago. Von Marburg shook his head, imagining the flag, along with a million others, being ripped down by whichever military first roared into Berlin. "God...please...let it be the Americans who take us," he whispered.

Upon entering the mansion, Von Marburg waved the various soldiers and civilians down after they had popped to attention. The interior of the building was as icy cold as it was outside, made worse by the conditioning modern humans have received to expect warmth upon entry. In essence, it felt colder. Just another subtle sign of the coming defeat.

He took the six flights of stairs, pausing to catch his breath on the upper landing. The guard at the top of the stairs, a tired old man from the Volkssturm home-guard, didn't even pop to attention until after he passed. Emil von Marburg ignored the lack of military courtesy. He navigated the long hallway, opening the door at the end, stepping inside. In the anteroom sat a beautiful, albeit thin, secretary. Same old Heydte—even in a war-ravaged country teetering on the brink of defeat, he could always find a looker.

"Hello darling," Von Marburg said without a smile. "Is he in?"

"Yes, sir, shall I buzz him?"

"Don't bother." The general burst into the room, closing the door behind him. Sitting behind the desk was Colonel Frederick Heydte, having been recently promoted. Heydte had his back to the door, reading with his feet propped up on his credenza. To his right, a fire crackled, the wood having to have been commandeered from an illicit stash.

"A little early for this, isn't it, *mein liebling*?" Heydte asked in a singsong manner. "You must not be as sore from yesterday as I thought."

Emil von Marburg shook his head. The country was going to hell and all this piece of crap could do was carry on a torrid affair with his secretary. Von Marburg chose to remain silent for effect. Eventually, Heydte spun his chair, his eyes bulging when he saw the general. He dropped the newspaper he'd been reading, popping to attention.

"Sir, I apologize. I don't know what you heard, but I was…well…of course—"

"Sit down, Frederick," Von Marburg said in a sharp voice.

Heydte sat, smoothing his hair. "What brings you here, sir? Aren't we due to meet on *Freitag*?"

"I've just come from Berlin."

"Yes, sir."

"Where I was *forced* to meet with your Führer."

Heydte's tone grew cautious. "Yes, sir."

"I had to sit there, with no warning, and listen to a general from the western front as he relayed intelligence he'd gathered from several credible sources. Do you know what he said, Heydte?" Emil von Marburg thrust a finger in his subordinate's direction, his voice rising. "Tell me, Heydte...do you know? Do you?"

"No, sir."

"He said two of *your* operatives, upon finding one another, decided to turn to the Americans. One, who has to be your boy Böhl, has given the Americans great detail regarding our intelligence network. The other, your 'can't miss' prospect Gerhard Faber, is now out on the front line, personally directing the Americans as they smash our armor to bits." Von Marburg massaged the bridge of his nose. "The descriptions of your men—who were supposed to be compartmentalized—are spot-on. There's no mistake. So, this means every single operative you trained...*every one*, has either failed or turned on us."

Heydte's mouth was open as if his jaw was made with no muscle for closure. His head quivered back and forth. "It's false information, sir. It's not true!"

"Then how come the descriptions, Frederick?" Von Marburg yelled. "How the hell would the intel sources *both* describe Faber and Böhl? The intel said one was a captain, with no leg, and the other a staff sergeant with green eyes—*jade* green eyes. You told me we made contact with Böhl in London, and that he'd lost his leg."

Heydte's hand went over his mouth as his eyes danced around the room. Finally he looked up at Von Marburg. "I don't understand how this could have happened."

Von Marburg made his response icy. "And neither does the Führer, who naturally wants *my* head on a platter."

"Sir, I'm so very sorry to have put you in such a situation. I would never have—"

Emil von Marburg stopped him with a gloved hand. "I did some further digging."

Heydte pulled in air through his nose.

"I learned that your boy Faber never killed his mother." Von Marburg made sure his smile was thin. "He never killed her and *you* gave the directive to cover it up for him." Shaking his head, Von Marburg said, "Then I talked to Bonitz. He informed me that Faber failed to eliminate his American wife when she blew his cover."

Heydte's face twisted as tears welled in his eyes.

"Even with these warning signs, you still pushed him into clandestine service of the Reich."

"I'm sorry," was all Heydte managed to whisper.

Emil von Marburg reached into his pocket, producing three amber capsules. He tossed them on the desk.

Heydte stared at them.

Von Marburg took a step closer, neatening the three glass capsules into a triangle on Heydte's blotter. "When you sent Faber to kill his own mother, wordsmith you are, you argued against my objections."

"But sir, I didn't—"

"And you termed it…what was it?…'a strategic disposal of an *insignificant* asset,' or something like that, didn't you, Frederick?"

Heydte stared down at the capsules, his breaths coming short and shallow. "Sir, please."

Emil von Marburg smiled. "Well, you're now an insignificant asset, Heydte. Hell…we all are."

Tears streamed down Heydte's face. "Please, sir…Emil…please."

"I'm doing you a favor. Would you rather the Führer decide your fate?"

Sniffles turned to outright weeping.

"Those glass ampoules are filled with laboratory grade saxitoxin, Heydte. One of the Führer's so-called miracle weapons." Von Marburg leaned forward, his gloved hands on the desk. His voice was a whisper as he added pauses between each word, saying, "It's the honorable thing to do, colonel. Put them in your mouth and crunch them all at once…they'll work faster that way." He straightened, did an about-face, and exited the office, pulling the door shut behind him.

The secretary, obviously a skilled social climber, put her hand to the back of her neck and batted her eyelashes. "How have you been, sir? I haven't had the stimulating pleasure of seeing you in quite some time."

"Fine, darling." Von Marburg removed a cigar from his pocket, thought better of it, and placed the last one of his American cigarettes in his mouth.

He crumpled the pack and tossed it in the garbage can. "Do you have a light, my dear?" The secretary handed him a pack of matches from a nightclub. He lit the cigarette and shook the match out, handing it back to her.

They made small talk for a few minutes, her suggestions getting progressively bolder. "Perhaps I might see you some time outside of these walls?" she eventually asked.

He shrugged. "Yes, perhaps, though I live up the road in Berlin."

"Getting there is no problem, sir. Not for a resourceful girl like—"

The loud thump made her stand from her seat. She stood behind her desk, her eyes wide as she stared at the door to Heydte's office. "Did that sound like the colonel fell in there?"

Emil von Marburg's calm expression didn't change at all. He blinked several times, glanced at the closed door and said, "It certainly did."

"Should I check on him?"

He shrugged again. "You can if you like." He stepped to the door leading to the hallway, turning back to the comely woman. "Or, if you want to save some time, just call the coroner."

General Emil von Marburg sauntered down the hall, finishing the last American cigarette he would ever have.

Das Ende

Acknowledgments

Doppelgänger is a highly-contrived work of fiction, not meant to be taken seriously. Although I had a great deal of help in preparing the novel for public consumption, any mistakes it contains are my own.

Two people gave me a great deal of help with *Doppelgänger*. The first, Bob Thixton, helped me when the idea for the tale was still in my head. His insights and historical knowledge were invaluable. The second, Phillip Day, taught me something about Gerhard/Gerald/Garland that I never would have thought of on my own. I owe both men a debt of gratitude for their help.

Thanks to Allison Walsh and Elizabeth Brazeal for their editing assistance and for their patience with my repeated blunders.

And to my beta readers—Linda, Phillip, Jan, Scott & Laura—your keen eyes helped me more than you know.

Finally, I owe so much to my friends and family for supporting me. When *The Diaries* was released, I was blown away by the support and encouragement I received. Writing is a very personal activity. Despite being fiction, it's still a piece of the author's brain. The reassurance I received from friends and family, as well as people I didn't even know before, is humbling. Thanks to each and every one of you.

Please, whether your opinion of this book is high or low, take a moment to write a review wherever you purchased it. It will help others decide whether or not it's for them.

God bless.

C.

About the Author

Chuck Driskell is a United States Army veteran who now makes his living as an advertising executive. He lives in South Carolina with his wife and two children. *Doppelgänger* is Chuck's second novel.

CPSIA information can be obtained
at www.ICGtesting.com
Printed in the USA
FSHW012354141218
54500FS